LUCKY BREAK

LUCKY BREAK

—

A.M. ARTHUR

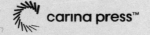

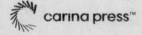

ISBN-13: 978-1-335-45947-3

Lucky Break

Copyright © 2019 by A.M. Arthur

www.CarinaPress.com

Printed in U.S.A.

Look out for the next book
in the Clean Slate Ranch series, *Hard Ride*,
coming February 2020.

Chapter One

Shawn Matthews glanced at the kitchen clock every few minutes while he worked, watching the long hand tick down the final two hours of his first season as sous chef of the Tango Saloon, a grim reaper inching closer and closer to Shawn's doom. Okay, so maybe *doom* was melodramatic, but today was the saloon's last day open for over two months, and Shawn had nowhere to go for the upcoming holidays.

"Eighty-sixing the buffalo burger," his boss, Miles Arlington, said from his position at the sizzling flattop. Their server, Annabelle, had just come back to fetch two slices of Vinegar pie, and she repeated what he'd said.

"I'll hard-sell the chili and Hangtown Fry," Annabelle said as she left the kitchen through the swinging double doors with her pie order.

Normally, eighty-sixing a dish from the menu this early, especially a dish as popular as Miles's buffalo burger, would have annoyed them all on a Sunday afternoon. But they'd underordered supplies this weekend so they wouldn't have too many leftovers when the saloon shut down for winter break. As it was, Shawn was down to one whole Vinegar pie, only a dozen biscuits, and three final slices of Mock Apple pie.

"Are you sure you're okay coming in tomorrow for a few hours to clean?" Miles asked after checking the temperature of his final burger. "I don't want to interrupt your plans, but I figured it would be easier than scrubbing the place down tonight after we've both cooked all day."

"Don't mind at all," Shawn replied, and he really didn't. It gave him somewhere to be for part of his day. The rest of the ten-ish weeks that the saloon would be closed? No idea, and he wasn't looking forward to living in his car all that time. "It'll be weird being up here without guests, though."

"Very true." Miles shot him a thoughtful smile. "It'll be weird not seeing you every day, too. You'll have to visit one weekend or something."

That was Miles's very unobtrusive way of inquiring about Shawn's plans while Bentley Ghost Town was shut down to tourists, so the actors and other folks who worked there could spend the upcoming holidays with their families. Mack Garrett, the owner of Bentley, had decided to close up starting the Monday before Thanksgiving, and then open again the final week in January. The break coincided with the closure of the nearby dude ranch Mack's grandfather owned, and where Miles's boyfriend—nope, fiancé now—worked as head cowboy.

Miles was excited to have lots of time with his guy. Shawn just saw a great, gaping maw of empty time waiting for him. Maybe he could drive into San Jose and pick up some temporary kitchen work to keep himself busy. God knew he'd need the money. Despite Mack offering a competitive salary, Shawn had meds to pay for, no insurance plan, and he had to send a good chunk of every paycheck home to help keep Granddad afloat.

Shawn didn't have the luxury of two months camping with a lover, riding horses, and being lazy. Not that Miles hadn't earned the break from real life, especially after the last few months of dealing with an abusive ex.

"We should definitely get together for lunch or something," Shawn hedged, uninterested in revealing to his boss that he'd been homeless for the better part of two years now. "It's not like we can't text or chat on the phone."

"Yeah. You can come up for movie night or something." Miles slid the burger onto its waiting bun. "Movies, popcorn, and drinks at Mack and Wes's place. We usually do it a few times a week so we can all catch up, and you're free to join us."

Shawn swallowed an irritated grunt, unsettled by the timing of these offers of friendship outside the saloon. Why had Miles waited until now? Pity? Shawn could entertain himself just fine, thank you. But Miles wasn't being overbearing or trying to pressure Shawn into anything. He was…being a friend.

"I appreciate it." The printer spit out a new ticket, and Shawn fetched the small slip of paper. "Two Hangtown Fries, hold the oysters in one, and a side of corn fritters."

Miles repeated the order and hit the small bell so Annabelle knew the burger order was ready. Then he reached for the eggs he needed for the Fry, while Shawn got to work on the fritters. In the eight months since the ghost town and saloon opened, their crew had created an easy, balanced work relationship, and they rarely had issues with getting food out. Okay, so maybe once Shawn accidentally made a batch of pies with salt in place of the sugar, but those mistakes were rare.

And funny, with the distance of time. In the moment,

Shawn had been terrified he'd be fired on the spot, and
he needed this job. He loved this job. He even loved the
tiny bit of acting he got to do during the noon holdup in
the saloon, where he had to pretend to be scared of the
"thieves." The cast and crew who kept the ghost town
going had become a kind of family all their own, and
he was so grateful to have that in his life again. It had
been five years since he'd truly felt accepted anywhere.

By four thirty, the last of Shawn's pies and biscuits
were gone, so he helped Miles with side dishes for the
final hour that tourists could order food. Most of the
prepared hot line was empty when the last ticket of
the season came over the printer. Miles blinked hard
as he plated another Hangtown Fry with a side of fritters, as if grieving the end of their first work season
here in the Tango Saloon.

Shawn's own chest tightened. He wouldn't be coming in tomorrow to cook, he'd be coming in to clean
and shut things down. They looked through the last of
the food on hand, fried up the end of the fritter batter,
scrambled the leftover eggs, and Shawn used the last of
the flour and butter to toss together a simple batch of
cheddar biscuits.

A few at a time, cast members came through the
kitchen like a small buffet and got food. Miles had suggested this to Mack last week, so they used up everything they could. Plus, free dinner as a thank-you for
everyone's hard work.

Mack and his boyfriend, Wes Bentley, were among
the last people to come through the line, and there wasn't
much left. Wes was also Miles's best friend, and the pair
hugged for a while, both men probably sad to see the
attraction they'd helped build temporarily shut down.

Shawn's own grief was less acute, tempered by simmering anxiety over his next paycheck. Shawn also hadn't been there at the start of the ghost town, only coming on as a cook about a week before they opened.

"You sure we can't help you guys clean up tonight?" Mack asked. "No one else has to drive up to do anything tomorrow, except me and some paperwork. Megan already closed up the general store for the winter."

"After Mack so generously bought the last of the consigned bread and canned goods to give away to the cast," Wes added with a lovestruck smile for his boyfriend. "Just when you think he can't get more generous."

Mack simply grinned.

Before Shawn could insist he didn't mind cleaning tomorrow, Miles shrugged and said, "I'm cool doing it tonight if you guys are volunteering. In terms of supplies, there's some flour, sugar, and baking powder folks are free to adopt, and I think some milk and half-and-half in the fridge. Forage away once we're done."

Shawn's stomach sank but he didn't contradict his boss. Instead, he started cleaning the line in a practiced, familiar way. Annabelle stuck around to help, and with five of them working, it didn't take long to scrub the place down, unplug equipment that wouldn't need to run, and scrounge up every last bit of stray food. Miles took a final trip out to the compost pile with the bus bin, which he then carefully washed and dried.

Annabelle hugged them all before she left, her eyes full of tears. "See you next year," she said as she walked out the kitchen's back door.

Their quartet left a few minutes later, slowly walking through the deserted town to the attraction's main entrance and gravel parking lot beyond. Shawn's feet grew heavier with each step toward his home for the next two months: a rusty hatchback that vibrated like crazy over fifty miles an hour and sometimes didn't have heat.

His entire life was in that car.

After a handshake from Mack and hugs from both Miles and Wes, Shawn slid into his car and sat there. Watched the trio of friends climb into Mack's pickup and trundle out of sight. Mack and Wes lived in a cabin off the road to the ghost town, and from there, Miles would drive an ATV back to the ranch where he lived with his own boyfriend. No one would care if Shawn stayed here for a while.

Not as if he had anywhere else to go, or anyone waiting for him to get there.

Except he couldn't linger long. Mack's cabin was out of sight of the road, but headlights and an engine too late at night might arouse suspicion, so Shawn turned his key in the ignition.

A gurgle and then nothing.

"Shit, not now." Shawn smacked the steering wheel and tried the key again. Nothing. Then he spotted the headlight knob—still pulled out from his morning ride through slightly foggy weather. He'd killed his own damned battery. "Goddamn it!"

Roadside service all the way out here would be expensive. Maybe he could call Mack and ask him to return for a jump start. Inconvenient, considering everyone's long day, but better than sitting up here all damned night. He palmed his cell—which was as dead as his car. The thing's battery wasn't holding its charge well anymore, and he'd forgotten to use the kitchen's charger today.

Anxiety rolled heavily through his chest and he fought against a rising tide of panic. With the car battery dead, his car charger wouldn't do him any good. Even if he could justify sneaking into the kitchen to use the charger, the doors were all locked in case anyone got big ideas about snooping around in the off-season.

He was well and truly screwed.

Shawn closed his eyes and took a few deep, centering breaths. He'd figure this out. He'd be fine. He'd been figuring his own shit out for years and was still standing, goddamn it. He'd figure this out, too.

Mack's house wasn't an unwalkable distance from the ghost town, but it was after eight at night, dark, with only a sliver of moonlight to guide him down the gravel road. Shawn wasn't afraid of the dark, but there were wild animals out here.

Flashlight. Do I have a working flashlight?

Granddad had given him an emergency roadside kit back when Shawn bought this car. He got out and opened the back hatch. Rummaged around his small collection of belongings until he found the kit. It had one of those battery-free flashlights, and after winding the crank a few dozen times, it finally shed dim light.

Better than nothing.

Shawn armed himself with his tire iron, not trusting the vast acreage of wild land all around him, and then set off toward the road. His feet already ached from a long day, and walking down heavy gravel wasn't helping his sore muscles or his roiling emotions. Anxiety over finding new work, plus anger at this unexpected expense, made his stomach hurt, and he had to pause once to work back the urge to vomit. He should have taken one of his meds before setting off on this hike, but he'd come too far to turn back now.

Except it seemed to take forever for the yellow reflectors marking the Garrett/Bentley driveway to finally flash in the distance. Shawn wanted to sob with relief, but he still had the long driveway to traverse. It dipped down and bent slightly, giving the house tree cover from the ghost town road.

He'd never actually been to the house before, despite a handful of invitations to dinner from Mack. Two stories, the exterior was very rustic-log-cabin, the beauty only slightly marred by the more modern deck furniture on the front porch. The pickup and another car were parked by the house, and lights blazed downstairs.

I might be inconveniencing them, but at least I'm not waking anyone up.

Shawn put his tire iron down, not wanting to appear threatening, and took a deep breath to steel himself before he knocked on the screen door. The interior door swung open a moment later, and Mack stared at him a beat. "Shawn? Everything okay?"

"No, and I'm sorry to bother you this late."

"It's no bother." Mack pushed open the screen door. "Come on in. Didn't hear you drive up."

"I walked." Shawn entered the house, a little surprised by the mix of boho chic décor and more rustic elements that was a perfect blend of the two occupants. A real home. "My car battery died, and then so did my phone battery, and I really hate to put you guys out because I couldn't remember to charge my phone, but I didn't know where else to go."

"Shit, that's a run of bad luck."

"Mack, who's—?" Wes appeared from above, where an open staircase led up to a loft area. "Hey, Shawn, what's wrong?"

"Dead car and phone batteries," Mack replied. To Shawn, he said, "You want a jump?"

"I know it's super late to ask, but I'd really appreciate it," Shawn said.

Wes trotted down the stairs, already out of his period costume and wearing only a pair of tight workout shorts. "Dude, it's after nine. Why don't you just crash here and Mack can jump you in the morning. Unless you've got cats at home that need to be fed or something."

Shawn nearly said he did, just so he could get out of this strange space and back to his familiar car, but he also didn't want to lie to their faces. "No cats or anything, but I don't want to be a bother."

"Don't even sweat it. We've got two guest rooms that barely get any use, unless Avery and Colt stay over together. You have got to be exhausted after today, and the last thing we need is for you to fall asleep at the wheel and crash."

"I agree with Wes," Mack said with a friendly smile. "It's really no bother. I was gonna drive back up to the site in the morning anyway, just to finish up a few things in the office, so you're on the way."

Shawn couldn't think of a good reason to turn down the offer, especially when all he wanted to do was lie down and sleep for a week. At least he'd have one night in a comfortable bed, instead of stretched across his two front seats, where he had no room to move. Sure, he'd gotten used to it over the last two years, but a bed? For one night?

"Okay, you have no idea how much I appreciate this," Shawn replied. *No. Idea.* And it wasn't as if Shawn had asked to stay; Wes had freely offered the room.

Wes showed him around the cabin, which only took

about a minute. The great room was a cozy combina-
tion of a living and dining area. Beneath the loft was
the kitchen, and tucked behind it were the downstairs
bathroom and two small guest rooms. "This one's got
the freshest sheets," Wes said about the room decorated
in deep shades of burgundy, purple, and gold that reminded Shawn of Bollywood films. "There are toiletries in the bathroom, so help yourself to a toothbrush
and a shower. Tonight or in the morning. Can I get you
something to drink?"

"Water would be amazing, thank you."

Wes left and returned with a chilled bottle. "So that's
some shitty luck, huh? Dead car and phone? Do you want
to use my charger?"

Shawn held up his flip phone. "You got a universal
charger?"

"Yup. I'll get it."

"Thank you." Shawn gazed around the room, a little
stunned at how generous Wes and Mack were being. He
was just an employee, but they were treating him like,
well, family. Part of the Bentley Ghost Town family,
and he didn't have the words to express his gratitude.
He'd fallen down, and for the first time in years, someone was there to help him stand up so he didn't have to
do it all on his own.

A fresh wave of tears strangled his throat and stung
his eyes. Tears of gratitude for the support, but also of
frustration for having to rely on other people's charity at all.

"Shawn?" Wes approached with the charger in one
hand and a pair of boxers in his other, his blue eyes wide.
"Are you okay? You are perfectly safe here, I promise."

"I know." Shawn blinked hard against those damned
tears, not afraid of his hosts in the least. "I'm just…not

used to having people around who'll have my back in a crisis. It's a little overwhelming."

"Oh, honey." Wes slung an arm around his shoulders. "You ever need anything, you can come to me or Mack. Definitely to Miles."

"Thanks." He carefully extricated himself from beneath Wes's arm, not much of a casual toucher. "I won't keep you from your, uh, evening. Thank you again, Wes. I mean it."

Wes's eyebrows furrowed briefly. "You're welcome. Sleep tight."

"You, too."

Shawn didn't realize until after Wes left the room how his actions could have been interpreted by Wes: a half-naked gay man side-hugging Shawn, and Shawn not wanting to be hugged. Crap. He hadn't meant to insult his host, but Shawn had never come out to anyone at the ghost town. Despite so many other queer people working there, it was no one's business. He was also too tired to try and explain himself tonight.

After a brief stint in the bathroom, where he changed into the boxers Wes had given him, Shawn slid beneath cool, fresh sheets. Stretched out on all sides on the queen-size mattress like a kid making a snow angel, happy to be in a real bed for a change. He closed his eyes and pretended this was his bed, in his own home, a safe place of his own. Not a one-night thing before he'd go back to sleeping in his car tomorrow.

For one night only, Shawn Matthews allowed himself to dream.

One of Robin Butler's favorite things about living in the last cabin on cabin row was the sunrises. His small porch angled to the east, his view not blocked by the main house like so many other employee cabins at Clean Slate Ranch. He leaned against the cabin's exterior wall, seated on the built-in bench, legs stretched out in front of him, and he watched the sun rise on the world.

The dark blue sky lightened with stripes of purple and red that melted into brighter orange and finally yellow. He snapped a photo just as the first rounded peak of the sun hit the horizon. The sky above the sun paled to its usual shade of blue, and Robin smiled at the lovely sight. Even on cloudy mornings, he loved knowing the sun had risen on another day. Another day on the second chance he'd been given to live.

He pulled his vape out of his jeans pocket and took a few drags. Sure, the thing wasn't much healthier than actual cigarettes, but Robin didn't like smelling like cig smoke around the tourists or horses. And he only used it in the morning as part of his sunrise ritual—or on the rare occasion a social situation worked his nerves too much.

At least his constant battle with insomnia was good for watching the sunrise.

Robin posted the sunrise photo to his Instagram account, something he'd created a few years ago as a way to honor Xander and his love of sunrises. He only had a few dozen followers, because he only posted once a day, but it was enough to do the familiar morning task. Every morning for the last two and a half years.

Didn't matter where he was, be it out in the wilds on an overnight camping trip with guests, or stumbling out of bed to get to the window after a hookup in the city. He captured each and every sunrise for Xander.

A strange thumping noise came from the cabin next

door, and Robin strained to listen. The ranch's den
mother, Patrice, lived in that cabin, as she had done for
as long as Robin had worked here. She cooked three
meals a day for both guests and staff, and she was a
mother figure to many of them.

Robin stood and took a few steps closer to her cabin.
She was an early riser, too, and watching her leave her
own cabin in the morning to start up breakfast at the
guesthouse was another familiar part of Robin's ritual.
About five feet of space stood between each small cabin,
and Robin crossed it to stand on Patrice's porch. That
thumping was a constant noise now. And louder.

He took a chance and knocked. The thumping got
even louder, and he swore he heard her shouting. With
his heart in his throat, Robin turned the knob, grateful
she didn't lock her door, either. Most of them didn't, because the staff at Clean Slate was a family who trusted
each other.

"Help me, please!" Patrice's shout chilled him to the
bone as he raced through the small living space to the
bedroom area beyond. The bathroom door was open and
spilled out yellow light. Patrice was on the tile floor, a
bath towel draped awkwardly over her middle, while she
held her right arm tight to her heaving chest.

"Oh, thank God." She started sobbing, and Robin
grabbed another towel to wrap around her damp shoulders.

"What happened?" Robin brushed a tear from her
cheek, unnerved at the way her collarbone was already
bruising.

"So stupid, I can't believe I did it. I slipped and fell,
and it all happened so fast. My right shoulder hit the side
of the sink, and I felt something snap. It hurts something

fierce, and I couldn't seem to get up. Started kicking the wall, hoping someone heard."

"I heard you. Do you need me to call an ambulance?"

"Lord, no, that'll just disturb the guests and get folks gossiping. Can you go wake Judson? Maybe the two of you can help me up and drive me to the hospital. Just don't make a fuss. Especially to Arthur, he doesn't need the stress."

Leave it to Patrice to be lying on the floor, half-naked with a possibly broken collarbone, and she didn't want them to fuss. Not liking her on the cold floor, Robin pulled the blanket off her bed and got her a bit more comfortable, before he took off for the back door of the main house.

He'd never been upstairs, so he didn't know which room belonged to ranch foreman Judson Marvel. Judson and Patrice had both worked for Arthur Garrett for decades, and the older trio had a unique bond. Arthur was also still recovering from a massive heart attack a few months ago, so no one wanted to stress him out. Robin paused in the downstairs kitchen and called Judson's cell. He heard it ringing somewhere upstairs.

"Robin, morning," Judson said in his familiar, gravelly voice. "Somethin' wrong?"

"I need you. Patrice fell in her bathroom and I need help getting her up and to the hospital."

"Shit, let me throw some pants on and I'll be right down."

"Don't tell Arthur yet."

"Won't, that's a promise."

Judson hung up and was downstairs in under a minute. Slipped on a pair of boots from the small row by the door, his sun-worn face a study of worry. "You say she fell in the bathroom?" he asked on their way out the door.

"Yeah." Robin described finding her.

Patrice's face was scarlet with embarrassment when they arrived. Robin gave the friends space while Judson got Patrice dried off and into a skirt. Then he helped Judson fashion a sling for Patrice's arm, hoping to keep it as immobile as possible for the ride, before Robin sprinted toward the car barn to get his ride. He'd never used his restored Mustang convertible to drive someone he cared about to the ER before, but hey, shit happened. Judson sat in the back with Patrice, who was working hard not to show how much pain she was in, especially during the initial drive down the dirt ranch road, which was bumpy and full of potholes. Once Robin hit the paved street beyond, Patrice relaxed a fraction and Judson called Reyes to fill him in on what was happening.

Reyes Caldero was head cowboy and in charge of all the horsemen, so he needed to know. Fortunately, the ranch was closed to guests this week for Thanksgiving, and half the hands had left to visit family, leaving a skeleton crew behind to care for the horses and land. Those remaining hands could scavenge for their own breakfast today, Judson said into his phone, and Reyes must have agreed, because the conversation ended shortly afterward.

"Can't thank you both enough for this," Patrice said, her voice fractured by pain, and so soft Robin barely heard her over the roar of his car's engine. "Hate it when folks fuss over me."

"You've spent decades fussing over us," Judson replied. "Let us fuss for a while."

She huffed. "Fine, fine, if you must."

Robin glanced at the older woman in the rearview, glad to see her sense of humor peeking out around the edges of her agony, and hating that she'd been hurt today. She truly was a mother figure to many, Robin included, who hadn't spoken to his own mother in…a long damned time. Not since Robin disappointed his entire family by leaving home to work on a neighboring cattle ranch, instead of their struggling hog farm. Following a dream of working with horses as a career.

After a lot of highs and some very low lows, Robin was back at that career again, and he was happy at Clean Slate. As happy as he'd ever be as a single man who longed for a real, human connection again, especially as he watched his fellow hands find love and relationships of their own.

He wanted to fall in love again, but how could he trust himself to keep his partner safe? Especially after what had happened with Xander. But that was a thought for another day. Right now, he had Patrice to look after, and until she was seen by a doctor and squared away, his nonexistent love life could wait.

Chapter Two

Shawn's plan to get his car jumped and head, well, somewhere, was thwarted first thing in the morning when
Miles showed up for breakfast. Mack had thrown together pancakes and fresh orange juice, and Miles arrived just as their trio was sitting down to eat. Shawn
had slept well and woken up sore from both yesterday's
long day and the soft mattress. His phone was also fully
charged with no waiting messages—not that he'd expected any. He also hadn't expected to be fed a full
breakfast, but refusing to eat would be incredibly rude.

Food, plus last night's lodging, had just been a favor
between coworkers, and Shawn had decided he could
trust Mack's and Wes's generosity.

Friendly greetings went around the table as Miles
filled a plate with food. "Reyes couldn't come?" Wes
asked. "And the ranch is closed to guests this week, so
he doesn't have that excuse."

"No, and I'm surprised no one called you yet," Miles
replied, his expression grim. "This morning, Patrice
slipped getting out of the shower, and I guess it took a
while for Robin to hear her screaming for help and go
next door. Robin and Judson drove her to the hospital

because of pain in her shoulder, and they suspect she fractured her collarbone."

"Holy shit," Wes said.

Mack made a growly noise that was a cross between anger and worry. "She okay otherwise?"

"Yeah, she didn't hit her head or anything." Miles winced. "Reyes and Arthur know, of course, because Judson called them when they finally got to the hospital. Reyes is at the ranch with Arthur to tell the other hands personally when they get real news, so they don't worry too much."

"Be right back." Mack excused himself from the table.

"Patrice cooks for the ranch, right?" Shawn asked, a tiny bit lost by all the names being thrown around.

"Right," Miles said. "She cooks all three meals for both the guests and the ranch hands, and she's done it for ages. I offered to cook breakfast for the skeleton crew, but Arthur insisted he and Reyes could handle it." Miles snorted. "My fiancé, who burns eggs, is going to help with breakfast. But Reyes also wanted me to tell you guys in person."

"This sucks so bad," Wes said. "If Patrice seriously hurt herself, who's going to cook for the guests next week? Arthur's a good cook, but he's not used to handling that kind of volume."

Shawn nearly shouted, "I volunteer!" but cut a bite of pancake instead, unwilling to show how desperate he was for something to do for the next two months. A paying job was obviously ideal, but if he could stay close to these new friends he'd found...

"I don't know," Miles replied. "Until we know Patrice's limitations, everything is speculation. I mean, if nothing else, I can certainly pitch in now that Tango Saloon is closed."

"Dude, this is your vacation." Wes stabbed at his pancake. "I just hope she's okay and recovers quickly. Patrice is amazing. She's, like, the mom of everyone on the ranch."

Shawn's heart thudded hard with grief. His own mother had passed away when he was ten, and despite that early parting, he remembered so much about her. Hours in the kitchen learning to properly cut cold butter into flour, in order to form the perfect piecrust. The right mix of butter and margarine in cookie dough for the best rise and texture. He'd lived more of his life without her than with her, but he still missed his mom.

"Reyes sounded confident it was just a fall," Miles said. "Even if she's out for a few weeks for a fractured collarbone, I'm sure she'll be fine."

They continued eating, and Mack didn't join them again until about fifteen minutes had passed. "She's definitely got a fractured collarbone. Right side. Doc's getting her set up with a sling, and it should heal in about four to eight weeks, but she's gotta take it easy with her dominant hand."

"Fuck, she can't cook for forty-odd people every week like that," Wes replied. "Even if it was her left hand, she'd need help. Or a temporary replacement."

"I know, and so do Arthur and Judson. We'll be okay this week, but come Sunday, we've got a new crop of guests who'll expect to be fed authentic cowboy dining."

Shawn glanced across the table at Miles, who was staring right at him, as if tempting Shawn to volunteer. And he should. The only thing that would change about his daily life was cooking three meals, seven days a week, but he'd be feeding fewer people per day than at the saloon. And he knew Old West food. It wasn't as if he had anywhere to go during his break. He hadn't been home to Breton, Nevada, in five years, and even if he'd had the extra gas money for the trip, his car was one more disaster away from falling apart completely.

Was luck finally coming through for him? Giving him an opportunity to spend his winter around people, instead of in his cold, lonely car? A chance to really matter? But how on earth had Miles known Shawn needed this chance?

"I'm not going anywhere while the ghost town is closed," Shawn said. "I can help out in the kitchen."

"Really?" Mack asked. "You aren't going home for Christmas?"

"No. I haven't been home in a long time, and that's a really long, intensely personal story." Shawn drew strength from Miles's supportive smile. "To be honest, I wasn't sure what I'd be doing while the ghost town is closed, and I'd like to hang around here if I can. Help out."

"You'd be compensated, of course. Judson would handle that negotiation, because no one expects you to cook for guests and hands for free, Shawn."

Relief flooded through him. While Shawn could probably eat the food he cooked for staff and guests, he still needed to put gas in his car. "I admit, a paycheck would be wonderful. I just really need to feel useful."

"Understandable. And it's not as if we don't already know you can cook."

"I don't have as much practice with savory as with desserts, though."

Miles waved a hand in the air. "You'll be fine. And

really, lunch is usually sandwiches and cold salads, so the most cooking you'd do is for breakfast and dinner. And your morning commute is basically the same, the hours are just a bit longer."

"I don't mind the work, honest."

As long as I don't spend another Christmas sitting in my car, all alone, I'll work twenty-four-seven in that kitchen.

"I'll talk to Judson, then," Mack said. "He's eaten your food, and one quick endorsement from Miles is all it'll take for him to hire you on. You're helping us out of a tight spot, Shawn, and I really appreciate it."

"It's okay. The timing is strangely perfect."

"It really is," Wes added. "Like an early Christmas miracle. It sucks donkey balls that Patrice got hurt, though."

Shawn winced, hating that his good luck had come at the expense of another person. He'd only met Patrice a handful of times, but she had always been supersweet to him.

"After breakfast," Mack said, "I'll drive you up to Bentley so we can jump your car, and then around lunch I'll meet you at the ranch. Show you around the guesthouse kitchen. Patrice has a routine she's stuck to for a lotta years, so I imagine she'll be jawing in your ear the first week or two, until you figure out a routine."

"I don't mind the help," Shawn replied. "But I do promise not to let her pick up so much as a soupspoon until her doctor says it's okay. Verbal help only."

"Good man."

It only then occurred to Shawn that Miles hadn't asked a single question about why Shawn was at Mack's house this early in the day, or about his car needing a jump. Wes had probably texted him. It made sense, but Shawn was a little uncomfortable knowing they'd talked about him.

Shawn volunteered to help with the dishes—a tiny fraction of repayment for his hosts' kindness—once breakfast was over, and Miles ended up joining him, drying after Shawn washed. "It's cool that you'll be around the ranch for the holidays," Miles said. "Here we were, worried we wouldn't see each other."

"Yeah, I'm excited to stick around."

"Because you don't have family in the area."

"Right."

Miles elbowed him and grinned. "Except you do now, dude."

Shawn returned the smile. "I guess I do. Thanks." Part of Shawn was still anxious about fixing his car without revealing he lived in the damned thing, but at least he had a job and a purpose for the next two months. He was still managing his own life and that was everything.

Once the dishes were put away and the kitchen clean, Mack asked if Shawn was ready to jump his car. They headed out in Mack's pickup, leaving Wes and Miles behind at the cabin. Shawn was grateful Mack didn't try to initiate banal conversation on the short ride back up to the ghost town—goddamn, that had felt like a much longer walk last night.

Mack parked next to him, and Shawn helped the guy fix the jumper cables on the correct parts of both batteries. If Mack had noticed the collection of belongings in the rear of Shawn's car, he didn't remark on it. Just completed the favor he'd come here to do until Shawn's engine roared to life.

"I really appreciate this, Mack," Shawn said. "All of it."

"It's not a bother to help out a friend," Mack replied. "Listen, you get that battery looked at. If you run over to Larry's shop in Daggett, just drop my name and he'll give you a good deal on any repairs you need."

"Thank you so much." He shook the burly man's hand before getting into his car. Drove down the gravel road while Mack headed for the town's office to do whatever work needed doing this morning.

As much as Shawn didn't want the expense, he couldn't risk his battery dying on him again, so he drove the familiar country road to Daggett, which was only slightly larger than Garrett. But it had a library, multiple restaurants, and a car repair shop. Larry was in, and about twenty minutes later, Shawn was relieved the only thing he needed was a new battery and spark plugs, and he got a good deal on the parts and labor. He hated dropping Mack's name for a discount, but pinching pennies was second nature by now.

"She's a classic in her own right," Larry said as he tapped the hood of Shawn's car. "Seen you drive her through town quite a lot these last few months. You local?"

"I work up at the Bentley Ghost Town." Shawn followed Larry into the shop's small, oil-stained office to settle his bill.

"Ah, of course. Went up with the wife for your July fourth celebration this summer. Had a hoot of a time."

"I'm glad. It's a wonderful place to work, and I'm grateful I'll still have a car to get me there."

"You ever think of selling, let me know. I've got a

friend who collects hatchbacks from the eighties, and I bet he'd be interested in an '85 Subaru like this one."

"Really?" The car had more rust than original paint, and what sane person collected hatchbacks of all cars?

"Sure." Larry handed him a business card along with his credit card receipt. "He'd give you a fair price for it. Keep it in mind, young buck, you hear?"

"I will, thank you, sir."

Shawn left the small lot, slightly buoyed by the conversation. He had no idea what a fair price for his car was, or if it would be enough to buy something better. It also wasn't a top priority right now. He texted Mack that his car was fixed, and that he'd be at the ranch in about twenty minutes. Halfway back, Mack texted that he'd meet Shawn on the guesthouse porch.

Mack and Reyes Caldero were both lounging on the three-story guesthouse's wide, front porch when Shawn parked nearby. The front circle of the ranch included the guesthouse, the barn and corral, and the main house, where the owner lived. There wasn't really a designated parking lot for the place, just dusty land full of tire tracks and buckboard wheel ruts.

Shawn was friendly with Reyes, because of the older man's relationship with Miles, and he shook Reyes's hand as Reyes thanked him for stepping up in the kitchen. "It's really not a problem," Shawn replied, "and I'm sure whatever salary Judson offers will be fair. Like I told Mack and Miles, I'm just grateful to spend the holidays around people I know."

Around a family, even if it wasn't his family.

"I understand." Reyes led them both into the guesthouse—Shawn's first time inside—and he took in the rustic décor. Fur rugs, a moose head, several deer heads, and a few other stuffed critters. Bookcase full of books and games tucked away waiting for the next crop of guests. Straight ahead was a big dining room with a long wood table, and beyond it, the kitchen. Shawn had worked in professional kitchens before, and this was a mix of pro and home, with a huge, eight-burner gas stove, four separate ovens, a long stainless steel counter, and a rack of pots and pans of all kinds. And stuffed in among the equipment and walk-in cooler was another dining table.

"The ranch hands eat their meals in here," Reyes said, "while guests eat in the dining room, all buffet style. It'll be hectic for a while, until you settle into the routine."

Shawn ran his fingers across the stove's shiny surface. The entire place was immaculate. "How does the food ordering work?"

"Once I've verified the week's reservations and any food allergies, Patrice makes up a list based on her weekly meal plan. Same meals each day of the week saves on guesswork, and we change how much we order based on number of guests. Amounts for the hands never changes. I'll need the final order on Thursday night, so I can place it and get the food delivered Saturday afternoon for the new week."

"Sounds good." The same meals each day of the week might get a tad boring for the ranch hands, but it certainly made Patrice's life easier. And Shawn liked the idea of a routine menu.

"Patrice also packs up the food we take out on the three weekly overnight camping trips," Reyes added. "It's usually easier stuff, like canned beans and biscuits, though, so nothing too taxing."

"Okay." This was starting to feel like a bigger chunk

than he could properly chew, but if Patrice could manage it then so could he. Shawn liked a challenge.

"Arthur and Judson almost always eat at the house, so no worries there. And we're light staffed until after Thanksgiving. You can ease your way into things with just breakfast and dinner. The guys know where sandwich shit is, anyway."

Shawn began opening cupboards and inspecting where Patrice stored the pantry staples, as well as how the utensils were stored, the walk-in organized, and how the dishwasher worked. Reyes walked him into the dining room and showed him where the bus bins would sit, so guests could put their dirty dishes in them after eating.

"We usually leave out fresh fruit and granola bars for snacking, too," Reyes continued, "and guests are pretty good about cleaning up after themselves."

"I love how this is set up," Shawn replied. Mack was in the corner of the dining room texting someone, so he mostly spoke to Reyes. "I can see why you guys have a steady influx of tourists."

"We offer something unique without being too far from the city. And now with the ghost town turning a profit…well, I'm hopeful Mack's plan to keep Garrett afloat for years to come is going to work."

"Same." Shawn wasn't as familiar with Garrett as Daggett, because Daggett gave him more places to park and hide for the night, but the tiny town of Garrett was important to Mack, Arthur, and the others. He was happy to do his part both here and at the saloon.

"You ride?" Mack asked out of the blue.

Shawn frowned. "Like ride a horse?"

Mack chuckled, a deep rumbling sound like thunder. "Yeah, like a horse. Wes and Miles want the four of us to go riding this afternoon, and Miles asked if you wanted to join us."

"I've never ridden a horse in my life." He wasn't afraid of the animals, he'd never had the chance before.

"Interested in learning?"

"Um, sure. Why not?" It wasn't as if Shawn had any pressing plans for the rest of his afternoon. And preparing supper later wouldn't be too monumental if he was only cooking for a handful of people.

"Excellent." Mack's thumbs flew over his phone. "Wes and Miles ate lunch at the house. Said they'll meet us at the barn in twenty. Plenty of time for us to make a sandwich or two."

Okay, then.

Somehow Shawn's future had turned from a gaping maw of uncertainty to a job and outdoor activities with men he considered friends. He'd still be sleeping in his car tonight, and that was okay, too. He wouldn't take a single moment of his newfound good luck for granted.

Shawn made a turkey on rye half sandwich for himself, mostly so he didn't stand out too much from the older, taller, bulkier men in the room. Or look rude by turning down food. He'd gotten used to a protein bar in the morning, a lot of water throughout the day, and a buffalo burger or bowl of chili midafternoon for his lunch/dinner. Couldn't exactly cook proper meals in his car, and he only needed enough food to fuel his body for the day.

Another hand came into the kitchen through the back door as they were finishing, and Reyes introduced them. Hugo Turner was the newest ranch hand, hired on last fall to replace Mack on the roster when he quit his duties as head cowboy to restore the ghost town. Newbie status put him on the skeleton crew over Thanksgiving.

Hugo was polite and earnest, and he shook Shawn's hand with enthusiasm on their way out.

The barn intimidated Shawn all over the place with its sheer size and number of animals inside. Big and dark, full of the odors of horse, dung, and hay, and enough exposed, rough wood to give a vampire hives just looking at it. Shawn wasn't exactly a city boy, having lived in medium-sized towns growing up, but he'd never been exposed to barns, ranches, and farms before now.

Reyes led him to a stall where a pretty paint mare stood watching them with huge, dark eyes. "This here is Valentine. She's a good horse, hard to spook. I think you'll do well on her today. Here." He held a sugar cube out to Shawn. "Put it on your palm and keep it flat."

Shawn did as told, his stomach squirrely as Valentine's big lips began swiping at his hand until she got the cube. Not a single tooth in sight. That wasn't so bad. He let her sniff his hand again, then chanced touching her nose. Smooth as velvet up the snout, with stiffer whiskers on the sides.

"Come on then," Reyes said. "You two can get to know each other while I brush her down and tack her."

"Okay."

Shawn did just that, petting Valentine's smooth head and neck, and even brushing her a few times, until Reyes had her properly tacked. Wes and Miles had shown up by then, and Reyes showed Shawn how to mount and ride while the others got their horses ready. It took him a few times to manage swinging his ass into the saddle, but Shawn got there. Being that high in the air on an animal ten times his weight scared him a little but Valentine was gentle and sedate.

"Hey, guys!" A new voice bounced around the corral where Wes was also getting used to riding again—apparently he didn't go out very often—and Shawn tracked it to the mouth of the barn, where a man was leading a gray horse forward, already tacked up.

Even beneath the brim of his cowboy hat, the newcomer was obviously good-looking, with a slick, I'm-sexy-and-I-know-it swagger to his hips and a crooked smile. Tall and well built without being too muscular. The exact type of guy who usually appealed to Shawn—except the last time he'd openly flirted with a straight dude, he'd nearly gotten his ass kicked, and no way in hell was every cowboy on the ranch queer.

The newcomer's smile dimmed when he spotted Shawn, and after staring for several beats, he looked away.

Okay, weirdness.

"Hey, Robin," Mack said. "How's Patrice doing?"

"Judson and Arthur have her settled in a guest room at the main house," the guy named Robin replied. "She's going to be on some major pain meds for a few days, which Patrice says she isn't used to taking, so they want to keep an eye on her."

"Good plan," Wes said. "Pain meds make me high as a kite, and it's not pretty. She should definitely be with her friends until she adjusts. So you're riding?"

Robin nodded. "Figured I'd take Apple Jax out for a ride to de-stress."

"Great minds think alike. Hey, have you met Shawn? He cooks with Miles up at the ghost town."

"No." Shawn prepared for a handshake, but Robin

nodded in his direction without making actual eye contact. "Robin Butler. Nice to meet you."

"Yeah, uh, Shawn Matthews." Okay, this was incredibly awkward, and Shawn had no idea why.

"Shawn's doin' us a huge favor this winter," Mack added. "With Patrice out, we're short a cook, so he's staying in the area and has agreed to be our guesthouse cook while the ghost town's closed."

Robin squinted at Shawn. "That's good timing."

"It's perfect timing," Wes said, completely oblivious to Robin's weirdness, and Shawn was eager to get this ride going and get away from Robin. "Hey, why don't you join us? It's Shawn's first time riding a horse, so he probably needs all the support he can get."

"Uh…" Robin seemed uncertain, and he wouldn't look at Shawn at all. Shawn tried not to take it personally, but Shawn wasn't exactly a troll. He'd showered this morning and worn deodorant. What was this guy's damned problem?

"Back off, boss," Mack said to Wes. "He might need to be alone."

"Not everyone needs people around him at all times," Miles teased. "Like you do."

Wes blew Miles a raspberry, then swung up onto his horse with a small boost from Mack. "Whatever, come along or not. I'm ready to go."

"You're only eager for this ride because you know you aren't camping at the end."

"This is very true."

Shawn bit back a grin. Miles had once confessed he truly enjoyed camping, especially with Reyes, and had joked about how dirtphobic Wes had been during their first vacation at Clean Slate a year and a half ago.

Wes had always struck Shawn as being somewhat high maintenance.

"It's cool. I'll come along," Robin finally said. "The more the merrier, right?" Except he wasn't smiling anymore, and Shawn couldn't help feeling as if it was his fault. But hey, Shawn had never met this Robin guy before, so fuck him if he had a problem with Shawn for no good reason.

Everyone mounted their horses, and Shawn was grateful when Valentine instinctively followed Reyes out of the corral and toward one of the marked trails. The horse knew these lands, so Shawn relaxed his death grip on her reins and tried to roll with the big beast's steps. The entire thing made him mildly seasick, so he studied the land while the others chatted away.

The Garretts apparently owned several thousand acres of land, a lot of it undeveloped and full of wild animals. Shawn had heard stories about coyotes and deer and foxes, and even one about Colt and a skunk, but all he spotted were birds and the occasional squirrel. His ass started getting a little numb after a while, and his inner thighs ached with how they were stretched, but there was something…peaceful about riding a horse.

At one point, Reyes led them off-trail, and Shawn's stomach ached with nerves. But Miles trusted Reyes, so Shawn could trust the man, too. Reyes wouldn't take them on a dangerous route.

Miles reined his horse over to walk beside Shawn's. "Everything okay with your car?" he asked.

"Yes, replaced the battery and spark plugs, so it should get me through the winter."

"That's great. I don't know what your commute is or

even where you live, but there isn't exactly a wealth of public transportation around here."

Shawn knew Miles well enough by now to see the subtle fishing. He'd put his Garrett P.O. Box address on his new-hire paperwork, and that's where his mail was forwarded now. Not that he got much mail, aside from the occasional card or letter from Granddad. "If my car breaks down again, I'll figure it out. Always do."

Miles nodded and let the subject drop. They talked about the meals Patrice typically cooked for breakfast, since Miles ate at the guesthouse with Reyes. Apparently she was a huge fan of both bacon and biscuits with sausage gravy. "Good, hearty food to keep you going for the day," Miles said in a slightly higher-pitched voice, imitating a line he must hear often from Patrice. "I actually modeled the sausage gravy we serve after her recipe, with Patrice's blessing."

Perfect. Miles's sausage gravy was amazing and he'd already taught Shawn the recipe. "I really am looking forward to the challenge of cooking for so many people."

"I bet. I mean, it's fantastic experience, and no one expects you to be my sous chef for the rest of your life."

He pretended to be offended. "Sick of me already, Chef?"

Miles chuckled. "No, just saying you're young, with a lot of potential, and that other opportunities might open up for you in the future. I stumbled into cooking by accident, but I love it, and I can't imagine doing anything else right now. Not only because I fell in love with Reyes, but because I love this land and the saloon. It's my home."

"I like it out here, too. The land is beautiful, and the people are great. Genuine." Unlikely to stab each other in the back, or kick a family member out onto the street because a new lover asked them to.

"The people are great. We've got each other's back, and we've got your back, too, Shawn. For anything you might need."

Fishing again, but Shawn wasn't about to tell his boss his living situation. If he did, Miles would try to fix it somehow, and Shawn could handle his shit. One of these days, he wouldn't need to send so much of his pay home to Granddad, and he didn't want to think about that inevitability today, either. Not when the sprawling mountains and valleys were so peaceful.

Shawn glanced around them. Robin and Reyes were riding ahead of the group; Mack and Wes had fallen behind and slightly to the left. "So what's Robin's problem?" Shawn whispered to Miles. "Back in the corral, he acted like I'd offended him somehow, and I had literally just met the guy."

Miles flinched. "You noticed that, too? I honestly don't know. Robin's a superfriendly guy, good friends with Colt. I've never heard him say a cross word to anyone. Then again, I've only known him for about nine months, so I can't say for sure. Maybe it's just the stress of Patrice's accident."

"Probably." Shawn hoped so. He'd be seeing the guy daily in the guesthouse kitchen, and Shawn didn't need attitude while he was figuring out a new job. Especially attitude from someone as attractive as Robin. But he was also rude—and probably straight, anyway—and Shawn wasn't here to flirt or date, he was here to cook.

"Come on, let's enjoy the day and not worry too much," Miles said. "Riding Tango always helps me forget my troubles."

Tango was Miles's horse, which was ironic, given the name of the saloon. Or maybe it was on purpose. Shawn had never asked. But rider and animal seemed to be in tune with each other as they moved with graceful ease, while Shawn was simply glad he hadn't fallen off his mount yet.

For now, Shawn would enjoy the sunshine, cool air, and gorgeous scenery. He'd worry about his new job cooking for the Clean Slate Ranch guesthouse later.

Please, let this run of good luck last. Please.

Chapter Three

Robin was losing his damned mind.

Taking Apple Jax out for a ride through the country-side to clear his head had been a great idea at the time. Like many of the other horsemen on the ranch, he enjoyed going out on his favorite mount when he wasn't seeing to guests. Enjoying the vast, open beauty of the land and the special bond between man and beast. Going out after this morning's scare with Patrice was exactly what he'd needed.

Until Shawn.

Robin had heard the guy's name in passing, always in reference to the ghost town, but he'd never actually met him before. Not until today when the smiling, dark-haired man sitting astride Valentine flipped Robin's life upside down. For one glorious—and horrifying—moment, Robin saw Xander sitting on the first and last horse he ever rode.

Robin thought his love had come back to him. His kind, energetic, willful Xander Peletier.

But no. Xander was dead, and this was someone else. Someone else who could have been Xander's twin, and the uncanny resemblance freaked Robin the fuck out. He hadn't wanted to engage with Shawn, and he'd silently cursed Wes's invitation to join their group. Not going would have been even more rudeness layered on his already rude introduction to Shawn, so Robin had agreed.

And he regretted it with every plod of Apple Jax's hooves on the hard-packed earth, because he couldn't get Shawn out of his head. It took all his energy to focus ahead and not look back. Not sneak glances at the guy riding behind him next to Miles, appearing perfectly at ease astride Valentine, despite it being his first time on a horse. Nope, he couldn't compare Shawn and Xander. Fate had just decided to take a big, fat dump on his head by putting a Xander look-alike in his life—a look-alike who'd be cooking meals at the guesthouse for the next two months, give or take, and that was bad.

Maybe I can buy a hot plate and live off canned chili and soup?

Nah. After eating Patrice's homemade chili, anything out of a can would taste like dog food. No, Robin could be an adult and ignore the guy. Ignore the way Xander's smile made his insides warm in a familiar way. Ignore the fact that everything about Xander appealed to him—wait, Shawn. Not Xander. Xander was dead, and having Shawn around the ranch was a living reminder of that fact. A reminder he needed to get out of his head somehow.

Robin was openly bi, and he had a regular city hookup with Wes's brother-in-law, Derrick Massey.

I should call Derrick, see if he's up for fucking my brains out later tonight.

Anything to get the memories of Xander, now superimposed with Shawn, out of his damned head. He'd worked too hard to put his past behind him, damn it.

"Robin? You awake, man?" Reyes said. He rode beside Robin on his personal horse, Hot Coffee, and he had apparently been saying something to Robin.

"Yeah, sorry, I spaced out. What?"

Reyes snorted softly. "Never mind. Wasn't important. You okay?"

"A little stressed about this morning still, I guess." Rushing a friend to the hospital would put anyone's mood into the shitter, and it was an easier excuse than telling Reyes about Xander/Shawn. No one in his new life here at Clean Slate knew about Xander.

"Not too surprised, but Patrice will be fine. She's a tough lady."

"Yeah, she is." Robin gave Reyes an exaggerated eyebrow wiggle. "You must be excited to have Miles all to yourself whenever you want for the next two months."

"Not really whenever I want, since I'm still working all but three of those weeks. But it'll be nice knowing he's nearby instead of up the mountain."

Robin nodded without comment, his brain flashing back to September, when he and Reyes had both heard a gunshot in the distance. Up the mountain toward the ghost town. They'd ridden bareback toward the sound, only to find a bruised and beaten Miles next to his unconscious stalker of an ex. Seeing Miles like that, stunned and bloody, had sent Robin right back to the day Xander died, and he'd frozen for an instant.

Reyes hadn't noticed, too focused on his damaged boyfriend, and Robin had righted himself quickly to help his friends. But sometimes those memories came back during the rare moments he slept long enough to dream, and he understood Reyes's need to make sure Miles stayed safe.

"You guys make any plans for Christmas yet?" Robin

asked, redirecting his morbid thoughts to the upcoming two-week December break for the ranch employees.

"Actually, if the weather is good, we talked about a horse ride out to the lake. Waking up on Christmas day in our favorite spot."

"You gonna haul a tree up there on your horse's backside?"

Reyes chuckled. "No. Neither of us has any big holiday traditions, and I like the idea of starting a new one of our own. Wes won't like it, but I can probably get him to back off by promising we'll be over for supper that night, or something. Besides, he gets to host Thanksgiving at the cabin."

"I can't wait to see the place."

Typically, the staff who remained behind at Thanksgiving ate a big feast in the guesthouse, because it had the largest seating area, cooked up by both Arthur and Patrice. With Arthur scaling back on excessive stress and exertion, Wes and Patrice had plotted to cook supper at Wes's house this year. The cabin apparently had a spacious interior and a long dining table that would fit everyone.

"With Patrice down for a while," Robin continued, "Wes'll have his hands full. I'd volunteer to help, but the best I can do for food is open a can of cranberry jelly."

"I doubt Patrice has ever allowed that canned stuff near her table," Reyes said with a soft chuff of laughter. "But Wes will have Miles to pitch in, and maybe even Shawn, now that he's sticking around."

"Yeah."

If Shawn's there, maybe I can fake a stomachache and hide in my cabin.

No, Robin could act like an adult and be around the

guy. He'd just…avoid conversation, that's all. Easy enough.

Maybe.

"So how about you?" Reyes asked. "Any plans for Christmas?"

Robin shrugged and stroked the side of Apple Jax's neck. "Not really. Might spend a few days in San Francisco, but I'll mostly just chill at the ranch. Don't mind being part of the skeleton crew who stays behind."

"Me, either."

Clean Slate Ranch was as much a person rescue as it was a horse rescue and rehab. A lot of the horsemen had stories, and some had even been incarcerated. But Arthur Garrett believed in second chances, and he'd pulled Robin out of the gutter (literally) and given him a fresh chance to start over.

Arthur had saved his life.

Robin also knew Reyes didn't speak to his blood family anymore—not the reason why, just the simple fact—and neither did Mack. Or Miles. The real outlier in their pack of cowboys was Colt Woods, who'd reconnected with his Texas family this past spring.

At least one of us gets to keep his family.

Robin had left his family behind as a young man, same as Colt, but Robin had no illusion of a warm welcome if he ever went back to Pall Flats. He'd be lucky he didn't get spit on and run back out.

A flash of rust in the distance caught his attention, and Robin caught the last glimpse of a fox darting across their unmarked trail. This one wasn't used by tourists, because it had more ups and downs, and it crossed the stream that wound through the land a few times. It was a private trail carved by friends, meant to be shared with friends.

Robin glanced over his shoulder at Shawn, who was gazing out at the trees around them, his expression… sad? Seeing Shawn sad made Robin want to fix it, because he'd hated it when Xander was sad, but that wasn't his job, damn it. Shawn wasn't Xander. Shawn and Robin weren't friends, weren't going to be friends, because Robin didn't need the constant, physical reminder of his former life right beside him.

His heart ached with old grief, and Robin bit the inside of his cheek hard. Anything to make that internal pain go away.

They stopped at one of the stream crossings to dismount and stretch, and so their horses could drink if thirsty. Wes complained about his sore butt, which Mack promptly smacked. Robin laughed at the pair, glad to be able to hang with Mack for a while this week. He'd missed the former head cowboy being around the ranch, and it amused Robin to see how carefree and affectionate Mack acted around his boyfriend. So different from the gruff, grumpy man he'd once been.

I want that.

Not that Robin was a grump or anything, but he did envy the happy couples all around him. And living in the middle of nowhere made it hard to meet people he could potentially settle down with. Man or woman, he wasn't picky, as long as he loved them, and they loved him back.

Except he wasn't sure he could stand the heartbreak of losing another lover.

Mack did and look at him now.

"Hey."

Robin turned at the sound of Miles's voice. Miles stood behind him with his arms crossed, expression firm but mild. "Hey, Miles."

"Can you do me a favor?"

"Sure."

"Can you please go make nice with Shawn for five minutes? He thinks he somehow offended you earlier, and I brushed it off as stress from Patrice's fall, but he's...taking it personally, I think. Please?"

Robin bit back a groan. "Yeah, I can talk to him. And he didn't offend me. We just met. How could he have?"

"Exactly, and thank you." Miles's expression clearly said he meant for Robin to do this favor right the hell now.

Shawn stood near the stream, nudging at rocks with the toe of his very worn sneaker, hands deep in his jeans pockets. Robin walked noisily so he didn't spook the guy, who seemed to be about Miles's age, but Robin had never been great at guessing that.

"Hey, man," Robin said. He pasted on a friendly smile and braced himself to look into Shawn's eyes. Instead of the dark blue eyes of his old lover, Shawn's eyes were a light brown that flirted with hazel. Instead of laughing and joyful, Shawn's eyes were wary and serious.

"Hi." Shawn stared at him.

Robin picked for his words so he didn't lie or reveal too much. "I want to apologize for earlier, if I came across as rude. I didn't mean to be—it's just been a really long day."

"I bet. And you were kind of rude, so how about we start over? Hi, I'm Shawn." He held out a pale hand to shake.

Robin took the hand, surprised by Shawn's firm grip

and work-rough skin. "Robin. Nice to meet you." And dear God, no, he did not feel any sort of electricity sizzle through his system from their touch. Nope. Not even a little.

He isn't Xander, you idiot, just a guy with a resemblance.

Shawn's eyes flickered to their joined hands briefly before he let go. "Same. So you're a cowboy, huh?"

The deadpan way Shawn said that made Robin burst out laughing. "What gave me away? The hat or the boots?"

"Mostly the horse, but the costume is good, too. Practical and fashionable."

"I aim to please, especially with the guests."

"I bet. Have you always wanted to work at a dude ranch?"

"Not specifically, no, but I've loved horses since I was a kid, and I dreamed of making some kind of career out of them. I just sort of ended up here, but I do love it."

Shawn nodded, a thoughtful smile on his face, and the more Robin looked at him, the less he saw Xander. Shawn's face was slimmer, less heart shaped. He had a mole on his left temple but no freckles on his nose like Xander had. Close up, Robin saw Shawn, and the guy was adorable in a geeky, boy-next-door way that appealed to him differently than Xander's exuberance for life had appealed to him when they first met eleven years ago. And Shawn might be outwardly appealing, but he was definitely off-limits.

"It's an easy place to love," Shawn replied. "I just sort of ended up here, too, so I know what you mean."

"Are you from Santa Clara County?"

"No." His expression shuttered, suggesting the past

was off-limits in this getting-to-know-you conversation. "You?"

"Nebraska, actually." Robin rarely delved into the intricacies of his past but his home state wasn't a big deal. "Probably why I love this hill country so much. Nebraska is flatter than big-rig road kill."

Shawn pulled a face. "I've never been but I've seen pictures."

"Then you know how boring it is." Robin winked. "Couldn't wait to get away."

"All the way to California?"

Some of his humor died off as Robin remembered why he'd landed in California to begin with. "Apparently so." Talking to and subtly flirting with Shawn was way too easy, so Robin needed to politely excuse himself. "Ready to hit the trail again?"

"Sure." Shawn seemed disappointed but hid it quickly. "This whole horse riding thing is actually kind of cool."

"Wait until you learn how to gallop. It's the most freeing thing in the world."

"Yeah? I'd love to learn how."

The simple statement, without a touch of flirtatiousness, still felt like a gong of doom to Robin. If Shawn wasn't straight, then hanging out with him would only deepen the things Robin already craved—connection, love, a long-term relationship. "I'm a little busy keeping all the horses looked after, but we'll see," he hedged. "Mack might be a better fit to teach you, since his lazy ass doesn't have to work for two months."

"I heard that," Mack said from over Robin's shoulder. "What am I teaching Shawn to do?"

"Gallop. Seems he's taken to riding."

"You don't have to," Shawn said to Mack. "I'll prob-

ably be too busy cooking to have time. Excuse me."
He strode to where he'd left Valentine and mounted the
horse like he'd been riding his whole life, and no, Robin
did not check out his ass.

Okay, yes, he did, and Shawn had a nice ass encased
in worn denim.

Robin *really* needed to stop perving on the new ranch
cook.

"You two okay?" Mack asked.

"Sure, I just wanted to clear up any misunderstanding from earlier," Robin replied with a casual shrug he
didn't really feel. "Are we all ready to head back?"

"Yeah, it's getting close to suppertime. All right,
folks, mount up!"

Robin rode behind their group on the return trip,
and it absolutely wasn't so he could stare at the back of
Shawn's head. Or watch the way his hips undulated in
the saddle with each step the horse made toward home.

I am definitely calling Derrick when we get back.

Shawn couldn't brush off the sense of being watched
on the ride back, which was a little silly, since he was
up front near Mack with four other people behind them.
Someone was likely looking at or near him at any given
moment. Didn't mean it was Robin.

Robin, who was even cuter up close, with his dark hair
and eyes, and the sun-bronzed skin of someone who'd
worked outdoors most of his life. Shawn wasn't great
at the whole dating thing, but he was moderately certain Robin had flirted with him a few times. So Shawn
had tried flirting back and he'd epically failed, because
Robin backed out of riding lessons so hard Shawn had

smelled the burned rubber. Robin was nice but clearly not interested.

Fine. Shawn had come to Garrett for work, not flirting, and he had work. Work he couldn't afford to lose if a fling went south, so better he keep his head in cooking and away from thoughts of flirting or anything else.

Back at the ranch, Miles showed him how to untack Valentine and return her to her stall. He even fed her part of a carrot as a thank-you for their journey together. She nickered at him and swished her long, black tail.

After he got a head count of who was eating in the guesthouse, Shawn and Miles headed for the kitchen. Shawn loved the idea of swapping roles, with Miles his sous chef tonight. Judson arrived around five to both officially introduce himself—they'd met very briefly during the July fourth celebration—and discuss a salary for Shawn's work. His offer was more than Shawn expected as a temp, so he didn't even negotiate.

"You'd need to be here by six thirty most mornings," Judson said. "Easy commute for Patrice, because she lives here on the ranch, but will that be too hard for you? Especially seven days a week?"

"It won't be a problem, sir," Shawn replied. If he had to, he'd park along the main road to the ranch and sleep in his car there. The plus side of taking your house with you everywhere you went was you made your own commute time. His only minor issue might be people peeking into his car and wondering why he carried so much stuff with him.

I'll just cover it with a blanket.

"And if you're ever too tired to drive home at night," Miles said a little too casually, "I'm sure you can crash on the ranch somewhere, or up with Mack and Wes."

"Ayup, that's never a problem," Judson added. "And Colt's still got himself a single cabin when his fiancé isn't staying over. You're doing us a huge favor, Shawn, so we'll work with you."

"You're doing me a favor, too, believe me." Shawn checked the flavor of the potatoes he'd been mashing. Maybe a bit more butter.

"Then I'll leave you to it. You'll be at Mack's place for Thanksgiving dinner, right?"

Shawn blinked hard. "Um."

"Oh, you have to come," Miles said. "Usually Patrice hosts it here, but Wes really wanted to show off the cabin to everyone with a big party, so she agreed to host it at Wes's this year. Wes already harangued me into helping him cook with Patrice out of commission. It'll be fun, and you won't be alone puttering around your apartment with a frozen turkey dinner, or whatever you'd planned."

How could he turn down an offer like that? "Okay, I'll be there."

"Perfect. Guests can arrive starting at noon, and dinner is at two."

"Got it."

At five thirty, a handful of ranch folk—both strangers and the hands he knew—started filing into the kitchen and filling plates with food. Shawn tried to remember everyone's name but it was going to take a while, and this was only a portion of the entire staff. Robin gave him a curt nod that Shawn returned. Once everyone had their food, Miles and Shawn each filled a plate. Well, Miles filled his. Shawn ate about what he thought he needed to hold him over until tomorrow's protein bar.

Mack and Wes ate with the hands, and Shawn suspected it was for nostalgia's sake, seeing old friends again now that the ghost town was shut down. Mack had been head cowboy here for a lot of years, according to Miles, and watching the older man interact with the hands felt a bit like watching a family reunion. Lots of joking and laughter and raunchy teasing. Wes talked a bit about an upcoming audition for a sitcom pilot he was excited for.

Shawn sometimes envied Wes his love of attention and being noticed. Shawn spent most of his time trying not to be seen. Trying to keep his head down, do his job, and be as unobtrusive as possible in the wider world. He'd had his fill of being the center of attention.

"Hey, Butler, what's up your ass tonight?" one of the hands asked Robin. The guy had his shirtsleeves rolled up, showing off tattoos from wrist to elbow on both arms. What was his name again? Quentin? "Usually can't get you to shut up at dinner."

Robin flipped him off. "Why don't you stick to strumming your guitar for the guests and let me worry about my own moods."

Even though he'd spoken in a teasing tone, Quentin scowled at the response. "At least I got talent at something other than showing greenhorns how not to fall off their horse."

The challenge made Robin look up from his plate. Something glinted in his dark eyes, and he seemed poised to comment. Then he shrugged and shoved mashed potatoes into his mouth. Shawn wasn't sure how to take the exchange, since he didn't know the different interpersonal relationships among the hands. But he imagined testosterone dripped off the walls on occasion, especially when someone's temper was up.

Wes redirected the conversation, and Shawn brushed

it away. But he couldn't help a glance down the long table to where Robin was sitting a bit away from the group, his eyes on his phone as he ate. Shawn wanted to crack into Robin's head and see what was going on inside it. Maybe even befriend the guy.

He also got the impression Robin didn't want to be friends, so Shawn paid attention to Wes's story and tried not to think about the hot, lonely cowboy at the other end of the table.

Tried...and failed.

Chapter Four

Cooking for the skeleton crew on Tuesday and Wednesday helped Shawn get a better feel for the routine he'd have to set next week when guests arrived. Reyes reported they had reservations for thirteen, which wasn't bad for this late in the year. Because of the way dates and holidays fell on the calendar, they had four more full weeks this year for guests, before the ranch closed until after the new year. While closed, the kitchen would again be feeding a skeleton crew.

Not bad, really, and Patrice had been allowed to observe him on Wednesday—from the rocking chair Arthur installed her in with a promise she would only get up to stretch or take a bathroom break. No cooking. Shawn had sworn to the man he'd only ask for verbal help, and he stuck to it.

The guesthouse kitchen was closed on Thursday for Thanksgiving, so Shawn ate his protein bar in his car, which he'd taken to parking in the bushes off the paved road that led into the tiny town of Garrett. So far, no cops or county sheriff's deputies had spotted him, and it made his commute easier. The nights had gotten chillier, so he'd dug out a fleece blanket from the back, and

Shawn kept it wrapped around his shoulders while the engine warmed on Thanksgiving morning.

Once he had hot air spewing from the vents, Shawn drove to the big interstate truck stop he visited several days a week to shower, buy drinking water, and maybe treat himself to a cup of coffee. He'd weaned himself off coffee once becoming homeless, because it was an expense he didn't need and he couldn't very well brew his own in the car. A long shower helped ease his sore muscles and woke him up, and he took advantage of the facilities until hanging too long looked suspicious.

Working boys sometimes hung around these truck stops, looking for quick cash or a ride elsewhere, and Shawn never wanted to put out that impression to the truckers who regularly came through. He'd never had to trick out for money or a place to sleep, and while he wouldn't judge anyone who chose to, he hoped he never found himself in that position.

He still had about two hours to kill before he could politely show up at Mack's place for dinner, so Shawn treated himself to a hot cocoa from the convenience store, parked his car in a sunny spot so he could turn off the engine and still stay warm, and pulled a library book out of the small stack on the passenger-side floor.

The Daggett librarians knew him by name now, because he went in every two weeks to get new books. Books kept him company at night when he couldn't sleep, because the car was too cold, or the seats too uncomfortable. Books helped him live happier lives, explore new places he'd probably never see with his own two eyes, and experience the world from new points of view.

"I have lived a thousand lives because I read books,"

Shawn whispered to his newest hardcover. If he ever got a tattoo—if his meager budget ever allowed it—it would be of that phrase. He'd seen versions of it online and it spoke to him more than almost anything else.

Shawn lost himself in the murder mystery, and when he checked his phone, it was already twelve thirty. Time to head back to the ranch. He'd have to find out who-dunit later. Showing up to a party without something for his hosts was bad manners, but alcohol was pretty easy to get in California, he'd learned. He picked up a nice-looking—if slightly dusty—bottle of wine from the convenience store before heading back to Garrett.

After working at the ghost town for the last eight months, Shawn had gotten to know the dirt track lead-ing to the ranch lands. Which potholes to avoid, which stretches he could go a little faster on, and soon he'd turned onto the ghost town road. Then the short track to Mack and Wes's house. The yard was already filled with cars and pickups, even two ATVs, and people lounged on the porch, enjoying the mild weather.

Shawn smiled at familiar faces but struggled to match them to names as he entered the cabin and sought out his hosts. He spotted Reyes, Colt Woods and Colt's fi-ancé, Avery Hendrix, first, hanging by the front door with drinks in their hands. Avery greeted him with a warm hug and pointed toward the kitchen.

Wes, Miles, Mack, and an older woman were danc-ing around each other in the okay-sized kitchen, manag-ing all sorts of pots, pans, and serving bowls. Miles was giving orders to everyone, and the woman introduced herself as Wes's mom, Leta. Wes took Shawn's bottle of wine with a grateful smile and added it to a folding table by the loft stairs that was the drink station. All kinds of wines and spirits, plus soft drinks, a bucket of ice, cups, markers for labeling, and even a cooler beneath full of beer and flavored ciders.

Shawn wasn't a fan of hard liquor, never had been, but he treated himself to a beer. It was a holiday, after all. Since the men he knew best were busy handling the food—and the house smelled amazing—he hung back a bit, unsure where to plant himself. Two familiar people approached him, and Shawn was proud of himself for recognizing Wes's little sister Sophie and her husband, Conrad. He'd met both on the ghost town's opening day in April, and the pair had come up to enjoy the site again back in August. Wes had shown them all the behind-the-scenes areas, including the saloon's kitchen.

"Happy Thanksgiving, Shawn," Sophie said as she gave him a big hug. Shawn wasn't used to all this hugging and wasn't sure how he felt about it. Not uneasy or anything. Simply…out of practice at human contact.

"Yeah, you, too." Shawn shook Conrad's hand. "So this is a big family event, I take it?"

"Yeah," Sophie replied. "When Wes said he wanted to do Thanksgiving here this year, Mom wasn't thrilled because we always have dinner at her house. But when Wes sold her on the idea of it also being a kind of housewarming party, she caved and agreed as long as she got to do the turkey."

Shawn's heart gave a funny pang at the easy way Sophie talked about family traditions and holiday plans, as if it was the easiest, simplest thing in the world. Especially when Shawn knew how complicated family could be. It had been too many years since he'd had Thanksgiving with anyone blood related to him. Even when he'd lived with his cousin Sheila, she never cooked more than a microwave meal for the occasion.

"I'm glad you guys could still be together today," Shawn said. He took a long pull from his beer bottle.

"So are you here with anyone?" Sophie asked.

"No, I'm just here as a friend of the hosts. I'm sure Wes told you I'm the temp cook at the ranch for a while."

"Yeah, that really sucks how Patrice hurt herself. I'm just glad everything worked out. Garrett is so remote, they'd have had a hard time finding a replacement this quickly."

"It was good timing."

A man similar in height and appearance to Conrad joined their group, and Shawn met Conrad's brother, Derrick. Derrick gave his hand a long squeeze as he held eye contact a bit longer than a straight guy would. "Very nice to meet you finally," Derrick said in a deep, oddly soothing voice. "I've heard great things via Wes."

Shawn couldn't stop a blush from heating his neck and cheeks. "Um, thanks. If you guys will excuse me a moment, um, do you know where the bathroom is?"

Sophie pointed at the hall that ran behind the kitchen. "The door on the right."

"Thanks." He escaped to the empty bathroom and took a few long, calming breaths. He'd taken his meds this morning, but all these people were still fucking with his anxiety. Everyone was friendly as hell but so many of them were strangers, and Shawn shouldn't have come so soon. They weren't eating until two, which meant too much time to kill with casual conversation.

You can do this. Don't let fear win. Be strong.

When someone knocked on the door, Shawn flushed and made a show of washing his hands, before relinquishing the bathroom to another guest—who happened to be Robin. For a split second, Shawn wondered if Robin had followed him. But Robin seemed surprised to see him, so Shawn slipped past the cowboy without a word.

Rude, maybe, but the best way for Shawn to curb his curiosity over the guy was to keep his distance.

Appetizers appeared on the long dining table: buffalo wings, hot dips and pita chips, a veggie platter, and a few things Shawn didn't immediately recognize but tried anyway. Grazing the food was a great excuse not to chat, but people found their way to him, anyway. He met Wes's dad, Avery's parents, a few Garrett locals Arthur had probably invited, and other employees of the ghost town who showed up over the course of the afternoon. The cabin had seemed huge on Sunday night, but today it burst at the seams with guests.

Wes was in his element as host now, leaving the others to finish the food, which was slowly finding its way to the other end the dining table. Shawn had expected a moderate-sized sit-down meal, but Colt and Reyes were setting up folding tables and chairs in different corners of the room, plus lap trays for others. Looked like they'd go buffet style and park wherever they could.

When two o'clock rolled around, Shawn didn't think another person could possibly fit into that house, and he'd met more folks than he could ever remember. Shawn had a good memory for food and recipes, but he'd never been good with names and faces. Wes stood on one of the long benches that lined either side of the dining table and let out an impressive wolf whistle that silenced conversation.

"Anyone who knows me knows I love being the center of attention," Wes said, to a scattering of agreeable laughter. "But I'll keep this brief, because everything smells amazing, and I'm starving. I'm not much for saying Grace or anything, but we must give credit where credit is due, and this wonderful Thanksgiving dinner wouldn't be possible without the capable hands of my lovely mother, Leta Bentley, my very best friend, Miles Arlington, my sexy boyfriend, Mack Garrett, and myself."

After a wave of applause, Wes continued, "And special thanks to everyone who brought booze, too. Now grab a plate and let's eat!"

Shawn hung back by a wall to avoid the initial throng of hungry people swarming the food, so out of place he half wished he'd lied about having plans today. Hugo, the new cowboy, came over and invited him to get in line. Shawn took small portions of most things, for the variety and so he didn't overdo it and make himself sick. The table seating was full, and so were a lot of the card tables, so he and Hugo went outside to eat.

They didn't really talk, which Shawn appreciated, happy to have a silent wingman. He felt less isolated, with the only other people he knew busy enjoying time with their families. They didn't need Shawn clinging.

"So I'm surprised no one lassoed you into helping cook today," Hugo said after several minutes of quiet eating.

"I'm sure Wes had his entire menu planned out before anyone realized I'd be around the ranch for Thanksgiving," Shawn replied. "I'm just grateful I was invited."

"The entire ranch was invited, and I'm glad. Even if I'd wanted to go home, I can't afford it right now."

"Same."

Hugo met his eyes and held his gaze for several long, meaningful beats. "Cool."

And like that, they kept eating. Shawn saw a possible kindred spirit in Hugo, just as he'd seen one in Miles their first week working together. He hoped Hugo's past wasn't as awful as Miles's or as frightening as Shawn's.

A few of the hands popped over to chat briefly between plates of food. Shawn didn't go back for seconds. He dumped his paper plate in the proper trash can and fetched himself a second beer. The comfort and camaraderie of the full house made him wish for home.

But which home? The home of his childhood, where he helped his mom bake pies and cakes and cookies for every county fair? The home of his middle school years, with a dad who was spiraling into opioid addiction but still loved his son? The home from high school, with loving grandparents and the worst two years of his life?

The only home he had left was with his grandparents, but as much as he loved them, that town had too many bad memories for him. Still, he needed to hear a friendly voice.

Shawn went outside and a few dozen yards into the backyard near the tree line. Checked his reception before placing the call.

"That you, Shawn?" Granddad asked in his familiar, cigar-raspy voice.

"It's me." Shawn blinked back hot tears. "Happy Thanksgiving."

"Here, one minute, and I'll put you on speaker for your nana."

"Okay."

Granddad fumbled with the landline, causing a few

amusing beeps before the line crackled a bit, and he said, "Go ahead. Guess who's called us, Irma?"

"Hey, Nana," Shawn said. "Happy Thanksgiving." Nana replied as best she could, and Shawn was able to translate the greeting as a return of the Thanksgiving salutation. Her speaking ability had deteriorated drastically over the last three years, and a lot of times Granddad had to translate for him.

Shawn was missing so much, and Nana didn't have many years left. She'd been battling the vicious, debilitating symptoms of Huntington's disease for fifteen years now, which was a long time considering how late doctors had caught it. She'd blamed so many things for her bad coordination, memory struggles, and sudden bouts of temper before relenting and having more in-depth tests done.

"So I have some interesting news." He told them about his new temp job.

"That's wonderful for you," Granddad replied. "It'll help keep your room paid up while the ghost town is closed."

Shawn flinched. The one big lie he'd told his grandparents was that he'd procured an affordable place to stay here in Garrett, so they didn't worry. The last thing Shawn needed was for Granddad to get noble about taking Shawn's money every month. They needed it more than he did.

He told them about today's party with as much added cheer as possible, desperate to always show how happy he was for their sake. And he *was* happy. Maybe not one hundred percent. Fifty-five percent? But they only ever got to see the hundred.

Nana said something Granddad translated as, "You seeing anyone down there?"

She always wanted to know if he was dating. "Nah, too busy right now, and I'll be too busy at the guesthouse going forward. But I'm not lonely, I promise."

Liar.

They shot the shit for a little while longer, until Granddad complained Shawn was wasting his minutes. Shawn didn't care. On this holiday, he needed to hear the voices of the only family he had left who gave a damn. Except…he had friends in the cabin behind him who gave a damn.

After Shawn said goodbye to Nana, the phone clicked off speaker. "You enjoy your life while you can, you hear me, son?" Granddad said softly. "Every single minute of it."

His heart sank. "How bad is she getting?"

"Medicine's got her moods more stable, but my back…not sure how much longer I'll be able to care for her at home. The last time she fell, I had to get a neighbor to help me haul her back up."

"Oh, Granddad." Huntington's affected muscle coordination as much as mind and speech, and Nana had suffered more than one bad fall over the years. "I can come home and help."

"No, Irma's my wife. I promised in sickness and in health forty-two years ago."

"There's gotta be some sort of help your insurance will pay for."

"Nothing that isn't hospice related, and I'm not ready for that yet. Don't want her to think I'm giving up. I'm not ready to let her go."

"I know." Shawn desperately wanted to reach through

his phone and hug his grandfather. "And she knows how much you love her, even on the days she forgets."

"Yeah. I'm just feeling down because it's a holiday. Don't mean to take it out on you."

"You can always vent to me, you know that. I get it." Shawn had been home for the worst of Nana's symptoms, while her neurologist experimented with medications and doses and time of day. He'd heard her screaming horrible things at Granddad, blaming him for past hurts long ago forgiven, even yelling and cussing at Shawn a few times. "I love you."

"Love you, too, son. You be happy where you are, okay? You're safe and away from Beck, and that's what counts."

"Yeah."

"You take care."

Shawn reluctantly said goodbye, and the second the phone was back in his pocket, his ass hit the ground. Energy gone, swamped with loss, grief, and so much loneliness he couldn't stand it. He pulled his legs to his chest and rested his forehead on his knees. Concentrated on breathing. Time and distance had taken the power Beck's name used to have to scare him. Now it only angered him that the asshole's continued presence in Breton compelled Shawn to stay away for his own safety.

"Shawn?" Robin's voice. Damn it. "Dude, are you okay?"

No.

Shawn shrugged without raising his head. He didn't want Robin to see the bad things that would be all over his face. All he wanted was to be alone for a while so he could work through his emotions. Except the air

shifted beside him, and he caught of whiff of something…cherry?

He looked up, surprised to see both Robin sitting
on the grass beside him, and a vape dangling between
Robin's fingers. Must be the cherry smell. It surprised
him that Robin smoked. Vaped. Whatever.

"Damn, man, someone die?" Robin asked.

"No." Shawn worked to school his expression but
he'd never been great at hiding his emotions, especially
when he was upset. "Just holiday blues, I guess. I miss
my grandparents."

"You talk to them today?"

"Yeah, just now. Guess it overwhelmed me." And
why was Shawn admitting all this to Robin? Robin Butler, cowboy, who wasn't interested, but who looked and
smelled really good up close like this.

"Are you guys, uh, close?"

For a guy who'd practically run away from him after
Monday's trail ride, Robin was acting like someone who
actually wanted to get to know Shawn.

*Maybe he has a thing for rescuing people in trouble.
He did help rescue Miles, after all.*

"They're the only blood family I have left who give
a damn," Shawn replied. "I haven't seen them in five
years." Now why had he gone and admitted that?

"Sorry, man."

"As my nana would say, that's the way it goes."

Robin smiled at him, and it spoke to something deep
inside Shawn. Something he hadn't felt in a long damned
time: hope. Hope that maybe he could find a friend in
Robin. Someone who'd listen without offering unsolic-
ited advice or trying to fix things.

"If it helps at all," Robin said, "I haven't seen my blood family in about thirteen years."

"Really? Why?" Shawn regretted the nosy question when Robin's expression shuttered. "Sorry, not my business. I appreciate that you kind of get it, though."

"Thanks. I'm like a lot of the guys at Clean Slate. Past is past, and the present is what matters."

"I like that idea."

Robin lightly bumped Shawn's shoulder with his own. "It's a good life motto. Hard to keep moving forward if you're always looking behind you."

"True. Have you called your family yet?"

"Nah. We're estranged in all the ways. I send my mother Christmas cards so she knows I'm alive but I've never gotten one back. It's complicated and messy, and it's too nice a day to get into all that crap."

"Okay." Shawn had never been the nosy, pushy guy, so he backed off on the personal questions. But he liked talking to Robin, and it was hard not to reach out and touch the man. To bump his shoulder again, just for the connection to another person. "So, uh, I guess you must really like working at the ranch."

"I do. I love horses, always have, so it's a dream job for me. Sometimes the greenhorns can be annoying, especially young guys who want to impress their friends, but for the most part I love it. And I work with some pretty terrific people."

"I feel the same. About the ghost town and my co-workers. Miles is great, and so are Annabelle and Emily. Plus Mack and Wes, and all the other employees. I lucked into a great job here." He'd been speaking to his hands, and when Shawn looked at Robin, Robin glanced away.

Weird. Robin was a mystery, running hot and cold,

and Shawn wasn't going to let that ruin the rest of his day. The food had been too good, the hosts too generous. "Well," Shawn said as he stood, "I should probably head out."

"Already?" Robin stumbled getting up and shoved that vape into his pocket. "They haven't served dessert yet."

"I'm not much for pumpkin pie."

"There's way more than just *pumpkin* pie, trust me." Robin tilted his head and offered Shawn a crooked smile. "Please? Have one piece of pie with me?"

This is a bad idea.

But it was only a bad idea if Robin was flirting, and Shawn couldn't figure out if he was or not. And if he wasn't, then maybe Shawn could score a new friend. New friends he could do, especially a friend who didn't like bringing up the past either, which meant Robin was unlikely to pry. Unlikely to poke into the parts of Shawn's life he kept private.

"Fine," Shawn said. "One piece of pie."

Robin's instant grin brightened that flame of hope deep down inside of Shawn, and he followed Robin back up to the cabin, grateful for the kind determination of his new maybe-friend. And eager to try someone else's pie for a change.

Robin hadn't meant to spy on Shawn. Nope, not at all. He'd come outside to take a few puffs on the vape, mostly as an excuse to stop being cheerful and chatting with anyone who approached him. Sure, the thing only released scented vapor, but after years of smoking real cigarettes, he couldn't do it indoors.

He'd spotted Shawn talking on his cell, his entire

slender body hunched and clearly unhappy. And when Shawn collapsed? Every instinct inside Robin had come to instant alert, because Shawn was hurting, and Robin had to fix it. But Shawn wasn't his to fix. They weren't even friends, for God's sake.

Remembering that didn't stop Robin from approaching the younger man, though, and making sure he was okay. Shawn had looked so sad, so completely wrecked Robin had faltered for the right thing to say. But he'd cheered Shawn up a bit and that was enough. Gotten Shawn to smile, and that beautiful smile had shown off a single dimple.

The house was still crowded when they went inside, full of conversations and food smells, and Robin led Shawn to the kitchen counter where an array of desserts had been laid out. All kinds of pies, a chocolate cake, a fruit torte, and a platter of homemade cookies. Mrs. Bentley was serving dessert, and she smiled at them both.

Robin asked for a slice of pumpkin pie covered in whipped cream, while Shawn chose a slice of peach, hold the cream. "Peach your favorite?" Robin asked as they looked for a spot to sit or stand.

"It was my mom's favorite," Shawn replied.

Sounded like a sad story there, so Robin didn't push. They found a place to stand near the loft steps. Miles and Reyes joined them with their own desserts. "Everything's been delicious today," Reyes said. He gave Miles a gentle elbow to the ribs.

Miles beamed. "It really has. Despite a few minor glitches earlier that threatened to send Wes into a meltdown, I think we pulled it off."

"Everything was terrific," Shawn said. "Thanks for inviting me."

"Of course. You're part of the Clean Slate family now, Shawn. Accept it."

Shawn smiled and ate his pie. His shyness over certain things was incredibly appealing to Robin, and he didn't understand why. Robin was usually attracted to guys with more energy, more exuberance for life. Shawn had a quiet strength that was hella attractive, though. As was his obvious independent streak.

"You think Wes and Mack will want to host every year now?" Robin asked the group.

Miles snickered. "I'm sure Wes will, but he'll probably have to flip a coin with Patrice going forward. Maybe they can alternate years."

Robin glanced at the living room sofa, where Patrice sat with her right arm pinned in a sling. Arthur and Judson were both being attentive to her, helping their one-armed den mother eat. The trio had been on the ranch together for a long, long time, and it made Robin intensely curious about their individual relationships. Arthur was gay, and Robin had heard a rumor that Patrice had a son who'd passed away.

Judson, though? Not a clue about his story.

"Well, I think their first year was a great success," Reyes said. "New home, new traditions." He smiled at Miles. "For all of us."

Robin glanced at Shawn, who was staring at his half-eaten pie. Robin hated seeing all this sadness on such a joyful day, and even without the words, it was obvious Shawn wasn't used to being around family and friends like this. Wasn't used to being included as part of a family. Had Shawn lived such an isolated life these past few years that he'd forgotten what it was like to be part of something bigger?

Robin had been lucky to go from a large extended family in Nebraska to the family he'd found as part of Lucky's Rodeo. The happy life he'd created with Xander. And then he'd stumbled into the Clean Slate family by sheer luck, after nearly losing everything, including his own life.

He gently nudged at Shawn's arm until Shawn looked up. "We've all got new things in our lives now," Robin said. His gaze flickered briefly to Shawn's pink lips before returning to his eyes.

Shawn's eyes brightened with something like hope and he nodded. "Yeah, we do."

Robin wasn't entirely sure what shifted between them in that moment, but he liked it. He hoped Shawn felt it too, and going forward they could be friends. And if their friends noticed, they didn't comment. Their quartet ate pie, chatted about simple things, and existed in that happy bubble for as long as possible.

Friends.

And family.

Chapter Five

Despite their peaceful interaction on Thanksgiving, Robin didn't see much of Shawn the next few days beyond the guesthouse kitchen. Shawn always had a friendly smile for him, but Robin wanted a chance to talk to the guy again. In private. Not with Patrice there, though, overseeing Shawn as he prepared himself for this Sunday's new crop of guests.

The ranch's horsemen flocked home from their vacations on Saturday night, including Robin's roommate Ernie Costello. Ernie had about ten years on Robin, and had initially been part of the horse rescue before transferring up to the ranch five years ago. They were friendly but not the best of friends, and they shared beers on the front porch while Robin filled him in on the events of this past week.

"Man, that's tough luck for Patrice," Ernie said. "Good thing you and your insomnia were awake, huh?"

Robin snorted. "Good thing."

"So the kid from the ghost town is cooking for us now."

"Shawn, yeah." He couldn't stop a smile. "I've gotten to know him a little this week. He's a nice guy and great cook. No one's gonna starve."

"Didn't figure we would."

They didn't talk much more after that, and the next morning, Robin walked into the guesthouse kitchen early, curious how frazzled Shawn was after cooking his first big breakfast for the entire ranch staff. Shawn was a little red-faced as he darted from an oven with sheet trays of biscuits to the serving basket on the back wall where hands got their food. The sausage gravy was already on its warmer, the kitchen smelled pleasantly of bacon, and Patrice presided over it all like a queen from her rocking chair.

Robin was the first one there, too. "Hey, morning. Need any help?"

Shawn tossed him a grateful smile. "Yes, please. Grab a towel and get the bacon out before it burns. Thanks!"

It took Robin a moment to find a clean towel, and then two tries to open the correct oven door. The bacon sizzled on sheet trays, and he carefully lifted them to the stovetop so he didn't spill bacon grease. Patrice had a Mason jar she collected it into for additional flavoring in some of her other dishes so that they always had a ready supply.

They also went through a lot of paper towels week after week, to drain the massive amounts of bacon their kitchen served.

Shawn pulled fresh fruit out of the walk-in and arranged it in another basket, while Robin dutifully piled the drained bacon and put it onto its usual platter for serving. He and Shawn moved with a scarily practiced ease, considering Robin wasn't much of a cook. But he'd seen Patrice do this dance for years, and Robin was a big fan of routines. By the time the other horsemen wandered in for breakfast, everything was set and waiting.

"Thank you so much," Shawn whispered. "I appreciate the assist. Still getting used to all this."

"Just wait until tomorrow when you're cooking for twice as many people," Robin replied.

Shawn blanched. "Ugh. I'll just have to get here even earlier to start prep."

"What time were you here today?"

"Six thirty, like Judson said, but I don't feel like it was enough time."

"Can't you do something the night before? Like biscuit dough?"

Shawn tossed him a thoughtful look. "Yeah, I can do that. They'll be extra flaky, too, if the butter is nice and cold when I bake them. You a chef in your spare time?"

Robin laughed. "No, I like to take as few steps in doing something as possible. Guess I'm a fan of instant gratification, rather than drawing things out." He glanced again at Shawn's lips, and Shawn flushed even redder.

"Morning, Shawn!" Miles's bright voice broke the spell, and Shawn looked away. "How was your first morning with the full staff?"

"Not bad," Shawn replied. "Um, Robin was kind of a lifesaver, because I didn't plan the timing properly."

"He did just fine," Patrice added. "He'll learn. I didn't fall into this job knowing how to cook for forty people each meal. You'll get there, sweetheart."

"Thank you."

Reyes was right behind Miles and said, "Wait, Robin helped? He can cook?"

Robin laughed. "I can pull things out of ovens and put them on plates. I was early so I lent a hand. No biggie."

Shawn's expression said it was a very big biggie, but he didn't say it out loud. Fortunately, lunch was a simple affair of lunch meat and cheese, bread, and cold salad sides—for hands and guests—so when Robin checked in around noon, Shawn was calm and collected and munching on his own lunch. And Robin couldn't swear to it, but he thought he felt Shawn's gaze on him the entire time Robin threw together a big sandwich piled high with ham, turkey, roast beef, and Swiss on rye.

He ate at the table with Ernie, Slater, and Colt, his entire body aware of Shawn's movements in the room, and that...wasn't normal. Part of him wanted to act on his physical attraction to the guy and flat out ask Shawn if he was into him. The rest of him was afraid of being turned down, and that was unusual for Robin.

Stop it. You're just infatuated because he reminds you of Xander. Focus on your damn job not your dick.

His cell rang with an unknown caller, so Robin sent it to voice mail, not interested in a telemarketer or wrong number. Sometimes if he was bored, he'd answer the calls and play along just to fuck with them. Today he wanted to hang with his friends and then go do his job.

He, Reyes, and Slater were teaching their guests to ride horses after lunch, which was always amusing in its own way. Superconfident guys who fell on their ass the first time they tried mounting a horse were his favorite. Humility was a great trait to have around those majestic animals.

With his plate empty, Robin had no excuse to continue lingering in the kitchen, so he put it in the bus bin. Turned in time to see Shawn look sharply away from him. He grinned. Maybe there was something here after all.

* * *

"The Pinkertons chased those bandits all across Garrett land and up into the mountains," Arthur said, his voice booming over the collection of ranch guests and hands listening to his story about the history of the land. "But when the Pinkertons finally found the thieves, they didn't have the gold on 'em."

Someone in the crowd gasped. Sunday evening was the big welcome barbecue for guests, and Shawn sat with Miles, Reyes, Mack, Wes, and Colt during Arthur's opening speech. He soaked in the gold myth like a guest might, eager for every word Arthur spun, delighted by the entire thing. Sure, some of the other hands looked bored, but they'd probably heard this story several hundred times before.

This was a whole new experience for Shawn.

And he didn't have to handle the food tonight. Shawn was only in charge of the side dishes, like Patrice's locally famous baked beans. Judson and Arthur were handling all the barbecued meats and grilled corn on the cob.

Being introduced to the guests as their guesthouse chef that morning, along with Patrice, had been mildly embarrassing, but it was also apparently part of the process. Getting guests acclimated to their week at Clean Slate and the people there to help them. Patrice was moving around more easily, so she was still their first contact with any issues, and Shawn was in control of the kitchen.

So far, so good.

He took his cues from Reyes and Colt, who were current employees at the ranch, and when they mingled with the guests getting plates of food, Shawn did the same. The barbecue smelled amazing, but he didn't gorge himself on the stacks of ribs, steaks, and burgers. Two ribs, one cob of corn, and some of the other vegetable sides were enough to satisfy him.

The guests seemed more interested in chatting with the cowboys in their Clean Slate polos and hats, and that was fine with Shawn. He sucked at small talk, which was why he worked in kitchens. No one expected you to chat up the prep cook or dishwasher. More than once, he looked up from his plate to find Robin watching him. A steady, curious look that held a hint of…intent?

It had been so long since Shawn had been with anyone. But possibly fucking around with a member of the ranch staff didn't feel illicit or thrilling. It felt dangerous. Shawn was only a temp and he couldn't afford to lose this job before the ghost town reopened in two months. And if he lost this job for inappropriate behavior, what was to stop Mack from firing him from the saloon? Nothing.

Flirting with Robin was one thing, maybe becoming friends, but that was as far as it could go.

As the meal died down, Quentin pulled out his guitar and started playing old-fashioned songs that some folks sang along to. The guests appeared to love it, and some of the hands even got into it, especially when the dancing started.

One big party and Shawn loved the entire thing.

"You dance?" Robin asked, practically in Shawn's ear. He'd slid onto the picnic table bench next to Shawn and grinned like a guy with a secret. Shawn's skin prickled with awareness.

"Not really," Shawn replied. "I have two left feet."

"Now that's a shame. How about a walk on one of the trails, instead?"

Shawn's brain stuttered at the question, which was innocent enough. But it was after dark, and those trails weren't lit by anything except the flashlight they might take. Was Robin trying to get him alone?

"Uh, don't we have to be here to entertain the guests?" Shawn asked, stalling for time. Living in his car, he'd gotten good at identifying dangerous people, and Robin definitely wasn't going to maul him in the woods. The fact that Shawn wanted to say yes was enough to throw him off-balance.

"Nah, as long as I get you back for cleanup, Judson won't mind you wandering off for a bit."

Maybe it wouldn't be such a bad thing to take a chance and try to make a new friend. "Yeah, okay, we can walk," Shawn said.

"Cool." Robin pulled up a bright flashlight app on his phone. "I'll protect you, promise."

Shawn chuckled. "I trust you." Because he did. He'd known the guy for a week and had no real reason to trust Robin other than instinct.

Years of learning to survive a big, scary world that could crush him in an instant if he ever let his guard down. Years to rely solely on himself to carry his burdens and get through each day.

The marked tourist trails were on the opposite side of the main yard from the barbecue, and they strolled side by side, setting an easy pace. Far enough apart they didn't touch, but Shawn could reach out if he wanted to.

Not that he wanted to.

Except I kind of do. I want to touch him.

He'd never been drawn to someone else the way he

was drawn to Robin. But was it really Robin? Or was Shawn attention starved and reading way too much into Robin's kindness?

The half-moon gave them a small amount of light beyond Robin's flashlight app, which he kept trained on the well-trodden path ahead of them. "You did great today," Robin said.

"I don't know how Patrice does it week after week." Shawn shoved his hands into his jeans pockets. "She's a hoot to talk to, though. So many stories."

"I bet. She's looked after this place for a long damned time. It was fucking scary finding her like that."

Shawn studied Robin's unhappy profile. He'd forgotten Robin had heard Patrice yelling for help and gotten her to the hospital only a week ago. Seeing a friend in pain like that had to stick with you. "I'm sorry for you, but glad for her," Shawn said. "You helped her."

"I guess."

"What do you mean, you guess?" Shawn took a step in front of Robin on the path, forcing him to stop. "You totally saved her. You aren't one of those guys who does false modesty just to get compliments, are you?"

Robin's frown eased into a flirty smile, and he winked. "Why? You wanna compliment me?"

Somehow he made *compliment* sound incredibly dirty. Shadows from their varied light sources made the planes of Robin's face even sharper, more handsome. Robin was taller than him by a good three or four inches, and he seemed to be trying to stoop so they were closer to the same level. It was both appealing and also a little scary, and Shawn wasn't sure what to do with it.

"I don't hand out compliments lightly," Shawn replied.

"Oh? So how do I earn one?"

"Why do you want one?"

Even in the bad light, Robin's eyes gleamed with amusement. They both knew they weren't talking about compliments anymore. "Because I suspect you give out great compliments, and I'm curious to know if I'm right."

Two could play at this game, and now Shawn was curious in return. It had been so fucking long and Robin was cute. Friendly. And the moonlight was playing havoc with his better judgment. "You always get compliments from guys?"

"Sometimes from girls. Depends on who I find… complimentary at the time. You?"

"Mostly girls, but I'd much rather share compliments with guys."

"Ever shared with guys?"

"Only once." Shawn's interest in this teasing deflated. "It ended badly."

"Oh." Robin slid into Shawn's personal space and rested his right hand lightly on Shawn's hip. "Pick the wrong person?"

"Something like that." Shawn swore he felt Robin's body heat, even though they were only touching in one place. Robin somehow surrounded him and Shawn should have found that scary but he didn't. He liked it. And damn it, he wanted more. Wanted to take a chance here, and that wasn't like him. "Can we stop talking now?"

Robin swooped in, and where Shawn expected a fierce kiss, Robin's mouth settled lightly over his. A hot press of lips that filled Shawn's senses with the man, and he relaxed. An arm circled Shawn's waist, hauling him closer as Robin's lips teased his own. A slip of tongue licked at the seam of Shawn's lips, and he parted them.

Robin didn't go far inside, though, mostly teasing, tasting. Fingers caressed the back of Shawn's neck. Blood rushed into his dick the longer the sweet, exploratory kiss went on.

And it went on. And on. And it was the most tender, most intense kiss of Shawn's entire life.

When Robin pulled back, pupils wide in the dark, he stared at Shawn with so much intensity his stomach wobbled. Robin whispered something, and it took Shawn a moment to realize it was a name.

Not his name.

His arousal died a swift death under rising anger, and he took a step backward, freeing himself from Robin's embrace. "Who the hell is Xander?"

Robin blinked hard several times. "What?"

"You just called me Xander."

"Shit, I did?" For a split second, Robin looked as if he might burst into tears, but it was probably a trick of the lighting. "I'm sorry."

Shame swamped Shawn's gut. He took two steps backward so he could circle Robin more widely, then stormed back up the path to the main part of the ranch. He'd been an absolute idiot to give in to Robin's flirting, to think this was anything more than Robin looking for a fun time with fresh meat. But hey, Robin had gotten his fucking compliment, hadn't he?

Fucker.

Robin gaped at Shawn's departing back, embarrassed and furious with himself for the slip. Sure, he still saw the physical resemblance Shawn and Xander shared, but he also saw *Shawn*. The young cook was shy and funny and hella cute. He'd leaned into the kiss and relaxed in Robin's arms, and it was everything Robin hoped it would be.

Naturally, Robin had fucked it up by getting lost in the kiss and forgetting the present. Falling into the past, where he'd been deeply in love with another man. A man he apparently wasn't over, even years later, if he'd whispered Xander's name in the quiet after the kiss.

"Damn it," he said, the two words bouncing off nearby trees, which seemed to mock him with their gnarled shapes and sharp shadows.

He considered chasing Shawn but didn't want to make a scene, especially when Shawn had every right to be pissed. Shawn had admitted, through their compliment banter, that he rarely kissed men, and what had Robin done? Kissed the guy and then insulted him by saying Xander's name.

I have to fix this. Apologize and fix this.

Frustrated with himself, Robin returned to the ranch only to find Miles and Reyes waiting for him near the trail entrance, and neither man looked happy.

Great. I'm going to get the "Did you hurt my friend?" speech.

"Well, this makes more sense, I guess," Miles said to Reyes, who grunted.

"What makes sense?" Robin asked.

"Why Shawn came back from the trail looking pissed off. He went right into the kitchen and won't tell me why he's upset. What did you do?"

Robin couldn't find enough energy to defend himself, because he'd hurt Shawn's feelings and was adult enough to admit it. "We went for a walk, and we had a misunderstanding."

Miles scowled. "The physical kind?"

"No, we were on the same page with, uh, kissing each other. I fucked it up after."

"You're into Shawn?" Reyes asked. "I thought you and Derrick Massey were a thing."

"Me and Derrick are just fuck buddies, not a couple. And yes, I'm into Shawn, and now I know he's into me, but like I said, I fucked it up." Robin looked around the yard, where guests still mingled, and some of the hands were helping Judson clean up after the barbecue. "I need to apologize to him."

"Maybe give it some time," Miles said. "Sometimes trying to apologize to someone while they're still upset can be counterproductive." Reyes gave Miles a knowing nod.

"I hate that he's angry with me for saying something that totally came out by accident."

Miles quirked an eyebrow. "Which was what?"

Robin's face got hot. "I, uh, said the wrong name." At Miles's openmouthed shock, Robin added, "But I swear I wasn't calling Shawn the wrong name. I just… said the name."

"Ouch, man," Reyes said.

"That's a pretty shitty thing to do, Robin," Miles snapped.

"I know!" Robin flapped both hands in the air. "I know it was shitty, which is why I need to fix it. It was such a great kiss and I totally fucked up."

"Look, I know you well enough to know you're not a dick to people on purpose, so I'm not going to warn you off Shawn. He can take care of himself. But without giving away too much of his privacy, Shawn was fucked over by someone in his past, and I get the sense it's stuck with him. Don't be someone else who fucks him over, okay?"

"I won't. Even if we just go back to being friends, I promise I'm not out to fuck him over." Hell, if Robin couldn't even manage a kiss without screwing up and chasing Shawn away, they were doomed from the start. Maybe he should back off and let their friendship run its natural course. Keep his distance for a while.

After he apologized, damn it.

"I believe you," Miles said softly, a lot of his outrage visibly deflating. "Look, Shawn was a really good friend to me this fall, so be gentle, okay?"

"I will. I promise." Robin let out a long, frustrated sigh. "Maybe this is the universe's way of telling me I'm not ready to date again, and I should just stick to fucking around."

Reyes's eyebrows winged up. "Date, huh? Do you know how to do that?"

"Not really. Only long-term relationship of my life started hot and heavy, and then we were just…together." And then Xander was gone. "Anyway, that was a whole other life that I left behind years ago."

"Sounds like it's still got some power over you."

"Some, yeah."

"Think maybe you should deal with that power before you go pursuing someone else?"

A fair, if annoying, question from his friend. "Probably. Shawn was unexpected, and it doesn't help that he reminds me of my ex. Physically. Everything else about them is hugely different, especially their personalities. I do care about Shawn, more than I thought I would after only knowing him for a week."

"Sometimes our hearts figure things out before our

minds do." Reyes draped a protective arm across Miles's shoulders. "Just be honest with Shawn, okay?"

"I can do that. I've been doing that." Robin ought to have felt foolish for baring his soul like this to his friends, but he didn't. They were listening and offering advice, not judging him. "Thank you."

Reyes nodded.

"For what it's worth," Miles said, "I hope you work it out. You and Shawn are both pretty terrific people, and if you make each other happy, then it's worth fighting for."

Robin had no idea if he was the guy to make Shawn happy, but he was interested in finding out for sure—if that's what Shawn wanted. If not, Robin would gladly return to his solitary life of wrangling horses, babysitting tourists, and flirting up a storm with anyone cute on two legs.

Maybe.

Probably not.

Chapter Six

Shawn usually woke to either the screech of his phone alarm or the bright glare of the rising sun—his car didn't come with curtains, after all—so the sound of someone pounding on his car window nearly scared the piss out of him. Literally. He jackknifed up to a sitting position, fleece blanket tangled around his torso, discombobulated by the strange noise—and then blinded by the flashlight beam in his eyes.

"Jesus." Shawn raised a hand against the glare, which shifted down, and he rubbed bright spots out of his eyes. The shape of a man came into focus on the other side of his driver's side window, and Shawn's heart fell to the floor.

A cop.

Shit.

He'd hidden in the guesthouse kitchen for as long as possible last night, cleaning and storing leftovers the hands could snack on at lunch the next day, hoping to avoid another encounter with Robin. And he'd succeeded. The asshole hadn't come near him again, not after that embarrassing moment on the trail, and Shawn had been grateful to leave the ranch with his dignity intact. After driving out to the truck stop for a shower to rid himself of the barbecue and wood smoke smell, he'd parked in his usual spot along the road from Garrett to the ranch.

The entire time, he'd replayed both the tender, amazing kiss with Robin, and also the zing of anger at being misnamed. He'd had more intense make-out sessions in the past, and not once had someone called him the wrong name, and what the fuck was up with that? He'd taken a chance, and it had blown up in his face, which had led to a very fitful, restless sleep, and now a cop?

Shawn rolled down the manual window with one hand as he rubbed sleep out of his eyes with the other. "Hi, Officer."

"You in some kind of trouble, son?" the cop asked. Middle-aged, thick around the middle, with a lot of silver in his mustache.

"No, sir. No trouble."

"You break down? I can get you a tow."

Part of Shawn wanted to lie and say yes, he'd broken down, but don't worry about a tow, he had a friend coming. Lies. Too many lies, and what if this cop checked for his car tomorrow night? Had his two-year streak of luck finally run out? He could fudge the truth, though, right? "No, I didn't break down. I just couldn't drive anymore tonight, so I pulled over. That's not illegal, is it?"

"Not in all places, but you see, this here is county property and it's not the first night I've seen your car parked here. Law says you need to be at a public rest stop less than eight hours, not parked on the side of the road night after night."

Shit, shit, shit, this is bad.

"I won't park here again, I promise," Shawn said, his

anxiety rising by the moment. The last thing he needed was a ticket or citation.

The cop had yet to ask for his license and registration—which were all current and valid, thank you—so he counted that as a win. "Since I know you aren't just passing through, you got work in these parts?"

"Yes, sir, I work up at Clean Slate Ranch." Shawn finally noticed a name tag on the guy's uniform: Bradley.

Officer Bradley frowned. "Arthur usually takes care of his people. How come you're down here sleeping in your car, son? You can tell me the truth. I'm here to help."

"I just…" Again, Shawn sucked at lying, and the truth was the easiest thing to remember. He'd gotten away with this for two years, and now he had to face the facts of his life. "I'm between places right now, sir. I can't afford any place to sleep right now except my car."

"Hmm. Does Arthur Garrett know one of his people is sleeping in his car?"

"No, and I was hired by Judson Marvel. No one knows I sleep in my car." *And I'd prefer to keep it that way, but that won't happen now.*

Officer Bradley stroked his mustache a few times. "Well, I can't just drive off knowing you're out here in the cold. Why don't you follow me down to the station so we can straighten this out for you?"

Shawn wanted to scream no and drive off in the other direction, but that would just get him into trouble. The cop would start looking for his car and stop him the next time Shawn tried to drive up to the ranch. No, he could be an adult and face what he'd done. He couldn't avoid his problems and hope they went away—a lesson he should have learned in high school while dealing with Beck.

"I can do that," Shawn replied, unhappy but resigned to whatever came next.

The station turned out to be a small office space in a tired-looking municipal building that also housed the mayor's office, town hall, and butted up against Garrett's tiny post office. The police station had a front desk—unmanned at three thirty in the morning—and two other desks behind it facing each other. Decades of old Wanted posters and missing person alerts covered the walls in fading layers, and the place kind of smelled like mildew.

"Have a seat, son," Officer Bradley said. "Help yourself to coffee, too." He pointed at a tiny table that had a coffeepot station at least twenty years old.

Shawn avoided the dark sludge in the pot and eased onto a wood chair against the wall. After Bradley fetched himself coffee, he sat next to Shawn and blew over the rising steam.

"Now, let's talk about you," Bradley said. "And as a reminder, you aren't in any trouble. Not under arrest, so anything you tell me is between us, okay?"

"Okay." Shawn wished he'd gotten coffee now just for something to hold with his hands, which were twitching with nerves. "I'm sorry for sleeping where I wasn't supposed to."

"I know, so let's forget about that. Garrett's a small town and I know everyone who lives here, but we've never met."

"No, I don't live here, so we wouldn't have met, I guess. I've been working up at the Bentley Ghost Town until we closed for the season, and now I'm helping out at the ranch guesthouse with the cooking."

"Ah, yes, I did hear about Patrice's accident. Such a fine lady."

"Yes, she is. I've learned a lot from her."

Truth. Patrice knew more about cooking than Shawn ever hoped to learn in his life, and not just about old-fashioned cooking. She knew French cuisine, and she'd told him a few stories of her early days cooking in Sacramento as a young woman, in a time when it was difficult being a woman in a professional kitchen. Shawn never asked why she'd given it up, because he suspected that was a sad story, and they weren't good enough friends yet to go there.

"So if you're working up at the ranch," Officer Bradley continued, "how come you're sleeping in your car? Arthur and Judson are good people. They'd give you a place to stay."

"I know they would, but...it's embarrassing being homeless." Shawn's face heated, and he tangled his fingers together on his lap. It was the first time he'd said the word out loud to another person. *Homeless.*

Bradley nodded, his expression thoughtful and without judgment. "Yep, it can feel that way—especially if you're used to taking care of yourself?"

"I am. And I make good money working for the Garretts—it's not that. I've just got...bills." So much easier than explaining his grandparents and their situation.

"I'm sure there are folks in town who'd rent you a room cheap. We take care of each other here, and if you work for the ranch, you're part of Garrett, too."

"I appreciate that, sir, I truly do. I just don't... I don't know."

"Don't know how to ask for help?"

"Yeah." Shawn hung his head, tired and scared and kind of thirsty. "I'm sorry to be so much trouble."

"You're no trouble. Most nights the biggest thing I've got going on is a feral cat fight keeping folks awake over on the south side of town."

Shawn chuckled at the idea of feral cats being the worst of this guy's problems.

"Now, you seem like a nice fellow," Bradley continued, "but I don't feel right sending you away and hoping you find a place for tomorrow night. So why don't you stay here for a few hours. The cot in the holding cell is actually pretty comfortable, and don't tell anyone, but I've slept more than a few shifts in there."

"Um."

"I'm not going to lock you in, I swear. But it's too early yet to call up to the ranch about you. Waking anyone up at this hour will just make 'em panic."

True, and Shawn was already going to become a burden to his friends. As much as Shawn wanted to flee the station the moment Bradley returned to patrolling, it wouldn't end well. Not now that the cop knew who he was and what kind of car he had. So he resigned himself to Bradley's plan and nodded. "Okay."

Bradley allowed Shawn to get his fleece blanket, pillow and a bottle of water from his car, plus his phone charger so he could keep the battery alive for what was likely going to be a lot of calls tomorrow. "I need to be at the guesthouse kitchen to cook by six thirty," Shawn said as he inspected the small holding cell. Just a square room with a barred window, a cot, and nothing else.

"Then I'll be sure to be back here by six to escort you up to the ranch."

"What?" Shawn's chest nearly burst open in a flash of panic.

"Not in the squad car, son, in my personal car. I just want to make sure the right people know what's going on, so they can help you. It's okay to ask for help."

Shawn took a few deep, calming breaths so he could answer. "Okay."

"Good. Now try and get some rest."

After Bradley left, Shawn wrapped the blanket around his shoulders and lay down, hoping to sleep a bit more. But now he was wired from panic and adrenaline, and he wasn't sleeping again anytime soon. So he lay awake and stared at the water-stained, Sheetrock ceiling, terrified of what his bosses were going to think of this news. That someone who appeared so put-together and on top of things was a homeless wreck who relied on expensive antianxiety meds to keep himself on an even keel.

That he'd spent two years living in his crappy car, showering at truck stops and eating from convenience stores. Occasionally at soup kitchens and free church dinners when he stumbled onto them.

Shawn was more exhausted when Officer Bradley returned than he'd been when the man left, and he dutifully followed his car up to the ranch. This was the very last thing he needed to deal with on his first morning cooking a full breakfast for both the ranch hands and their thirteen guests, but it was a simple enough menu. Hopefully, Shawn could cook and explain himself at the same time.

He didn't expect to see Judson, Miles, and Reyes waiting with Patrice in the guesthouse kitchen when Shawn entered with Bradley behind him. With Bradley in uniform, Shawn felt like a complete fool—and like he'd somehow committed a crime. But no one looked upset or annoyed, merely curious.

The cop must have called ahead to warn them. *Great.*

When no one said anything, Shawn walked directly to the walk-in to get the biscuit dough he'd prepared last night. It needed to warm slightly before he could roll it, or he'd never get them thin enough to cut into—

"Shawn?" Miles said, "I'm not going to ask why, because God knows I'm famous for not liking to be guilt-tripped into talking about personal stuff when I'm not ready. But you can talk to me about anything."

"I know," Shawn told the bowl of dough. He fetched the big package of ground sausage so he could start the gravy. Miles helped by getting the stockpot out and onto the front burner of the stove.

"You are not sleeping in your car another night," Judson said firmly. "We'll find a place for you here at the ranch until you get your affairs in order. While you're cooking here, or at Bentley, I won't allow anyone who's part of this family to be without a bed and roof every single night."

Shawn's eyes burned and not from the onion he was dicing. All he could manage was an exaggerated nod that he understood. While he and Miles cooked breakfast, the other three men confabbed by the kitchen door, and Shawn tried to ignore them. He hated knowing he was being discussed. Hated. It. But he'd kind of done this to himself by not speaking up and asking for help.

Then again, asking for help only ever seemed to land him in a worse mess.

Not here, though. He knew in his heart he could trust

these people. He just had to get his stupid head on board with it.

"Gonna head out," Officer Bradley said as Miles slid two big sheet trays of biscuits into the oven. "You take care of yourself, Shawn, you hear?"

"I will, sir. Thank you," Shawn replied, and he was forever grateful that Reyes and Judson left with the man. He and Miles continued cooking, with Patrice a silent onlooker, and they had everything out and waiting when the first ranch hands and guests came around seeking coffee and food.

Reyes came around again with Colt, Ernie, and Robin, and the quartet sat down to eat with Miles, while Shawn busied himself checking on the food and guests. One of the ladies complimented him on the biscuits and gravy, which of course made him blush, so he excused himself back to the kitchen.

No one at Miles's end of the table gave Shawn knowing looks, which boosted his hope that they weren't gossiping about him. Then again, neither Miles nor Reyes had ever come across as gossipy, not like some of the other ranch hands. The only person who did seem to pay him extra attention was Robin, the big jerk, and Shawn really didn't want to hear any excuses about last night's kiss.

Thankfully, Robin didn't linger or try and speak to him, and he left with the group he'd come to breakfast with. Miles stayed behind—because of course he did— and helped Shawn clean up. Even though Shawn was being paid to be here, Miles wasn't. Shawn appreciated the extra hands as he acclimated to the sheer volume of dirty dishes he had to deal with at the end of the meal.

Patrice instructed him how to best fit everything into

the massive dishwasher so he only had to run it once. Some of the bigger pots he'd cleaned as he went, and they were drying for use tonight at dinner. With lunch such a simple affair, Shawn didn't need verbal direction in peeling potatoes and dicing veggies for the cold salads, so Patrice excused herself to take a nap.

Miles stayed behind. "You've got choices," he said when they were alone in the kitchen. "About where you'd like to live. If Reyes and I had a place of our own, I'd insist you stay with us, but we still share a two-man cabin."

"And I appreciate that, truly," Shawn replied, daring to meet Miles's eyes. His friend's expression was open and curious, giving Shawn the same patience and attention Shawn had given Miles a few months ago. Allowing Shawn to speak up when he was ready. "It's not an easy thing to admit. That you're homeless."

"I can't imagine it. I could talk to Mack about your salary at the saloon."

"No, don't do that. Mack's more than fair with what he pays. It isn't that. I just have extra expenses, and that money does more good elsewhere than paying for a motel room or cheap apartment nearby. Ever since I left home, I've lived as cheaply as possible, and it's become a habit I can't seem to break. Even when I feel like I might have a little extra, I don't keep it."

"Do you want to talk about why?"

"It's a lot of things." Shawn sat in one of the chairs and Miles sat opposite him, still nursing a glass of orange juice. "The big thing is my grandparents. They live on a fixed income, a mix of social security, disability, and my grandfather's pension, but it's not enough. My grandmother is ill and he insists on caring for her at home. Their lifelong home, which is old and falling apart in places, so I send every penny I can spare home to help them out. They raised me when my parents died."

"I'm sorry to hear about your parents."

"Thanks."

"Do your grandparents know you're homeless?"

"No." Alarm jolted through Shawn, but Miles had no way of contacting his grandparents to spread the news. No one at the ranch did. "No, and I won't ever tell them. It'll only make Granddad feel guilty for taking my money, and I'm giving it freely."

"That is incredibly generous, Shawn. I mean it. I just…" Miles sighed. "I can't believe you were living in your car this whole time."

Shawn shrugged. "I had a routine that kept me in clean clothes, showered, and perfectly capable of cooking each day. The worst part was honestly our two-day weekend, because I had nowhere to go except the Daggett library, or to drive into San Jose. But I hate wasting gas, so a lot of the time I'd park somewhere and read."

"Well, no more of that, okay? Like Judson said before, we can figure out you living somewhere on the ranch. I know Mack and Wes would take you in and give you a guest room."

"I'd feel horrible asking them to do that. They haven't even lived in that house for a year yet. No one wants a semipermanent houseguest, and I have no idea when my financial situation will change so I can afford my own place."

"What about sharing a cabin with Colt? I'm not sure if any of the other hands have open bunks in their cabins right now, but I can ask Judson."

"Doesn't Colt have a boyfriend? Fiancé?"

"Yes, who has an apartment in the city they share basically every weekend."

Shawn didn't like the idea of crashing with a guy who probably had routines and expectations of alone time when his fiancé came to visit. "I don't know." He picked at the worn inseam of his jeans, confused and annoyed by his secret coming out, and now everything seemed to be riding on this choice. The last thing he wanted to be to anyone on the ranch was a burden who had to bounce around from bed to bed until he could get his shit together.

But his shit *was* together, it was just...money.

Too bad he hadn't managed some sort of lucrative career that could afford him the best home-care nurses and helpers available. No, he was baker at a saloon, and while he loved this job and the ranch, someday something was going to give.

"Well, think about it, okay?" Miles said. "You've got all afternoon to think about it, and if I come up with a genius plan of my own, I'll tell you."

"I will think about it, thanks. What are your plans for the day?"

"Probably go chill up at Wes's house for a few hours. I'm going on tonight's overnight camping trip with Reyes and whichever guests sign up, so no matter what, you could always crash in our cabin. Since it'll be empty."

"Okay. I appreciate that."

"Not a problem at all. But if I know Reyes and Judson, they've got their heads together about your living situation."

Other people planning my life for me. Lovely.

Except...it kind of was a lovely gesture. Having people who cared enough to really consider Shawn's life and to try and help him out of a tough spot. He wasn't used to this, and his independent side resisted the handling.

His exhausted, stressed side accepted it wholeheartedly.

"Thank you for everything, Miles," Shawn said. "For being supportive, but also not pressing into my personal life."

"You're welcome. And if you ever do want to talk, my door's always open."

"I know. You're a good friend, and I haven't had one of those in a really long time."

Miles grinned. "Then consider yourself stuck with me."

They shook hands and Miles left. Shawn set about working on the salads for lunch, plus the list Patrice left for the overnight campers and what he'd need to pack into the chuck wagon. He had no idea what a chuck wagon looked like, but one of the hands was supposed to bring it down around eleven. The campers left after lunch.

So he worked.

And he was not happy that the cowboy who brought the chuck wagon around at eleven was Robin, wearing a charming smile Shawn wanted to smack off his face. "Special delivery for our chef," Robin said. He stood in the kitchen doorway and jacked his thumb over his shoulder. "For the overnight trip."

"I know," Shawn snapped. "Patrice told me what to do, so you don't have to stay."

"I owe you an apology for last night."

"No, you don't." Shawn didn't look in his direction as he continued preparing lunch. "Last night was a mistake, and it won't happen again."

"It wasn't a mistake. The kiss wasn't, I mean, and I really want to explain myself."

Shawn hated the soft, pleading tone coming from the tall, sexy man, but he was holding his ground, damn it. "I'm working, and so are you."

"Can we talk when you're done after dinner? Please? Pretty please? Just hear me out, and if you want after, we can go our separate ways. Don't even have to be friends, but I'd like if we could."

Shawn wasn't sure he'd ever heard a grown man say "pretty please" before and it destroyed his resistance. "Fine, we'll talk after dinner."

"Thank you. I mean it, Shawn, thank you."

"You're welcome."

Robin left, giving Shawn space to get not only lunch fixings out for the hands and guests, but also to pack the chuck wagon. It had taken him a bit of practice to get used to the meat slicer, but Shawn had agreed with Patrice's explanation that it was far easier and cheaper to buy the deli meats and cheese in bulk than buy it all presliced. Plus, the food lasted longer and he could add more to the buffet if one thing seemed more popular than another.

The same familiar faces filled the kitchen for lunch, and Shawn did better at remembering names. Robin simply offered him a polite smile before making a sandwich. Shawn flittered in and out of the kitchen, watching the food in the dining room like a nervous waiter so nothing ran too low. He was proud when the guests ate almost the entire bowl of potato salad, because he'd cribbed a bit from Patrice while adding a few of his own favorite ingredients. She hadn't come down to supervise him today, which he found a little odd, but he wasn't complaining.

For someone who'd run this kitchen her own way for possibly decades, her trust meant the world to him.

Once the dining room and kitchen cleared out, he started on cleanup. Right before he began pondering Monday night's supper menu, Judson, Arthur, and Patrice came into the kitchen through the back door, all smiling.

"I'm sorry I missed lunch," Patrice said. "I was busy at the house with a small project."

"Project?" Shawn parroted. "I thought you weren't supposed to be doing anything but resting and supervising."

"Oh, she supervised all right," Arthur said with a chuff of wheezy laughter. "So did I, actually. Poor Judson there did all the work."

Judson did look a bit red in the face.

"All what work, if I may ask, sir?" Shawn said, crazy curious what the trio had been up to.

"Oh no, don't go sir-ing me, young buck." Arthur waved a hand in the air. "We don't have to be formal at all, not with you joining the family."

"The family?" Shawn was so confused right now, and he needed someone to explain what was happening before he had a meltdown. "I don't understand."

"I made a decision today that I've been pondering for some weeks now," Patrice said, "so don't go thinking this is all about you. I'm moving out of my cabin and into Arthur's house permanently."

"You are?" Shawn stared stupidly at the woman. "Because of your collarbone?"

"That's part of it, but like I said, I'd been thinking on

it for a few weeks now, and Arthur's been offering me a room for years. I think part of me worried at losing my independence by accepting, but if falling and hurting myself has taught me anything, it's that it is absolutely okay to accept help when it's offered. So Judson moved my things out of my cabin and into the house."

"Wow. Um, congratulations?" And why on earth would Shawn think this was about him? Patrice had obviously been considering it for a long time—oh. Oh! But they hadn't offered yet, and Shawn wasn't going to ask first.

"Patrice's cabin is free for you to live in, if you want it," Arthur said to Shawn. "And I hope you take it. When Judson told me about your situation, I felt awful for not knowing sooner. I'm not a rich man when it comes to money, but I will always share what I have with folks who need it worse than me."

"Me too," Patrice added, her smile so bright and genuine that Shawn wanted to hug her. Maybe even cry a little.

And Shawn couldn't say no to their collective generosity. His pride wasn't too big, not this time. Not when he had a real chance to live in a tiny home of his own, with a bathroom and a bed, and it was almost too much. He rubbed at both eyes as he struggled to hold tight to his emotions. "I'll take it," he finally managed. "I'm not too proud to take the cabin, thank you. God."

Patrice came over and squeezed his elbow with her left hand. "You aren't alone anymore, Shawn, not by a long shot. This ranch is famous for taking in strays who need a second chance. And as Arthur said before, welcome to the family."

Family.

Shawn did shed a few tears then, and he accepted a one-armed hug from Patrice. He relaxed into the older woman's embrace, calm for the first time in...probably years. A temporary calmness but one he held on to for as long as he had it—until the real world crashed back in and he had to let go.

But even after Judson and Arthur left, and Patrice settled in to supervise supper prep, Shawn found himself smiling as he worked. Smiling and calm, and maybe even a little bit...happy?

Sooner or later, something would burst that bubble, but for now Shawn held on tight and hoped for a happy future here with his new family at Clean Slate Ranch.

Chapter Seven

Robin had spent the last two hours practicing his apology in front of the horses he was exercising, and he was still a nervous wreck. His mouth was dry and his hands a little clammy, and Quentin and Scott gave him funny looks as their trio walked up to the kitchen for supper. But if Shawn was willing to listen, he was confident he could make it through a proper apology without hurting Shawn's feelings worse than he already had.

Robin was surprised—and a little annoyed—not to see Shawn anywhere in the downstairs of the guest-house. Patrice and Miles presided over the kitchen, with Judson as backup, and what the actual hell?

Was Shawn sick? Hurt?

"Hey," Robin whispered to Miles, "where's Shawn? He okay?"

"Yeah, he's fine. Moving into his new digs, so we gave him the night off."

"New digs?"

Miles just smiled at him.

Okay, whatever. I can take a hint.

Robin grumped his way through dinner, though, frustrated now because if Shawn was off the ranch lands and moving his stuff, he might not come back for their post-dinner conversation. And that would really, really suck.

I should have gotten his cell number but no way will Miles give it to me. Not after last night.

He hung around the guesthouse as long as he dared after dinner was over, and no Shawn. At seven, he gave up and headed down the well-trodden path from the kitchen to the cabin row behind the main house, disappointed in not being able to apologize. Halfway there, a familiar figure appeared, heading in his direction, and Robin froze.

Shawn walked with his head down, hands in his hoodie's pockets against the evening chill, and he didn't look up until he nearly walked into Robin. "Oh hey," Shawn said. "I was coming to find you."

"Yeah?" Robin glanced behind him. "Did you try my cabin first?"

"Huh? No." Shawn bit his lower lip, and that wasn't all kinds of cute or anything. "No, I actually just moved into one of the cabins for a while."

"Really? Miles said you were moving into your new place, but he didn't mention it was here on the ranch. Did you lose your old place?"

"Something like that. But I remembered my promise to talk to you tonight. I got a little lost unpacking and relaxing, and I'm glad I didn't miss you. Um, to talk to you."

"Same." Robin grinned, relieved Shawn was giving him this chance to fix things. "So, where do you want to talk? We could take a walk or go down to the barn."

Shawn shrugged. "We can talk outside my cabin, I guess. I didn't realize the cabins all have these little built-in seating areas on the porch."

"Yeah, they're handy." Especially when Robin put his to good use every morning as the sun rose. "Come on."

Shawn pivoted, and they strode down the path together, close but not touching like last night on the trail.

"So who are you living with?" Robin asked. The only guys he could think of with single cabins were Colt and Quentin, and Quentin was only alone because they'd lost a guy this summer to another job opportunity in his home state of Montana.

"No one," Shawn replied, head still tilted so he was practically speaking to his feet. And it didn't help that Robin was so much taller. "Patrice decided to move into the main house permanently, and she offered me her cabin. The whole thing happened today and it's been a little overwhelming. I needed some time alone to get myself together."

With his head ducked, Robin couldn't get a good look at Shawn's expression, but his voice held inflections of awe and...grief? "Wow, dude, you're just being smiled on by the universe, huh? First the guesthouse job, and now a place to live with a two-minute commute? Wanna share some of that good luck?"

"I would if I knew how. I'm not used to all this good luck, believe me."

Robin did believe him, and it was a damned shame Shawn seemed to have had a bad run of luck before now. They walked the rest of the way to Patrice's—nope, to *Shawn's* cabin in silence, and then stood awkwardly on the porch for a minute. Ernie wasn't haunting theirs, and it was chilly enough most of the horsemen weren't on their own respective porches, giving them a bit of privacy.

The lights were on inside the cabin, and it gave the

porch a pleasant yellow glow near the window. Robin used it to study Shawn, who was definitely less angry than the last time Robin spoke to him. Maybe he'd been stressing about a new place to live and Robin's epic name-fail had only made that stress worse? Time to repair some of the damage he'd done.

"Okay, first of all, I am so sorry about calling you the wrong name last night," Robin said, practiced words suddenly tumbling out in a rush. "And I wasn't really calling *you* his name, I just got so into the kiss, and then I got lost in the past and it just sort of came out, because I've only ever kissed one other guy like that, and it was Xander, and I am so fucking sorry I insulted you, because I really like you."

Shawn watched him with a blank expression, but his eyes were…amused? He was such an interesting contradiction of emotions. "Thank you, and apology accepted. The kiss was a mistake anyway."

Robin's heart hit the floor with a sad plop. "I disagree."

"You disagree?"

"Yes, I do. I felt something last night, Shawn, and I think you felt it too, but you're scared of it."

And you're not the only one.

Shawn's eyes narrowed. "You think I'm scared?"

"You're not?"

"Tell me more about Xander."

The non sequitur threw Robin for a beat, and it took him a split-second to realize Shawn had avoided answering his question about fear. "What do you want to know about him?" Robin could think and talk about Xander more easily now, even though he tried hard not to do either. He wanted to stay rooted in the present, not focused on the past.

"Were you lovers?"

Robin's left pinky rubbed his empty ring finger out of habit. "We were married."

Shawn's lips parted and his eyebrows jumped. "You were?"

"Yeah." Robin sat on the small porch bench and stretched his legs out in front of him. "For two of the eight years I knew him."

"Are you, uh, divorced?"

"No." He held Shawn's eyes as old grief washed through his chest without warning. "Widower. He died about three years ago now. Three years Christmas Day."

"Holy shit. I am so sorry, Robin." Shawn sat next to him, then lightly squeezed Robin's right wrist before releasing him. "I didn't mean to bring up a painful subject."

"I know. I guess technically, I'm the one who brought it up last night." And every time Robin thought he was ready to move forward, all the old love came rushing back, followed by the grief, and it kept him firmly planted in place. Static. He needed to break that cycle somehow and learn to carry those things with him, instead of letting them keep him stuck in one place.

"Still. I'm sorry you lost your husband."

"Thank you. Everyone here has a past, and Xander is part of mine. The day I met him, I knew he was someone special. Someone I could love, and I did love him. Hard, and for a lot of years. And then he was gone, and I didn't handle it well. At all. Took me a long time to get my shit together, and it's not hyperbole when I say this ranch saved my life. Got me on track to living in the world again."

"I think I get it a little bit. I get loss, anyway. We all handle loss differently, and I can't speak to losing a spouse, but both my parents died by the time I was thirteen. No siblings, no extended family in the area who cared besides my grandparents. Then it was just the three of us until I had to leave town."

"Had to leave?"

Shawn heaved a deep, weary sigh. "Long story, not going there."

"Understood, and I won't push. And in the interest of full disclosure, one of the reasons I was so pissy to you when we first met is because of how much you initially reminded me of Xander. The resemblance threw me off, and seeing you up there on a horse just…sent me back to a bad place."

Back to the day Xander died.

Shawn squinted at him. "So are you only interested in me because I look like Xander?"

"God, no. I mean, once I talked to you and saw you up close, the resemblance isn't as strong. And you have such a different personality from Xander. It's not about you being like him, it's just…you. I like *you*, Shawn. I like you more with every conversation we have. Xander had a big personality, and a smile and joke for everyone, and I loved that about him. You have this beautiful inner strength that you try to hide but can't, because it shines through in everything you do."

"Oh." He couldn't tell in the dim light but Shawn might have blushed. "Thank you."

The conversation was getting a bit too serious for

Robin, so he pulled out his inner flirt. "What's something you like about me?"

Okay, that somehow came out more awkward and less charming than Robin had hoped, but Shawn still laughed. "Well, you're blunt, which is nice. Honest and open about what you want. I'm gay, but I've never had good luck with my gaydar, and more than once I've flirted too much with a straight dude who didn't appreciate it. I guess I'm attracted to the wrong type of guy."

"Really? Am I the wrong type?"

"Probably." Shawn's gaze dropped briefly as he very openly cruised Robin. "Physically, you are definitely my type. I think I'm a little intimidated by your age and experience."

Robin pretended to be offended. "Woah, I'm not exactly at my expiration date."

"I didn't mean it like that. Yeah, you're older, but you've been married and had this whole other life before now."

"Well, so did you. Where did you go when you left your hometown?"

"San Francisco, to live with a distant cousin. We weren't friendly, but it was a place to live, and I worked any job I could get, so I could send money home. I tried taking college courses, but they didn't seem to do anything for me but cost money. I learn things better hands-on, and kitchens were a good place to hide."

Robin didn't like Shawn's frown. "Hide from who?"

"People in general, I guess, and it was an old habit from before I left home." Shawn nibbled at his thumbnail. "One of the reasons I left was because of a semi-public…incident that made me famous in my hometown, and not in a good way. People were coming down hard, on my side or against me, and it sucked."

It took all of Robin's self-control not to ask about the incident, because Shawn looked absolutely miserable now. Robin chanced sliding an arm across Shawn's shoulders, and he was relieved when Shawn didn't pull away. He didn't lean into Robin, either, but he did accept the comfort.

"I'm sorry that happened," Robin whispered.

"Thanks."

"Is that why you never visit home?"

"Pretty much. My grandparents never stopped supporting me but it embarrassed them, I could tell, and they lost some lifelong friends over the whole thing."

"Guilt can be a powerful thing. Trust me, I know guilt." Guilt kept him awake at night. Literally. "But you're here now. Safe and sound."

And right next door to me.

"Yeah." Shawn's lips twisted into an adorable half smile. "The ad for the saloon job was a random find for me, and it's completely changed my life."

"Same. Both things. Random find and changed my life."

Shawn's hip pinged, and he slid out from under Robin's arm to check his phone. "Miles. He's asking me to his cabin to watch a movie. Guess Reyes is on the overnight without him."

Robin didn't want their conversation to end yet, but this one had given him hope. Shawn had forgiven him, hadn't turned him down flat, and they'd shared things. Personal things. He could be patient and go at Shawn's pace. "You should go. Hang out with your friend."

"Are you sure?"

"Yeah. I mean, we said what we needed to say." His heart sped up as his nerves got the better of him. But Shawn had said he liked Robin's bluntness. "I'm still attracted to you, Shawn, and I'd like to get to know you more. Maybe kiss more, too, if you're okay with that?"

Shawn nibbled on his thumb again. "I'd like that, I think. Definitely getting to know you. Maybe kissing. Um, are you out?"

"Sure. Once I got settled here, I never made it a secret I'm bi. Honestly, most of the guys who work here aren't completely straight, and it's been great living in a place where everyone is tolerant and accepting of all sexualities."

"I imagine it is."

"Are you out?"

"No, not really, but if anyone asked, I wouldn't lie."

Robin winced. "Yeah, about that, I sort of outed you to Miles and Reyes last night. They confronted me after you stormed off the trail, and I said we'd kissed."

"I don't care what they know. Miles is discreet and a loyal friend."

"He definitely seems to be. Go watch a movie. I can entertain myself."

Shawn still hesitated, and Robin really hoped it was because he'd enjoyed their conversation, too, and didn't want it to end. "Okay, thanks. Um, see you at breakfast?"

"Absolutely." He watched Shawn rise and walk down cabin row, not hiding his appraisal of Shawn's departing backside. Shawn was slender but not skinny, and he moved with purpose, intent on his destination and aware of his surroundings at all times.

It made Robin wonder about this horrible incident in Shawn's past, and a desperate need to protect Shawn took hold. Protect him from the past, the future, from anyone who tried to hurt him. But Shawn wasn't his to protect—not yet—beyond a casual friendship. Robin longed for a permanent person in his bed at night. Someone to fall asleep with, wake up with, watch the sun rise with.

Someone to fully share his life. Maybe Shawn Matthews was that person, maybe not. But for the first time since Xander died, Robin had genuine hope he could finally move forward.

Shawn was so muddled by his chat with Robin that he'd knocked on two different cabin doors trying to find Miles's, without realizing he had no idea where he was going. The cabins weren't numbered, and the only things that seemed to set them apart on the outside were small items, like a potted flower or wind chime.

Fortunately, the second door he knocked on was Colt's and Colt politely pointed to the cabin next door. When Miles opened his cabin door with a wan smile, it really hit Shawn that Miles was supposed to have been on the overnight with Reyes but wasn't. It hadn't even occurred to him earlier when Miles offered to take over dinner so Shawn could move into his cabin.

"Hey, you okay?" Shawn asked. "I thought you were camping."

"Yeah, I'm fine now." Miles let him in and shut the door. "Something I ate at Wes's for lunch upset my stomach, so I decided not to be miserable miles away from my bed. Slept it off earlier, though, and I'm just nursing it with hot broth and crackers. But it's not contagious, I promise."

"Okay. I'm sorry you got sick."

"Believe me, so was Wes. But he didn't poison me on purpose, and now you and I get to hang on your first night here."

"True." Shawn studied the cabin, which had the same basic interior layout as his. Sitting area out front with two chairs, a small table, and a mini fridge with a coffeepot on top. In the back half, two twin beds had been pushed together on one side to create a larger bed, and beyond it was the bathroom. The place didn't have a lot of personal things in it, though, which Shawn found odd. Especially knowing Reyes had lived here for years before Miles moved in.

Guess none of us are fond of holding on to useless trinkets.

"You weren't busy, were you?" Miles asked. "We can totally watch a movie some other night, if you want."

"No, it's fine." Shawn had been somewhat grateful for the excuse to get away from Robin and his cheeky, adorable smiles. Finding out Robin had once been married had been an odd gut-punch, and Shawn still wasn't sure why. Perhaps it was knowing the older man had already had one love of his life, and he was unlikely to find another, so maybe all they'd ever be were friends.

But that warm, heavy arm across his shoulders? Shawn had barely resisted leaning into the man's broad chest for more of that comfort and warmth, and that was an odd response for Shawn. Then again, how much genuine physical affection had he had these last five years?

Practically none, and that's all it is. I want affection and Robin is giving me some.

"Okay, something has you distracted right now." Miles circled Shawn and planted himself in his direct line of sight. "Did you talk to Robin about last night?"

"Yes. He apologized and explained himself, and I forgave him."

"Really? For calling you another guy's name?"

"His dead husband's name." Oh shit, Shawn probably shouldn't have blurted that out.

Miles's green eyes went impossibly wide. "Seriously? Wow."

"Yeah. I get the feeling it's really, really complicated and it hurts to talk about, so I didn't push him, and he didn't push me, either, when I told him some stuff about my past."

"Did you tell him about living in your car for two years?"

Shawn flinched. "No, and please don't. All I told him about my moving into the cabin was that I needed a place to stay, and he didn't press me for details. He's superrespectful about the past, and I think it's because he's got a lot of his own demons he doesn't like talking about. And I have the cabin now, so there's no reason to bring up the homeless thing."

"Maybe not with Robin, but I do wish I'd known sooner. We'd have helped you, Shawn."

"I know. But I was managing, and now I'm here."

"So…are you and Robin a thing?"

"No. I don't think so." Shawn flopped into one of the sitting chairs. "I'm attracted to him, and he flat out said he's attracted to me." *And that he wants to kiss me again.* "I think I'd like to try dating but… I'm scared." Something he couldn't bring himself to admit to Robin earlier. "Every good thing I've had in my life ends up ripped away from me."

"Your job at the saloon hasn't been ripped away, and

it won't be. You're a fantastic cook, and you have a job there for as long as you want it."

"Thank you. Old fears, I guess."

"I get old fears, believe me. But part of moving on and being happy is putting the past behind us and only looking forward. It's what I've done with Dallas. The only thing that matters now is the life I've built here with Reyes, Wes, Mack, and everyone else. You can have that, too, Shawn."

"I do want it. I guess I'm not used to things going so well for me, you know? I've got a job I love, a safe place to live with a bed in it, and a cute guy who's interested in me. I can't help waiting for that other shoe to drop."

Miles waved both hands in the air. "Ignore the shoe. There is no shoe. Just embrace this new life here and live it. You deserve it." Then he chuckled. "Man, I'm starting to channel Wes and all his positivity now."

"Not a bad thing."

"I guess not. So I'm assuming you aren't out?"

It took Shawn a few seconds to catch up with Miles's train of thought. "You mean as gay? Not really. For a while, I thought maybe I was bi, but nah. It's just… I've never actually had a relationship with a guy before."

"But you're into Robin."

"Yeah. I mean, he's hot and funny, and he has this easy charm that appeals to me. I'm attracted to him. It's just…there are so many new things going on right now, with the guesthouse kitchen and moving into the cabin. I don't know if I can juggle a boyfriend, too, if Robin even wants that."

"He's a fan of clubbing in the city with Colt, but that doesn't mean he isn't itching to settle down again. Especially if he was married once already."

"That's what worries me, though. When Robin talked about his husband, he got all dreamy, and I could tell how much he loved and still loves the man, dead or not. How do I compete with a ghost?"

"You don't compete." Miles perched on the other chair, elbows on knees, his expression serious. "Mack was still nursing a broken heart when he first met Wes, and maybe Mack hadn't been married to his ex, but he still loved the man. Wes was himself with Mack. Didn't try to compete, and he didn't relent when he decided he wanted Mack."

Shawn let out a frustrated breath. "You make it sound so easy."

"It's not, and it can be a lot of work. And even after you get together, it's work. Reyes and I are crazy in love, but we don't always agree. We argue and then we talk. Mack and Wes fight, and I always know because Wes comes right to me to vent. So if you and Robin do try to date, or whatever, you can always come to me to talk."

"Thanks, Miles. I don't know what I really want, other than to watch a movie and then go to bed."

Miles grinned. "That's a good start. What are you in the mood for?"

They climbed onto the bed, which had so many pillows piled on, it looked more like a sofa and made it feel less weird that it was a bed. On the wall directly across was a mounted smart TV. Miles turned it on and brought up a streaming app, and Shawn was a bit jealous of the setup. He'd never owned his own TV before, and the wall mount was still up from where Patrice had taken hers down.

Maybe one day he'd have extra cash to buy a TV of

his own. Or even a small tablet would work just fine for him.

They agreed on a recent comedy, both in the mood to laugh, and Shawn settled in next to his friend, ready to do nothing more taxing than relax for two hours. He'd figure out this thing with Robin another time.

Shawn slept fitfully that night, unused to having room to wiggle and stretch. And the ranch was just so...quiet. He was used to the occasional car driving past, or the loud screech of crickets or frogs outside the car. Maybe he'd buy a small desk fan just for the noise. But getting up and being able to stumble into a bathroom first thing? To pee in a toilet, wash in a real shower, without worrying about the other, bigger men using the facilities?

Perfect. And very much missed.

It hadn't taken him long to unpack his car last night, because he didn't have a lot. The gym bag where he kept all his clothes and a few personal items he kept with him. His little basket of toiletries. The stack of library books. His saloon costume. Everything stored away in a manner that would make packing it all back up quick and painless. After keeping his clothes in a gym bag for the better part of two years, he'd only been able to put his socks and underwear in a drawer. The rest of the bag sat on top of the dresser for now.

Floor-plan-wise, this cabin was the same as Miles's, but Patrice had definitely styled it to her own preferences, with a small couch instead of two chairs that faced the TV wall mount. And she'd had a full-size bed opposite a long, nine-drawer dresser with a mirror.

Waking up to his own reflection was a little weird,

though, so he'd probably have to throw a towel over the mirror.

And now he had an easy commute, so at about six fifteen, Shawn left his cabin—only to nearly fall off his own porch from fright at the sight of someone awake and watching from the cabin to his left. The last one on the row.

Robin.

"What are you doing?" Shawn asked.

"Watching the sun rise." Robin had his phone in his hand but didn't seem to be actively using it.

"The sun doesn't usually come up until seven."

Robin smiled and shrugged. "It's my porch, so I can wait it out. Always get a great view from here."

Shawn took a few steps closer so they weren't speaking quite so loudly to hear each other. People were still asleep all along cabin row. "Early riser?"

"Something like that. I don't sleep well anymore, and it's become a habit to sit out here and wait for the sun." He held up his vape. "And take a few puffs on this."

"Another habit?"

"Trying to kick it. Started smoking because I'd hoped it would help kill me faster, and it's a hard habit to break. At least this thing smells better."

"Very true." Shawn kind of wanted to stay and keep talking to Robin, but he had a house full of guests who'd be wanting their breakfast. "Well, I guess I'll see you up in the kitchen."

"Count on it." Robin tipped an imaginary hat at Shawn.

Shawn waved meekly, feeling a bit dumb, and walked away. He definitely got the sense of being watched, too, and it didn't bother him this morning. After last night's conversation with Miles, the two things Shawn needed to focus on most were the kitchen and settling into life on the ranch. His friendship with Robin was a distant third.

Chapter Eight

Shawn's first week cooking for both the full ranch staff and guests came to a happy close after breakfast on Saturday—yay for lunchtime sandwiches and salads!—because he was exhausted in the very best way. He hadn't been so worn-out since the day of their July fourth celebration at the ghost town, and his bed was a much nicer thing to collapse onto than his car's front seat.

Which he did collapse onto around one thirty, after lunch was over and all the fixings put away, for a two-hour nap. A nap over way too soon, and then he was hoofing back to the kitchen to learn what Patrice called Leftovers Pie. It was basically a casserole of anything left over from the week for the hands to eat that night. Their grocery delivery came, too, driven up from town by a nice kid named Juno, who always seemed worried he'd gotten something on the list wrong.

Poor kid. But Shawn imagined finding a steady, paying job in a town the size of Garrett wasn't easy, and Juno didn't want to mess up and get fired.

Neither did Shawn, but so far so good.

Only a handful of the hands came through for supper. Saturday was the only night everyone had off, so the cowboys often scattered once the guests left at three.

Either into San Jose or San Francisco for fun, or even just to more local bars to drink and blow off steam. So it surprised Shawn when Robin was one of the guys who ate at the guesthouse.

Not that Robin couldn't have plans later, and he probably did. Miles, Reyes, Mack, and Wes had gone into San Jose to meet up with other friends. With his closest friend off the ranch, Shawn had big plans to read in bed until he fell asleep.

Robin didn't openly flirt with Shawn while he ate, and Shawn wasn't sure how he felt about that. Maybe he was being respectful because Shawn wasn't really out? Or maybe Robin had decided he didn't really want to kiss Shawn again.

Whatever. Distant number three.

Once the kitchen was cleaned up and shut down for the night, Shawn took a longer, slower route back to the cabin row that swung closer to the big barn. Not for any particular reason—he was just stretching his legs. He hadn't gone near the horses since that first ride two weeks ago, because he'd been too busy. But he had enjoyed riding and wouldn't mind doing it again one day.

Robin was on his own porch, long legs stretched out in front of him, doing something on his phone, and he didn't look up when Shawn stepped onto his cabin's porch. Shawn started to say hello when something on his bench caught his attention. He picked up a single red rose—only it wasn't a real rose, it was carved out of wood and painted to look like one. He ran his fingertips over the smooth wood, which was sanded down beautifully, even the thorns. The petals were defined, some so thin Shawn wasn't sure how the carver had done it.

It was breathtaking.

"You like it?" Robin asked. He'd stood and leaned against his porch's support post, hands deep in his jeans pockets. Tentative.

"It's beautiful. Wait, did you make this?"

"Yeah. Old hobby I picked up from an uncle when I was a kid. It's hard to find fresh flowers way out here, even wild ones this time of year. Plus, that'll last longer."

"You made it for me?"

"Of course." Robin's tentative smile dipped into something more flirty. "Can't romance you without flowers, can I?"

"You…" Shawn studied the older man, who'd kept a quiet distance from him since their Tuesday morning conversation. Had he planned all this? Giving Shawn space, only to drop something superromantic on him during their free night off? "I love it. No one's ever given me a flower before, real or fake."

"I'm glad you like it. Had to start over three times to get the petals just right, and the only thing the general store in town had was a kid's watercolor set, but I think I did okay. I don't usually paint things, but I wanted it to look real."

"You did an amazing job." Shawn moved closer to him, the rose clutched to his chest, drawing Shawn toward Robin like a magnet. He wanted to thank Robin with something bigger than words, but that was too much, too soon. Right? "Thank you."

They met on the strip of ground between their cabins. Shawn's heart ached with gratitude for the thoughtful, handmade gift. "I can't remember the last time I was given something with any real meaning," Shawn said, barely able to get his voice above a whisper. The moment was too special.

"Happy to." Robin's gaze drifted to Shawn's mouth and back up, his eyes glittering with want, and Shawn kind of wanted, too. "I'll carve you an entire bouquet if it'll make you happy."

"When did you find the time?"

"I don't sleep well at night, and I like sitting out on my porch, listening to the land whisper to me."

Shawn blinked hard. "The land whispers?"

"If you listen the right way, it does. Carving gives me something to do with my hands. Want to see some of my things?"

Dear God, that doesn't sound like a come-on or anything.

"What things?" Shawn asked.

"The things I've carved over the years. They're in my cabin."

"Okay."

Belly flipping with nerves, Shawn followed Robin into his cabin, which was somehow cozier than Miles's, and smelled like a mix of cedar and leather. And he left the door open, which made Shawn feel less trapped and isolated. A TV was mounted on the wall in front of the sitting chairs, and a large, handmade bookcase stood to the right. Instead of books, it housed carved figures of all sizes and shapes. Animals, plants, inanimate objects, most of them unpainted and in their raw, unpolished form. All of them beautiful.

"Wow." Shawn put his rose into his back pocket so he could pick up a horse the size of his hand. The details were exquisite, down to a visible mane on the horse's neck. "You should sell these at a craft show or something. They're incredible."

Robin, for all his bluster and self-assuredness, blushed. "Nah, it's just a hobby."

"Are you fishing for compliments? Because this is art, Robin."

"Compliments, huh?" There was the confident, flirty Robin. "I'd love to earn another compliment from you."

"Well, your rose definitely earned at least one." Distant number three was catching up fast and overtaking his other two priorities, and Shawn was okay with that. It was Saturday, he'd had a long week, and Robin's gift was so thoughtful and romantic he could spare a "compliment."

Robin stepped closer, right into Shawn's personal space, bringing with him the scents of cherry, leather, and horse. "Only one compliment?"

"Do a good job with the first and you might get another."

"Hmm."

Shawn's pulse jumped a moment before Robin cupped his jaw in one hand and kissed him. Warm lips played atop Shawn's. Another hand squeezed his hip as Robin deepened the kiss, licking into Shawn's mouth. Bringing a new, more intense flavor of Robin that overtook Shawn's senses. He breathed in the sexy cowboy, his own hands clasping the front of Robin's polo. The kiss went on and on, and Shawn was only vaguely aware of moving. Then his shoulders hit a solid surface and—

"Ouch, shit!" Shawn pushed Robin away as something sharp poked his ass. He reached around and pulled the carved rose out of his back pocket. "I got stabbed by a thorn."

Robin chuckled. "Sorry about that."

"It's okay." Shawn was glad the rose had broken them

apart, because that kiss had fried his senses a little. He was already half-hard and didn't want to give Robin the wrong impression. As much as getting off appealed to Shawn, he really didn't know the man that well, and Shawn wasn't about to become another notch on Robin's headboard—especially knowing more about his weekend clubbing history. Shawn wanted more than a sweaty weekend hookup.

"That was a fantastic compliment, by the way." Robin glanced to the left, where a clock carved from a piece of log hung. "If we want to keep, uh, complimenting each other, we might want to go hang in your cabin. Ernie will be back soon."

Ernie? "Oh, your roommate, right. Sure, we can hang in my cabin. Just for compliments, though, right? No other, uh, demonstrations?"

"Only what you want, Shawn."

Shawn studied Robin's eyes, so full of desire but also of kindness. If Robin just wanted to get laid, Shawn had no illusions the man could go find someone. But he was here. With Shawn. The lonely part of him didn't spend too much time pondering why. "Okay."

Rose in hand, Shawn led Robin to his cabin and they settled on the couch close enough that their knees touched. Shawn wished for a radio, or even a damned fan to break the silence of the cabin. "It's so quiet here at night," he blurted out.

"It can be, especially inside." Robin settled one hand on Shawn's knee. "It's why I like sitting outside."

"Because the land whispers to you."

"Yup. Some nights she's got a lot to say, too."

"Like what?"

Robin quirked an eyebrow. "You'll have to sit up some night with me and find out."

"We'll see. I do have to be up early for work, you know."

"At least we'll always have our good mornings in passing."

Shawn glanced at Robin's lips, wanting them on his again but too uncertain to make the first move. "We do have that. May I have another compli—?"

His words were lost beneath the hard claiming of Robin's mouth. Shawn fumbled getting the rose onto the back of the couch and out of his way so he could grab Robin's shoulders and hold on tight. Robin knew how to kiss, to seduce with his mouth, and he did. Very, very well. Shawn reacted instinctively to the seduction, relaxing in Robin's arms, slowing going under. He eased onto his back and pulled Robin down with him, both of them hard in their jeans. And Shawn wasn't scared, wasn't nervous, because…it was Robin.

He trusted Robin, despite only knowing him for two weeks, and his body was very on board with everything happening. Robin held Shawn by the neck and hair, and Shawn wanted those hands to explore but Robin wasn't going below his shoulders. Wasn't doing more than seducing his mouth and rubbing their erections together, and this was as far as Shawn had ever gone with a guy.

I want more but I don't know if I'm ready.

He was twenty-four fucking years old; he should be ready for more.

Robin broke away and rested his forehead on Shawn's, hot breath gusting over Shawn's kiss-bruised lips. "Hot damn, but I do love kissing you. Wow."

"I like it, too. A lot."

"I can tell." He gave Shawn's dick a deliberate grind. "But I don't want to push you too far, too fast. This is… kind of new for you, right?"

"Yes." Shawn wasn't embarrassed to admit that to Robin, because they'd already sort of talked about it. His lack of experience with men. Or rather his lack of positive experiences with men, and he was so not bringing up Beck tonight or in the near future. "It's not that I'm scared of sex with guys or anything. Before I left home, there was never an opportunity for more than stolen make-out sessions, because it was a small town. When I lived with my cousin, I worked so much I couldn't meet people, never mind bringing a hookup to her place, and I wasn't about to go home with a strange guy. When I did have sex, it was always with a girl, and then these last two years I didn't—" Shawn caught himself before he admitted to living in his car. "I bounced around from place to place too much to really get to know anyone."

Robin nuzzled his nose. "Because you aren't a once-and-done guy like me?"

"Yes, and I'm not judging you for liking sex, I swear. I like the sex I've had, I just…need intimacy first." Shawn groaned. "Do I sound as corny as I feel?"

"Not corny at all." Robin shifted so their dicks weren't rubbing so directly together and raised up to peer down at him. Only affection and understanding shined in his eyes. No judgment or amusement. "We like what we like, and right now I very much like you right where you are."

"I like me here, too. It's kind of surreal having my own space again. Space to just…exist."

"And swap compliments?"

Shawn chuckled. "Yeah, that, too."

"Do you think maybe you haven't felt comfortable

doing more with a guy because you haven't felt safe where you are?"

"Oh, that's definitely part of it. I mean, I didn't feel unsafe with my cousin, exactly, but I was kind of forced on her, so I didn't feel welcome, either. But here... I have friends here. People who really, truly have my back. People who will believe me if I say something bad is happening."

Robin traced a single finger down Shawn's cheek in an oddly electric touch. "You can tell me anything, Shawn. Past, present, anything, and I'll listen. I like listening to you. Talking to you."

"Kissing me?"

"Definitely that, too." He brushed his lips over Shawn's, his weight a comfortable blanket over most of Shawn's body. "What can I carve for you next?"

"Surprise me." Shawn didn't care, because everything Robin did was a work of art, and he'd love it no matter what.

"Okay. What's your favorite color?"

"What does my favorite color have to do with you carving something for me?"

"I'm getting to know you. Isn't that what people who flirt and compliment each other do?" Robin wiggled his eyebrows, and Shawn kind of adored that expression. It kept serious things light and made Robin look carefree—especially when sometimes, if he didn't think Shawn was watching, he looked so sad.

"I don't know if I have a favorite color really," Shawn said after a moment. "I like blue. Blue goes with everything."

"Does it?"

"Sure." He tugged on one of Robin's belt loops. "Jeans are blue and they go with pretty much everything."

"This is true. Favorite movie?"

"Gosh, I don't know. I don't watch a lot of movies or TV, to be honest. Mostly I read."

"Yeah? Favorite book?"

"I couldn't possibly choose. I read all kinds of books. Fiction, nonfiction, travelogues, biographies, you name it. Depends on my mood at the time, I guess, and I'll go on reading splurges where a certain topic captures my attention, so I'll find everything I can at the library and check them out."

"Like what? For example."

Shawn should have felt strange having this conversation on his back, with Robin on top of him, but he didn't. It was incredibly comforting and…right. "The last big binge was true crime bios written by the victim themselves, like the girl in the box, and then that serial killer in Philadelphia in the eighties. Gary Heidnik, I think? The Daggett library didn't have a lot of those books, but they ordered some in from other county branches."

"Huh. I wouldn't have pegged you for liking gruesome stuff."

"Gruesome stuff is part of life. I'm not big on horror novels, but the things in those true crime books actually happened. It's also an interesting study in human psychology, you know? How incredibly warped some of those perps' minds were."

"Makes sense."

"Do you like to read?"

"Not really." Robin seemed embarrassed for a beat. "Never was a fan of books, not even as a kid. I always had trouble making the words make any damned sense

and barely passed classes that required a lot of writing.
I'd rather be outside doing things than inside reading."

"That's cool. People don't always like the same stuff."

"We don't seem to have a lot in common, do we?"

Shawn rested a hand on Robin's hip. "Don't they always say opposites attract?"

"Some do."

"Attract or say they attract?"

Robin laughed, then rubbed their noses together in an affectionate gesture Shawn was really starting to enjoy.
"Both."

"So I have a very important question to ask you."

"Okay." Robin gazed down with intent in his eyes.
"Hit me."

Shawn worked to keep his expression serious. "Can you cook?"

He laughed again, and Shawn enjoyed the way the sound rumbled from Robin's chest into his own. "Yes, I can cook. Sort of. Nothing fancy, but I wouldn't have to exist on frozen dinners if I ever found myself living off the ranch. Quite a few of the hands can cook, and we've all volunteered to help Patrice over the years, but she loves what she does."

"Mothering forty people a week?"

"Yup."

They both went silent, and Shawn wasn't sure who began their second round of kissing but he was glad for it. Glad for the way Robin's taller body cocooned Shawn, keeping him safe and comfortable as they ground their erections together. Moved together in a wonderfully arousing way without pushing too hard, too far. Not enough to get off, but enough to feel it while they explored each other's mouths. Sensual and sweet and oh so perfect. Like nothing Shawn had ever experienced before, and he liked it. A lot.

Shawn's hands wandered first, stroking across Robin's ribs and back, along his spine as he arched and ground. Robin mostly kept to Shawn's neck and shoulders, less freedom to touch from his position on top with half of Shawn's body hidden by the couch cushions. The fun bits weren't hidden, and Shawn silently thanked Robin for his restraint, when Robin had to crave an orgasm as badly as Shawn did.

Why am I resisting him so hard?

Because the last time he'd said yes, his entire world had imploded in the aftermath, and he couldn't risk losing this beautiful slice of heaven he'd found at Clean Slate. He really shouldn't be doing this now, but it had been so damned long since someone had taken care of him like this. Put Shawn's needs above his own.

The endless kiss left Shawn panting and desperate when Robin finally pulled away, his mouth puffy and damp. Pupils blown. He stopped rubbing against Shawn, too, leaving their groins pressed close. "We need to stop," Robin said. "Fuck, I want you so bad."

"Same, but it's too soon."

"Okay." Robin kissed his forehead and nose before lightly brushing their lips together. "This was wonderful."

"Yeah, it was. Thank you, though, for, um, stopping?"

"You don't have to thank me for that." Robin helped him sit up, which was a tad uncomfortable with his raging boner, but at least Robin had the same issue. "I respect limits, Shawn."

"I know. I do. It just can't be easy for you. Going slow."

Robin shrugged, never losing his easy smile. "It's different but worth it. When I first met Xander, it was instant attraction and desire, and we had sex within twelve hours of knowing each other. At first, all we really had in common was sex, and in that first year we were together, we hit a lot of rough patches trying to figure each other out. Maybe if we'd gotten to know each other first, we wouldn't have fought as much as we did that first year."

"But you worked things out."

"We did. But I've always regretted the fights, because they were as passionate as our lovemaking."

A bolt of alarm shot through Shawn's gut. "The fights weren't physical, were they?"

"Lord no. I mean, Xander threw a book once, and I might have punched some drywall but we were never physically violent with each other, I promise. The only two times I ever hit someone else was during drunken bar brawls."

"You were in drunken bar brawls?" Shawn didn't like knowing Robin had punched people before, but people did do pretty stupid shit when drunk.

"Yeah. Strangely, both the guys I punched were co-workers, but tempers can really get up when you're traveling in close quarters with bull riders."

"You...punched a bull rider?" Wait a second. "You worked with bull riders?"

Robin pressed his lips together, expression pinched, as if unhappy he'd revealed such a thing. "Yeah. Part of my old life, and how I met Xander. Lucky's Rodeo was a traveling attraction. We went to state and county fairs all over the Midwest and South, put on trick riding, roping, and skill demonstrations. I was with them over eight years. Left after Xander died."

"Wow." Shawn was impressed Robin had lived a nomadic life for so long, putting on a show for crowds of strangers. "It was your dream job of working with horses?"

"Yeah, it was. Loved everything about it, especially being able to travel. See the United States firsthand, instead of just in books or on TV. There's nothing quite like coming up on the Rocky Mountains for the first time."

"I can't imagine it." Shawn had never lived outside of Nevada or Northern California, much less traveled across the country, and he envied Robin that experience.

Robin still seemed down and a bit wistful over his old life with the rodeo. Shawn got the impression his past was a tender subject, so he stopped pressing on the bruise. "Thank you for sharing that with me."

"You're welcome. I should probably go."

Shawn kissed him at the door, which did wonders to reengage his flagging erection. After Robin left, he bolted into the bathroom to jerk off. Hand on the wall over the toilet, Shawn fisted his erection, closed his eyes, and remembered how it felt when Robin kissed him. Rubbed against him. Made love to his mouth in a way that was both aggressive and tender. Imagined this was Robin's hand on his dick, stroking him just right, no thought for anything other than Shawn's pleasure.

"Oh shit." Shawn bit his forearm as he came, the release washing over him like a breaking wave—a powerful force that soothed into a calmer, rolling pleasure. "Damn."

It had been ages since his own hand had felt so good, and it had everything to do with Robin. His kindness and kisses and expressive eyes. The way he looked at Shawn and *saw* him.

He carved me a rose.

Shawn cleaned up so he could fetch his rose and sniff it. It smelled like wood and paint, but also like a promise. A promise to be gentle with Shawn's heart as Robin slowly but surely began to steal bits of it for himself. And Shawn was very much okay with that. He was finally in a stable place where he could stay for a while. Find safety and friendship, and maybe even offer his heart to another person.

Another man for the first time. But Robin's wistfulness over his past lingered in the back of Shawn's mind, and it made him wonder. Would Robin eventually get itchy feet and want to travel again? Nah. Robin seemed settled here. Shawn had to trust in that.

"Be gentle with my heart and I'll be gentle with yours," Shawn told the rose. "I promise."

Chapter Nine

Robin sauntered into the kitchen Sunday morning in a terrific mood after last night's couple of hours with Shawn. Not only because Robin had come like gangbusters in his own cabin afterward—and again this morning in the shower—but because of the trust he'd established with Shawn. Shawn struck him as a guy used to depending on himself and slow to trust that other people wouldn't fuck him over.

Like the person in his past who Miles had mentioned. It had been a bit of a struggle for Robin not to pry into that last night, and then the conversation had flipped itself into Robin's painful past, instead. But Shawn hadn't pushed too hard, and his own restraint helped Robin fall for the guy a little bit more.

And dear God, but he couldn't wait to make out with Shawn again. Soon.

Sunday breakfast was informal, since some of the horsemen were still straggling home for work after a night out, and a small group had gathered at one end of the table. A table captained by Mack, which threw Robin for a moment. Hadn't he been out of town with Wes last night? Why was he back at eight in the morning and at the guesthouse, instead of his own home?

"Hey, Robin, join us!" Mack said the instant he spotted Robin. "After you get food, of course."

"Okay." He eyeballed the other people in the huddle as he plated some food, surprised to see Colt and Avery both in the mix, along with Wes, Shawn, and Slater. He slid into a seat next to Slater, wishing he could be next to Shawn instead. "What's going on?"

"My overachieving boyfriend," Wes replied, "is already brainstorming next year's seasonal reopening of the ghost town."

"Yeah, I am," Mack said. "I don't wanna do it all last minute like the July fourth thing. Even though that went great, I stressed out a lot of people, including our cooks."

Miles and Shawn exchanged knowing looks. Robin could only imagine how stressed out both men had been cooking for so many extra people on a week's notice. He'd been up at the site along with that week's guests, and it had been crowded. And a lot of fun, too.

"So what are you going to plan?" Robin asked as he spread blackberry jam on a piece of toast. "Another barbecue?"

Mack shook his head no. "I was thinking something along the lines of a rodeo with riding and roping tricks, maybe even a greased pig catch for the kids. Something like an Old West show but also interactive."

Robin's stomach shrank into a ball of ice and he put his toast down, the rest of his insides shaking. "Rodeo?" He felt Shawn's eyes on him, but Robin couldn't turn his head. Couldn't do anything except see Xander on that horse…

Voices kept talking around him, and the kitchen was suddenly too damned small. Too small and Robin needed air. Needed quiet and air and not to see Xander on that fucking horse. He was pretty sure he excused himself before walking away. Blindly away from the kitchen, and he nearly walked into a damned tree before he stopped. Leaned one shoulder against it and sucked in big, deep breaths. Pushed them out on long exhales.

He closed his eyes and listened to the land whisper around him. The rustle of air through the leaves. The steady hum of the earth itself until he could reasonably react to other humans again. He stared at the ground, annoyed now by his reaction, but goddamn. Why did Mack want to do a fucking rodeo?

Not that Mack knew shit about his past, because Robin didn't talk about it. Not with anyone. Not until Shawn.

"Robin?"

The only voice Robin wanted to hear in that moment drifted over from his left. Shawn stood a few yards away, openly concerned, and he was alone, thank Christ. "Hey."

"I'd ask if you're okay, but that seems like a stupid question right now." Shawn came a few steps closer. "Forgive the expression, but when Mack mentioned the word *rodeo*, you looked like you'd seen a ghost."

"I did." Robin shifted so his entire back was resting against the tree. "How badly did I embarrass myself back there?"

"You didn't really. You said something about feeling queasy and needing air, and then Colt made a joke about you drinking too much last night."

"Oh. Good." He'd nursed more than one hangover at that kitchen table in the past.

"I'm sorry Mack upset you."

Robin waved a hand in the air, then beckoned Shawn

closer. "It wasn't Mack's fault. He doesn't know my past."

"Really?" Shawn stood in front of him, hands in his pockets, and Robin really wanted to hug the guy for the simple comfort and contact. But they were outside where anyone could see, so he'd let Shawn reach out first. "You've worked here a long time."

"We've all got pasts, everyone who works here does. Some of the guys are more open to sharing things, and some of us don't go there. Ever."

"But you went there with me."

"Yeah, I did."

"You know you can trust Mack, too, right? You've probably got all kinds of knowledge and experience that would help him pull off a kick-ass rodeo day."

"I do. And I know some tricks of my own." Robin peered over Shawn's shoulder to the big corral. Every week, he was in that corral doing roping demonstrations for the guests, showing off his lassoing skills and even doing a few riding tricks. But that was only a small slice of the things he'd learned after eight years on the road.

I wonder if Levi would come help.

Robin hadn't consciously thought about his brother-in-law in ages. Levi and Xander had been incredibly close brothers, born only fourteen months apart, growing up together in the traveling entertainment field. Levi had been as crushed as Robin over Xander's death, and he'd quit the rodeo, too. They kept in infrequent contact over email, but rarely discussed anything except surface stuff. Other than Arthur and Judson, Levi was the only other person who knew how far Robin had fallen before hitting rock bottom.

Before Robin chose to live.

"Maybe helping Mack with a rodeo will be therapeutic for you," Shawn hedged.

"Maybe so." Robin studied Shawn's hesitant posture and half smile, and he no longer saw a Xander look-alike. How had he ever thought they were the same person? The man in front of him, boosting him up, was his Shawn. No one else. "I, uh, might even know someone I can call for more ideas. For a phone conversation, if nothing else."

"Great." Shawn grinned at him. "For what it's worth, I think a rodeo is a really fun idea, and it could be a great way to reopen the ghost town."

"I agree. Thank you. For coming after me."

"Of course. Ready to go back?"

"Definitely."

Bolstered by the conversation, Robin returned to the kitchen with Shawn by his side. Shawn had finished eating, so he sat next to Robin instead of his former spot on the other side of Slater. Under the table, Robin gave Shawn's thigh a quick squeeze.

"You feeling okay, man?" Colt asked.

"Yeah, better now," Robin replied. His toast was cold, but he nibbled on it anyway. "So a rodeo show, huh? How accurate is that to the time period of Bentley?"

"It's not superaccurate," Avery Hendrix replied. He was the historian who'd helped Mack bring the ghost town to life, and he had a head of knowledge that rivaled even Robin's smartphone. "However, it also isn't outside the realm of realism. The first advertised Wild West show was put on by Buffalo Bill Cody in 1883, and it had demonstrations of prowess at shooting, riding, and roping skills."

Avery scowled at no one in particular. "However,

the shows were incredibly racist and portrayed Native Americans as savages and the cowboys as heroes, and they were used as propaganda in support of Native genocide."

"And we're not looking to do anything remotely like that part," Mack said. "Just the skills demonstrations and things tourists can participate in that aren't dangerous. Sharpshooting is an idea but I'm worried about using live ammunition anywhere near people. I'd rather stick to horses and ropes and bypass gun use."

"Totally understandable." Avery's gaze landed briefly on Colt, and Robin followed his gaze. Colt had been shot in the back less than a year-and-a-half ago protecting the ghost town site from vandals, and the former SWAT officer was now skittish around gunfire.

For a good damn reason.

"I've got experience with doing rodeo shows," Robin said before he could change his mind. "Riding, roping, making an audience gasp and cheer. Way more than the stuff I do here for the guests."

"Really?" Wes sat up straighter. "Like what? Can you show us?"

"I'm way out of practice. It's been years since I've done some of those tricks, and I'm more likely to fall on my face. Plus, the horses I rode were trained to perform. I'm not sure the trail mares here would work well, but you might be able to rent show horses locally."

"Would you be willing to perform again?" Mack asked Robin, his expression neutral. Completely open to Robin saying no, even though Robin suspected Mack was internally overjoyed at Robin's experience.

Robin wanted to say no way, forget it, but Robin had brought it up. And part of him missed the adrenaline rush of doing those tricks. Of knowing he could be seriously hurt if his horse deviated or spooked. Of the applause after he was finished. The fans, both male and female, who wanted to buy him drinks after the show, despite his wedding band.

"I would, yes," Robin replied, more confidence in his voice than his heart. "I've also got a friend who was in the life with me who may be able to offer ideas on punching up the act."

"That's a fantastic resource," Avery said.

"Look at you, enthusiastic about horses," Colt teased Avery. "That mean you wanna go riding again soon?"

"Not a chance."

"So what exactly can you do?" Wes asked Robin. "Can you, like, stand on two different horses while they run side by side?"

"I could once upon a time," Robin replied, grinning at the way Wes's eyes lit up. "I fell on my ass a lot learning that one, and again, it takes well-trained horses. It's been close to three years since I've tried anything like that, though."

"Tude was a show horse before she came to the rescue," Mack said. His personal horse, Attitude, Tude for short.

"I didn't know that about Tude," Wes replied to him.

"Yeah, she did dressage and even won some ribbons. Then after the incident that put all those scars on her legs, her asshole owners decided she wasn't worth keeping. Sold her to an even bigger asshole, who kept her locked in a stall, didn't treat her wounds well." Mack grunted, his anger at Tude's former owners clear on his face. "Anyway, point is Robin might be able to work with her. She ain't afraid of people or a shy horse."

"Maybe," Robin said. He'd exercised Tude before but hadn't ridden her himself. "If you don't mind, I'll take her out for a run this afternoon. See how we fit."

"Wouldn't have offered her if I minded."

"Thank you."

"So, Rodeo Man, what else do you know how to do?" Robin grinned.

As Shawn listened to the other men talk about the rodeo and make plans, he also cleaned up the kitchen, a strange feeling buzzing in his chest that he tried to ignore. Breakfast was over, and the crop of guests would arrive in about ninety minutes. Reyes excused himself from the group to help Judson hitch up the buckboard. Shawn was starting to get used to this part: welcoming and being introduced to the guests. Getting to know the new arrivals he'd be cooking for all week.

He also kept half an eye on Robin, grateful he seemed to be easing into the rodeo conversation when it had initially driven the man right out of the kitchen. Shawn couldn't forget the way Robin said, "I did," when Shawn said he looked like he'd seen a ghost.

Had he seen Xander? Shawn hadn't asked how Robin's husband had died, and he had a horrible gut feeling it had something to do with the rodeo.

No wonder Mack's idea spooks him so badly.

But Robin was facing his ghosts, dealing with something in his past he'd probably never faced before. He'd run from this thing, just like Shawn had run from his own past. But Shawn didn't know how to face a past or present where half a town thought he was a vindictive liar trying to get a fast payout.

Shawn also couldn't help worrying that participating

in this rodeo show would fuel Robin's nostalgia for the traveling lifestyle and take Robin away from the ranch. From him. Yes, Shawn had been the one to urge Robin to participate, to face those ghosts head-on, because he sensed it was what Robin truly needed. Didn't mean Shawn had to like it. Everyone Shawn loved eventually left him, anyway, so why wouldn't Robin, too?

Stop anticipating the worst. Enjoy the happiness you have now.

Shawn turned on the dishwasher, pivoted, and his elbow smacked into Wes's chest. "Crap. Sorry, Wes."

"No problem." His blue eyes were serious, though, and Shawn inwardly groaned. "So what's up with you and Robin? You chased after him a while ago."

"I didn't chase after him. I went to check on a friend."

"Friend, huh?"

"Yes, friend." Shawn did not need his private business gossiped all over the ranch by Wes while Shawn and Robin were still figuring things out. "Our cabins are next door to each other, and we talk like neighbors do."

Wes studied him a beat. "Well, if you're just friends, make sure Robin knows that, because I caught some of the looks he's thrown your way recently. Maybe shut him down gently?"

Shawn stared, a little confused by Wes's comments— until Shawn remembered that night at Wes's house and the way he'd brushed off Wes's arm. "Listen, I'm not… the night my car battery died and you put your arm around my shoulders, I didn't brush you off because you're gay, or anything. I am, too, actually. I'm just… I'm not used to being touched."

"Oh, okay." Wes's expression brightened. "Thanks for that. I mean, I never pegged you as being a homophobe.

I just didn't want Robin barking up the wrong tree and getting hurt. He's a nice guy."

"He's a great guy, and I enjoy his company, and that's all I'm going to say about it."

"Message received. So what do you think about the rodeo?"

"I think it could bring in a lot of new business to Bentley, and it's a good idea. Not that I'll get to see it, since I'm sure Miles and I will be stuck in the saloon's kitchen, but someone will film it, I'm sure."

"Oh yeah. Well, I'll see you around, okay?"

"Sure. Bye, Wes."

Wes gave Mack a kiss on his way out of the kitchen, destination unknown. Mack, Avery, Colt, Robin, and Slater continued talking in a huddle at their end of the kitchen table, and Shawn took a moment to study Robin's expression. Open but still a bit wary. Avery had a tablet out and they were watching videos, with Robin pointing different things out. Since planning the rodeo wasn't his business, Shawn finished cleaning up the kitchen.

They were still at it when Patrice joined him with the welcome packets that week's guests would need, and twenty minutes later, the buckboard rolled up outside. Shawn lost himself for a while meeting the guests, having them sign waivers and get their packets. They had one family this week, young parents with ten-year-old twins, a girl and boy, and they were assigned the third floor. Reyes escorted them upstairs.

It was a small group this week, only twelve in total for their twenty available beds, but it was also December, getting colder, and Christmas was steadily approaching. Next week was their last week open to guests before the ranch closed until after the New Year. Shawn was eager for the break from cooking for so many people, but not because he didn't enjoy the work.

Less work in the kitchen meant more free time to spend with Robin. Keep getting to know the man who turned a stick of wood into a beautiful rose.

Guests were free to explore until lunch at noon, and after that they'd get riding lessons in the big corral from Reyes, Slater, and Scott. While Reyes was always present for the first lessons, the other hands alternated by week. As Shawn learned the pulse of the ranch, he understood how things worked more. Some of the guys, like Colt, strictly worked in the barn or did handyman stuff, while other hands took turns with the different tourist options, like camping and trail rides.

It would probably be a great week's vacation; too bad Shawn would never get to experience it as a guest might. He'd just content himself with watching from the sidelines.

Around eleven, Shawn started organizing the lunch buffet, and he spotted the twins out in the main guest-house living space with one of the games. Curious, he crossed the dining room until he could see which game: chess. The boy—Eric?—was reading the directions, while his sister arranged the pieces completely wrong on the board.

Shawn's heart trilled at the sight of the game. He and Granddad had sat up many nights playing chess, battling each other to the final checkmate, sometimes keeping one game going for days at a time. In no hurry, no real strategy, because it was how they spent time together. It wasn't about winning.

"This is too hard," Eric said. "Let's do something else."

"It can be a little daunting," Shawn said without thinking. "You just have to learn how the pieces move first. Then you can focus on strategy and winning."

The girl looked up from the board and smiled. Ellie, he thought. "Can you teach us?"

Shawn glanced at the clock on the wall. "Tell you what. Give me twenty minutes to finish getting lunch out on the buffet, and then I'll teach you. Keep reading the instructions, though, and there should be a diagram for how to place the pieces on the board. Black on one side, white on the other."

"Okay, thank you."

Excited by the chance to introduce someone to his favorite game, Shawn got the lunch fixings out in record time—Patrice no longer spot-checked him on lunch, since it was just sandwiches—and was back to the kids. Ellie had the pieces in the right order, thankfully, so Shawn went over each piece, how they moved, and how important they were.

"The bishop can go diagonal forward or backward," he said, "and how I remember that is because of the spire. It's kind of like a point or an angle. It's opposite the rook, which is flat on top, and can only go straight forward or backward, but not at an angle. Make sense."

Ellie nodded along but Eric seemed dubious. "Why is it so hard?" Eric asked.

"That's what makes it such a fun challenge. It's a game of patience and strategy, and of thinking ahead. I learned when I was about your age, so you should be able to pick it up. The first step is learning the pieces and how they move. Strategy comes later."

The knight was the hardest to explain, but it was also Shawn's favorite piece, because your move could completely ruin your opponent's strategy, especially if it was in a position to take two different, big moves. The siblings sat on opposite sides of the board, and Shawn coached them through moving the pieces, remembering who went where, that pawns could only move two spaces on the first move, and then one space after.

Guests began filtering into the dining room, and Shawn announced it was a sandwich buffet and to please help yourself. Patrice was in the dining room chatting up the guests so Shawn didn't have to. The twins' parents told them both to go eat and stop bothering the cook. Shawn assured them he was happy to teach them chess, and they weren't interfering in his duties.

Shawn fixed his own plate and ate in the kitchen. Robin and Colt weren't there, and Shawn couldn't help wondering if Mack had kidnapped both men to talk more about the rodeo idea. Colt had grown up on a working cattle ranch, if Shawn remembered correctly, so he might have ideas of his own. Hiding his disappointment over not seeing Robin and missing his granddad terribly, Shawn threw himself into work and tried not to think for a while.

Easier said than done.

He did find an hour that afternoon to continue coaching the twins in chess, in between their riding lessons and Shawn needing to get side dishes started for tonight's welcome barbecue. Ellie took to the game much faster than Eric, and Shawn got the sense Eric was only doing it to please his sister.

Melancholy followed Shawn into the evening, a feeling only exacerbated by Robin's continued absence, and that also kind of pissed Shawn off. Not that Robin was busy doing his job and/or helping Mack, but that Shawn had already become so dependent on Robin's smile and presence that the lack of both was affecting his mood at all. He'd relied on himself for the last five years, and two weeks around the cowboy had Shawn…what? Pining?

Fuck no.

Robin returned to the ranch in time for the barbecue, but Shawn ignored him and focused on his duties with the food. Then he used Judson's opening barbecue speech as an excuse to hide in the kitchen and call home.

"Good to hear from you, son," Granddad said in a near whisper. "She just dozed off, so don't wanna wake her."

"It's fine. Just give Nana a kiss for me tomorrow." Shawn sat on the floor and leaned his back against the walk-in. "I just needed to hear your voice. Been thinking about you a lot today."

"Oh? My sturdy good looks?"

Shawn chuckled at the joke. Granddad had a chunk of his neck missing because of throat cancer twenty years ago, and he'd often used it to great effect on Halloween when Shawn was young. "Definitely your good looks. I taught two kids how to play chess today, and it got me thinking about you and me. Sitting up late at night playing. Snacking on Ritz crackers with peanut butter and cheddar cheese."

Still a favorite snack, and one Shawn hadn't had in far too long. His cabin had a mini fridge like the others. Maybe a trip in town to the general store was in his near future.

"Those were good nights," Granddad said. "You have some for me, okay? Can't really indulge with my cholesterol."

"Yeah, I will."

"How's that new job of yours treating you?"

"It's fantastic." Shawn talked more about this week's guests and about Mack's idea for a rodeo show at the ghost town.

"Sounds like that boss of yours is full of good ideas."

"He is. One of the ranch hands used to perform with a traveling rodeo show, too, so Robin's giving Mack all kinds of pointers."

"That's some good luck for Mack."

"It is." Clean Slate had been providing a long run of good luck for its residents recently. Could a patch of land be the opposite of cursed? Blessed maybe, by previous residents? Sure, the land had its fair share of trouble, but things always seemed to turn out good in the end.

Especially for Shawn.

They chatted about nonsense for a while, just to hear each other's voices. Shawn kind of wanted to tell Granddad about the carved rose, but it was still too personal. Too intimate. If Shawn told his grandparents about his... thing with Robin, he needed to be sure they were an actual, committed couple. At this point, Shawn wasn't even sure he could define what they were doing as dating. They were friends who kissed.

His phone beeped with a text, and he stupidly hoped it was Robin—stupid, because they hadn't exchanged phone numbers. Why call when they were neighbors?

Miles: Are you feeling okay? Don't see you at the barbecue.

Shawn considered lying so he could head to his cabin early, but that just wasn't him. He had a job to do, and he'd do it, damn it. He replied he'd be down in a minute, then pocketed his phone. Drank a glass of water from the sink. Made sure he didn't look as messy on the outside as he felt inside.

He found Miles with the usual crew at a picnic table, but a quick scan of the area showed no Robin. Huh. Probably for the best. Shawn got a small plate of food and joined his friends, who were still talking all things rodeo.

Maybe it all overwhelmed Robin, and he'd gone back to his cabin?

Good chance. Today must have brought up all kinds of sad memories for Robin. Shawn wanted to check on him but he also needed to be here to mingle and for cleanup afterward. Later on, when he finally headed to his own place to crash, he was disappointed not to see Robin on his own porch. The cabin itself was dark, so Shawn went into his.

Alone.

It was for the best. He was getting too attached, too quickly.

And for someone like Shawn, who was used to managing his own life and being able to leave at a moment's notice, getting attached was a very bad idea. If he fell for Robin and then was run out of Garrett like he'd been run out of Breton, his heart wouldn't survive the loss.

No getting attached. Complimentary friendship was better.

Right?

Chapter Ten

By the Sunday night barbecue, Robin was a fucking mess, and all he wanted to do was to get into his car, find the nearest bar, and get hammered. Really, truly hammered, until the ghost of his dead husband stopped haunting him from afar, mocking Robin for not saving him. For being the reason why Xander died in the first place.

He'd been screaming internally ever since agreeing to help Mack plan the rodeo that morning, and it had only gotten worse after lunch, when Robin put in his promised phone call to Levi. Levi had answered after only two rings. "What's wrong?" he'd asked.

"Nothing's wrong, old friend," Robin had replied. "I know we don't usually call each other, and it's been a long time."

"A really long time."

Robin had bitten the inside of his cheek to stave off tears at the sound of Levi's voice—a voice that reminded him so much of Xander it hurt. Probably why they emailed each other instead of doing this. "How've you been?"

"Not bad. Got my two-year chip last week."

"That's excellent news." Robin was outside on Mack's

porch making the call, and he tilted his face to the slightly gray sky. "I'm proud of you. He would be, too."

"Yeah. How's life on the ranch?"

"It's great, really great. The ranch is actually why I'm calling, and you can tell me to go fuck myself if you want."

Something rustled on Levi's end of the phone. "Okay, now I'm intrigued. What's going on?"

Robin briefly outlined Bentley Ghost Town, the successful July fourth day, and Mack's hope to do a rodeo of some sort to celebrate reopening the town. Levi listened without asking questions, and he was silent for a while after Robin shut up.

"What exactly are you asking from me?" Levi asked.

"The most I'm asking is for you to talk to Mack and Avery about some of the stuff you did with Lucky's, maybe offer them advice on how to pull this together." And even asking for that felt like the biggest favor on the planet. They'd grieved Xander's death together, before that grief pushed them apart and to completely opposite coasts.

"The fact that you're asking at all tells me this is important to you."

"It's important to people I consider family. Mack has done so much to keep the ranch and neighboring town alive. I want to help, and a friend thought that…helping might help me deal with my grief better."

"That's reasonable. And I can definitely talk to Mack, but have you given any thought to calling Dad?"

"No." Not at any point had Robin considered reaching out to his former father-in-law, who'd inherited Lucky's Rodeo from his own father, and who'd been devastated when Robin and Levi both walked away from the show.

But the show had continued, after a three-month hiatus to grieve and replace his lost performers, and that had hurt Robin intensely. To be so easily replaced.

Even Xander had been replaced...

"Robin?"

"Huh?"

"I said Dad would do it if you asked. Bring the show to California. He's not mad anymore."

"Maybe I'm still mad," Robin shot back.

"Just think about it, okay? You'd have trained riders and performers, so the risk to your local horsemen and horses would be minimal. Hell, if you dedicate the show to Xander, Dad will probably do it for free and thank you for it later. He misses you."

Robin pinched the bridge of his nose, unwilling to say how much he missed the Lucky's gang. Doug Peletier had been a demanding boss, but at the end of the day when the boots and spurs came off, he was a loving family man who'd adored his sons. Levi, Xander, and even Robin. And every other man and woman who'd worked for him had been part of that family. The kind of extended family Robin had finally found again here at Clean Slate Ranch.

"I'll think about it," Robin replied. "Do you want me to set up a time for you to conference call with Mack and Avery?"

"Who's Avery again?"

"The historian who's marrying one of Mack's best friends."

"Oh, right. Would you— Never mind."

"No, ask me. Would I what?"

Levi let out a deep breath. "Would you mind at all if

I flew out to visit you sometime? Maybe for the rodeo, whenever it is?"

"I wouldn't mind at all." In the years since they'd gone their separate ways, they'd never discussed getting together in person again. As if they'd both known it would be too painful. Maybe Robin was truly starting to move on and deal with his grief, because he really did want to see Levi. To hug the man he still considered a brother.

"Good, okay. We'll talk about it. Maybe Christmas? We can just call and check in?"

Robin pinched his nose harder, this time to stave off tears. "Yeah, we can do that. Definitely. Thanks for doing this for me."

"Like I could ever say no to you. It was great to hear your voice again, Robin."

"Same. I'll have Mack text you about setting up that chat, okay?"

"Yeah, of course. Please take care."

"I am. You do the same."

They didn't say goodbye when they hung up, and Robin leaned his elbows on the porch rail. Stared out at the trees and let a bit of old grief work itself up and out. Grief over how horribly Robin had acted after Xander's accident, not only to Levi, but also to Doug. At everyone who worked for Doug. At the whole world, really.

Shawn's right. I do need to do this. Face the rodeo life I left behind and put it all firmly in the past.

Finally, Robin could confront the worst emotional wound of his life head-on: the day his husband gasped out his last breath and died in Robin's arms.

The screen door squealed open and shut. "Everything okay?" Mack asked.

Robin cleared his throat hard before straightening to

face Mack. "Yeah, it's fine. Levi agreed to talk to you and Avery."

"Great news, but are you sure you're okay with making that call? You look a little spooked."

"Levi and I were really good friends years ago, and hearing his voice hit me kind of hard, I guess." Robin had been vague about who Levi was to him, and now wasn't the time to unload a lot of personal baggage on his friend. "He did bring up a fair point, though, about hiring trained performers to do your show, instead of trying to teach amateurs."

"Hiring folk costs money, and while we did okay our first year open, I don't want to start the season in a big financial hole."

"Understandable." Robin could potentially get a free performance if he could find his balls and make a simple phone call, but it was too soon for that. "I mean, I guess it depends on how flashy you want this thing to be, and how well I can train a horse in the next two months."

"Speaking of that, I did kidnap you when you said you wanted to take Tude out."

"It's early yet. I still can."

And he did. Robin returned to the ranch and spent a few hours out on the land with Tude, testing her at running and with doing jumps and hard turns, and she worked with him, her big body moving beautifully. She didn't like every single adult she met, but she was a dream with kids, and Tude had always seemed to like Robin.

He could work with her for sure, and after he'd put Tude back in her stall, he checked who was still around. The tourists were in the corral learning how to ride some of the horses. Tango and Hot Coffee were off-limits because they belonged to Miles and Reyes, respectively. His own preferred horse was Apple Jax, but she was sensitive to loud noises, so applause and cheering would freak her the fuck out.

Zodiac nickered from her stall, so Robin went over to rub her forehead. She was a good horse, strong runner, very calm. And young, so still trainable. Robin tacked her up and took her out onto the trails and beyond. Testing her ability to do jumps and hard-turns the same way he'd tested Tude. Being out on the land, riding alone, helped calm some of his emotional turmoil, but not all. He kind of wished Shawn was out here with him, but Shawn had a job to do down at the ranch.

A job Robin had to do, too, but Mack had cleared his absence with Judson so Robin wouldn't get in trouble for not being around this afternoon. As the sun dipped low, marking the start of evening, Robin headed back to the barn. The scent of grilling meat made his mouth water, and by the time he had Zodiac back in her stall, the barbecue was in full swing.

Robin got a small plate, his insides still twisted up with so many things, and he ate with his friends. But Shawn was nowhere to be seen, and it hurt Robin's feelings in a way that made no sense, so he excused himself from the barbecue early. And then he'd spent a long time pacing the cabin, reliving the past, unable to focus on the here and now in a manic way he hadn't felt since his first few weeks here. Detoxing from his final attempt at ending his own miserable existence and adjusting to this new life.

Levi was right that asking Lucky's Rodeo to do the show was the safest, easiest route, but that meant reaching out to Doug. The last time Robin had spoken to

Doug, Robin had been so consumed by rage and grief that he'd shoved the older man. Called him every awful name Robin could think of. Told him to get the fuck out of Robin's life.

Levi said Doug misses me. What if it's true?

He could easily solve Mack's problems with organizing his own rodeo with one simple phone call. Hell, maybe Levi would come too, and they'd all teach locals to do the tricks. Train them so Mack could put on his own show next time, or work them into the daily ghost town routines. Mack was all about doing things right so no one got hurt.

But first, Robin had to swallow his pride and call his former father-in-law—and hope the man didn't hang up on him.

Not tonight. Robin couldn't handle anything else tonight, so he paced in the dark until he'd exhausted himself. Took a piss and crawled into bed. He slept a little but mostly he tossed and turned, fully aware when Ernie returned to the cabin. At midnight, Robin gave up, grabbed his knife, vape, and a piece of wood from the basket under his bed, and went outside.

He whittled at the wood and listened, but tonight, the land had nothing to whisper to him. Only silence.

Monday morning, Shawn tamped down on another wave of disappointment when Robin wasn't parked on his bench with his vape, as he had been every morning for the last eight days. That disappointment dried up, however, when Shawn spotted the small carved object on his own porch bench seat. He picked it up, and it took him a moment to identify it as a slice of pie with a perfect lattice top, which made him chuckle

Pies had been his specialty at the saloon.

Only about three inches long, the wooden pie slice fit easily in his jeans pocket, so he carried it with him to the kitchen and got started on that morning's meal prep. Patrice showed up at six thirty like clockwork to chill in her rocking chair, even though Shawn saw how hungry she was to help. He imagined after doing this for so many years, she couldn't stay away, despite being unable to assist him.

Maybe in another week, she could help stir the reconstituted orange juice in its pitcher. Simple tasks she could complete with her left hand only.

The rooster call went off at seven fifteen, which helped wake up guests for breakfast at eight. The first time Shawn had heard the thing, it had scared the shit out of him but now he knew to expect it. Every Monday, though, Patrice said at least one guest complained about falling out of his or her bunk.

Robin showed up a little later than the other hands, and he flashed Shawn an apologetic smile that silently promised they were going to talk about yesterday. Good. Shawn had hated feeling like Robin was blowing him off, and the whittled pie slice had been a good step toward closing whatever distance yesterday had created between them.

After breakfast Robin stuck around to help Shawn clean up, and they worked in companionable silence until Patrice excused herself. Once they were alone, Shawn turned to face Robin, and they both said, "I'm sorry about yesterday," in stereo.

"You don't have to apologize for anything," Robin said. "Yesterday was all me."

"I could have knocked on your cabin door, or gotten your phone number from someone and called you."

"I was not in a good head space yesterday. Keeping my distance was so I didn't take my bad mood out on you. But I do think now you were right about me helping Mack with the rodeo. I think it'll help me heal and let a few things go."

"Really?" Shawn's heart gave a happy lurch. "I'm glad."

"Yeah." Robin leaned his hip against the counter. "I called my former brother-in-law yesterday. Xander's older brother. To see if he'd offer his thoughts, too."

"Yeah? How did that call go?"

"Really well, actually. We'd stopped talking for a while because hearing his voice hurt too much. But... we're going to get together at some point. Be friends again. I've missed him."

The wistfulness in Robin's voice wrapped a slim tendril of jealousy around Shawn's heart. "That's great."

"It is. After talking to him, though, I needed to be alone, so I took two horses out to see if I could work with them on riding tricks. But I was still a little worked up after and when I didn't see you at the barbecue, I went back to my cabin to be alone."

Shawn squeezed Robin's forearm. "I was hiding in here during the barbecue because I was anxious about you avoiding me all day, so I think we're even."

"I guess. And how about we exchange phone numbers, so at the very least, we can text if we can't talk in person?"

"Great plan." They did just that. Shawn swapped out his phone for the pie slice. "I love this, by the way. Thank you."

"You're welcome. I wasn't sure what to carve, and pie seemed appropriate." Robin's gaze dropped to Shawn's mouth. "Care to compliment the carver?"

Shawn grinned and leaned in.

"Mr. Shawn?" Ellie's voice broke them apart. The girl stood in the frame of the kitchen doorway, hands clasped in front of her. "I know you're working and stuff but will you keep teaching me and Eric to play chess?"

"Of course I will," Shawn replied. "Are you guys doing the camping trip today?"

"No, Mom says it'll be too cold, but the weather looks better for the Wednesday trip."

"Okay, then why don't you go set up the board, and I'll be out in a few minutes."

"Okay!" She darted out of sight.

"You're teaching kids to play chess?" Robin asked.

"Yeah, I saw them fiddling with the game yesterday and ended up showing them how to move the pieces and think ahead." Shawn paused before sharing this bit of himself. "I used to play with my grandfather at night. Just the two of us, snacking on cheese and crackers, not really playing to win. Just to spend time together. I haven't played since I left home, and to be honest, I was a little down yesterday because I started missing my family."

"I'm sorry I wasn't here for you."

"It's okay, you had your stuff to deal with." And Shawn was fully capable of dealing with his own stuff without Robin's help. "I did call Granddad, though, just to hear his voice."

"I'm glad you can still call him. Hear his voice."

Shawn leaned his shoulder against Robin's. "Thanks.

So we were both off yesterday, and now we're back on the same page."

"Yes, we are. I'm also doing the overnight camping trip tonight, but do you wanna hang out together tomorrow night?"

"Definitely."

"Excellent." Robin gazed around the empty kitchen, and then he planted a soft kiss on Shawn's mouth. "I'll be back with the chuck wagon in about an hour."

"I'll be here."

Shawn briefly admired Robin's ass as the man left the kitchen, before heading into the main area to teach the twins more about chess. And as it turned out, no one signed up for that night's camping trip—it was supposed to be cold and windy—so Shawn got the pleasure of chatting with Robin over lunch and dinner that night. Robin even helped him clean up so they could go to Shawn's cabin together.

Where they made up for barely speaking yesterday by making out for hours on Shawn's couch. Their erections rubbed together, and very soon Shawn wanted to get his hands on that—and get Robin's hands on him. Not yet, but soon. It was too huge of a step for Shawn to rush into it.

Their week took on a similar pattern of sharing meals, Shawn teaching the twins chess, and making out in Shawn's cabin every night. Miles and Reyes were out in the wilds on a three-day horse ride/camping excursion, and Shawn kind of missed his friend but he wasn't lonely. Colt kept giving them significant looks, but he wasn't nosy about how close Shawn and Robin were now, and Shawn appreciated that.

Shawn was also getting friendly with some of the

other hands, including Hugo and Robin's roommate, Ernie. And the humor wasn't lost on Shawn when he belatedly connected the fact that Clean Slate had two ranch hands named Bert and Ernie. And Robin carved him two more gifts: a chef's knife and a small mug. Shawn wanted to display his collection of wooden objects on the bookshelf, but they were too precious to forget if he had to leave quickly. So he wrapped them in an old T-shirt and kept them in his gym bag.

By the end of the week, Shawn's great mood was slightly soured, knowing Ellie and Eric were going home today. He'd enjoyed teaching them the game, and Ellie was keen to keep practicing. Eric less so, and Shawn truly hoped she found a good chess partner. He'd miss playing, too. Maybe someone else on the ranch knew how.

Then again, Shawn was also eager to spend as much of his free time as possible with Robin—especially since he didn't get a lot of it. Thankfully, once the Saturday skeleton crew finished their supper of Leftovers Pie, Robin surprised Shawn with the offer of a proper date.

"Let's go into San Francisco for a few hours," Robin said while he helped Shawn load the dishwasher, which was starting to become a new routine of theirs. "We can go to some of the clubs, I can show you off. Show you around."

Shawn was intimidated by the idea of going to a gay club, and he admitted as much. "I've never been to one, never danced and flirted like that. Is it how they show on TV?"

"Depends on where you go. Trust me to keep you safe?"

"Of course." Shawn was nervous about going out but

also excited. He couldn't remember the last time he'd been out on a proper date, and especially not with a guy he was so into. Grinding with Robin on a dance floor was sounding more and more like the best idea ever.

They returned to their respective cabins to change. Shawn didn't own any sexy club clothes, so he slipped into a clean band T-shirt he'd picked up at a thrift store and finger-combed his hair. Robin had changed into much tighter jeans and a torso-hugging black tee that made Shawn's mouth water. His dark hair was slicked back, giving him a slightly dangerous look.

Yum.

I want him. And he wants me back.

Robin shocked the hell out of him in the barn-shaped garage where everyone parked their vehicles by leading Shawn to a beautiful, fully restored, cherry-red Mustang convertible. He nearly swooned at the polished interior and leather bucket seats.

"Holy crap, this car is amazing." Shawn ran his fingers across the shiny radio.

"Thank you. Colt calls it my midlife crisis car. I'd always wanted to own one, so I started saving my salary and bought it."

Shawn couldn't imagine having enough money to buy a car like this. Even though he was saving about a hundred-fifty bucks a month by no longer living in his car, burning gas, and buying protein bars, it would take years to build into a significant savings. Arthur and Judson insisted Shawn could live in the cabin rent-free when the ghost town reopened, but Shawn wasn't sure he could do that. He'd find a way to pay a small amount of rent, even if it was only the hundred bucks he wasn't spending on gasoline.

He could accept the charity while he worked for the ranch, but after he was no longer directly contributing, Shawn wouldn't mooch.

He fawned over every detail of the car on the long drive down the dirt track to the main road. And once Robin hit the interstate, Shawn settled into his seat and enjoyed the smooth ride, while a classic rock station played over the radio. "So why this specific car?" Shawn asked.

After a few moments of silence, Robin said, "Saw one on the road once when I was a teenager and it spoke to me. I lusted after this car for years but could never afford it. When I was with Lucky's, money was tight in the winter, so I saved whatever I made to get through the tough times. After Xander died, it didn't seem important. Not until I got my head back on right."

The post-Xander period of Robin's life intrigued Shawn, because Robin always brushed up against the time period without really talking about it. But were they good enough friends now for Shawn to directly ask? No, that story was one Robin could share when he was ready. It wasn't as if Shawn had ever admitted to his two years of homelessness.

Some things were private. Period.

They kept up lighter chatter about the present and stayed out of the past for the rest of the drive into San Francisco. Shawn had always looked at the city through the lens of someone trying to keep his head down and survive. Tonight, he gazed out at the lights, buildings, trolleys, and people with a new perspective: that of a tourist. Someone out to enjoy the sights and sounds with a friend. A maybe boyfriend?

Robin took him on a bit of a tour before finding public

parking in a very active area. Even on a cold December evening, people were out all over the place this Saturday night, so Shawn stuck close to Robin. And after Shawn saw multiple same-sex couples openly holding hands, he took a chance and held Robin's.

Robin squeezed back and grinned at him.

They'd both eaten at the guesthouse, so their first stop was a colorful place for drinks and bar nuts, while they talked. Nothing serious really. Shawn talked a bit more about teaching the twins to learn chess, and Robin told him a story about an eighteen-person bridal party they'd hosted two years ago who'd driven the entire ranch nuts with their demands. Polite demands, mostly, but apparently, they'd even tested Patrice's temper.

Shawn sipped at a virgin margarita while Robin nursed a beer. One of the bartenders was friendly with Robin, which suggested this was a place Robin frequented. After they finished their drinks and paid the tab, Robin led him around more, pointing out stores and restaurants he liked. Their next destination was Club Base, a place that thrummed with music, alcohol, and a sea of dancing men. Some women dotted the crowd, but not many.

"Wanna dance, hot stuff?" Robin asked.

"Uh, can we watch for a while? I've never really done this kind of dancing."

"Sure. I'm going to get another beer. You want something?"

Shawn wasn't much of a drinker, but a little liquid courage went a long way when it came to trying new things. Problem was he didn't really know what was good beyond a margarita. "Sure, pick something you think I'll like." He winked to suggest the challenge was flirtatious, rather than because Shawn was an idiot about certain things. Sometimes he still couldn't believe someone as mature and caring as Robin wanted him, but here they were. Together. On a date.

Robin grinned and headed for the bar. Shawn hung out near the entrance, where people were mostly standing in clusters, rather than dancing. A few guys openly cruised Shawn, which was…kind of nice. Usually, Shawn didn't want to be noticed, but he was in a safe place surrounded by other gay men who wouldn't be offended if Shawn flirted with them. Not that he wanted to flirt with anyone except Robin tonight.

"You look pretty terrified, honey," a deep voice said behind him. "First time?"

Shawn turned and blinked at the handsome man in a tight, sparkly purple shirt and multiple facial piercings who gave Shawn a deliberate up-and-down look. "Um, yeah, first time here."

"I knew I smelled fresh meat." Purple Tee slid in closer and put a light hand on Shawn's shoulder. "Buy you a drink?"

"I have a friend bringing me one, but thanks." Was he supposed to introduce himself? Invite the stranger to join them? Ignore him until he went away?

How can I be twenty-four and this socially awkward? Ugh.

"Shame," Purple Tee said. "How about a dance? I'd love to see you all hot and sweaty."

Okay, yeah, the guy was flirting with Shawn. Practically propositioning him, and while the guy was good-looking, and Shawn was flattered by the attention, he was also taken. "No, thanks. I'm here with someone."

"Even married guys still dance with other men."

The stranger's inability to take Shawn's "no" at face value and buzz off started fucking with Shawn's fight-or-flight instincts. But Shawn was no longer a vulnerable, impressionable fifteen-year-old who couldn't afford to lose his job. He was an adult who could defend himself, and he adjusted his posture, hoping he went from uncertain to determined.

"I said no," Shawn snapped. "Thank you but no."

Purple Tee frowned. "Yeah, whatever."

"Problem here?" Robin slid right up beside Shawn and draped an arm across his shoulders. Kissed his cheek. "Sorry I took so long, baby."

"No problem." Purple Tee turned and melted into the throng.

Annoyed by Robin playing hero at the last minute, Shawn ducked out from beneath his arm and glared. "I had it under control, Robin."

Robin gaped at him for a beat. "Sorry, I just…you looked tense, and we're supposed to be out having fun. It was instinct."

"I don't need to be saved. I've been taking care of myself for the last five years."

"Okay, and I really am sorry." He held out a tall clear glass with something turquoise in it and fixed on an adorable pout. "Peace?"

Some of Shawn's temper slipped away; Robin's charm was hard to resist. "Peace." He sniffed the drink. Kind of fruity. "What is it?"

"Blue Lagoon. It's a sweeter drink, so it made me think of you. Plus, you said your favorite color is blue."

That was way more thoughtful than Shawn had expected, so he thanked Robin by kissing his cheek. He sipped the drink, surprised by how much he liked it.

The flavor of the liquor was strong to his unpracticed tongue—or maybe the bartenders poured generously here? "It's really good."

Robin beamed, clearly proud he'd chosen well. "While I was waiting, my friend Derrick texted me and mentioned he'll be here tonight. You mind if I tell him we're already here? He's a chill guy and a lot of fun to dance with."

Shawn wanted to say no, this was supposed to be their date, but Robin's big grin never fell away. Robin was clearly excited to see this friend, and Shawn didn't want to disappoint Robin, despite a fresh flare of jealousy. "May I ask you a question first?"

"Sure, ask away."

"How are you going to introduce me?"

Robin's smile gentled into something tender. Sweet. And he leaned into Shawn's personal space. "As the guy I'm seeing, unless there's a bigger word I can use."

Shawn's pulse leapt. "A bigger word than *guy*? Homo sapien?"

"I was thinking *boyfriend.*"

Warmth spread from Shawn's chest all the way to his fingers and toes, and he nudged his way closer to Robin. Put his free hand on Robin's hip. "I like that word. Is it too soon, though? This is our first date."

"I dunno, I like to think of all the evenings we've spent together this past week as dates. We've spent time together, made out a lot, watched movies, and talked. All things boyfriends do."

"True." Shawn chanced kissing Robin in such a public space, and Robin opened for him. Shawn tasted beer and Robin and it was perfect. His nerves hummed a bit, but Shawn didn't regret it for a single instant because he was falling for Robin. Robin made him feel safe. Settled. At home. Even if he was a little overprotective at times. But it was a sweet sort of overprotectiveness, not the smothering, manipulative kind like with Beck. Robin actually gave a damn about Shawn.

I want to keep him.

"Text your friend," Shawn said. "I'm okay with it."

"Thank you."

Shawn held Robin's beer while he texted. Then they waited together, hips touching, while they nursed their drinks and watched other people dance. Shawn listened to the techno music piped over loudspeakers and observed how the beat affected the dancers. He kind of sucked at dancing, in general, but maybe he could do this sort of frenetic, unpracticed dance. A dance that was more of a seduction than anything else.

"Hey!" Robin shouted to someone in the crowd. "You didn't say this was a foursome."

Shawn followed his gaze to two men making their way toward them, one more familiar than the other, and his heart sank a bit, sure what had briefly been a wonderful date had just come to a screeching end.

Chapter Eleven

Derrick Massey had openly flirted with Shawn back at Thanksgiving, and he was the friend Robin mentioned had texted him earlier. The face Shawn did not expect to see trailing Derrick was Colt's. The pair was decked out in tight club clothes, and wasn't Colt engaged? Why was he here?

"Last-minute decision," Colt replied. "Avery's got some kind of bug, so he didn't want me sitting on my ass, possibly getting infected. He gave me permission to come out and dance with Derrick."

Gave him permission?

Shawn had met Avery several times in person, and the guy was slender and demure—not someone Shawn could see giving other people orders. Then again, he didn't know crap about the relationship dynamic between Colt and Avery, and it wasn't his business.

"You mind?" Colt asked Shawn directly.

"Of course not." Shawn did mind that their twosome was now a foursome, but the other three men seemed excited to be there together.

"Cool," Derrick said. "Nice to meet you again." He squeezed Shawn's hand longer than necessary. "Wanna dance?"

Shawn held up his drink. "In a bit but thanks."

"Cool. Mind if I steal your boyfriend for a few rounds?"

Robin choked on his beer, then glared at Colt. "Dude."

Colt only shrugged while fixing on an innocent smile. "Come on, anyone who sees you two together can tell something is going on. Plus, I'm getting really good at telling when one of my friends is secretly dating someone. I totally called it early with Miles and Reyes."

That didn't surprise Shawn in the least. Colt had always struck him as a people watcher. "Yes, we're boyfriends," Shawn said, surprised at his own boldness. But the word felt right. "So no poaching."

Colt hooted. "No worries, I've got my own great guy at home. Just keep your eye on this one." He elbowed Derrick. "Might get jealous now that you've stolen his fuck buddy away."

Oh? Oh! Yeah, okay, no wonder Robin wants Derrick here. One more night out with his former fuck buddy before settling in as my boyfriend.

Robin smacked Colt on the back of his head. "Dude, really?"

"What? It's the truth," Colt replied. "Come on, let's dance. I've got energy to burn."

Colt grabbed Derrick's hand and led him into the dancing throng. Robin hung back and asked, "Are you mad?"

Shawn shook his head. He wasn't mad, exactly, but he also wasn't okay. Confused mostly. Robin had declared them boyfriends but he'd also invited an ex to join them? "No, we're here to have fun, right? Go have fun."

"Come with me."

"In a few. I don't want to waste my drink."

Robin hesitated a beat before taking his half-empty

beer bottle with him and joining his friends. Shawn hung back and sipped his Blue Lagoon, mixed-up and unsure of his place here tonight. He'd begun this date on cloud nine, happy to explore the city with Robin, and now he was watching other people dance while he held up the wall.

Is this normal in gay relationships? One guy goes out with other people while the other stays off to the side?

No, maybe that was how Colt and Avery rolled, but it couldn't be everyone. Miles and Reyes didn't. They were so closely knit and in-synch they were practically one person. No, Shawn had stupidly hoped for a two-person date with just him and Robin, but Robin had other ideas. Ideas that included a former fuck buddy.

Shawn gulped down the rest of his drink, then ordered another at the bar. Gulped that, too. The liquor took the edge off his confusion and made the lights seem brighter, more interesting. The dancing, too. He eventually found his way to Robin, Colt, and Derrick, and he was included in their mix of grinding bodies. Shawn wasn't very good but he tried. Being tipsy helped, and eventually a shot of something—had Colt said SoCo and lime?—burned down his throat.

That helped, too. It mattered less that Shawn was surrounded by strangers.

Robin held him by the hips and crushed their groins together in a simulation of sex that both turned Shawn on and made him self-conscious. But this was something Robin enjoyed doing, so Shawn would try. Robin was also a hell of a dancer, moving fluidly from Shawn to Colt to Derrick, and then back again, changing his dancing style to match his partner's with an ease Shawn envied.

Other men drifted in and out of their quartet, and Shawn occasionally found himself ass-to-groin with a stranger. It unnerved him at first, until he caught Robin's hungry gaze on him. Watching. Apparently enjoying the view. Shawn had never been much of an exhibitionist, but he didn't mind performing a bit for Robin. This was a completely new experience for him, and Shawn rode it for all it was worth.

At some point—and after Shawn tossed back at least two more shots—Derrick and Robin ended up thrusting groin to groin, practically fucking with their clothes on, and a hot flash of jealousy burned through Shawn's chest. Jealousy he wasn't sure what do to with. Hadn't Shawn consented to all this dancing and groping by joining in without a word? Could he tell Robin this was too much, when they'd only known each other three weeks? Only been boyfriends for two hours?

Colt draped himself over Shawn's back in a light hold, hands on Shawn's hips but he kept his groin out of things. "They're sexy together, aren't they?" he said into Shawn's ear. "We've all been coming out like this for about a year."

Shawn had no idea what to say to that. It was simple information about the two men, but what was Shawn supposed to do with it? Was Colt telling him Robin would always want to club? To fuck around? Would Robin be exclusive with Shawn? Had he been since they met?

The idea of Robin fucking around with other people while they were figuring things out horrified Shawn. If Robin still had fuck buddies on the side, maybe that was why he was fine with them just making out and not having sex. Maybe Shawn was just a fun distraction for

Robin, and Shawn had read too much into their relationship. A cold flash of anxiety shot through his chest, and Shawn's hands started trembling.

"Shawn?" Colt turned him around to face Colt, his blue eyes wary. "You're not used to this, are you?"

"No." Shawn didn't know exactly which "this" Colt was referencing. Dating? Dancing? Being with a guy period? But his answer applied to any possible question. "I'm not used to this at all. Any of this. It's like an alien planet."

"Does Robin know that?"

Shawn shrugged, trying to tamp down on his urgent need to flee. To find a dark corner to sit in until this episode passed. "I don't know. Probably not. But he was excited to do this tonight, so I thought I'd be a good sport and play along. I guess I'm not used to all this open display of affection. Touching and stuff."

"Got it. It can be a culture shock if you aren't used to it. Small-town dude?"

"Living in a lonely world."

Colt laughed at the song reference. "Just don't take any midnight trains on your own. Do you wanna stop dancing and get a drink? Don't worry, if you and Robin are solid all he'll do is dance. He's a good guy."

Shawn was definitely thirsty and needed the distraction, but… "I don't think I should have any more alcohol. I feel fuzzy."

"We'll get you a water then. Come on." Colt steered him toward the bar and the sweet relief of a chilled bottle of water, while Colt ordered a beer. They silently watched their friends dance, and that cold flare of panic in his chest battled hotly with the jealousy burning in Shawn's gut.

* * *

Robin noted when Shawn and Colt left their throng, and he was silently grateful to Colt for sticking close to Shawn. Shawn had been a confusing mix of excited and wary all evening, especially after Colt and Derrick joined them. And okay, it wasn't the best way to spend a first date, but Robin had every intention of making it up to Shawn when they were alone again.

Plus, he hadn't seen Derrick in a couple of weeks, and it had been ages since he, Robin, and Colt had all been out together like this.

Derrick's hands squeezed the top of his ass in a familiar way as they moved to the music, groin to groin, chest occasionally bumping. It reminded Robin of all the fantastic sex they'd had off and on this past year, hooking up to help the other scratch a particular itch. They were both bi and both frequently into women, too, but damn if Derrick didn't know how to fuck Robin into the mattress.

But Derrick was off-limits now that Robin had a boyfriend, and he still couldn't quite wrap his head around that. Boyfriend. It had been a long damned time since Robin had been anyone's boyfriend, but so far he seemed to be doing an okay job of it.

"This doesn't seem like Shawn's scene," Derrick said now that they were alone. "You didn't have to bring someone to make me jealous, you know I'm a sure thing."

"To what?" Robin nearly tripped over his own feet. "What do you mean make you jealous? Shawn and I are dating."

"Sure you are, Mr. Sex Without Complications."

Okay, so Robin had said that a lot to Derrick in the

past. A guy could change his mind, though, right? "I like Shawn. A lot."

Derrick's eyes narrowed and his movements slowed. "Why? Don't get me wrong, he's cute and all, but he doesn't seem your type."

"Why?" Robin teased. "Because he's not a big, buff guy like you?"

"Yes."

"We talk about things. Real-life things that matter, not just surface stuff. He makes me feel good about myself." Robin couldn't believe he was having this conversation in the middle of a dance floor, surrounded by hot, gyrating men, any one of whom Robin could probably seduce on his worst day. Hell, he had a hot, gyrating man in his arms right now.

But there was only one guy Robin wanted to go home with and seduce tonight, and that guy was off somewhere else in the club.

"You've been a good friend to me," Robin said closer to Derrick's ear. "A really good friend, and I want to stay friends. But I'm dating Shawn and no one else. Okay?"

"Yeah, okay." Derrick grinned, disappointment shining in his dark eyes. "I can respect that."

"Thank you." Robin planted a big, wet kiss on his cheek before pulling away. "We'll always have our good times here, but I need to go find my guy."

"Sure. Go." Derrick slid easily into the arms of someone else, so Robin didn't feel bad about leaving him behind.

He turned and scanned the crowd. Near the bar, Colt and Shawn stood close together with drinks, Colt's arm across Shawn's shoulders in a too-friendly way. Their heads were ducked low, as if they were in an intense conversation, and something possessive woke inside Robin. He didn't like that arm where it was, didn't like that they could turn their heads a few inches and be able to kiss—not that Robin thought Colt would ever cheat on Avery, but still.

Shawn's my *guy.*

Riding this new emotion and needing to stake his claim, Robin wove his way to their location, gently tugged Shawn into his arms, and planted a big kiss on his boyfriend. A long, claiming kiss full of tongue, hands tangled in Shawn's thick hair, tasting fruit juice and the essence of the man himself.

Someone nearby wolf whistled.

Shawn clutched Robin's waist, and when Robin pulled back, his face was stained red. But his eyes gleamed with arousal and surprise, and so many other positive things that Robin knew he'd done the right thing. "I missed you," Robin said.

"Clearly." All the uncertainty that had clung to Shawn since Colt and Derrick joined them melted away under a bright smile. "I missed you, too."

"You two go have fun," Colt said. "I'm gonna go dance some more." He eased his way into the sea of dancers to find their friend.

Robin looped both arms around Shawn's waist and kissed him again, gentler this time. "You ready to head back to the ranch?"

"Yes." Shawn rested his head on Robin's shoulder. "I'm glad I got to experience this with you. To see and try something you enjoy, but I'm not sure it's my thing. Too many people, too crazy."

"I get it." Robin was a little sad but also glad to have learned this thing about Shawn. They'd probably never be a couple who enjoyed clubbing together, like Mack and Wes, and that was okay. He and Shawn were creating their own relationship, and this was how they learned things about each other.

Robin was slightly overheated from dancing, and the chilly night air outside helped bring his temperature down on the walk back to his car. Halfway there, Shawn took his hand and held it in a loose grip that made Robin smile. They existed in a comfortable silence until they reached the car. Robin had just slid his key into the ignition when Shawn said, "I got jealous tonight."

"Really?"

"Yes. Watching you dance with other guys, especially Derrick, because you guys have history."

"It's just dancing, and I wasn't going home with anyone except you tonight."

"I know." Shawn shrugged, embarrassed now—Robin saw it in his slumped shoulders and twisted mouth. "I guess when you really like someone, certain reactions are kind of irrational."

"But also hella appealing." Robin reached over to squeeze Shawn's hand. "And in the interest of full disclosure, I got pretty jealous too, when I saw you and Colt all cozy by the bar."

Shawn's eyebrows crept up. "We were just talking."

"I know but he had his arm around you and it just… You guys looked intimate, and I didn't like it."

"So you're okay if I'm grinding against another guy, but a side-hug from a friend sets off your jealous side?"

"Yes?" Robin had never been jealous like this before, not even over Xander. Lucky's Rodeo had been a hotbed of no-homo straight guys, so it wasn't as if Robin had had any competition for Xander's attention. They'd also burned hot and heavy from the start, unlike this slower dance with Shawn. Xander had been someone he'd had to keep up with, while Shawn moved at a slower, more careful pace.

New rules, new reactions.

"If it helps at all," Shawn said, "I'm not big on casual touching. I think Colt realized I was getting overwhelmed and was trying to keep me calm. I've battled anxiety for a lot of years, because of bullying in high school and that thing in my past, and sometimes it gets bad."

"I didn't know you struggle with anxiety." Robin was a tiny bit hurt Shawn hadn't shared that, but it also sounded intensely personal. Not something Shawn shared lightly. "Thank you for telling me."

"It's something I have an emergency stash of meds for if an episode gets really bad, like it did when I was first kicked out of my cousin's place. But I don't have insurance so I've mostly learned to manage it on my own. Routines help, and so does work that doesn't require me to really interact with people too much, which is why I enjoy kitchen jobs."

"I'd have never guessed. You always seem focused and put together." Except for Thanksgiving, when Shawn had been so down after talking to his grandfather.

"Focused and put together is a part I play most days."

Robin leaned over to kiss Shawn lightly on the lips. "You don't ever have to play a part around me, Shawn. Just be yourself. I won't judge you."

"Thank you. In that case, can we go home? Please?"

"Absolutely." After another kiss and hand squeeze, Robin got them on the road. Once he was out of the city and back on the interstate, Robin took Shawn's hand again and held it the rest of the drive back to Clean Slate. Held it on the walk from the car barn to Shawn's cabin. From the cabin door inside to the couch.

Robin urged Shawn to sit, then said, "I'll be right back. I need to go get something."

"Okay."

He retrieved his gift from the spot he'd hidden it under his bunk, mostly so Ernie wouldn't notice and tease him. Robin hadn't been able to find a box, so he'd wrapped them in one of his bandanas, and Robin put the package in Shawn's waiting hands. Sat beside him and tried not to panic now that the moment was here.

"More carvings?" Shawn asked with a wink.

"Yup."

Shawn carefully unfolded the bandana to reveal two hand-carved chess pieces: a king and a queen. Robin had given both pieces a light varnish but hadn't otherwise touched the natural wood grain of the piece of black walnut he'd chosen for the project. Shawn held them with slightly trembling fingers, his eyes wide with wonder.

"They're beautiful," Shawn said. "Wow."

"I looked up different designs on my phone, and I liked these best. I'll do a darker stain on the opposing set of pieces."

"Huh? You're carving me an entire chess set?"

"Yes. Maybe one day you'll be able to take it home and play with your grandfather."

Shawn's eyes went liquid. He put the pieces on the arm of the couch, and then he tackled Robin flat onto his back. Kissed him hard, first on the mouth, then dropping kisses along Robin's cheeks and neck. Robin submitted to this new, more aggressive side of Shawn.

"You're amazing," Shawn said between kisses.

"They're so thoughtful. I love them, thank you. Thank you."

"You're welcome." All the friction was doing wonders to bring Robin's erection back full-force, and soon they were rubbing their hard cocks together through their jeans, Shawn on top with all the power. Robin squeezed his hips. "Get off with me, Shawn."

Above him, Shawn froze.

Shit, I fucked this up.

Shawn gazed down at Robin, whose earnest expression was as endearing as it was sexy as hell. Same as his bluntness in asking for what he wanted. And Shawn wanted it, too. He trusted Robin and he wanted to take this next step with his boyfriend. "Yes," Shawn said.

Robin's smile widened. "Yeah? How?"

Heart trilling with desire and nerves, Shawn sat up. "In the bed."

"Really?" Robin sat up too, and wrapped an arm around Shawn's waist. "You ready to do this in your bed?"

"Just getting off, though. No, you know, penetration."

"Only what you want, Shawn, I swear. I'll follow your cues, and if I do anything you don't like or want, tell me and I'll stop and we'll talk. And if there's something you do want, tell me that, too. Open communication every step of the way."

Some of Shawn's buzzing nerves calmed under Robin's expected declarations. Robin had always gone at Shawn's pace, and his trust in the older man swelled. "Why are you so amazing and patient?"

"You make it easy." Robin rubbed his nose against Shawn's.

Perfect answer. They both took a moment to remove their shoes and socks. When Shawn preemptively took off his belt, too, Robin followed suit. He led Robin to the full-size bed, and then drew the bigger man down with him.

The kissing was practiced and easy, and they had more room to play on the bed. To pinch and touch above their clothes, until Shawn wriggled out of his shirt, leaving him bare-chested. Robin gazed at him with hungry eyes. Shawn nodded at Robin, who whipped his own shirt off. Shawn stared at the broad, tan chest on display. Dark nipples and work-ripped abs and a dark happy trail that disappeared into Robin's jeans. So much gorgeous skin that Shawn's mouth nearly watered.

"Wow," Shawn whispered.

"You're pretty wow yourself." Robin trailed his fingertips across Shawn's collarbone. "I can't wait to lick every single inch of you. When you're ready."

Shawn shivered and his dick swelled at the mental image of Robin licking different parts of his body. His pecs. His abs.

His dick.

God yes, I want that. Soon.

For tonight, Shawn wanted to get off with his boyfriend—a boyfriend he desperately wanted to see completely naked. This first sip had him addicted. "Will you…" Shawn blushed. "Will you take the rest of your clothes off?"

Robin was gloriously naked in about five seconds, kneeling in the middle of the bed, his erection seeming to point right at Shawn. "You can touch any part of me you want," Robin said, his voice slightly wrecked.

Shawn knew the mechanics of sex with guys—hello,

online porn—but he had no actual experience with it.
Not with a naked man in his bed ready to give Shawn
anything he wanted, and with Shawn completely unsure
what he *did* want. Other than an orgasm, and he trusted
Robin to get them both there.

Trusted Robin to stop if Shawn wasn't ready for
something.

"Will you be in charge?" Shawn asked before he
could second-guess himself. "Please? I'm not exactly
sure what to do here."

Heat flared in Robin's eyes. "Are you sure?"

"Yes."

"Jesus." Robin grabbed both Shawn's hands and
placed them on his pecs. "Do you have any idea how
much I want to turn around and bend over for you?"

Shock jolted down Shawn's spine. "You're a bottom?"

"Mostly. I'll top when I'm in the mood, but I love getting fucked by men and women."

"Women? How does that work?"

Robin slid Shawn's hands down so they now rested
over his abs, his skin smooth and warm and Shawn
wanted to feel more of the man. "Ever heard of peg-
ging? The lady wears a harness and fucks the guy with
a dildo. It's crazy hot with the right person."

"Wow." Shawn had just learned something new, and
he had a feeling he could get quite the sexual education
from Robin. "So you'd really want me to fuck you?"

"Definitely." Robin released his hands, which Shawn
left on his abs, and cupped Shawn's cheeks in work-
roughened palms. "And if you want the opposite, I'd
love to do that with you. Be your first."

Shawn released a long breath of relief. "Oh wow. I…
maybe, God, I'm an idiot."

"Why's that?" Robin readjusted them so they were sitting with Shawn practically on Robin's lap, and it wasn't even weird to be sitting on a naked man.

"Stereotypes, I guess." Shawn studied Robin's neck so he didn't have to meet his eyes. "I guess I assumed that because I'm the younger, smaller one, I'd have to take it. I mean, that's all you really see in porn."

"Oh, baby." Robin nipped at his chin in a playful way. "I have so much to teach you about sex, starting with size doesn't matter when it comes to preferences. It's all about what you want, what makes your body feel good. Is that why you've never had sex with a guy before? You were scared to bottom?"

Shawn hadn't consciously thought that, no, but the way Robin laid it out made perfect sense. Sure, his housing situation had been a convenient excuse not to bother looking for someone to date. A conscious reason to avoid this exact situation—except Robin didn't expect Shawn to bottom. Hell, Robin was eager to bottom for Shawn!

"Yes?" Shawn replied. "Yes, I think it was."

"Then I'm glad you waited until we met. People have sex all the time for all the wrong reasons, and I will never pressure you into something you don't want to try. I don't want to scare or hurt you. I care about you too much."

The truth of those words shined in Robin's eyes and they wrapped around Shawn's heart. Stole a bit of it away and gave it to Robin with open arms. "I care about you, too."

I might even be falling in love with you, but it's way too soon to say that.

Robin kissed him. "I'll also tell you something you

might not know about sexual relationships between guys: they don't all include anal penetration."

"They don't?" But… "So they just do blow jobs and rubbing off?"

"Yup. Anal can be messy and painful, and for some guys it just doesn't work. Or they flat-out don't care to try it. Sex is a lot of things, Shawn, but at the end of the day, it's feeling good and making your partner feel good, and there are a lot of different ways to make a guy orgasm."

Shawn turned all that over in his mind, stunned by everything he'd learned in the last five minutes. And kind of embarrassed. He pressed his forehead against Robin's neck. "I must seem like some naïve, country-bumpkin kid to you right now."

"Nah." Robin skated warm fingertips across Shawn's back. "Maybe a little sheltered, but you've been in survival mode for a lot of years. Years other guys spent exploring their sexuality and learning about themselves. What they like and don't like. Believe me, I am more than happy to help you explore yourself."

"Because you get to explore me, too?"

"Absolutely. I was lucky to have a safe place and person to explore the guy side of being bi, and I'd love to give you that same safe place."

Shawn kissed him before Robin saw the huge swell of emotions that had to be all over his face. Gratitude and joy and curiosity and something tender that felt like it could one day grow into love. The kiss deepened, and Shawn relaxed as Robin carefully kissed him onto his back, Robin's beautiful, naked body blanketing his. So much tan skin to touch and explore, and Shawn did his best with fingers and palms, while Robin licked every inch of Shawn's neck and shoulders.

"I'm going to play with your nipples now," Robin said.

It was both a statement of intent and a silent question. "Okay."

Robin brushed a thumb over Shawn's left nipple. An odd shock of pleasure jolted through him, and he gasped. "Oh yeah?" Robin said with a sly grin. "Tell me more."

Shawn didn't censor his cries or gasps as Robin drove him out of his mind by pinching, pressing, and then biting both of his nipples. Shawn thrust his hips, desperate for more pressure on his cock, but Robin had shifted in such a way that Shawn only had his own jeans to press into. God, he'd never realized his nipples were this sensitive, and he was so close to coming in his pants that he shouted, "Stop!"

Robin raised his head immediately. "Too much?"

"It felt amazing. I don't want to come in my jeans."

"May I take them off you?"

Shawn's belly swooped at the idea of being fully naked with another man for the first time in his life, but wasn't this what he wanted? To explore, experience, and get off? Robin was an amazing man, who'd only ever respected Shawn and his wants, needs, and desires.

I'm safe here.

"Yes," Shawn replied. "Take off my pants."

Chapter Twelve

Robin held Shawn's wide, wild eyes for several long moments, but he saw no hesitation or fear. Only trust. And that trust beat wildly in Robin's heart as he reached for Shawn's fly. Undid the buttons with a few short tugs, his eyes never leaving Shawn's. Robin had never been the teacher before, the one who helped another man explore sex, and he didn't want to fuck this up. It was too damned important.

He gently eased those worn jeans down Shawn's narrow hips, leaving a pair of sexy blue briefs on for now, taking small steps. So many things Shawn hadn't said suggested he'd been scared enough in his past. All Robin wanted to do was make Shawn happy and keep him safe.

Those jeans came down lean, pale legs and then completely off, leaving Shawn almost completely bare. Robin's hole clenched with the need to be filled by the erection pressing against Shawn's briefs. A damp spot betrayed Shawn's intense arousal, but Robin left the briefs in place for now.

He gazed up the length of Shawn's body, taking in the taut lines of his belly and chest, the smooth planes of his skin. His legs had a thin smattering of hair on the calves and upper thighs, while his chest was smooth

Shawn watched Robin with open curiosity and arousal, so emotionally naked Robin had to kiss him again.

Robin crouched over Shawn and captured his mouth. Sucked on his tongue. Explored as deeply as he could while Shawn gave back with gusto. Shawn hitched his knees up, inviting Robin closer, so Robin lowered himself. Situated his naked cock near Shawn's covered one and pressed. Pleasure pulsed in his blood at the contact, and Shawn nearly bit his tongue.

"Oh God," Shawn panted. "Feels so good."

"Yeah?" Robin thrust his hips once, and Shawn gasped. "That feel good?"

"All of it. I need to come."

"You will. Eventually."

Shawn tried to thrust up, the brat, and take over, but Robin settled him with a firm grip on his hips. "Let me drive, Shawn," Robin whispered. "I promise you'll get there."

"It's so intense."

"I know. It's chemistry." He sucked on the side of Shawn's neck until Shawn whined. "Haven't felt this in a long time and I'm not wasting it by going too fast."

Shawn looked equal parts annoyed and in love. "You're killing me."

"It'll be worth it in the end, trust me."

"I do." He wriggled his hips. "I kind of hate you right now but I do trust you, Robin."

"Good."

Robin took his time kissing his way from Shawn's mouth to his navel, pausing to torment both nipples, to trace the lines of his pecs and down through the valley of his abdomen. Shawn was a slender guy, bordering on too skinny, with jutting hip bones Robin licked and made love to. His chin bumped the head of Shawn's cock more than once, and each time Shawn tried to get more friction.

With his own throbbing erection desperate for friction, too, Robin hooked his thumbs in the waistband of Shawn's briefs. Met Shawn's wide, needy eyes. Shawn's nod answered his silent question. Robin slid those briefs down and off without ever breaking eye contact. Shawn's chest heaved once but he never looked away. Only nodded again, reaffirming his consent.

Chest burning with desire and other, sweeter emotions, Robin bent his head and took Shawn's entire length into his mouth.

Of the handful of women he'd dated in the past, only two had gone down on Shawn, and while he'd liked it and gotten off, there was something to be said for patience and chemistry. When Robin wrapped his mouth around Shawn's cock, Shawn's mind exploded a little bit with the intense heat of it. The way Robin's lips created a steady pressure, while his tongue rubbed and teased. And Robin took all of him at once without a single gasp or choke.

Holy fucking shit!

It was almost too much to bear. Not only the intense way Robin had taken Shawn apart with his mouth, tongue, and fingers, but for the emotions involved. More than lust and desire, there was also trust, connection, and care. They both wanted to come, and yes, that was half the point. The other half was building their relationship in their own way. Taking time instead of rushing to climax. Making the entire thing less about sex and more about growth. Generosity

Love?

One day, definitely love.

Robin had slowly deconstructed him tonight, and Shawn wasn't sure who he'd be tomorrow, only that the new Shawn would be a better person. A happier person who'd learned so much about himself after a single encounter that wasn't even over yet, because Robin somehow knew how to squeeze Shawn's dick to stave off his orgasm. Robin sucked him until Shawn wanted to weep for all the endorphins and desire heating his blood, slowly making him insane with lust.

And then Robin sucked on his balls, and that was it. Shawn shouted as he came, his entire body spasming and jerking as he turned inside out with pleasure. The world fuzzed out a little, and when his vision cleared, Robin was carefully licking every bit of spilled semen off Shawn's belly and chest.

Shawn had forgotten the English language, so all he could do was tremble and pluck at Robin's shoulders. His hair. Anything to get his attention. Then Robin licked at his softening dick, and Shawn thrashed, a sharp whine tearing from his throat. Too much and not enough, and he lurched for Robin, dragging the bigger man up the bed so Shawn could kiss him. Silently thank him for such a tremendous gift.

They kissed until Shawn could think clearly. Feel the hard dick riding his hip, evidence that Robin still needed to come. Shawn snaked his right hand between them and grasped the hot length of Robin's erection. He was average in length and girth, which gave Shawn hope he might one day be brave enough to bottom for Robin. In porn, the tops were always huge and it looked so freaking scary… But not Robin.

Robin was perfect.

"Yeah, twist your wrist," Robin said, hot breath panting against Shawn's cheek. "Like that."

Shawn tried doing what he liked while jerking off, but the position was weird. "Roll onto your back."

Robin did as asked without a word, stretching out on his back, hands folded behind his head in a position that gave total control to Shawn. Shawn straddled him and sat on his upper thighs, a bit self-conscious in this position, but Robin watched his face not his body. Shawn clasped Robin's heavy cock again in a surer grip and stroked, curious what Robin's face looked like when he came. Desperate to see it now. To get Robin off and know Shawn had done that.

"So close," Robin panted. "So fucking close. Oh fuck." He thrust up into Shawn's grip, eyes rolling back in his head. Fingers clutched at the blanket beneath him. His entire big body thrummed with energy as his climax built. Teased. Shawn stilled his hand completely and Robin cursed.

Shawn smiled at the sight of his cowboy losing his goddamn mind over a hand job. "You ready to come?"

"Fuck yes, please."

The "please" did it, and Shawn had mercy, stroking Robin until the older man painted his own chest with pale ropes of come. Shawn wasn't sure about cleaning him with his mouth, so he swirled his fingers in the load, rubbing it around Robin's nipples as Robin came down off the high of release.

Robin gazed up at him with a naked expression. So naked Shawn bent to kiss him, sure those same things were in his own eyes and smile. He loved the way Robin held him tight, smashing Shawn to his damp chest, smearing them both with Robin's come. Their spent dicks rubbed a bit, too, and Shawn relaxed against Robin. Tucked his head under Robin's chin and breathed in the man beneath him.

"How do you feel?" Robin asked after an eternity of silence.

"Good. Really good. You?"

"Fantastic." Fingertips skated up and down Shawn's back, a lazy caress that felt as if Robin simply couldn't stop touching him. "A guy could get used to this."

"Regular sex?" Shawn teased.

"Sex with you." Robin kissed the side of Shawn's head. "While hookups with strangers can be sexy and fun, there's definitely something to be said for knowing the person first. Having a connection with them before the sex happens."

A bit of uncertainty crept in and made Shawn blurt out, "Is that why you hooked up with Derrick a lot? You guys were friends?"

"That was part of it, sure, but me and Derrick are just friends now. No more hooking up, I promise. You are the guy I want, Shawn, not him. Hell, he even flirted with me tonight, but I shut that down fast."

"He came on to you?"

"Yeah, but that used to be our thing. Now we're friends only, because he knows I'm taken. And taken by a pretty incredible guy, for putting up with a dance club when you didn't really want to be there."

Shawn seesawed between annoyed at Derrick for trying to poach and proud of himself over Robin's praise. "Club Base is a place you love, and I wanted to experience it with you. It's not my thing, but once in a while, I wouldn't mind going there with you."

"Really?"

"Yes. Robin, I don't want to be the reason you deny yourself things you love doing, and this is still too new to make big, grand promises. How about we just keep talking? About everything."

"I can definitely do that." Robin squeezed Shawn's waist. "Can we clean up before we talk more? We're both kind of sticky."

"Good idea."

The tubs in the cabins weren't really big enough for two grown adults to have any reasonable amount of room, so they took turns rinsing off before wrapping towels around their waists. Shawn's first instinct was to get dressed, but he liked the ease with which Robin moved around the small space in just a towel, so he followed suit. They cuddled up on the couch with a throw blanket over their shoulders and held each other for a while.

Shawn marveled at what he'd experienced tonight. From his minor meltdown at the club to the beautiful sex they'd shared. The things he'd learned from Robin. The intense orgasms they'd each had. Shawn could see a future with Robin on this ranch: Robin working with tourists and Shawn cooking at the ghost town. Coming home to each other in this cabin. Something similar to what Miles and Reyes shared, but also incredibly different because it was Shawn and Robin.

And Shawn had never expected Robin. Never expected to fall for someone so handsome and strong and take-charge. Someone as haunted by his past as Shawn and just as reluctant to talk about it. But also strong enough to get back up when life knocked him down. Brave enough to start over.

Shawn rolled with every punch that came his way and had never, ever quit.

"Penny for your thoughts," Robin said.

"Just marveling at where I am, safe and sound with you." Shawn nuzzled Robin's throat. "Happy. All I wanted when I came to Garrett was a job and I found you. And a family."

"That's the magic of this land. She gives you what you need, and for most of us, it's family. And for a lot of us, too, second chances. Arthur created something incredibly special here when he turned a failing cattle ranch into a horse rescue and vacation spot."

"Yeah, he did. God bless Arthur Garrett." And Shawn meant the words. Arthur turned eighty years old next year, and he'd already had two heart attacks. Shawn couldn't fathom what would happen to this patchwork family if they ever lost their patriarch, and he hoped he didn't find out anytime soon.

"God bless Arthur," Robin said, and then kissed Shawn soundly on the mouth. "And bless us, too."

Shawn wasn't much for religion, but he said, "Amen," anyway.

Please, God or whoever's out there, let me keep Robin. I need him.

I'm falling in love with him.

Robin woke to the steady cadence of Shawn breathing beside him, and it took him a moment to understand why that was strange. Not because he'd spent the night in Shawn's bed, but because Robin had slept. Actually slept. He carefully reached for his phone on the shelf above the bed. The cabin was pitch-black so it was still early yet.

Four thirty. They'd finally tumbled into bed a little after midnight, after talking for a while about life and nonsense, and Robin had nodded off quickly with Shawn in his arms.

I slept for four hours straight.

He couldn't remember the last time he'd slept that long in one go, not even after an incredibly gymnastic round of sex with Derrick. And he usually dozed, unable to truly relax in a bed not his own, but tonight he'd slept. With Shawn.

As Robin's eyes adjusted to the small bit of light from the cabin's two front windows, he studied the man who'd given him this gift. Shawn was still asleep on his side facing away from Robin, one arm under his pillow and the other tucked close to his body, fist beneath his chin. Face smooth, completely unencumbered by stress or fear. Robin wondered if Shawn remembered his dreams; Robin rarely slept long enough to find true REM sleep and dream himself. Often they were nebulous thoughts that trickled in and out of his mind as he edged close to sleep, before sleep flittered away again.

He'd been spending time with Shawn this entire week, and Robin's insomnia hadn't changed. But last night had been unique. Not only had they made love but Robin had stayed and slept over with his boyfriend. He hoped to do it again and again, but he didn't want to pressure Shawn. Shawn wasn't used to relationships—hell, Robin had only ever had one that lasted—and Robin couldn't risk pushing Shawn too far, too soon.

He couldn't risk losing Shawn.

How did I fall so hard, so fast? It's only been a few weeks.

It didn't seem possible.

Fully awake now, Robin played a game on his phone for a long time. As sunrise approached, he eased out of bed, slipped into his clothes, and went out onto the porch. Over to his porch. Phone ready, Robin sat and watched today's sunrise. The horizon was a bit hazy but the colors changed in familiar ways, and Robin snapped two pictures in a row. The first had a stunning swath of ruby red in it, but the second showed the first orange curve of the sun. On a whim, Robin posted both to his account.

He didn't even miss the puffs on his vape until he was walking back to Shawn's cabin. The puffs had been about tradition more than anything, and this morning he'd already broken tradition by posting two photos instead of one.

Change is good.

It wasn't until a light clicked on in Shawn's cabin that Robin remembered the time. Breakfast on Sunday for the hands was a casual thing but Shawn liked being in the kitchen when food was being handled—a trait he'd probably learned from Patrice. Robin opened the cabin door to find an empty bed and the bathroom door shut. A toilet flushed and water ran, and Robin's brain flashed to that moment three weeks ago when he'd found Patrice on that very bathroom floor, hurt and scared...

The door flew open and a now-dressed Shawn let out a yelp when he saw Robin. "Jesus, I thought you'd gone home," Shawn said, his face bright red and angry.

"No, I woke up and couldn't go back to sleep, so I sat outside for a while. It's tradition." He'd never told Shawn about his Instagram account for Xander, and this morning didn't seem like the right time.

"Oh." Shawn's anger shifted into embarrassment. "I thought you'd sneaked out."

"I didn't, I promise. Not like that." Robin closed the distance between them and wrapped his arms around Shawn's waist. Gave him a soft, sensual good-morning kiss. "I'm sorry I hurt your feelings."

Shawn rested his own hands on Robin's shoulders. "It's my insecurity, I guess. But when I woke up to an empty bed, I didn't know what else to think. I didn't even remember your insomnia problem."

"No reason you should."

"Yes, there is. You carve me beautiful mementos when the rest of the world is asleep."

"Not the whole world. Only our little slice of it." Robin kissed him again. "I'll meet you up at the kitchen. Probably shouldn't show up to breakfast in my club clothes."

Shawn laughed. "Probably not. I'll see you there."

They left together, going in opposite directions. Robin quietly let himself into his own cabin, grabbed jeans and a fresh long-sleeve ranch polo, and headed into the bathroom to change. Ernie snored away on his bunk, and he was still asleep when Robin had cleaned up and dressed. The guy was a heavy sleeper and had snored his way through Robin sneaking home on dozens of occasions. Ernie was older and more likely to head to nearby bars for a beer and pool than go to the city like the younger horsemen.

To each his own. Guy probably sowed enough wild oats in his day.

Shawn was rolling out biscuit dough when Robin arrived, and he helped himself to coffee from the industrial maker. Patrice wasn't there supervising him, and that was a great sign. She still showed up for meals, but Robin suspected it was more about socializing with the guests and hands than any need to check on Shawn's cooking.

No one was likely to come in for a while yet, so Robin blew on his coffee as he watched Shawn work. "So sitting outside to watch the sun come up isn't just something I do for shits and giggles," Robin said. "Watching the sun come up was one of Xander's favorite things to do, and while I was getting my shit back together after he died, my shrink suggested I work through my grief by continuing to share the sunrises with Xander."

"You saw a shrink?" Shawn asked.

"A few times, and it did help. She was someone Judson knew and trusted. So I set up an Instagram account in Xander's honor, and every morning I post a photo of the sunrise to it. Hot, cold, rain, wind, whatever, I'm out there. Haven't missed a morning since I started doing it."

Shawn gaped at him over a row of cut biscuits. "Wow. That's…beautiful. Thank you for telling me, and now I'm glad you woke up. I'd have felt terrible if I was the reason you missed the sunrise."

"It wouldn't have been your fault, and Xander wouldn't have been mad. Neither would I. I think if he saw how happy you make me, he'd completely understand. The photos are something I do, but not something I need. Not anymore."

"It's part of the healing process."

"Exactly. I'll still take them but if I miss one? Especially because I'm with you? How could I possibly be upset?"

Shawn leaned up to kiss his lips. "You're kind of amazing. And you make me happy, too. Really happy. Last night was…fantastic. You took care of me."

"I'm happy to. You took care of me, too, Shawn."

After another shared kiss, Robin helped Shawn get the sheet tray of biscuits into the oven. Shawn didn't make the sausage gravy, only set out the block of butter to soften, plus a few jars of jams and jellies. Robin enjoyed not only watching Shawn cook, but also assisting him. He could see them in the future, doing this dance around a kitchen of their own, cooking a big meal for friends and neighbors.

A real life. And a home of their own, which was something he'd never really had with Xander. Only an RV they shared with Levi and another performer. As much as Robin had loved living on the road and seeing the country, he liked having roots again.

Robin saw a real home for himself and Shawn, maybe somewhere in Garrett. A few of the horsemen and most of the rescue workers lived in town or near it. A little home all their own, with a little porch facing east, so they could still watch the sunrise if they chose to.

And Robin would do everything in his power to make that precious dream a reality.

Shawn helped greet the new crop of guests a little after ten, a bit sad that this was the final week for guests before closing for Christmas and New Year's. They only had nine reservations, though, so it was for the best. Arthur was probably paying his staff more this week than he'd made in guest payments, and Shawn made a quiet comment about it to Patrice once the guests were settled in their rooms and free to explore.

"Arthur's made a few investments over the years," Patrice said with a fond smile. She was leaning against the counter, watching Shawn shred cabbage for lunch's fresh batch of coleslaw. "Things were a bit tight a few years ago, but we all weathered it thanks to those investments, and now with the ghost town bringing in more tourist dollars for both attractions, things are looking better than ever."

"Good on Arthur." Shawn had never given a thought to investing money. Hell, he didn't have a savings account, only the checking attached to his debit card.

"If you ever have questions about where to put your money, feel free to ask him. Arthur loves handing out advice on topics he's familiar with."

"I'll keep that in mind, thanks." Not that Shawn would have any questions in the near future, but having a resource available was a good start. One day he wouldn't have to live like a pauper, but it wouldn't be today. Maybe not even two years from now.

He started grating carrots for the slaw. Extra work but way cheaper than buying coleslaw mix in a bag, and Patrice had even taught him her homemade dressing which was delicious. Just the right amount of sweetness and tang. And Robin was a huge fan of it, if the amount he ate at lunch these past three weeks was any indication, so Shawn didn't mind the effort.

He also kind of loved the way Robin helping him out at breakfast was slowly becoming a shared thing. Shawn wanted to watch a sunrise with Robin one of these days, but his prep schedule had Shawn in the kitchen around dawn every morning in order to feed guests and hands. Maybe one morning next week, when all the guests were gone and the hands were down to a skeleton crew.

"You really have eased into this job," Patrice said once the coleslaw was mixed and chilling in the walk-in. "You are so much more confident than during your first week with guests."

"I like routines and knowing what to expect day to day." Shawn checked on the potatoes boiling for potato salad. Still needed a few more minutes. "I had to get my feet firmly under me, and now I know what to do, and in which order, for the best results. It's kind of like juggling the line in a kitchen, but with less surprise in what I'll be preparing dish to dish, you know?"

"I do remember those days. Very well, in fact. I love knowing the industry had changed in recent years and that women get much more respect in professional kitchens, but I'd never go back. I can't imagine being away from this ranch now."

"May I ask how long you've worked here?"

"Oh, let's see." Patrice settled into her rocking chair, her expression distant. "It'll have been twenty-seven years this past summer. Kerry would have been forty-five this year."

"Kerry?" She never mentioned that name before.

"Yes. My son."

Shock jolted through Shawn's middle. Patrice had a son? He turned the burner off under the potatoes and paid closer attention to the older woman, really seeing her age for the first time as grief settled over her. If her son was forty-five, she was in her midsixties, at least. Older than he would have guessed for her energy and lack of wrinkles or gray.

"I didn't know you have a son?" Shawn said tentatively. Unsure if this was an okay conversation topic, but she'd brought it up.

"I used to. He died in Desert Storm." Her dark eyes glistened, and Shawn handed her a paper towel. "All he talked about growing up was being a soldier like his father, and when he turned eighteen, he enlisted. Two months before that goddamn war started, and six months later he was dead."

"I'm so sorry, Patrice."

"He's been gone now longer than I had him in my life, but he was my baby boy. It's still hard to talk about, and most of the boys here don't know."

"Thank you for trusting me." Shawn squeezed her good wrist. "I mean that. And I won't tell anyone else, I promise."

Patrice turned her hand around to clasp his. "I trust you. You remind me of Kerry a bit, and I'm truly glad you ended up here, living in a safe place."

"So am I. Glad, I mean. Is losing Kerry why you left San Francisco?"

"Yes. I wasn't married to Kerry's father, and we had a strained relationship as he grew. Our grief drove us apart completely. But Judson was an old friend of mine from high school, and we'd kept in touch over the years, writing letters back and forth. When he heard about Kerry, he told me about the ranch his friend Arthur was renovating. I packed a suitcase and never looked back."

"Wow. So you've been friends with Judson a really long time."

"Most of my life." She smiled and some of that grief slipped away. "He and Arthur have been amazing friends. Lifelines, really."

"I can't imagine." Except Shawn kind of could. They'd taken him in, too, hadn't they?

"Careful, you'll overcook the potatoes."

Shawn jolted for the stove so he could drain the pot. The serious conversation seemed over for now, so he focused on finishing up lunch prep. Since they had half the guests Patrice's recipes usually fed, any extra salads would go into the walk-in for tomorrow's lunch and cut down on his midmorning prep.

Robin entered the kitchen with Reyes, Miles, and Colt. He heaped coleslaw onto a plate with a piled-high sandwich and a giant dill pickle from the barrel Patrice kept for the hands. Everything was under control, so Shawn fixed himself a turkey half sandwich and a small scoop of slaw. Robin waited for him to sit and then slid into a chair right next to him. Colt smirked at them from the opposite side of the table, and Shawn ignored him for now.

"Excited to teach the new guests how to ride?" Shawn asked.

"Not sure yet," Robin replied. "Reyes says the five guys who reserved together are college friends, and those guys are usually superrespectful and eager to learn, or they're arrogant douche-bros."

Miles spoke up. "We had a pair of those during our vacation here. God, what were their names? Liam and... something. All week they kept talking about searching for Arthur's mythical gold."

Reyes chuckled. "I remember those two. Liam and Miller. They signed up for my overnight camping trip and were right pains in the ass. Miller scared you with his comment about bobcats coming near our camp."

"I can't believe you remember that."

"I didn't like him scaring you."

The pair shared a lovesick smile and continued eating. Shawn glanced at Robin, who was staring at Shawn's plate. When Robin looked up and met his gaze, Robin's eyes seemed to say, "Eat your lunch." So he did. It also occurred to him that Colt was currently the only person on the ranch who knew Shawn and Robin were dating. Not that Shawn planned on making a huge announcement—he was still a tiny bit worried that if this blew up in his face, he'd somehow lose this job— but Shawn was also a little jealous of how openly affectionate Miles and Reyes were.

Then again, Reyes was head cowboy and the best friend of the ranch owner's grandson. His job would always be safe.

No, Shawn had to stop waiting for the other shoe to drop. He really did, just like Miles told him to. Embrace this new life instead of expecting it to shatter. Even if he and Robin didn't work out long-term, Robin was a genuine guy. Not the type to insist Shawn be fired so they didn't have to work together or live near each other. And Miles would fight for Shawn's job at the ghost town.

Shawn simply wasn't used to stability in his life. But maybe…just maybe he could truly have a stable life and future here.

Chapter Thirteen

Their final week with guests ran smoothly and was also kind of boring. With nine guests and much colder weather, they were only offering the Wednesday night camping trip, since it had the warmest overnight temperature. Robin wasn't on that one, and they couldn't take guests to swim at the lake anymore, so Robin mostly worked with the horses all week long. Exercising them, mucking their stalls, keeping all the gear clean and polished.

And he spent as much of his downtime as possible with Shawn. He haunted the kitchen between meals, and Patrice picked up on their relationship quickly. Other horsemen did, too, and Robin didn't mind. Shawn was very hands-off when they weren't alone, which was fine by Robin because Shawn was very tactile when they *were* alone. Robin loved knowing he was helping Shawn get used to physical connections again, even something as simple as holding hands.

No one gave them shit, other than Ernie once teasing Robin about his cock-hunting days in the city being over.

They also spent a lot of time naked in Shawn's bed, fooling around and existing together as a couple. Talking about everything and nothing, and Robin stayed over a few times but not every night. He also noticed a slight change in the cabin: the gifts he'd carved for Shawn were now proudly displayed on the bookshelf next to Shawn's library books.

On Friday, after a fun round of rubbing off together, they were lazing about on Shawn's bed. Robin on his stomach, Shawn on his side with one hand drawing shapes on Robin's bare skin. In all the times they'd played around in bed together, those curious fingers never strayed lower than the small of Robin's back, and he kind of wished they would. Other than a few ass pinches and gropes through underwear, they hadn't explored each other's bare butts yet.

But Robin wanted this to work, so he'd be patient and go at Shawn's pace.

Shawn's finger traced a line on the left side of Robin's ribs. "What's this scar from?"

Robin had a handful of scars from various accidents over the years, and he knew exactly which one Shawn had asked about. "First time I got thrown standing on the back of a galloping horse."

"Really? You told me you can do riding tricks, but I guess I never pictured it until now."

"It can be dangerous and I was showing off that day, so I wasn't totally surprised to find myself thrown and trampled. I was lucky the horse didn't break my ribs, just broke the skin in a few places. That one was the deepest. Hurt like hell for weeks."

Shawn leaned down to kiss the scar, and the sweet gesture sent warm, gooey feelings through Robin's chest. "I'm glad you were okay. Were you showing off for Xander?"

"Yeah." Talking about Xander with Shawn didn't hurt

as much as it once had. Xander was his past, and while he would always own a small piece of Robin's heart, Robin still had plenty left over for Shawn. And Shawn was surely stealing it, bit by bit. "He was so pissed at me for taking a risk, and it made him even more afraid of horses than he already was."

"Wait a sec." Shawn urged Robin to sit up with him. "He worked for a traveling rodeo but was afraid of horses?"

"Yup. Xander grew up in the life, same as his brother, Levi, but Xander just…didn't like horses. Levi told me once he had the vaguest childhood memory of Xander being kicked by a horse when he was maybe three, so it could have been one of those subconscious fears."

"So what did Xander do in the rodeo?"

Robin grinned as so many wonderful, funny memories flooded back. "He was our clown. He opened every show with magic tricks, some acrobatics, and told jokes. Warmed up the crowd for the show to come. And he was good at it. Great, actually. It never felt forced or fake. He knew how to get everyone excited, no matter where we traveled. It was his gift, connecting with people through humor. He could always make me laugh when I was having a bad day."

"He sounds like an amazing person. So have you, um, talked to Levi again since that first phone call?"

"We've texted a few times." Robin was glad to have renewed his friendship with Levi, and he'd put Levi in contact with both Mack and Avery about the rodeo idea. But he wasn't sure he was ready to see his former brother-in-law again. Not yet.

And Levi's suggestion that Robin reach out to Doug rang in his head. It really was the easiest solution to the rodeo problem, but…how was Robin supposed to mend fences with Doug when Robin was the reason his son was dead?

"Hey, where'd you go?" Shawn cupped his chin in a cool palm. "Robin? Did I say the wrong thing?"

"No. Certain parts of my past are just…hard to think about."

"I get it. Trust me." Shawn's expression shuttered for a brief moment, and it took all of Robin's restraint not to ask about that mysterious incident from Shawn's past. They both had painful things they didn't like talking about, but maybe one day, when their relationship wasn't still so new, they'd finally share those secrets.

"I know you do." Robin kissed Shawn's nose. "Any other scars you want to know about?" He pointed to a pale line on his lower belly. "This one is my appendix. It nearly burst when I was fourteen. Only time I've ever had surgery."

"I've never had surgery before. Never even been in the hospital overnight."

The overnight remark stuck in Robin's head, suggesting Shawn had been in the hospital briefly for something. Maybe the emergency room? Shawn didn't add to his comment, though, and Robin left it alone. For now. They'd had such a wonderful night, and he didn't want to spoil it with unhappy things.

"I'm almost done another chess piece for you," Robin said. "Should be done in the morning. Maybe." He'd been sleeping way better on the rare night he stayed over here, usually in three-to-four-hour bursts, but he still often woke hours before the rest of the ranch and carved away on the front porch.

"Oooh, which piece?"

"You'll have to wait and see."

Shawn blew a raspberry but didn't stop smiling. "Well, it's been almost a week since I got the king and queen, so I'm going to guess the knight, because they tend to be the most intricate."

Robin forced back a grin at Shawn's perfect guess. "Stop fishing or you don't get your present until… Sunday."

"Okay, okay." Shawn twisted around so he could sit with his back to Robin's chest, butt on the bed between his spread legs. Robin wrapped his arms around Shawn's waist and held him close, loving this position. Loving how easily they could sit, totally naked, in each other's arms. "It's going to be weird not having guests for three weeks."

"It does feel a little strange, I'll give you that, especially when the hands who are traveling elsewhere leave. Gets real quiet, but it's also peaceful in its own way. Just the land and the horses and a few close friends." He kissed the side of Shawn's neck. "And this year my boyfriend."

"Does it ever snow?"

"Very rarely. Mostly it rains, so it's a good thing the ghost town is closed when it is. Tourists aren't likely to walk around in rain and mud."

"Good point."

"Why? Did it snow where you grew up?" Robin had no idea where that was, because Shawn always seemed to sidestep the question. More than once, Robin had been tempted to search Shawn's name on the internet to find clues about his mysterious past, but that always felt like an invasion of privacy. Even if anything was online, it was up to Shawn to tell Robin about his life and any skeletons still rattling around in his closet.

"Yeah, a lot most winters." Shawn rested the back of his head on Robin's shoulder. "Northern Nevada. I grew up near a small ski resort."

"Ah." The cabin was a bit chilly, so Robin wrapped the bedspread over his shoulders and pulled it around to fold over Shawn's lap. "Can I ask you something personal?"

"Sure."

Robin hesitated, hoping he didn't overstep with his question. "If you had the money for the trip, would you go home to see your grandparents?"

Shawn let out a long, low sigh. "I want to say yes. I miss them, especially Granddad, and my nana isn't well. Hasn't been for a long time. But I have so many bad memories of that damned town." He twisted around to hug Robin properly, and Robin held him tight, wishing he knew this secret. "Maybe if I could sneak back for a few days with no one seeing me. A secret mission."

"What if we can?"

He sat up straighter to look Robin in the eye, brow creased in confusion. "What do you mean?"

"I mean, living here at the ranch has given me the chance to save up my pay. Arthur doesn't charge anyone rent and he feeds us through the guesthouse, so even though our hourly is minimum wage, I don't have much in the way of expenses except my phone. And with Christmas in ten days, I can reasonably take a few days away from the ranch. So can you, if we talk to Judson and Patrice. If you want to see your grandparents, of course."

I'll do anything to make you happy, Shawn. Promise.

* * *

Shawn gaped at Robin, confused and surprised and awed by the man's generosity. Robin was volunteering to pay for a trip to Nevada, so Shawn could see his family again. All without knowing a single real detail about why Shawn had stayed away for so long. Hell, Robin hadn't even asked about Nana not being well or what that meant.

"I want to see them again, more than almost anything," Shawn replied. "But I also left town and stayed away for a reason."

"Do you want to talk about that reason?" Robin's expression was so open and gentle. Very much an *I'll listen if you want to talk* expression, rather than an *I want the gory details* one.

Shawn didn't want to talk about it. At all. Not ever again. The only person in Garrett who'd ever gotten a smidge of that story from him was Miles, and Shawn had been incredibly vague. Nowhere close to the whole truth. And Robin had never looked at Shawn like an immature kid for not exploring his sexuality until he was twenty-four, but what if Robin got tired of waiting for Shawn to get his act together about anal sex and possibly topping Robin?

Maybe he could give Robin a little bit more of his truth.

"I was about eleven or so when my nana first started showing bizarre symptoms," Shawn said. "She resisted seeing her doctor for a long time, but when she started losing control of her hand movements and had trouble writing, she finally went to a neurologist. I was thirteen when two things changed my life: my father died of a heroin overdose, so I was given to my grandparents, and then Nana was diagnosed with Huntington's chorea."

Robin's eyes went liquid. "I'm so sorry about your father."

"Thanks." It wasn't lost on Shawn that Robin hadn't asked what Huntington's was. Most people didn't have a clue, but maybe Robin had heard of it before. "My dad and I weren't close. My parents divorced when I was still a toddler, and I lived with my mom full-time until she passed away when I was ten. Then my father took me in until he died, so I got used to being shunted from place to place pretty young. And used to loss."

"Were you close to your grandparents before you lived with them?"

"Not exactly close, but I knew them. Mom and I lived about a hundred miles south of them so we got together on holidays and birthdays, and we talked on the phone. They probably would have taken me in when she died, if the courts hadn't been able to locate my father. Nana was diagnosed about a year and a half after I moved in. So much had changed in my life in less than five years, and then I was in high school and noticing boys, and the very last thing I wanted was the complication of being gay, on top of being an orphaned transplant with bad skin and prone to social anxiety."

High school had been a living nightmare for Shawn, both before and after the incident with Beck, and in some ways, he'd been anxious to turn eighteen and leave town. Leave behind the whispering, the taunts, and the angry looks from townsfolk who'd lived in Breton their entire lives and hadn't liked some scrawny newbie coming in and making accusations.

True accusations, but whatever.

"I can relate to that a little bit," Robin said. He stroked a hand through Shawn's hair. "Growing up in a small town and hiding your sexuality. Being eager to get away and be my true self. Except I ran away from home because I wanted to. Sounds like maybe you felt forced to?"

"I did." Shawn burrowed a bit deeper into the blanket and Robin's embrace, finding it easier to say more by looking at Robin's shoulder than his eyes. "Long story short, something happened, and it pit my word against the word of someone a lot of townsfolk loved and respected, and it made things worse. It put my grandparents in an awkward position and embarrassed the hell out them, and Granddad was also dealing with getting Nana's medications sorted and her symptoms under control. Even though I only ever told the truth, I felt like the outcast villain."

Robin kissed the side of his head. "So you left?"

Bless you for not asking what exactly happened.

"Yeah. My mom had a cousin who lived in San Francisco and Granddad got me in touch with her. Sheila. She wasn't thrilled by the idea but she agreed to let me live with her, as long as I got a job and paid rent. My only truly useful skill was baking, which I'd learned from my mom, so I was able to get a good job in a bakery. And the early hours meant I only really saw Sheila around dinnertime when she got home. I paid my rent, my car insurance, even paid for some community college courses, too, and whatever I had extra I sent home to Granddad to pay for the second mortgage he put on his house for my legal fees."

He'll ask now.

But Robin didn't. He held Shawn, a silent protector, and listened to whatever Shawn told him. Shawn's heart squeezed with tender feelings for the man and his discretion. But Shawn still couldn't find the courage to admit that after Sheila kicked him out, he'd spent the next two years living in his car. Until fate stepped in in the form of Officer Bradley, and now he was here. Safe and warm and cared for. Maybe even loved.

"So you haven't seen your grandparents in five years because of this incident that turned the town against you?" Robin asked after a few moments of silence. "And it's why you're scared to go back."

"Yes. I love that you're offering to take me back but I can't. Not yet."

"Not even for Christmas?"

Robin scowled. "Are you going to see your family for Christmas?"

"My family is right here in Garrett. I don't need to travel anywhere to find it, other than maybe up the road a ways. You still love and miss your grandparents."

"I do but…after Mom died, the holidays have always been the worst time of year for me. We used to spend an entire weekend baking. Dozens of cookies, all different kinds, and we'd make up platters. Drop them off at local businesses, shelters, neighbors, anywhere she thought needed some holiday cheer."

"Sounds like your mom was a generous lady."

"She did her best as a single working mom. Pinched her pennies and saved up money all year to buy the stuff she needed so we could bake." Grief tightened Shawn's throat. "When she got sick, all those people rallied to help. They dropped off casseroles and chicken soup and cleaned the apartment for us. Those were some of the best people I've ever known until I moved here."

"I'm glad you had that support, and I'm sorry the holidays make you so sad."

"Thanks. I used to make Nana and Granddad's favorite cookies for them for Christmas but it's not the same."

"Have you thought about baking some this year for the ranch hands?"

Shawn sat up straighter and met Robin's curious eyes. "No." In the past, the idea of baking for multiple people hurt too much and made him miss his mom. But right now? He liked the idea of starting a new tradition. "Would you want to help me?"

"Definitely." Robin flashed him his trademark charming smile. "I have to admit that I've never baked a cookie in my life, not even the store-bought dough kind."

"Then I can teach you something new." A trade for all the new things Robin was helping Shawn learn about himself. "Maybe we can drive into town and buy some stuff after the guests leave tomorrow? I don't want to use the flour and sugar Arthur buys for the ranch."

"I can't imagine Arthur would mind, seeing as you'll be sharing the cookies with the hands, but I also don't think Patrice keeps a ready supply of chocolate chips."

Shawn laughed. "Doubtful since I've yet to stumble over a hidden stash anywhere in the kitchen. Hold on a sec." He climbed off the bed, his naked skin immediately too chilly, and bolted to the dresser, where he'd put his stash of personal items and mementos. He removed a small metal box that he brought back to bed with him. Under the warmth of the bedspread, Shawn opened the box. "These are my mom's recipe cards."

"Oh wow." Robin thumbed through them. "All pastry?"

"Pretty much. We ate pretty basic foods to save

money but I never went hungry, and she made every meal feel special, even if it was only boxed macaroni and cheese with cut-up hot dogs." All this reminiscing left Shawn both missing his mother, and also able to look back on the good times with fondness and a tinge of nostalgia. "Were you close with your parents?"

Robin was silent for a moment, his expression giving away nothing. "I guess it depends on how you define *close.* They were caring people but they expected their kids to do as told, and once we were big enough, to help out on the family farm. We got a cake on birthdays and presents at Christmas, but they didn't throw any kind of elaborate parties or make a fuss over any particular milestone, other than maybe high school graduation. They were good parents but I can't remember any real, personal conversations I ever had with them, beyond the basic sex talk. So I guess, no, we weren't very close." He plucked a recipe card from the box. "Snowballs?"

Shawn didn't have to glance at the card to know that one. "They were one of Mom's favorites. They're these crispy little cookie balls full of chopped pecans, and you dust them with powdered sugar."

"I love pecans, so we're definitely making these. Any other favorites?"

"The Magic Window cookies were always a hit. It's a shortbread-style cookie you cut out with cookie cutters, and then you use a knife to cut interior bits out of the dough. Crush up different colors of LifeSavers and sprinkle them into the holes, so when the cookies bake, you have this opaque candy middle."

"Like a stained-glass window. I love it. So we'll probably need to buy cookie cutters, too. Unless Arthur has some at the main house."

"Why would Arthur have cookie cutters?"

Robin shrugged. "Dunno. Doesn't hurt to ask."

Shawn shook his head. "No, I'd rather buy my own. Then I'll have them for next year, too."

"I guess you didn't keep any of your mom's?"

"I didn't even think to. She passed away in July, and I had no thought of Christmas at all. My father said I could take whatever I could fit into one suitcase, so all I could think to grab from our kitchen was her recipe box. Everything else he sold through an auction company, I think."

And then shot the proceeds right up his arm.

He was a bit surprised Robin hadn't commented on the fact that Shawn said his father died of a heroin overdose, but Robin was shockingly discreet about certain things. Maybe because he had his own painful past he didn't like talking about.

"I'm sorry you didn't get to keep more," Robin said.

"It's okay, it just meant fewer things to drag around with me. And I still have all the memories." Shawn was tired of focusing on bad things, so he refocused the subject. "So there are ten days until Christmas. Since we aren't starting until tomorrow, let's pick out nine cookies to make and do a different batch each day."

"Sounds like a plan to me. We already have Snowballs, and Magic Window cookies are definitely on the list."

They spent at least an hour going through the recipe tin, comparing and contrasting, and Shawn shared more than one story about making a particular cookie with his mom. And doing the entire thing while naked with his boyfriend in bed? Priceless. Shawn hadn't been this settled and content in...well, about fourteen years. Since

Mom died and his life blew up completely. He'd gotten used to things changing on a dime, loved ones being taken away, and ending up struggling simply to survive.

Tonight…he had hope. Real hope that maybe this life would be the one he could keep. That he had a solid boyfriend in Robin, an ongoing job at Tango Saloon, and friends who wouldn't turn their backs because of a secret. Just maybe, Shawn had finally found a place to put down roots and be happy—an ending he'd never once stopped fighting for.

Please let this be my future. Please?

Chapter Fourteen

Saturday was bittersweet for Shawn. Not only because the last batch of guests for the next three weeks climbed onto the buckboard for their ride down to their cars, but because a good two-thirds of the ranch hands were also gone by three thirty. All but the skeleton crew was ready to head out for the holidays, and Shawn sort of envied them a place to go to. Families to visit, old traditions to uphold.

But he also liked knowing he had new traditions of his own to begin with Robin. After Shawn accepted the kitchen's weekly supply order from Juno—way smaller than even last week's small order—they took Robin's car into town for cookie supplies. Shawn had been through Garrett multiple times but he hadn't really explored the place much. The general store was charming, and Shawn had put together a shopping list based on their combined recipes so they didn't overbuy or forget anything.

Robin pushed their cart while Shawn tried to navigate the unfamiliar aisles and the entire production was kind of hilarious. And domestic. And right. No one gave them odd looks, and Robin still wore his Clean Slate long-sleeved shirt, so maybe they assumed both men were buying things for the ranch. Either way, Shawn relaxed and enjoyed shopping for cookie supplies with his boyfriend.

"Why are there so many different types of sugar?" Robin asked. "Light and dark brown?"

"Dark brown sugar has a stronger molasses flavor than light," Shawn replied. "And this is nothing compared to all the varieties a chain grocery store carries. They have tons of different all-natural sweeteners and syrups made from different plants and fruit."

Robin picked up a two-pound bag of plain white sugar. "This is all I need for my coffee. Right here."

Shawn laughed. "We need three of those." He grabbed light brown and confectioner's sugar, and added them to the cart, while Robin hefted in the big bags of white. The small store didn't have the best selection of nuts or chocolate chips, but Shawn made do with what they offered. Besides groceries, the store also had a selection of toiletries, some basic clothing items, and a pharmacy in the back, so he imagined shelf space limited the variety of certain things.

Near the single checkout counter, he noticed a small display of Christmas items: greeting cards, premade fruitcake, small figurines, boxed ornaments, and even outdoor string lights. It hit Shawn then that he needed to get Robin a Christmas gift of some sort, but what? Nothing in the store really appealed to him, so he'd have to think it over and look online. Maybe something to do with his woodcarving.

Yes.

The carved knight Robin had presented to Shawn that morning was beautiful, with a detailed mane and tiny little nostrils on the horse's nose. Robin truly made art, and if he ever gave up being a ranch hand, he had a future selling his pieces in a gallery or an artist's collective—one more thing that could take him away from Clean Slate.

Nope, not going there today.

Shawn picked up a set of Christmas-shaped cookie cutters from the display, though, and that completed their list. The total for their grocery haul made Shawn's bank account nervous, but Robin insisted on paying half since Shawn would be doing extra work teaching Robin how to bake. Shawn was not too proud to let Robin slide his debit card, too. Juno brought two sturdy boxes out of the stockroom for all their sugar and flour, so they didn't bust the store's plastic bags, and then he helped them load up Robin's car.

"We appreciate the help," Robin said as he slipped Juno a cash tip. "Merry Christmas."

"Merry Christmas, Robin. Shawn." Juno blushed and ducked back into the store.

Shawn chuckled to himself. Juno was somewhere around his age, maybe a bit younger, and he always seemed nervous when he delivered their groceries to the ranch. Patrice had told him how Arthur used to input their orders up until about a year and a half ago, when he started making big mistakes and underordering staples. After that, the task was assigned to someone else. Shawn imagined jobs were hard to come by in Garrett and Juno hadn't wanted to mess up or get fired.

In the guesthouse kitchen, Shawn had already cleared a spot in the pantry and walk-in for his personal cookie supplies, which he and Robin promptly put away. Except for what they needed to make today's batch of Magic Window cookies. Shawn talked Robin through crushing the LifeSavers and measuring dry ingredients, while

Shawn put together that night's Leftover's Pie casserole for the skeleton crew's dinner, plus a pan of corn bread.

Mom used to make great corn bread, but Patrice had told Shawn her secret ingredient to make it so addictive—a secret Shawn promised to reveal to no one.

The kitchen smelled amazing by the time they had two sheet trays of cutout cookies ready for the oven, but Shawn decided to wait until after dinner to bake them. The small group of hands came through and ate their dinner, and no one noticed the cookies. They'd be ready and waiting in the morning at breakfast. Miles and Reyes didn't show up, so they were probably at Mack's place or in the city with their other friends.

Shawn did miss seeing Miles every day. He'd gotten so used to cooking with and talking to the man at the saloon that it seemed odd not to. They'd have to plan another movie night or something, just the two of them.

Robin was crazy excited when the timer went off, and they pulled the first two sheets of cookies from the oven. Put them on wire racks to cool. Robin reached for one, but Shawn lightly smacked his hand. "They need to cool almost all the way before you can pick them up, or the candy won't set," Shawn said.

"Oh. That makes sense." Robin gazed at them like a kid at Christmastime. "They look really good. Can't wait to try one." He reached around Shawn to dip his finger into the half-empty bowl of cookie dough. Before Shawn could warn him, Robin licked his finger and pulled a face. "That's...not great."

Shawn laughed. "The cookie is closer to a shortbread than a sugar cookie, so it's less sweet. But it works with the melted candy, because that's supersugary. It's all about balancing flavors, even in pastry. Not everything in dessert has to be incredibly sweet."

"Got it."

"Here." He handed Shawn the rolling pin. "Your turn to roll out the dough while these cool."

Robin managed the task without much fuss, and he flicked flour into Shawn's hair to tease him. They got the second batch into the oven, and Shawn tested the other cookies. Peeled one shaped like a church bell off the waxed paper and handed it to Robin. "Here. Enjoy."

"Finally." Robin took a big bite out of both cookie and candy center. Shawn heard an audible crunch, and Robin made an incredibly endearing "yum" sound. "Oh wow." He offered the cookie to Shawn.

Shawn took a smaller bite, and the familiar flavors sent him right back to baking with his mom. Full weekends with the house smelling like sugar, cinnamon, chocolate, and spice. He remembered his mom's bright red apron, her hair up in a messy bun of brown curls, and her laughter—and it didn't make him sad. Not like it used to. Because he was making new, happy Christmas memories with Robin, here in the present, and this was everything.

"Thank you," Shawn said. He kissed Robin, tasting sugar and candy on his lips. "For today. It's been a lot of fun."

"Yeah, it has." Robin wiggled his eyebrows. "Wanna fool around while the cookies bake?"

Shawn didn't want to get too frisky in Patrice's kitchen, and despite there being several couches in the dark guesthouse living room… "We can't. The cookies only take ten minutes and they can burn pretty fast if we forget about them."

Robin slid into his personal space and rested a hand on Shawn's hip, so close Shawn felt his body heat. "So I'm a distraction?"

"A very addictive distraction. Don't worry, we'll be alone in my cabin shortly. First, we need to clean up."

"Always the professional cook." Robin kissed the tip of his nose before reaching for the empty dough bowl to wash.

Their dishes were done by the time the last batch of cookies came out, and Robin used the very real need to let them cool to tempt Shawn into fooling around on one of the couches. And why not? No guests tonight or any night for the next three weeks. There was no reason for any of the ranch hands to come inside, and even if one of them wandered into the kitchen for any reason, the living area was dark and deeply shadowed.

The illicitness amped Shawn up a bit, and he dragged Robin down on top of him, enjoying the way the taller, broader man covered him. It made Shawn feel protected and safe, and he trusted Robin completely. Robin thrust his groin against Shawn's own thickening cock before swooping down for a hard kiss full of tongue and lips, and Shawn gave as good as he got. The more time he spent with Robin, making out and having sex, the braver he got. Easing into the things they shared helped him trust it. To trust Robin. Someone looking for a Christmas fling wouldn't be so patient and attentive to a lover.

Shawn wanted to take a new step tonight. Something new so Robin didn't get bored with just frotting and hand jobs. Something he'd been too nervous to share with Robin until now. Something he'd only ever done once before and not by choice. He kissed his way across

Robin's cheek to his ear and whispered, "I want to suck you tonight."

Robin went perfectly still but didn't tense up. He just stopped moving for several moments before turning his head to meet Shawn's eyes. Robin's own eyes danced with desire and surprise. "Are you sure?"

"Yes. I want to. Please?"

"Of course." Robin rubbed their noses together. "I'd love for you to go down on me, but it's not a deal breaker if you change your mind, or don't like doing it. I'm a patient man, Shawn, you don't ever have to push yourself sexually for me."

I'm a patient man.

"I just don't want you getting bored with the way we have sex," Shawn blurted out. "I'm not ready for anal yet but I do want to try this."

Robin stroked his cheek. "I am not bored with the sex we have. Everything about it is spectacular. There are plenty of people, gay or other, in perfectly healthy relationships that never have penetrative sex. I'd love to go there with you, but I am not going to dump you if you are never comfortable doing anal, I swear. I'm with you for who you are inside, Shawn, not what we do with our bodies."

Those perfectly chosen words strengthened Shawn's decision to try this new thing and go down on Robin. He hadn't enjoyed it the first time, because it hadn't been his choice. Not exactly. It had taken him a lot of years to truly accept that making a decision under the coercion of someone with power over him wasn't making a decision at all. Some days he still struggled with it, though.

Not today.

Today he was going down on his boyfriend because he wanted to. A lot.

Shawn didn't go right to it, though. They kissed more and rutted their hard dicks together through their jeans, not enough to get off but definitely enough to feel it. He loved this sort of lazy friction the most, because it wasn't them speeding to a quick climax. They were building something between them, and the eventual release was always worth the wait.

He tugged Robin up into a sitting position, Robin's feet on the floor. Shawn straddled his lap, enjoying the way he fit perfectly against his boyfriend, their groins once again pressed together. Kissing Robin this way was fun, too, because Shawn could touch his hair and neck and shoulders better. He got rid of their shirts because that fabric was in the way, and Shawn licked Robin's nipples, loving the way Robin gasped and thrust his cock against Shawn's.

"Bite them," Robin said. "Not too hard."

Shawn did, pinching one taut nub with his teeth, and Robin moaned, so Shawn did the other one. Then he slid off Robin's lap and knelt between his spread legs. The submissive position sent a gurgle of anxiety through Shawn's stomach but he ignored it. He wanted to do this. He wasn't here because someone older with power over him told him to be; he was here for Robin and he was here for himself.

My boyfriend. My choice. My gift to give.

He unbuckled Robin's belt, and Robin lifted his hips, helping Shawn get his jeans and boxers down to midthigh, baring his cock, which Shawn immediately wrapped his left hand around. He stroked Robin a few times, enjoying the sight of the small drop of clear fluid that pooled at the slit. Proof of his boyfriend's arousal. Curious, Shawn leaned over and licked that bit of fluid. Bitter but not unpleasant, and with it came a stronger flavor of Robin himself.

A flavor he enjoyed, and Shawn wanted to know more. He wrapped his lips around the head of Robin's dick to get more of that addictive flavor, the scent of Robin's bare skin filling his nose. The slide of flesh over Shawn's tongue was odd but good, and he licked at the underside of the glans. Robin moaned a bit too loudly and slapped a hand over his own mouth. Shawn chuckled around his mouthful of cock, and Robin stifled another loud noise.

"Feels so good, baby," Robin said. "Fuck, yeah."

Pleased with himself for igniting such reactions from Robin, Shawn took a bit more into his mouth. Robin's dick was heavy and warm on his tongue, not demanding or rough. Robin watched him with a mixture of arousal and protectiveness in his eyes. Eyes that saw Shawn as a real, sexual being and not a pawn to manipulate. It fueled his desire to continue pleasing his boyfriend.

Shawn pulled back to lick the slit before going down again. Not far, because he didn't want to ping his gag reflex and choke himself, so he used his hand to stroke what his mouth couldn't reach. Robin squeezed his shoulders in a gentle, grounding touch that didn't demand or direct. The blow job was unpracticed and a little messy, and it was…kind of perfect. No anxiety, no fear. Robin's touches were soft and careful, and it meant the world to Shawn. It also fueled his burning need to bring his boyfriend to orgasm.

He rolled Robin's sac with his right hand and sucked harder on just the glans, until Robin said, "Fuck, gonna come." Shawn pulled back, both hands still working Robin's body, and he watched as Robin painted his own chest and thighs with his release. Robin gasped and twitched, his own hands gripping the couch cushions hard in a white-knuckled grip.

I did that.

Shawn couldn't hold back a smug grin. "Sit tight, I'll go get a rag so you don't get come on Patrice's couch."

Robin pouted. "Kiss me first?"

Unable to resist that adorable pout, Shawn stood and leaned over, hands braced on the back of the couch. Robin attacked his mouth, fingers combing through Shawn's hair as Robin kissed him until Shawn's back ached from the position. He fetched Robin a damp washcloth and a dry towel so Robin could clean himself up.

Once Robin's tackle was tucked away and his jeans done up, Robin yanked Shawn back down onto his lap. "Please tell me I get to blow you back," Robin said. "Please?"

"Oh, you absolutely are."

And he did. While Shawn wasn't quite ready to swallow Robin's load yet—they'd had the test status conversation a few days ago—Robin eagerly took everything Shawn gave him when he found his own release. They spent a few minutes cuddling on the couch, existing in the lovely memory they'd created.

Until Robin started chuckling. "Goddamn, I'll never be able to walk into the guesthouse and see this couch without thinking of you."

Shawn laughed and kissed Robin's neck. "Same. No regrets, though."

"Me, either."

"You ready to put the cookies away and head back

to my cabin? Maybe we can find a Christmas movie to stream."

"Sounds like a perfect plan."

They did exactly that. Robin found an old Steve Martin comedy called *Mixed Nuts* that Shawn had never heard of, and it had him laughing so hard he cried and his stomach ached. "How am I just learning about this guy now?" Shawn asked. "He's hilarious."

"Steve Martin?" Robin feigned shock as he sat up on the bed where they'd been lounging against the pillows. "Come on, you aren't that young and sheltered, are you?"

"I mean, I probably saw a few of his movies when I was a kid, because Mom watched them, I guess, but I never paid attention before. We are definitely tracking down more Steve Martin movies."

"We can do that. He has a pretty eclectic backlist depending on what kind of story you prefer. *Three Amigos* is a sort of satire about old silent Westerns, and *Father of the Bride* is a middle-aged man realizing his little girl has grown up and is getting married. Or you've got megaclassics like *Dirty Rotten Scoundrels* and *Planes, Trains and Automobiles.* So many great movies."

Shawn grinned up at Robin, content to stay relaxed against his pillows. "Sounds like you're a fan."

"He was a big part of my '90s. Wait." Robin's eyebrows knitted together. "How old are you, anyway?"

"Twenty-four. Why? How old are you?"

"Thirty-two."

Shawn's lips parted, a little stunned at the age difference. Not that eight years was that huge, but it was more than he'd expected somehow. And yet, not really, given the world-weary air Robin had about him some days. Not often but, once in a while, his history showed through in the crinkling at the corners of his eyes, or the way he talked about his life with Xander.

Beck had been in his thirties, too.

Nope, Shawn wasn't going there. This thing he was creating with Robin was completely different in every single way from what happened with Beck—except for them both being dudes, obviously. Robin gave generously, when Beck had only taken. Robin made Shawn feel safe, when Beck had pushed his anxiety to nuclear levels.

"Didn't realize I was dating someone so close to retirement," Shawn teased, mostly to take his mind off the bad things in his past.

Robin growled softly before pouncing.

The Magic Window cookies were a big hit at breakfast, and Robin proudly took half credit for concocting the tasty treats. When he and Shawn admitted their plan of baking new cookie varieties until Christmas Day, the skeleton crew got even more excited—especially Hugo, who was quiet around Robin but seemed to have befriended Shawn in recent weeks. Hugo even asked if Shawn needed any help baking.

Shawn politely turned him down—this was his and Robin's thing, after all, and Robin cheered internally at it remaining theirs—and somehow managed to redirect the question into Shawn volunteering to teach Hugo chess.

Hugo eagerly accepted the offer.

Robin pretended to grump over that, not happy with sharing his Shawn-time with another guy, but they did have more hours in a day now that the ranch was closed to guests. And Shawn was now preparing meals for less than ten people a day. Leftovers were easier to stretch, especially the lunchtime salads and coleslaw, according to Patrice.

It also occurred to Robin that Shawn was one of the few people on the ranch close to Hugo's age. The rest of the hands were Robin's age or older, so he imagined Hugo was a bit starved for friends his own age.

After breakfast, Robin had a meeting he wasn't exactly dreading, but he also wasn't completely excited about. Mack had invited him up to the house for a rodeo planning meeting with himself, Wes, Avery...and Levi via Skype. Since Colt and Avery hadn't been at breakfast in the kitchen, they'd probably stayed over at Mack and Wes's house last night. Robin kissed Shawn lightly on the mouth before heading to the ATV shed.

On the drive up to the house, Robin thought back to last night's illicit doings in the guesthouse living area, and he smiled at the scenery over the blow job. He had genuinely not been expecting it, and it had shown Robin proof of something he'd heard from others but hadn't actually experienced himself: technique meant nothing when genuine attraction was involved. Maybe Shawn wasn't great, technically, at giving head, but who the fuck cared when Robin got off so hard he'd wanted to cry?

The entire encounter had been perfect. Because it was them. And Robin loved that Shawn was willing to take new steps and try new things. To keep exploring his sexuality at his own pace, trusting Robin to prop him up if he stumbled and help him up if he fell. To never laugh or make fun of Shawn's lack of experience. He was also grateful Shawn hadn't been annoyed at Robin for making absolutely sure Shawn wanted to blow him, and that he hadn't found Robin's questions overbearing.

Robin believed Shawn knew his own mind, but in that moment Robin had needed the reassurance.

As much as part of Robin longed to be bent over and fucked again, he genuinely loved the relationship he was building with Shawn. All couples—gay, straight, lesbian, whoever—navigated sex in their own unique ways. Ways that brought them together as partners, creating a pleasurable experience for them both. Robin and Shawn were here, happy, and building this with each other.

There was no reason to rush anything.

Wes opened the door before Robin could knock, likely tipped off by the ATV's engine. "Hey, good morning," Wes said with a cheerful grin.

"Morning." Robin shucked the coat he'd worn to protect himself from the chilly December air during the drive. Wes hung it in the closet by the loft stairs. More greetings were shouted from the dining table, where Colt, Avery, and Mack were already seated, facing a mounted tablet.

"So how's the ranch feel with no guests and half the hands gone?" Wes asked as he led Robin to the table.

"Kind of like a ghost town," Robin quipped.

Wes laughed.

"Perfect timing," Mack said, indicating Robin join them on their side of the table. "We were just about to call Levi."

Robin's stomach squirmed, and he eased onto the bench on Mack's left. "Okay. Great."

"We've been chatting a bit on the phone this past week," Avery added with a familiar eagerness. The guy got excited over anything historical, but especially the Old West. "It sounds as if Lucky's Rodeo is an amazing show. I watched some of the clips on the website."

Robin frowned, surprised Levi had talked about Lucky's. But why wouldn't he? That's where Robin and Levi had learned everything they knew about roping, riding, and tricks. It had been Levi's entire life experience until three years ago. "It was an amazing show," Robin replied.

"Have you seen it in person?"

For a split second, Robin thought he'd lost his mind. He'd told these guys he had experience doing rodeo shows…but not that Robin had been part of Lucky's. And it sounded like Levi hadn't let that tidbit slip, either. Not wanting to drag his personal past into this planning session, Robin hedged his answer. "Yeah, a few times. It's how I met and got to know Levi."

"Excellent." Avery grinned and flipped to a clean sheet of paper on the yellow legal pad he'd been keeping his notes on. "Then let's get started."

Mack nodded and placed the call.

Robin bit the inside of his cheek to keep his expression as schooled as possible. The screen flashed, and then Levi Peletier's smiling face filled the tablet's screen. "Mornin', all," Levi said, his gaze shifting in such a way that Robin was positive Levi was staring directly at him. "Hey, Robin. Long time no see."

"Yeah." Robin wanted to reach out and touch his friend's face, to show this wasn't his imagination—which was stupid, because tablet and pixels. "You look great."

"You, too." Levi was thinner in his face than Robin remembered, his dark hair short and trimmed, instead of the shaggier style he'd once sported. But he otherwise still looked like himself. And like Xander. The brothers

had always had a strong family resemblance and time
hadn't changed that.

"I'm real grateful to Robin for putting us in touch,"
Mack said to Levi. "You've been a terrific asset so far,
and I'm excited to do more work on our plans today."

"I'm grateful, too. It was real nice hearing from Robin
again. Talkin' to someone who remembers the lifestyle.
Traveling ten months out of the year ain't a life all folks
can handle. But I was, well, lucky that my family went
with me everywhere I went."

"Sounds like the ideal job. My family's here on this
land and I can't imagine being anywhere else."

Levi's smile went soft. Almost wistful. "I can hear
it in your voice whenever you talk about the ranch and
ghost town. It's why I'm more than happy to help you
pull this show together." His gaze flickered to Robin
and seemed to silently ask if Robin had reached out to
Doug yet, and why not?

Pride, that's why, Robin tried to put into his own expression.

"So let's talk horses," Levi said.

Robin and Mack both talked a bit about Tude and
Zodiac, and their belief both horses could be trained
for some of the roping tricks. Robin was pretty sure he
could train Tude for a running mount, and maybe even
to be ridden by a standing rider. Now that the ranch was
closed, he'd have more time to work with the horses—
especially with Shawn's new Hugo hobby.

*Don't be jealous, we both need friends and activities
to do apart from each other.*

Colt opened a laptop and chat window, and Levi sent
them links to several online video demonstrations that
showed different tricks step-by-step. "You can learn a

lot from tutorials," Levi said, "but most folk learn these things best by doing. My dad is one of the best teachers I've ever known. He's had offers from more than one place to teach there if he ever retires from the life."

"You think he ever will?" Avery asked.

"Doubt it. He doesn't perform as much now as he used to because he dislocated his left shoulder last year."

Robin's hands jolted in his lap. Doug had been injured? How come Levi hadn't mentioned it before?

"Sorry to hear that," Mack said. "Is he on the mend?"

"Thank you, and yes, he's healed but doesn't have the same dexterity or strength in that shoulder as before. But Lucky's is his family, and he'll tour until the end of his days." Levi's lips twitched.

Robin remembered countless times Doug had spoken about touring until "the end of my days," and wanting his ashes spread along the side of the road on the way to the rodeo's next destination.

"I imagine his expertise is in high demand," Avery said with a thoughtful expression.

"He is." Levi glanced at Robin again, his meaning very clear. They both knew Doug would bring the entire rodeo to Garrett for a free show if Robin reached out and asked. But Robin couldn't do it. Plus, he had no idea how Mack would react to that kind of charity—especially with Mack wanting to make the show a regular thing at the ghost town. They needed to learn the tricks.

They can more easily learn from professionals than from me.

No, good old Butler pride kept Robin's mouth firmly shut on the topic of his former father-in-law.

Their group brainstormed for another hour or so before Levi had to go. Once he'd signed off, Robin excused himself to the front porch for a few puffs on his vape. He used it less and less, but kept it in his pocket out of habit. The vapor did nothing to soothe his ruffled feathers but it was a good prop.

The screen door squealed. "You okay?" Mack asked.

Robin put his vape down on the porch railing and pushed both hands into his jeans pocket. "I guess," he told the front yard.

Mack's heavy steps approached until the man stood beside him, looking out at the yard and trees beyond. "I'm gonna guess there's some hidden history between you and Levi?"

"Oh yeah."

"He an ex?"

"No, nothing like that." Robin had admitted the truth of his past to Shawn weeks ago; he could tell his friend, too. "I used to work with Levi in the rodeo. Lucky's. We both quit about the same time three years ago." He straightened his spine and turned to face Mack, whose expression was open and calm. "We quit when Levi's brother, Xander, died. We all worked for the rodeo and—" he gulped hard for air "—Xander was my husband."

Mack's bushy eyebrows rose into twin arches. "Damn, I'm so sorry to hear that, Robin. I had no idea you'd been married."

"No one does. Well, Arthur, Judson, and Shawn know, but I never wanted to talk about it. Talking about Xander used to be too damned painful. And staying on at the rodeo, being around Levi and Doug and all the reminders of Xander was too hard. I lost touch with Levi for a while, because he looks so much like Xander did, and we both hit rock bottom in our own ways. Arthur saved my life when he brought me here."

Mack's dark eyes were liquid and sad. "This ranch has saved a lot of souls from runs of bad luck, myself included. I never expected to fall in love again after Geoff was killed, but I did."

Robin nodded. "I never expected Shawn. That first day we met in the corral? I was kind of an asshole to him because at first, he reminded me so much of Xander. But then I got to know Shawn, and he's this incredibly strong, brave, generous guy. Guess it's the magic of the ranch. To help lost, wounded souls find each other and build each other up again."

"Guess so. So I assume this rodeo stuff is stirring up your past in a not-great way, huh?"

"It hasn't been easy, but remembering Xander doesn't hurt like it once did. And it got me back in real contact with Levi again, and I am forever grateful for that. We were terrific friends once, and I'd like to be again."

"Glad to hear it. When you think of someone like a brother, it hurts like hell when you lose them." Mack's gaze went distant, likely remembering the huge fight he'd had with Colt last year. It had taken months for the pair to fix their broken friendship, but they had. "Are you sure you still wanna help with this rodeo? I'd understand if it's too hard."

"I'm sure. Honest, Mack, I want to do this. The more we talk about it, the more I remember why I loved that life so much. Seeing the country, the adrenaline rush of doing a dangerous stunt, and the thrill of the applause when I succeeded."

"Think it's a life you'll ever go back to?"

"Dunno. Doing that kind of stunt work is a lot easier

in the body of twenty-two-year-old than a thirty-two-year-old."

Mack chuckled. "I hear that. And I look forward to working with you on this project, Robin."

"Thanks. So do I."

"You staying up for lunch?"

"I can't, I promised Shawn I'd be back to eat with him."

"Good man. You treat Shawn right, you hear me? He's a good friend of Miles's and I'd hate to have to sic Reyes on you for any reason."

Robin grinned. "I hear you. Reyes has a scary temper I don't ever want to see aimed in my direction. Hey, where are Reyes and Miles? They aren't here and I didn't see them at breakfast."

"Went into San Francisco for a few days away. Now that we're shut down, you should think about maybe taking your guy away for brief vacation."

I'm trying to, but Shawn doesn't want to go see his grandparents.

"I'll keep that in mind," Robin said instead. Besides, Shawn's reasons were personal and not Robin's to spread around.

After Robin collected his coat and said his goodbyes, he took the ATV the long way back, down the ghost town road to the main ranch road, instead of through the woods. Not for any real reason other than to enjoy the cool air and sunshine, and to breathe in the magic that was Clean Slate Ranch.

Chapter Fifteen

The first week with no guests flew by quickly for Shawn, and not because he was busy cooking for a bunch of people. With Patrice's collarbone mending—but her arm still in a sling for a bit longer—she was lending herself to more of the prep, and with Shawn so used to the full, forty-mouths recipe batches, they had leftovers frequently enough he rarely had to worry about slicing lunch meat. The hands helped themselves to the fridge and nuked their own plates of food.

Shawn's free time was what helped speed the week along. He was able to read more frequently during the day, and he'd managed a trip to Daggett Library to swap out his old titles, which were a week overdue. The librarian teased him about having left the state with the books, and Shawn just said his life had gotten incredibly busy. And he promised to return these books on time—one of which was the biography of a famous woodcarver.

He also spent about two hours a day tutoring Hugo in chess, baked cookies with Robin, and hung out with Miles, usually riding the trails. Shawn had asked Robin once if he wanted to go horseback riding with Shawn, but Robin had abruptly changed the subject.

Whatever. Miles loved riding, and he was teaching

Shawn how to tack his own horse—he definitely liked
Valentine, but he also had a fondness for Duchess, too—
and they were working up to galloping. Slowly. Miles
loved showing off his skill with horses, and Shawn was
a little surprised Miles wasn't participating in the rodeo
in some way. But dressage stuff was different than rodeo
stuff, he guessed? Miles also wasn't an exhibitionist or
a performer.

He kept his head down and out of the spotlight like
Shawn.

Robin spent a chunk of his free daytime hours working with Mack, Colt, and some of the horses. Planning
where on the ghost town property to host the various
events, deciding what needed to be built—which was
where Colt, their handyman, came in. Robin was a little down sometimes when he got back from the site, as
if mired by the memories of his old rodeo life. A life
Shawn was scared Robin might be tempted back into,
but Shawn had quickly learned that a blow job perked
his boyfriend right back up. They watched movies every
night, took walks on the trails, and sometimes did nothing more exciting than sit on the porch bundled up in
sweatshirts and stare up at the stars.

It was the kind of peaceful, domestic life Shawn had
never imagined for himself, and he was terrified of losing it. So he concentrated on existing in every moment.
Enjoying every laugh and touch and fun new memory.
While sex hadn't progressed beyond Shawn fingering
Robin during blow jobs, Robin never showed any frustration with Shawn's slow pace—as if every single touch
and kiss was a precious gift he could lose at any moment.

On the twenty-first, they drove into Daggett to visit
a discount store for decorations. Robin put up a small

Christmas tree in the sitting area of Shawn's cabin, while Shawn festooned the walls and bookshelf with shiny garland. They'd chosen classic red, green, and white ball ornaments for the tree, and Shawn had too much fun draping the tree in that silver, icicle stuff—and draping Robin's hair with it.

That move got Shawn tickled to the floor until he was howling with laughter. Then they lounged on the rug together, taking in their tree. Shawn's first Christmas tree in more than five years.

The next evening, Arthur, Patrice, and Judson cooked an early Christmas dinner for the ranch hands at the main house, and it was a crowded affair. Seven staff, plus Mack, Wes, Colt, Avery, and Miles. They hosted it a few days early, because the next day, Colt and Avery were flying to Texas to spend a few days with the Woods clan. And Reyes and Miles were leaving on a two-night camping trip out at the pond, and would be back late Christmas Day.

Shawn didn't see the appeal of waking up on Christmas in a tent, on the hard ground, but camping was their thing, not his.

On Sunday, as the two couples fled the ranch, Robin seemed to…shrink? Shawn couldn't find the right word but his mood definitely shifted downward. Was it because his friends were leaving for a few days? Or was it old memories of Xander kicking back up, thanks to Robin's work on the rodeo exhibit? Shawn tried asking a few times but Robin just flashed him a flirty smile and said he was fine.

Shawn wasn't so sure, so he kept his boyfriend as distracted as possible with sex. He also kept an eye on his hiding place so Robin didn't peek at his two wrapped gifts. Earlier the previous week, his online orders had come in—both of his planned Christmas gifts for Robin. The first gift was a highly rated seventeen-piece wood-carving tool kit, complete with waterproof case and two whetstones for sharpening, plus sandpaper in different grits. And he'd ordered it after double-checking with Ernie that Robin only ever seemed to use a basic wood-cutting knife on his projects.

The other gift—and he hated thinking of it as a gift, but Shawn couldn't think of a better day than Christmas to take this step with Robin—was lube and condoms. Shawn was ready to be inside Robin. To finally share this new-to-him thing with Robin.

On Christmas Eve morning, after baking their last batch of cookies—Robin had wanted to try his hand at Oatmeal Scotchies—they cleaned up the guesthouse kitchen and headed for cabin row. Hugo had invited them to his cabin to watch Christmas movies for a few hours, along with Quentin and Slater, and the marathon was supposed to begin at eleven.

Just as they reached the part of the path that started bending behind the main house, the sound of a car engine stole their attention to the main ranch road. They stopped walking, both of them curious who was here. The ranch probably didn't get many unexpected visitors. Unless Judson or Patrice had invited a friend to spend the holidays.

Shawn bet Patrice missed her son like crazy around the holidays.

An unfamiliar blue sedan trundled up the road toward the house and the wide parking area in front of it, where it pulled to a slow circle. The engine shut off, and the driver's door opened. Robin let go of Shawn's hand and took a step forward. A man of average height and build with short brown hair stepped out of the car and straightened.

"Oh fuck," Robin whispered.

Shawn looked at Robin's pale face and slack jaw, stunned by the reaction. Equally stunned when Robin bolted forward and swept the stranger up into a bear hug, lifting him right off the ground. Both men were laughing and hugging, and Shawn had never felt more confused and out of place in his entire life. It couldn't be one of Robin's long-lost siblings, could it?

Robin put the guy down, and Shawn got a better look at his face. Familiar enough in shape and angles and hair color that it hit him right in the gut: Levi. Robin had admitted to first keeping his distance from Shawn because of his resemblance to Xander, and the man holding Robin by the forearms couldn't be anyone except Xander's brother, Levi.

"Jesus, you look amazing," Robin said. "So fucking healthy. Wow."

"Thank you," Levi replied. "So do you. This ranch definitely agrees with you."

Shawn wanted to walk away and give the pair their space, but he didn't like the wide-eyed way Levi was looking at Robin. Something ugly and dark reared up inside Shawn, and he let it carry him twenty feet to the car. And to his boyfriend.

Robin noticed Shawn immediately, and he let go of Levi. He did not, however, reach for Shawn. "Hey, sorry," Robin said, "I didn't mean to run off like that. I'm just in a little bit of shock here."

"I bet," Shawn replied. "I'm Shawn Matthews."

"Levi Peletier," Levi said. He shook Shawn's hand

in a firm, work-calloused grip. "You must work here at the ranch with Robin."

Shawn's entire body went rigid. Robin hadn't told Levi about him? Uncertain how to reply to that—and a tiny bit hurt—he looked at Robin for guidance.

"Shawn works in the guesthouse kitchen right now, but he usually cooks up at the ghost town when it's open," Robin said to Levi. He reached out and purposefully took Shawn's hand. "And he's my boyfriend."

Hope bloomed in Shawn's chest at Robin's firm declaration, chasing that ugly thing away.

"Oh." Levi's friendly smile dimmed. "I mean… congrats? You guys look happy."

Since defensiveness and jealousy were not attractive traits, Shawn reined his in hard. "We are, thank you. Robin is amazing."

"Aw, shucks." Robin planted a wet kiss on his cheek. "You make it easy, hot stuff. Levi, what are you doing here?"

"Came for Christmas," Levi replied, his smile tentative now. "We sort of talked about seeing each other again, and I figured I'd just get back up on the horse, so to speak. Come see you."

Robin shivered; Shawn clutched his hand tighter, unsure what the physical reaction meant. "It's just so unexpected," Robin said. "I mean, I guess you can stay in my cabin since my roommate's off the land until January. I usually sleep over with Shawn, anyway."

"Cabin? I'm sorry, I suppose I didn't rightly think this through. Guess I thought you had a place of your own." Levi gazed around the property. "It's lovely land."

"I'll take you out on a trail ride, show you around. It's beautiful here."

Shawn resisted the urge to bristle. Robin wanted to take Levi out on a ride, but not him? What the hell?

Robin pointed. "The main house there is partly office and canteen, and the owner, Arthur, lives in it with his ranch foreman, Judson, and the guests' den mother, Patrice. That big house is the guesthouse, but we don't have any guests for a while, and Shawn's been the guesthouse cook for the past six weeks, while Patrice heals from a broken collarbone. All the hands live back yonder." He jacked his thumb at cabin row. "Mostly two-man cabins, but Shawn lucked into living alone. Kind of."

The flirty smile Robin tossed Shawn's way eased his discomfort with this situation. A little. He'd been seriously looking forward to spending Christmas with Robin, and Levi had just crashed his perfectly planned party. But Robin and Levi had a long history Shawn couldn't deny, and the excited smiles they shared tempered Shawn's disappointment.

"Most of the ranch hands are away for the holiday," Shawn offered. "Including Robin's roommate, Ernie. I'm sure Arthur won't mind if you stay for a few days."

"The ranch owner," Levi said.

"Yup."

"I don't want to put anyone out."

Then why did you drive up on us without a phone call first?!

"You aren't," Robin said. "With Christmas tomorrow, the staff is small and people are away with other families. It's no inconvenience at all. Hell, Shawn's used to cooking for upward of forty people a week, so eight instead of seven is nothing."

Shawn didn't like Robin speaking for him, but he also couldn't begrudge Robin his excitement at seeing an old family member again. Much. "It really isn't a bother," Shawn said. "But if you're uncomfortable, there is a motel in town."

Robin frowned at him, but Shawn ignored it. He was only pointing out Levi's options.

"In that case, let me grab my bag," Levi said. "Um, should I park my car somewhere else?"

"Nah, right here's fine," Robin replied. "No one's using the buckboard for a while so you aren't in anyone's way."

"Cool." Levi grabbed a small duffel bag out of the backseat. "Lead the way."

While Robin showed Levi to his and Ernie's cabin, Shawn ducked into Hugo's to beg off the movie marathon. Their afternoon had just taken a huge swing into left field, and Shawn wasn't sure what would happen next. He found Levi admiring Robin's bookshelf of carved figurines, while Robin stood nearby, hands in his jeans pockets and shoulders hunched like he was…shy?

Weird.

"These are so good, bro, I mean it," Levi was saying. He turned his ever-present, cheerful smile to Shawn. "I mean, he used to whittle for fun while we were on the road, but Petey used to complain about stepping on the wood fragments, so Robin didn't do it much. And you got so fuckin' good at it. Wow."

"I needed something to do at night when I couldn't sleep," Robin said. He shared a long, meaningful look with Levi that made Shawn feel invisible.

"Who was Petey?" Shawn asked.

"He shared the RV with me, Levi, and Xander when we traveled. And don't think I didn't step on his clipped toenails more than once because he missed the trash can."

"He was incredibly farsighted and had a hard time focusing up close," Levi said with a chuckle. "But he was a good guy, great around the horses."

"Was he a trick rider?" Shawn asked.

"Yup, that man was an expert with roping, especially on horseback. Dad said he moved on from the show about two years ago. Finally found a woman who'd marry him, and they have a newborn."

"Good for Petey," Robin said in a wistful voice.

Does Robin want kids? I sure as hell don't, but... what if?

They'd never talked about that before.

"So how about I give you the dime tour of the ranch?" Robin said to Levi. "You can see some of our horses, meet the two I've been working with for Mack's show."

"Sounds great," Levi replied.

To Shawn, Robin said, "You don't have to come if you'd rather go to that movie marathon. It's not like you don't know the property by heart."

Shawn shoved against another flash of hurt at what felt like a dismissal, rather than an actual choice in his afternoon activity. Levi had come all this way to hang out with Robin, not Robin and his boyfriend, and the pair probably had things to talk about. Private things. "Yeah, okay. When you're done the tour, you guys should stop by. Meet some of the guys."

"Will do." Robin kissed Shawn lightly on the mouth. "See you soon."

"Yeah."

He watched the pair leave the cabin with an odd pit in his stomach, frustrated by being so easily replaced by another man. A man with whom Robin shared a lot of history and hadn't seen in three years. They'd both loved and lost Xander, though, and Shawn could be an adult about this. Give Robin the space he obviously needed to get to know Levi again, because at the end of the day, Robin would go to sleep in Shawn's bed, not Levi's.

Right?

Robin's mind was still reeling with the same shock he'd first felt when Levi got out of his rental car and Robin realized who he was, and the whole thing had left him slightly dizzy and drunk with joy. More joy than he'd imagined possible when he saw Levi again after all these years. When Levi first floated the idea of meeting up again, Robin hadn't been sure he could handle it.

Now?

Best Christmas present ever.

In some ways, it felt as if no time had passed at all. Robin looked at Levi and saw his former best friend and brother-in-law, and all the happy memories flooded back. The rodeo shows, the practice sessions, the jokes and laughter and shared meals. Remembering didn't hurt like he'd expected it to.

Probably because I have Shawn and am moving on.

Looking at Levi also reminded Robin of the huge loss they'd suffered exactly three years ago tomorrow. It felt right that Levi was here to share that anniversary, especially with Robin finally settled and happy. Levi's ring finger was empty, and he hadn't mentioned meeting anyone in their infrequent emails, so on the walk from cabin row to the barn, Robin started fishing.

"So did you have to beg anyone back home for permission to skip Christmas there?" Robin asked.

Levi snorted laughter. "Nah, I have a neighbor checking on my three cats, so as long as they're fed and watered, they won't attack when I go home."

"Three cats? You really have retired from traveling the country."

"Technically, I'm not. I bought a tiny house last year, plus a pickup to haul it around with. Right now I'm in an RV park in Colorado."

Robin paused at the mouth of the barn. "You have three cats in a tiny home? Don't tell me you had it customized with a composting litter box."

Levi laughed. "No, I did not. One of the things I picked up on in recovery was the importance of relationships and the value of the things and people in my life. Found all three cats in a cardboard box on the side of the road one day, after I'd been sober about six months. Felt like a sign they were meant to be mine, so I honor that gift by keeping their box clean and feeding them the best food."

"Huh." This new, more spiritual side of Levi fought a bit with the wild child Robin remembered from their rodeo days. They'd all been wilder back then, unbroken by the burden of loss and grief. "What are their names?"

"Ginger, Sporty, and Baby."

Robin groaned. "You named your cats after Spice Girls?"

"Sure. Ginger is a ginger kitty, so it fit perfectly. The other two just…came to me after I had them for a few days. Sporty loves to climb on things, and Baby loves to cuddle. So you obviously don't have any pets."

"I've got twenty-five of the best pets in the world right here." Robin swept his hand at the barn entrance. "Let's go meet 'em."

No one else was in the barn at the moment but that could easily change. All the horses were regularly exercised by the skeleton staff, so everyone got out once a day, not just the horses favored by hands who wanted to go riding. Robin showed off Apple Jax first, since she was his favorite, and then introduced Levi to Tude and Zodiac. Blizzard seemed annoyed at being ignored, so Robin petted her long forehead and ran his fingers through her mane.

"You feel like a ride?" Robin asked.

Levi smoothed his hand down Zodiac's snout. "I haven't been on a horse in three years."

"Really?" His heart hurt for the grief in Levi's voice, and he squeezed his shoulder. "Sorry, bro."

Levi shrugged. "Can't seem to bring myself to do it, but I'm real glad you could. Workin' with horses was always your dream, and you're still livin' it."

"Almost didn't live it. I was truly lucky to end up here when I did." Robin didn't think it through before the words popped out of his mouth. "I bet Arthur wouldn't mind if you parked that tiny home on his land and stayed awhile."

"I don't know, Colorado is beautiful."

That wasn't a no, and Robin was getting attached to the idea of Levi moving closer. Of them being brothers again. Of Levi meeting all the other hands and their significant others, and being part of the Clean Slate family.

"Maybe before I think about moving to a dude ranch," Levi said with a silly grin, "I should get my scaredy-cat ass back up on a horse first."

Since Tude was sometimes picky about the adults who rode her, they saddled up Zodiac for Levi to ride and Tude for Robin. Levi saddled her like the pro he used to be, and they led their horses out the north-facing side door. Robin waited, watching Levi as he gripped the pommel and settled one sneakered foot in the stirrup. Levi closed his eyes and inhaled a deep breath that he released slowly. This was a huge step for the man, and Robin was grateful to witness it. Levi had loved riding once and he'd been damned good at it. Hopefully, he'd learn to love it again instead of fear it.

Levi stood there for so long Robin started doubting he'd do it—then Levi bounced on his right foot, gripped the straps, and hauled himself up without a single struggle or hesitation. "Thank you, lady," he said as he stroked Zodiac's neck. "Thank you for allowing me to ride you."

Robin quirked an eyebrow at the Zen-like words and mounted Tude. He led the way to the tree line and toward the path that led up to the ghost town. They'd created it for the buckboard, so it was wide enough that they could ride side by side and Robin paid attention to his friend's mood. Levi was a little tense but he relaxed the longer they rode, taking in the scenery all around them, soaking in the peaceful quiet. The less-dense, hillier trails the tourists rode on were to the east, and he'd probably lead them home that way.

"This is somethin' we rarely got to do," Levi said after long minutes of silence. "Leisurely rides through the woods or mountains. We were always boltin' from one venue to the next. Didn't really slow down enough to enjoy the world around us."

"I hear that. I've said it before but there's something magical about this land. It gave me what I needed to turn my life around. I'm grateful Mack and Arthur are of the same mind about preserving the land and the creatures who live here."

"Creatures like what?"

"All kinds, but don't worry. Never had a problem with a coyote or mountain lion in all the time the ranch has been open. Might see some tracks up at the ghost town site, though, since it's been shut down since Thanksgiving."

"Is that where we're headed?"

"Yeah, thought I'd show it off. I don't have any specific chores this afternoon other than helping feed the horses tonight, so we can ride for a few hours." Robin winked at his friend. "Or until your unpracticed ass gets too sore."

The old Levi would have flipped him off, but the new Levi just smiled. Robin caught a glimpse of Xander in that familiar Peletier smile. He still missed Xander. Part of him would always miss Xander, and that was okay. Grief was a process, and Robin was forever grateful to continue healing with Levi.

"Thank you," Robin said. He pulled Tude to a stop, and Levi did the same with Zodiac. "Thank you for surprising me with this visit. I didn't know how much I missed you until you showed up again, and I'm glad we'll be together tomorrow."

"Same." Levi's blue eyes sparkled in the sunshine. "I almost talked myself out of getting on that plane more than once, but we've avoided each other long enough. Xander's gone but we're still family, Robin. I want us to be family again."

"So do I."

"Good. So tell me more about Shawn. How'd you meet?"

Robin pressed his heels into Tude's flanks, and the big horse started plodding up the path. Zodiac followed instinctively. He nattered on about Shawn being hired to do pastry at the Tango Saloon, and having never actually met the guy in person until that November day in the corral. He left out the whole "I thought he was Xander on that damned horse again" bit, but detailed their flirtation, Shawn moving into the cabin next door, and Robin basically romancing him with wood carvings.

"Look at you, turning into a romantic sap," Levi teased. "I think the only thing you ever carved for Xander was that dick and balls he glued to the RV's dashboard just to annoy Petey."

Robin laughed out loud at that memory. "It was right after I did that dumb trick and got trampled by my horse, so I was laid up for a few weeks. Xander started complaining he wasn't getting any dick, so I made him one and gave it to him."

"Yeah, you did." Levi snorted. "Although Xander *was* kind of a sex fiend."

"Don't I know it." Xander had been a firecracker in bed from their very first fuck, and it had been one of the things that had charmed Robin about the guy. Xander was secure in his sexuality, knew what he wanted, and he went for it. He'd also been a firecracker when they fought and then had make-up sex. Everything about his relationship with Xander had been so different from the one he was building with Shawn.

And that made what he had with Shawn even more special.

"Hey," Levi said. "Where'd you go?"

"Thinking about Shawn."

"Why? He a sex fiend, too?"

"No, kind of the opposite, actually. He's also a bit younger than me, but we click in our own unique way."

Levi stroked the side of Zodiac's neck. "How much younger?"

"Eight years."

"Holy hell, bro." Levi held up a hand. "Sorry, not judging. It just surprised me."

"Surprised us too when we realized, but what does it matter? His boss, Miles, is with a guy eleven years older than him, and I've never met a more in-sync couple in my life."

"Miles is the saloon chef?"

"Yeah, he's out camping with his boyfriend right now, but you'll meet him tomorrow night. Mack and Wes invited everyone to their place for a Christmas night dinner."

"You want me to go?"

"Of course. You're family, remember? Besides, I talk so rarely about my past that I'm sure my friends will enjoy the chance to grill you. Didn't even tell anyone about Lucky's until Mack brought up the rodeo idea. And a few people know about Xander, but only that his death was an accident. Not…how it happened."

Familiar grief tightened his chest, and Robin shoved it away. Not today. Today he got to enjoy his time with Levi. There'd be enough time for grief tomorrow.

"Got it," Levi said. "I won't say anything. Promise."

"Thank you."

"Does Shawn know?"

Robin shook his head. "No. Not yet. And he's also superrespectful of limits when it comes to my past, so he doesn't push."

Because he has secrets of his own he hasn't shared, either.

Maybe one day, when they'd been together longer,

they'd both share those final, dark parts of their pasts. He hoped so.

"I guess you get regular updates about folks from your dad," Robin said, changing the subject entirely. "Is Howie still obsessed with pistachios?"

"Absolutely."

Levi launched into a story, and Robin listened with peace in his heart, happy to exist with his brother for the rest of the afternoon.

Chapter Sixteen

Shawn didn't technically need to cook a guesthouse dinner for the ranch staff that night, because the walk-in had plenty of food they could reheat, but he needed the excuse to get out of Hugo's cabin before his temper exploded. He'd honestly been fine over the idea of Robin showing Levi around the ranch, even if he'd felt somewhat dismissed. But when Bert joined their group only ten minutes after Shawn, he'd mentioned seeing Robin leaving the barn with two horses and a stranger.

Robin couldn't be hassled to go riding with Shawn, but he could go out with Levi? What the actual hell was that?

Not even the hilarity of *Home Alone* could lighten Shawn's mood or his sense of betrayal. He made it through half of *Elf* before excusing himself to the guesthouse kitchen, where he concocted a version of Leftovers Pie to warm in the oven. Then he paced the kitchen for a while, upset and unsure what to do about it. He had no worry that Robin was cheating on him with Levi, but damn it, why could Robin ride with Levi and not with Shawn? It made no sense.

And it hurt.

Part of him wanted to escape to his cabin and read,

immerse himself in someone else's story, someone else's problems, but his whirring brain wouldn't be able to focus on the words. Hell, he could barely focus on pacing without tripping over his own ankles.

The hands who eventually came through for dinner were surprised by the Leftovers Pie, and Shawn had enough that there would be leftovers of it for tomorrow, when he wasn't required to cook at all. Besides, tomorrow's dinner was being handled by Mack and Wes, and the few who'd stayed behind on the skeleton crew could forage for breakfast and lunch. Plenty of sandwich fixings and leftover biscuits.

"Are you okay?" Hugo asked as he put his dirty plate in the dishwasher basket. "You've been off all day."

"I don't know." Shawn wasn't sure he was good enough friends with Hugo to discuss today's events, but they had bonded a bit over chess this past week. "An old friend of Robin's showed up today, and they're out riding together."

Hugo's eyebrows went up. "Old friend as in ex?"

"No, nothing like that. They never dated, they just haven't seen each other in a few years." Shawn let out a harsh breath. "I guess I was looking forward to spending Christmas Eve and Day with my boyfriend, and he's been out all afternoon with Levi."

"That sucks. But if they haven't seen each other in a while, I guess they've got catching up to do."

"I guess." Shawn didn't bring up the weird "not riding with Shawn" thing, even though it was the crux of his confusion over today's events. "I'm sure you're right. My relationship with Robin is just so new, and we've all got other friendships and stuff, right?"

"Exactly. And it's starting to get dark so they'll be

back soon." Hugo winked. "Then you can tell his Levi character to buzz off so you can spend quality time with your boyfriend."

Shawn chuckled at the determination in Hugo's voice. "I like that idea. Thank you."

"Not a problem. It's nice having someone closer to my age to talk to, you know? I mean, the guys I work with are great, but they're old."

"Happy to help." And Shawn kind of agreed. He'd have totally been picking Miles's brain about this if the guy wasn't out camping under the stars. "Merry Christmas, okay?"

"Yeah, man, Merry Christmas."

Hugo was the last hand to leave the kitchen, and Miles was about to store the rest of the Leftovers Pie when Robin and Levi walked in, both of them laughing. "Oh, hey, good," Robin said. "Food. I'm starving."

"You're starvin'?" Levi retorted. "The last thing I ate was a stale bagel at the airport at eight o'clock this mornin'."

"Okay, you win." Robin slipped an arm around Shawn's waist and grinned. "Hey, you. Missed you."

Shawn's heart gave a funny lurch. "Yeah?"

"For sure. We got a little carried away riding around the property, and I totally lost track of time, or we'd have been back sooner."

"Riding, huh?"

Robin didn't catch the subtle inflection in Shawn's tone. "Yeah." He kissed Shawn's temple, then went to fetch two plates. One went to Levi, and they both got food. The petty side of Shawn didn't want to hang around while they ate, but he also wanted to be near Robin. So he put the last of the leftovers away and fussed around the kitchen, wiping clean counters and annihilating every last bit of dirt or grime.

The pair didn't speak while they ate, but they'd also been together all afternoon and had probably talked about everything under the sun. Shawn kind of wanted Levi to go away so he could ask Robin about their day, but he couldn't figure out how without sounding like a jealous brat. So he stayed quiet until both men put their dishes in the basket, and Shawn set the wash cycle.

"Thank you for the meal, Shawn," Levi said. "It was very good."

"You're welcome." Shawn shook the hand Levi extended toward him.

"I think I'll head back to my cabin now. Haven't ridden that long in forever, and my butt could use a rest."

Shawn chuckled. "I remember the feeling. I was pretty sore after the first time I ever rode a horse. Merry Christmas, Levi."

"Merry Christmas." Levi clapped Robin on the shoulder as he passed on his way to the door.

Once they were alone, Robin pulled Shawn into his arms and kissed him thoroughly. "Hey, you. You have fun at the movie marathon?"

"I guess."

Robin squeezed his hips, his expression dimming. "What's wrong? I know Levi dropping in like this was a shock, and I'm sorry I got carried away with him today. It was like we'd seen each other yesterday, and even though we've both changed a lot, some things felt exactly the same."

"I get that. He was a big part of your life before Clean Slate. I'm glad you can be his friend again without it reminding you of sad things."

"Yeah. Yeah, we were able to talk about the past without it hurting like it used to. We talked a lot about Xander, and it helped us both. A lot."

"Good."

"But something's still bothering you."

Shawn shrugged, and when he tried to pull away, Robin held him tighter. "It's not that big of a deal."

"If it wasn't a big deal, you'd say it. You can tell me anything, Shawn."

"Fine." Shawn looked Robin right in the eyes. "When Bert said he saw you and Levi riding off together, I got jealous. Really jealous."

"Oh, Shawn, my relationship with Levi is nothing like that. I'd never cheat on you. Not with him or anyone else. When I commit to a person, they're it. You're my guy, no one else."

"I know, and that wasn't it. It's just…the few times I've asked if you want to go riding, you always turn me down. We haven't been out together once as a pair, and I get that you like riding solo so you can listen to the land and be alone, so it upset me when you went riding with Levi less than an hour after he got here."

Robin's eyes softened with a kind of grief Shawn didn't expect. "I see. When I took Levi down to the barn, I wanted him to meet the horses, specifically Tude and Zodiac, since they'll be part of the show. I never intended for us to do more than maybe walk them around the corral, let Levi see how they move, but when Levi admitted he hadn't been on a horse in three years… I had to go out on the trails with him.

"I know you just met Levi, but the man grew up on and around horses. He's one of the best trick riders I've ever seen in my life. Call him a horse whisperer if you want. So to hear he hadn't been around these animals who are in his blood because of Xander's accident? I needed to do something to help."

Shawn's heart broke wide-open for the fresh wave of grief that flashed across Robin's face. God, Shawn was being such a selfish jerk over this, not giving enough consideration to Robin's past with Levi and the pain they still shared over losing Xander. "I'm sorry, Robin. I'm glad you were able to help Levi."

"Me, too. Thank you for understanding."

"You're welcome. He's your family."

"Yeah." Robin sucked in his lower lip, eyebrows furrowing.

"What?" Shawn asked, giving Robin's hip a light pinch.

"Levi's been urging me to reach out to his and Xander's dad. Doug and I had a huge fight after Xander died, and we haven't spoken since. Levi insists Doug has forgiven me and he's ready to move past it, but…"

Shawn took a chance. "You haven't forgiven Doug?"

"I haven't forgiven myself. For my part in Xander's accident." Robin didn't add more, which was frustrating on one level, but Shawn also didn't push. It was Christmas Eve and not the time for sad things. Besides, their relationship was barely a month old. Robin would tell him when he was ready.

I hope.

"Do you think spending time with Levi will help you forgive yourself?" Shawn asked.

"I hope so. Guilt's a heavy thing to carry around. Today definitely helped. And having you in my life helps more than I could ever say." Robin tucked him close and Shawn melted against his warm chest, grateful for the perfectly chosen words. "Thank you for being you."

"I don't know how to be anyone else."

That got a soft chuckle from Robin and broke some of the seriousness of the conversation. "Let's go back to my cabin and enjoy our first Christmas Eve together."

"Yeah."

They did exactly that by spreading a blanket out on the sitting area rug and relaxing together under their tree. Christmas music played softly on Robin's phone. All lights in the cabin were off except the tree's lights, and they cast a beautiful glow around the small space. A peaceful glow that seeped away the last of Shawn's tension over Levi's arrival under its spell.

Eventually, they went to bed and took their time sharing blow jobs. Worshipping each other's body with their lips and tongues and fingers. Shawn gently fucked Robin with two fingers, staying shallow because the lube was still tucked away with the condoms. He probably wouldn't give that to Robin tomorrow, but soon. Tonight, he took Robin apart moment by moment, until Robin shot hard down his throat. Robin sucked on Shawn's cock and balls, and even licked his taint a few times, and he swallowed Shawn's load with a wicked smile.

It was perfect. The most perfect Christmas Eve Shawn had experienced in a long, long time, and he couldn't wait for tomorrow.

Robin woke on Christmas morning a little after five, impressed he'd slept for so long. But he tended to sleep for longer, more restful periods of time when he slept over with Shawn, and it was becoming a habit he really wanted to make more permanent. But asking Shawn if Robin could move in with him was way too soon, too serious, especially when Robin only lived five feet away from his boyfriend.

And it wasn't only having Shawn's slim, warm body nearby that helped Robin sleep. As he slowly began to unwind his own guilt and self-loathing over Xander's death, his mind was less troubled at night. More able to settle and allow deep, dreamless sleep to take him. He was losing whittling time, and that was okay. He'd figure out how to do it more often and in sunlight, rather than moonlight.

Robin eased out of bed, slipped on a pair of sweatpants, and walked to the cabin door. The sun wouldn't rise for another ninety minutes or so, and it was too cold to sit outside for that long without a few layers. But he also wanted to listen to the land for a while so he slipped on his shoes and Shawn's hoodie, and he took his phone outside with him. He walked quietly over to his own porch and sat in his favorite spot. Closed his eyes.

Peace washed over him like a cool, soothing breeze, and Robin sighed. Allowed his muscles to relax, his breathing to even out. This was right. Being here with Shawn. Talking to Levi again. Learning to forgive himself for his past mistakes. Allowing himself to love again. He sat and soaked it all in.

"Robin?" Shawn's tentative voice should have startled him but it didn't.

Robin blinked his eyes open. Shawn stood on the ground by the porch, dressed in jeans and another sweatshirt, hands tucked beneath his armpits. Robin smiled and scooted over on the bench. "Join me."

"Thank you." Shawn sat beside him, and Robin draped a possessive arm across his shoulders, so grateful to have his boyfriend here. Today. To share this moment. "This is the first time I don't have to be up early to cook. I can watch the sunrise with you. If that's okay?"

"I would love nothing more in the world." Especially today; Xander would approve. "We can both watch the sun rise on our first Christmas together."

"The first of many more to come?"

Robin kissed his temple. "That's the plan."

"I like this plan." Shawn snuggled in closer, and Robin soaked in his warmth and scent, loving everything about this.

They sat in silence for a while as the starry night sky lightened from navy to a rich purple, with streaks of red that turned into orange. When the first arch of the rising sun appeared on the slightly misty horizon, Robin opened his camera app and raised his phone. Waited for the perfect moment when the first streak of real sunshine brightened the sky, and he hit the button several times, giving himself a few shots to choose between.

He didn't look right away, though; he sat there with Shawn in his arms and enjoyed the lovely sunrise. The wide-eyed joy on Shawn's face. The way the new morning sun reflected in his brown eyes. The way his lips parted just so…breathtakingly beautiful.

"Thank you," Robin said. "For sharing this with me."

"I wouldn't be anywhere else. Merry Christmas, Robin Butler."

"Merry Christmas, Shawn Matthews."

They kissed under the steady warmth of the rising sun for a long while before parting. They scrolled through the sunrise shots Robin had taken and chose their favorite together. Robin added the caption: *Sun rose on a new chapter in my life today, and I am forever thankful to be here.*

Shawn smiled and nodded his approval before Robin uploaded it.

His cabin door swung open, and Levi stepped out dressed in sneakers and running gear. He didn't seem surprised to see them on the porch, and his sunny grin made Robin smile right back. "Hey, Merry Christmas," Levi said.

They both returned the salutation.

"Going running?" Robin asked, despite it being some-what obvious.

"Yep, I try to run every mornin'. It's gets my engines going."

"Better you than me. The hiking trails are good for that. They start on the other side of the main house. You'll see the signs."

"Awesome, thanks. I'll see you both later?"

"Sure, we'll be around."

Levi tucked earbuds in and sprinted off toward the trails.

"I have to admit," Shawn said, "I kind of admire people who can get up early just to exercise every day."

Robin chuckled. "Me too. But if running is what helps get Levi through the day, more power to him. He went to a really bad place after Xander died, just like I did. I'm happy to see him enjoying his life again." He kissed Shawn's temple, not wanting to dwell on that now. "How about we go inside, brew some coffee, and open presents."

"Sounds perfect."

Shawn had put his gift for Robin under the tree before going outside to watch the sunrise—an action he'd second-guessed more than once, uncertain if Robin would want him intruding. Then he remembered the

different times Robin had invited him to share that moment, and it was now Shawn's new favorite memory of
them together. He'd also done one smaller, but no less
important, task before going outside—put the last of
his summer clothes still lingering in his gym bag into a
drawer, and tucked the bag under the bed. This was his
place now, and he wasn't going anywhere.

Robin had to duck into his own cabin for gifts, and he
brought over a long, narrow box about the size of a loaf
of bread, and a small, rectangular box, both wrapped
in red-and-green-striped paper. They sat opposite each
other in front of the tree, and Shawn felt a slight pang of
guilt at Robin getting him two things, when he'd have
been perfectly content with another chess piece.

"Me first." Robin handed the larger box over to
Shawn, his eyes shining with delight.

The weight surprised Shawn, and he pulled the paper
away to reveal a sturdy black canvas case. Before he
unzipped the case, Shawn knew, and his heart started
beating double time with surprise and wonder. It was
a gorgeous, nine-piece, stainless steel Japanese knife
set. The kind professional chefs used in their kitchens.

"Holy crap," Shawn squawked, because he knew how
expensive this particular brand name was. "You didn't
have to do this."

"Yes, I did. Every chef needs his own knives."

"But I'm a pastry chef. Miles doesn't even have
knives like this."

Robin chuckled. "I guess that depends on what Reyes
put under their tree for him. And you're more than just
a pastry chef, Shawn. You deserve to have something
like this, since I know you'd never treat yourself to it."

Grateful tears stung the corners of Shawn's eyes, and

he reached over to plant a thank-you kiss on Robin's lips. The gift meant the world to him, and it also made his twenty-buck woodcarving kit feel dinky and cheap. And the condoms? Even cheaper, despite the meaning behind them.

"Do I get my present now?" Robin asked.

For a split second, Shawn thought Robin was talking about sex—but Robin didn't read minds, and he was eyeballing the box Shawn had wrapped poorly in some green tissue paper he'd gotten from Patrice. "Yes, for you." Shawn deposited the much lighter box onto Robin's lap.

Robin ripped the tissue off like an eager kid, and his eyes went wide as he figured out what it was. "Shit, this is awesome. Look at all these tools! And sandpaper, too? Dude." Robin tackled him to the rug with the force of his hug and dropped kisses all over Shawn's face like an excited puppy. "I love them, thank you."

"I can tell. I mean, they aren't pro tools like you got me."

"They're meaningful tools, and that's what matters. I can't wait to use them and keep carving your chessboard."

Shawn turned his head and eyeballed the other box. "Does that mean I get new pieces today?"

"Maaaaybe." Robin sat up, and Shawn followed, sitting so they were side-by-side, hips touching. "I wanted to do something really nice for you, again, because I know your finances are tight. But you deserve this, too."

Shawn's stomach quivered with unease at that preface. "Okay." With nervous fingers, he unwrapped the gift—which was a box showing off this year's newest smartphone model.

No, that wasn't right. He'd just put Shawn's real gift inside the phone box, because he didn't have anything else to use. Except when Shawn opened the box…the phone was inside. He gaped at it, rocked to his core, his emotions pinballing all over the place. "You…got me a phone?"

"Yeah. It's got all the latest reading and music apps, and you can use the Wi-Fi here to download any games you want. Plus, the battery life is amazing, and you're always complaining about keeping yours on the charger all the time. And you'll never have to worry about being stranded at the ghost town again." Robin's cheeky grin did not dislodge the chunk of ice in Shawn's stomach.

"I understand all that, but a phone, Robin?" Shawn put the box down. "Those things are expensive, not just the payments but also the monthly charges."

"I added the line to my plan, so it really didn't cost as much as you think." Robin's delight over the gift was slipping off his face, probably because of Shawn's poor reaction. "You don't like it? We can trade it for a different phone if you want."

"The model of the phone isn't the point. You bought me a phone I never asked for and put me on your plan. Yes, I gripe about my phone, but it's what I can afford. I don't need charity."

Robin's lips parted. "Hell, Shawn, this isn't charity. It's a gift. I wanted to do something nice for you. I don't understand why you're mad."

"Because I can buy my own goddamn phone." Why was this so hard for Robin to understand? His hands started shaking, and Shawn cursed the impending anxiety attack. "I love the knives, but I cannot accept this." He put the phone on the floor. "I'm sorry."

Robin scowled. "Because of your pride? I know you're used to doing for yourself, and supporting yourself, because you think you have to all the time. But you really don't. Part of being in a relationship is supporting your partner. I have the means to make your life a little bit easier, so I did. I in no way intended the gesture to suggest you're weak or unable to manage your life."

Shawn studied the hurt in Robin's expression and believed him. Robin wasn't a manipulative jerk like Beck. He wasn't trying to "buy" Shawn with expensive gifts or trick him into feeling obligated. He wasn't trying to run Shawn's life by upgrading his phone. That wasn't Robin. Robin wanted to do something that would make Shawn's life easier, and Shawn was being a brat about accepting the gift.

"Thank you," Shawn finally said. "Thank you for the phone. I wasn't expecting anything this extravagant, and I'm honestly still not used to people being generous without expectations in return. But that's not you."

The hurt drained from Robin's face, replaced by a wry smile. "I mean, I was sort of hoping for a kiss in return…"

Shawn laughed and kissed him. Thoroughly. "Thank you. Sorry for being a jerk about it."

"I get it. Truly. If it helps, I used to do these grand gestures for Xander, too. I guess it's my way of making sure the people I love are taken care of." Robin's face went slack and then he blushed.

Unsure if it was a slip of the tongue, or if Robin really was in love with him, Shawn let the turn of phrase slide for now. "And then there's me," Shawn said. "Not used to being taken care of anymore. But I will pay whatever my share of the monthly data plan is. You can pay for the phone as a Christmas gift, but not the data."

"Deal." Robin pressed a gentle, loving kiss to his lips. "See? We had a crisis, we talked it out, and we solved it. I think we've got this."

"Hope so. I'm really starting to like the way you take care of me." Shawn's stomach chose that moment to let out an impressive hunger growl, and they both laughed. "Breakfast?"

"Sounds good."

They showered and dressed in proper clothes for the day, and then walked hand in hand to the guesthouse kitchen to forage for food. Shawn ended up mixing a bowl of blueberry pancake batter, and he made pancakes that they shared with Hugo, Slater, Bert, and Quentin, with syrup, butter, and fresh fruit from the walk-in. Levi joined them near the end of the meal, rosy cheeked and smiling, and Robin introduced him to their coworkers.

Hugo and Levi seemed to hold eye contact for a split second longer than anyone else when they shook hands, but it was probably Shawn's imagination.

With nowhere to be for a few hours, Shawn, Robin, and Levi spent the morning hanging around on Shawn's front porch. Existing together. Shawn played with his new phone, figuring out the apps and adding his different log-in information, while Robin tested out his new carving tools on a piece of scrap wood. Levi kept up casual conversation, engaging them both in surface topics, keeping things light.

But as lunchtime approached, the other two men grew quieter. More solemn. And Shawn could guess why, but he needed to know. "What time of day did he die?"

Robin tilted his head in Shawn's direction without

meeting his eyes. "Twelve sixteen. I was facing the arena's big scoreboard when it happened, and I saw the clock. Vividly."

"I'm sorry." Shawn checked the time. Just about noon. "Do you guys want to be alone for a little while?"

Please say no, please say no, please say—

"For a little while, yeah," Robin replied. "Meet you at the kitchen for lunch around one?"

"Okay, sure." Shawn had been the one to offer, but he felt kind of foolish for it now. With his new phone in his pocket, Shawn trod up the worn path from cabin row to the guesthouse kitchen, unsurprised when Hugo joined him halfway there.

"So Robin was in a rodeo, huh?" Hugo asked. "That's wild."

"Pretty wild. He doesn't talk much about it, but I think having Levi here right now is helping him deal with some stuff in his past."

"He's cute."

"Who? Robin? Duh."

"Levi."

Shawn cast Hugo a curious look, and Hugo waggled his eyebrows. "What?" Hugo asked. "I notice attractive people."

"Not judging. He is cute, and he's also Robin's former brother-in-law, so I'm not worried about them being alone together."

"Cool. I mean, you and Robin seem pretty solid. He get you anything good for Christmas?"

Shawn couldn't hold back a smile as he flashed his new phone at Hugo. "He kind of spoiled me."

"Damn, dude." Hugo plucked it out of his hands and started thumbing through the apps. Shawn hadn't set a lock screen password yet, since he didn't have anything salacious or private to protect. "My phone is, like, three generations old. This is wicked."

"Well, my old phone was dying a slow death, and it barely held a charge for longer than three hours. Robin just wants to make sure I don't get stranded without a working phone."

"Yeah? He didn't have to buy you a top-of-the-line model to do that. I think I'm jealous."

In all their prior conversations, topics tended to stay mostly surface, so Shawn didn't have a clear idea of Hugo's sexuality. Many of the men at Clean Slate seemed to fall in the 2 to 5 range on the Kinsey scale, and were fairly open about attraction. Maybe Hugo was still figuring himself out. Finding his footing here, like Shawn.

"Maybe you'll meet someone someday soon who will buy you an expensive phone," Shawn teased as they walked in the kitchen door.

"Or I'll land in a profession where I can afford my own expensive phone."

Shawn laughed as he surveyed the kitchen. Work like this was unlikely to ever provide Shawn with that sort of income, but he loved what he did every single day. And he'd keep loving it as long as he was here in Garrett, no matter where his relationship with Robin went—or where Robin went.

Whether here at Clean Slate Ranch, or up at Bentley Ghost Town, Shawn was finally, truly home.

Chapter Seventeen

The barn's main corral seemed like the most appropriate place for Robin and Levi to end up after Shawn gave them some privacy. After all, Xander's short life had ended in hoof-trodden dirt like that, almost exactly three years ago. All because Robin had asked for an impossible gift from his husband, and Xander had said yes.

No one had expected that incredibly explosive truck backfire.

"Sometimes I can still feel him," Robin said to his feet. "The way his hands were so limp after. How still he was in my arms."

"Yeah." Levi slung an arm across Robin's shoulders, and Robin leaned into his friend's chest. "It all happened so fast, but it replays so slow in my head. The first time I finally talked about Xander at a meeting, I burst into tears but I got through it."

Robin was impressed Levi had been able to stand up in front of a roomful of strangers and talk about the most painful moment in his life. "I've only ever told Arthur and Judson how he died."

"You really should tell Shawn. This is only my experience, but talking openly about a painful thing can take some of its power away."

"I guess." He scuffed at the dirt with his boot. "You know, the first time I laid eyes on Shawn, he was up on a horse, and I swore I was looking right at Xander. It terrified me to my bones, and I was so rude to Shawn at first. Eventually, I apologized and he forgave me."

"And look at you now. Do you love him?"

Robin met Levi's open, curious gaze. "On some level, I do. Not sure if I'm completely in love or not but I know I can love him."

"Good. You deserve that joy again, Robin. No one would judge you for moving on from Xander and being happy with Shawn. Not me, especially not Dad."

Not wanting to have the "call Doug" conversation again, Robin checked the time on his phone. 12:14. Close. "I'll always love Xander," Robin said softly, the ranch suddenly too quiet for loud words. "I'll always miss him. But I don't have to mourn him for the rest of my life." He closed his eyes against a flash of hot tears. "I love you, Xan, and I hope that wherever you are, you're at peace. Please, be at peace."

Levi whispered something in a language Robin didn't know, but the words sounded nice. Like a prayer.

A gentle breeze ruffled the hair at Robin's neck, and he shivered. Then he smiled. It was Christmas Day. Today wasn't about mourning or loss or grief. It was about gratitude for everything Robin had and the people in his life. This ranch had given him so much. The Garretts and Judson and Patrice and Shawn and Mack… they were his family.

Family helped family.

Before Robin could voice his decision to call Doug, Levi's phone rang. Levi smiled at the display a moment before answering, "Hey, Dad, Merry Christmas."

Robin's heart sped up.

"Yeah. Yeah, I'm with a friend, remembering Xander." Levi met Robin's gaze; Robin nodded. "Actually, I think he'd like to say hello." He held out the phone.

Robin took it with trembling fingers, proud to have found his own courage, and a little nervous over what Doug might actually say. "Hey, Dad."

Doug made a choking noise. "Robin? Am I dreaming or is that really you?"

"It's me." So many rioting emotions tangled inside Robin's chest, and they all tried to strangle him at once. "Merry Christmas."

"I just…" Doug coughed hard, his voice rougher now. "It's so damned good to hear your voice, son. Words cannot express it enough."

"I feel the same. My pride and hurt kept me from calling for too damned long, and I'm sorry about that."

"I'm sorry, too, about a lot of things. Things we can't change, but there's no sense in dwelling on old hurts. I forgave you a long time ago, and I apologize for my part in our fight. I never meant to drive one of my sons away."

Robin nearly burst into tears at the tender, loving way Doug called him his son. They'd been family for eight years, and Robin had nearly lost this forever. The naked joy on Levi's face only reaffirmed his decision to reach out. "I forgive you, too, Dad. For all of it. We should have been there to support each other in our grief, and I'll always regret that we weren't."

"Same. Same. So you and Levi are friends again?"

"Yes, we reconnected on the phone a few weeks ago, and then he surprised me by flying in yesterday so we could spend Christmas together."

"I'm glad to hear that. Levi told me you ended up on a dude ranch?"

Robin spent a few minutes detailing the ranch and his work here, pacing the corral a bit until he eventually leaned his back against a post.

"I can hear how happy you are in your voice," Doug said when Robin paused his storytelling. "It does my weary heart good to know that."

"I am happy." Robin decided to go all in. "I'm also… I've met someone. His name's Shawn, and he makes me happy, too."

"Good. You're too fine a lad to stay single. Now can you do something about Levi?"

Robin laughed out loud—a thing he never imagined doing when he reconnected with Doug—and he finally, truly understood the power of forgiveness. "I don't know, I think Levi ever getting a love life is a lost cause."

Levi blew a raspberry at him from his perch on the mobile steps short riders used to mount the horses. He was simply listening to Robin talk, his smiling face bathed in sunshine.

"Well, I'm glad you boys are all together today," Doug said.

"So am I. Um, when you spoke to Levi last, did he happen to mention he's been consulting with the ghost town owner on an opening day event?"

"It didn't come up, no. What sort of event?"

Robin told him about Mack's plans for a rodeo-style event. "He's worried about training the horses and riders, so no one gets injured. And we've only got about five weeks left to pull this all together."

"Hell, son, you say the word, and I'll bring Lucky's up there and do a full show for free."

Robin sank into a half-squat, his back still against the post, as gratitude and love for the man nearly cut his legs out from under him. Despite Levi assuring Doug would come, hearing it from the older man's lips drove it all home. Doug was still his family. His father in so many ways beyond blood or law.

"Will you come to Garrett?" Robin asked after he'd gotten himself under control again.

"Absolutely. Let me talk to Potter about scheduling. We don't have our first booking until early February, so I don't see a problem. What about our animals? We've got our portable shelters, but I don't know the weather where you are."

"We average low forties to high fifties in January, so they should be fine in the gated tents." Robin had once been the fastest tent erector in the crew, despite the weight of that reinforced canvas. "But if we happen to have a cold snap, I'm sure we can find space for them in the barn."

"Sounds good."

"Let me get in touch with Mack about this. I know he had his heart set on training his own people, so they could do another show next year, too, or add acts to the ghost town, but I just don't think there's time."

"I'll talk to my people, too. If we can get up there early enough, we can definitely work with Mack's people. Teach them some things while we're there."

"Yeah?" Robin wished Doug was there in person so he could hug the man for his generosity. "Thank you. I don't wanna bother him right now, but I'll see Mack later tonight for dinner. I'll call you when I talk to him."

"Sounds good. Merry Christmas, Robin. I can't say how much this conversation has meant to me."

"Same, Dad."

Doug coughed. "Can I have Levi again for a bit?"

"Of course." Robin somehow got to his feet and ambled over to Levi. "Your turn."

Levi winked as he took his phone back. "Surprise!"

Robin chuckled as he walked away, giving Levi privacy to speak with his dad. He wandered into the barn and down to Apple Jax's stall. She nickered at him and seemed unhappy he'd been neglecting their time together. All the horses were regularly exercised, but all the horsemen had their favorite mounts. Maybe now that Robin had worked through more of his grief and reconnected with Doug, he could stand to see Shawn up on a horse. Maybe they could go riding together, the way Robin had wanted to with Xander three years ago...

Small steps. First, he got to hand Mack the good news about Lucky's and take some of the pressure off his shoulders. Keep him from having to juggle training riders with the regular stress of reopening the ghost town. Robin was happy to do that for his friend.

His text alert chimed.

Shawn: First text from new phone a success. You okay?

Robin finally realized it was a few minutes past one, and they were due for lunch. He shot off a quick On our way very soon message, a little surprised time had completely gotten away from him. He turned, prepared to collect Levi, but the man was ambling down the barn toward him with a relaxed expression.

"You know you wanna say it," Robin said.

Levi's blue eyes danced. "I told you so."

"Yeah, you did. Thank you. You helped me get my

head out of my ass about this, and now I think it'll be exactly what Mack needs to really kick off his second year in business."

"I agree. And I think it'll do Dad a lot of good to see both his sons again."

Robin blinked back more of those damned, happy tears. "Me, too."

Shawn tamped back his annoyance at Robin being late for lunch, because it wasn't really Robin he was annoyed at. It was mostly himself. He hadn't been in the kitchen more than a few minutes before realizing he'd left his old phone in the cabin, and his granddad didn't have this phone's new number. Unsure when he'd be able to switch his old number to the new phone, Shawn excused himself from Hugo and went into the empty living area.

Granddad predictably let the unknown number go to the answering machine. "Hey, it's Shawn. I have a new phone."

The line crackled. "Shawn? Good to hear your voice, son, Merry Christmas."

"Merry Christmas, Granddad."

"I'd put you on speaker, but Irma, she just did nod off. Had a bit of a hard time sleeping last night."

"That's okay. You can call me back later when she's awake."

"I'll do that. You say you got a new phone?"

"I did." Shawn detailed his morning with Robin, his initial hesitation over the gift, and finally his agreement to accept it. "It's so strange having someone in my life who… I don't want to say he puts me first, but after I put my pride away, it was so generous and thoughtful. He didn't do it to show off, he did it because he cares."

"This Robin sounds like a special fellow. I'm surely glad you have him. You know I wish I could do more."

"I know, and I'm glad I have him, too." The *L*-word rang in his head like a bell. "I don't know if this is forever, or just for now, but I care about him a lot."

"Then you hold tight. You'll have struggles, but in the end, the love is worth it."

"I hope so." They hadn't spoken in a while, so Shawn told him what was happening at the ranch, including last Saturday's big dinner, and tonight's dinner at Mack's place. Talking about these people—his family—made it hurt less that Shawn's blood family was so far away at Christmas.

Maybe I should let Robin splurge on a trip north.

No, Robin's splurge had been the new smartphone. No trips unless Shawn could afford to pay for it. And he had no idea the price difference between the minutes he was used to buying, and the data plan he'd just insisted he pay for himself. Ugh, why couldn't he have just allowed Robin to pay for it all?

Because then I'd be completely dependent on Robin for my phone.

He kind of was now, anyway. If they broke up, would Robin cut him off?

Shawn decided to keep his old phone for now, just in case.

"So when did you say your ghost town opens up again?"

"Last week in January. I'm looking forward to it. As much as I enjoy cooking in the guesthouse, I think Patrice is getting antsy about getting her kitchen back, and I miss the solitude of the saloon's kitchen. I don't have twenty-odd employees parading in and out at each meal."

Granddad chuckled. "You sound so happy and confident when you talk about that place. I'm real glad you landed there, son. Real glad."

"So am I." A pang of guilt over never admitting he'd been homeless for two years before landing here soured Shawn's stomach. "You know, I've been thinking of maybe coming out for a few days before the saloon opens."

"Oh? That'd be nice, but only if you're sure."

Shawn sighed. "I'm not sure, which is why I've only been thinking about it. But I miss you guys, and I'd love to see you."

"We'd love nothing more than to see you again, too, but you need to think of yourself first. You hear me?"

"I hear you. And I love you both."

"We love you, too. You take care of yourself."

"I will. Kiss Nana for me."

"Will do."

They both hung up, and a cloud of annoyance and melancholy drifted over Shawn's head. It stayed put while he cooked up grilled ham and cheese sandwiches for lunch, with some help from Hugo. When Robin and Levi finally joined them, the sandwiches were warming in the oven, and they shared from a big tin of kettle-style potato chips Shawn had added to last week's supply order. Chips were easier than fixing up a cold salad side.

Robin looked excited about something, but he didn't share and Shawn didn't press until the meal was over, and Hugo had excused himself. Then Robin shared the Lucky's Rodeo news, while Levi smiled at them, clearly pleased. And Shawn was happy for both men, especially Robin. When he talked about Doug Peletier, Shawn heard his affection for the older man and how

much Robin had missed him. Robin was reconnecting
with the family he'd lost.

A family Robin had once traveled all over the country with, touring and putting on shows. A family who
would be here in a few short weeks to put on another
show…and steal Robin away?

No. No bad thoughts like that. Robin was staying
here. With him.

Right?

Their trio ended up at Shawn's cabin, because he had
the bigger TV, and they watched movies until it was
time for dinner up at Mack and Wes's place. Levi volunteered to drive his rental. Mack was predictably thrilled
by Doug's offer to both put on a show, and to train local
folks in the tricks Mack was interested in for the attraction. He spent most of the meal and the evening goad-
ing stories out of Robin and Levi, and they wove a lot
of fun, fascinating tales of life on the road.

Shawn also saw the nostalgia sparking in Robin's
eyes, and he didn't like it. Not that he'd begrudge Robin
a future that made him happy, but Shawn really wanted
that future here. With him. Miles picked up on Shawn's
mood, but Shawn brushed him off. He did, however,
show off his phone to Miles, who acted like the gift was
as good as a marriage proposal.

That was easy enough to laugh off. Maybe Miles and
Reyes were engaged, but Shawn was nowhere near the
neighborhood of that step with Robin. Hell, not even in
the same state.

Over the course of the next week, Shawn was pretty
sure they weren't in the same country anymore. Levi
stuck around, despite having three cats at home he said
he adored, and he spent a lot of time with Robin when

Robin wasn't busy working. It gave Robin and Shawn less time alone, but Robin was also happy. He practically vibrated with joy now, so Shawn accepted this new dynamic and quietly prayed Levi went home soon.

Which he did. The day before New Year's Eve. Finally.

Levi promised to return for the opening day festivities, but Shawn had a feeling he'd be back before then. Likely whenever Lucky's Rodeo rolled into town. And that was fine, because it gave Shawn a few weeks with his boyfriend so they could…take new steps. He still hadn't given Robin his final Christmas gift. New Year's seemed like a good opportunity to begin on a brand-new note.

On New Year's Eve, Wes predictably threw a party at his and Mack's cabin, and even though Shawn wouldn't have minded a quiet night alone with Robin, Robin threw on his best pout and won Shawn over. A new crop of guests was scheduled to arrive this coming Sunday, so a lot of the absent hands had returned to the ranch, and Robin wanted to hang with his friends.

And to be fair, Shawn didn't mind a chance to chill with Miles, Wes, and Avery. Their quartet ended up drinking wine in the kitchen, while the cowboys took up the living room with beer and other assorted liquors. Since Shawn rarely drank alcohol, his first glass of wine went down a little too smoothly, and he followed it up with a second. He rarely relied on his meds anymore to regulate his anxiety attacks, which were fewer and further between the more settled he became. Apparently, having a stable place to live and friends all around did wonders for his nerves.

And while that box of condoms continued to mock

him from its hiding place, Shawn's life was...pretty good. Not perfect but how could he really complain? He still missed his grandparents, but he had a good life here in Garrett, with steady employment and a family who cared about him.

And a boyfriend who spent a lot of his free time reminiscing about his wanderer days with a former best friend, and a whole lot of personal self-doubts.

A big group of the guys got together in the living room to play *Cards Against Humanity* but Shawn wasn't in the mood. He ended up in one of the downstairs bedrooms with Miles and Avery, and ten minutes into them streaming hilarious cat videos—apparently Avery and Colt had adopted a cat online recently—Shawn got a little maudlin, and he ended up venting his frustrations to both men. Avery was kind of an accident, because Shawn didn't know him very well, but he knew and trusted Miles.

Shawn probably overshared a bit, but he told them what he knew about Xander and Robin, and Shawn's own hesitation over anal sex—hesitation he still couldn't fully explain to himself, much less his friends. The way Robin and Levi had bonded again and Shawn's fears of Robin getting itchy feet. Of Robin wanting to go back on the road for a more exciting life than here at Clean Slate, especially with Lucky's coming to town in a few weeks.

"Speaking as someone who knows what it's like to have a long-distance relationship," Avery said, once Shawn's rambling drunk brain cut off his words, "how do you think you'd handle it if Robin decided he wanted to travel?"

"I don't know," Shawn replied. "Robin is the only real boyfriend I've ever had, and all I know is having him nearby. I think it would hurt a lot if he went away, especially if was for months at a time."

"It can be a challenge, believe me. But today's technology makes it very easy to see each other face-to-face, even if it's only in pixels."

"True."

Miles was watching him in that quiet, assessing way of his. "Shawn, do you think this fear of Robin leaving stems from your, uh, living situation before moving to the ranch?"

Even Shawn's wine-soaked brain understood that Miles was trying not to share Shawn's secret homelessness. Guess Miles and Reyes weren't gossips, even with their closest friends. "Probably. I'm used to the people I love either leaving me, or me having to leave. It's hard to believe this isn't a temporary relationship."

"Could that be why you're so hesitant to go all the way with Robin and have anal sex? Once he gets that one thing from you, he'll lose interest?"

"Yes. No. Maybe?" Shawn stared into the ruby remnants of his wine. "Robin isn't with me for sex. We have great sex. And he totally wants to bottom for me, so I'm not worried about being on the receiving end. I want to go there with him."

"So what if the opposite is true," Avery said. "What if this hesitation is over what a powerful symbol having sex with Robin is to you, and that it makes your relationship even more permanent. Which means any possible breakup will hurt even more."

Shawn turned that over in his head, and it fit better than Miles's assessment. "That sounds about right."

"Then wait," Miles said sharply. "There is no rule that says gay couples have to have anal sex by a certain time in their relationship. Hell, there are plenty of guys who go out and have it, and they never see their partner again. The one great thing I learned while navigating my relationship with Reyes is that you have to create a dynamic that works for you both. No two relationships work the same way."

Avery nodded. "Agreed. Relationships also change when circumstances change. Colt and I got back together knowing we had hundreds of miles between us. Things just worked out in our favor and I was able to move closer for a better, more stable job. What if some hotshot celebrity chef ate at the saloon and loved your food so much he tried to woo you away with a high-end restaurant job?"

Shawn snorted and downed the last dregs of his wine. "That's more likely to happen to Miles, not me."

"You don't give yourself enough credit," Miles said, then knuckled his shoulder. "And Avery is making a valid point. Even if Robin doesn't get itchy over the rodeo life, something could happen down the road where either one of you has to make a choice about staying or leaving the ranch. Hell, all three of us could face that at any time. It's part of life and part of being with someone else. Part of loving someone else."

"I don't know if I love Robin. I think I do, but I've never been in love before."

"Then enjoy what you guys have in the moment. Something I learned the hard way with Dallas is life can flip upside down and take everything away from you in a second." Miles snapped his fingers, his green eyes glittering with bad things that faded quickly.

Or maybe it was the wine, Shawn wasn't sure.

"Trust me," Shawn said, "I know how quickly life

can take a giant shit on your head. I lived in my car for the last two years, remember?"

Avery's eyebrows rose.

Shit, I didn't mean to say that.

"You did what now?" Robin's shocked voice came from the open bedroom doorway. He stood in the hall with a bowl of popcorn in his hands and a strange look on his face.

Shawn's cheeks burned with humiliation. Of all the stupid-ass things to come out of his mouth thanks to drinking, it had to be that. Except— "Were you eavesdropping?"

"What? No. It's thirty minutes to midnight, and I came to tell you guys we're putting the TV on for the pre-ball-drop show."

"Oh."

"Avery, why don't we give them a minute," Miles said. The pair silently slipped out of the room, and Miles plucked the popcorn from Robin as he passed.

Robin came inside and pulled the door mostly shut, and then stood there with a dumbfounded expression. "What do you mean, you lived in your car these past two years?"

Shawn flopped backward onto the bedspread and stared up at the plain white ceiling. "Exactly what I said. After Sheila kicked me out, I couldn't find a room or place I could afford, so I lived in my car."

"For two years?"

He couldn't shrug well on his back so Shawn raised both his hands in an I-give-up gesture. "I figured it out and made do. Rent in San Francisco is insanely expensive, and living in my car helped me send a little bit more money home."

"But your car?" Robin eased onto the bed near Shawn's head, and Shawn couldn't bring himself to look at his boyfriend. "Did your grandparents know?"

"Hell no, and I'm never telling them." Shawn sat upright and reached for Robin's wrist. Squeezed. "Granddad doesn't need to know. Him and Nana will just get upset, and I did it knowing full well what I was doing."

Robin's grief-stricken expression was almost too much for Shawn to bear. "So all of last year while you were working for Miles, you lived in your car?"

"Yeah. I parked for the night along state roads, or outside Garrett. Daggett, too. It got hot in the summer, but I showered at a nearby truck stop, and I got used to a certain way of eating. I didn't want anyone to know. I wanted to prove I could handle everything on my own."

"Until the day after we kissed and you moved into the cabin?"

Shawn hazarded a peek at Robin's eyes and wished he hadn't. Robin looked one wrong word from bursting into tears. "If it helps at all, it wasn't about you calling me Xander. A local cop who'd seen me parked on the road before woke me up in the dead of morning, and he decided to help. Got Reyes and Judson involved. Miles, too. I think Patrice and Arthur are the only other people who know, except now obviously you and Avery."

"Homelessness is nothing to be ashamed of, Shawn."

"It's not that I was ashamed." Yeah, that was part of it, but so much more was his damned pride. "To be honest, I didn't want exactly what happened, which was near strangers changing their own lives around to accommodate me. I know Patrice said she'd been thinking of moving into the big house for a while, but would she really have done that if she hadn't broken her collarbone? Given her cabin to me?"

"I think she would have because that's who Patrice is. The minute anyone here knew you lived in your car, they'd have found a way to get you a place to live that isn't on four wheels. Be it Mack and Wes's guest room, or even a permanent bunk in the guesthouse. Bentley's a separate business from the ranch, but we're all family. We'd have helped you."

Shawn believed that deep down, especially after living here for nearly six weeks and seeing how the staff supported each other.

"I wish you'd trusted me enough to tell me sooner," Robin said in a soft, almost sad tone.

"I do trust you, Robin, I swear. But I never told anyone except that cop, and after that, people found out because they kept getting involved in my situation. I want to be able to say I'd have told you sooner or later, I mean it. But I also wish no one had ever found out at all."

"Why, though?" Robin sounded less upset now and more confused. "People fall on hard times, especially in this economy, and especially with people your age. And just so we're clear? I will never make fun of you, shame you, or belittle you for having problems. We all have things we're dealing with, Shawn. Emotional, financial, spiritual, whatever it is, that's why we keep people close who will support us. I'm guessing until you landed in that cabin, you were used to not having support of any kind."

Shawn nodded, his throat tightening with emotion. "It's hard to trust that support is completely altruistic when the first person who offered help —" he made air quotes on the word *offered* "—preyed on my trust and manipulated me."

Robin studied him a beat. "The person from your past?"

"Yeah." Shawn didn't want to unpack the details of Beck's manipulations so close to the New Year. Maybe some other time when he was clear-headed. He scooted closer to Robin and rested his head on the taller man's shoulder. "I know you aren't like that, and I'm trying. I'm also sorry I didn't tell you I'd been homeless sooner. I just…"

"Don't like to talk about it?"

"Yeah."

Robin's arm looped around Shawn's waist in a supportive side-hug. "I get it. I'm sorry I had to find out by accident, but thank you for telling me now."

"You're welcome." In some ways, Shawn was glad this particular secret was out in the open. Maybe it would make the whole Beck disaster less huge when (if?) he found the courage to explain it all to Robin. But Shawn was in no hurry to go there, especially with his persistent doubts about the long-term future of his relationship with Robin.

Shawn desperately wanted to believe they'd get the same happily ever after that Miles and Reyes got…he wanted to believe it.

But he wasn't sure if he did.

Chapter Eighteen

Despite the semi-serious conversation about Shawn's two-year stint living in his car, the pair managed to join their friends and share a New Year's kiss when the ball dropped at midnight. Other than a few fumbled kisses at high school parties with casual friends, this was Shawn's first New Year's kiss, and it was wonderful. He usually wasn't much for public displays of affection, but they weren't the only queer couple in the room doing it, so Shawn enjoyed the long, toe-curling kiss Robin planted on him.

Plastic flutes of champagne went around the cabin. Shawn hugged a bunch of people before finding his way back to Robin, who hugged him tight and kissed his temple. They stayed for another hour or so, until they were both yawning more than talking. Since they'd driven up in Robin's car along with Ernie and Hugo, Robin collected their inebriated friends and they went home.

Robin tucked Ernie into their cabin, while Shawn helped Hugo to his, before they were finally alone together in Shawn's place. Shawn didn't have to be at the guesthouse to cook until lunch, since no one was likely to be awake before ten anyway, but he was too tired to do more than climb into bed with Robin and kiss for a while. When Shawn was too sleepy to do that, Robin curled around his back and held him close.

"I'm so glad you stayed safe," Robin whispered. "You stayed safe until I could find you and love you."

Shawn smiled against his pillow. "Me, too. All of it."

Sleep took hold fast, and Shawn woke later to the unfamiliar situation of sunlight in the cabin and Robin still asleep beside him. He'd rolled away sometime in the night and slumbered on his back, one arm thrown across his eyes. The moment was so peaceful, so beautiful, Shawn knew it was time. He carefully slipped out of bed and retrieved the other now-belated Christmas gift from his dresser.

The sheets rustled. Robin had rolled toward Shawn's side of the bed, and one hand was rubbing the spot he'd left moments before. Seeking. Robin muttered something as he came awake, and then he spotted Shawn at the foot of the bed. "Hey, morning," Robin said.

"Good morning. Did you get your sunrise picture? First of the new year?"

"Nope. I've decided that my first resolution is to take those photos if I happen to be awake, but it's okay if I'm not."

Shawn nodded, nervous now, but as Robin sat up and the blanket fell away, his obvious morning wood got Shawn's own libido into the game. "So I was going to give this to you on Christmas, but then Levi showed up, and I chickened out and doubted myself, but after last night, I know this is right. I'm ready."

Robin's sleepy smile went a bit more alert. "Oh?"

"Yes." He climbed back into the bed and handed Robin the box. "For us."

"Hmm." Robin tore the tissue off and found a plain

brown shipping box. Shawn had torn off the label and opened it to check the contents, and he'd resealed it with a single piece of tape. Robin popped it open and pushed aside the packing peanuts. His lips parted and both eyebrows went up.

Shawn's belly quivered with nerves when Robin didn't say anything, but he wasn't going to let his anxiety win. "I want to take this step with you. Penetration. Obviously, only if you're into it, too, so if you aren't—mph." He hit the bed on his back, Robin smothering him into the mattress with the force of his kiss, morning wood riding Shawn's thigh.

Robin kissed him thoroughly, with long pulls from his lips and slow drags of tongue, until Shawn's own dick was thick and straining in his boxers. "Yes, yes, I am so down with this plan," Robin finally said, a bit breathless. His dark eyes glistened with joy and lust...and love? "I've dreamed about what it'll feel like with you inside me." That joy tempered into something more serious. "This isn't because of our conversation last night, is it?"

"Yes and no. Mostly it's me going all-in with us as a couple. I want to do this, Robin. I've imagined it myself."

"Yeah?" His eyebrows waggled. "What position did you like best?"

Shawn laughed. "All of them. What's your favorite?"

"I'm a big fan of being bent over and fucked from behind, but I think we need something more intimate for our first time."

Gooey feelings overtook the last of Shawn's anxiety. "How about like this?"

"This sounds perfect."

Kissing each other out of their clothes was practiced and easy, and they spent a long time touching, kissing,

and playing. Enjoying each other's body, making the
other man feel good. Robin sucked his dick and played
with his balls until Shawn thought he was going to come.
Then Robin squeezed the base of his cock and the release backed off a little. Robin had done this more frequently lately when they made love, pushing Shawn to
the tip of orgasm and then stopping. Every action was
familiar and loving, and they relaxed Shawn by degrees
for what was yet to happen. Going so slowly meant this
was exactly what the words said: making love.

Shawn played with Robin's stomach, licking the
ridges of his defined abs and dipping his tongue into
Robin's navel just to hear him laugh. He never imagined
he'd laugh or make his partner laugh so much during
sex, and it was one of his favorite things. An expression of pure joy. He drifted lower to Robin's dark nest
of pubes and gorgeous cock. Licked the glans while he
rolled Robin's sac. Small motions more about sensation
than getting Robin off. He'd learned that Robin liked
being teased, and Shawn enjoyed teasing him. Learning all the little tics and quirks that made the whole of
the man Shawn was falling in love with.

A spit-wet finger rubbed Robin's taint, and the bigger man's thighs quivered with need. Shawn was a little
nervous—but way more excited to be taking this step.
To try this new thing Robin loved and explore a different kind of pleasure between them. Done because Shawn
wanted to, not because he was being pressured.

Robin nudged the lube at him, and after a brief battle
with the plastic seal, Shawn rubbed a lubed finger over
Robin's hole—such an intimate place to touch someone,
and Robin clearly loved it.

"Oh yeah," Robin said. He drew his legs up and open,

holding them by the backs of the knees. Opening himself for Shawn to really see what he was doing. He pressed against that tight muscle, curious and aroused and so fucking happy to have gotten over himself and made this choice. "Harder, one won't hurt me."

Trusting Robin to know his body's limits, Shawn pushed harder. It was easier with real lube and not just spit. Robin bore down and then Shawn's finger pushed into tight heat. So tight he couldn't believe his dick would fit inside. Shawn pushed in deeper than he'd ever dared before and Robin moaned. "Feels okay?" Shawn asked, unsure if that was a good moan or a pained one.

"It feels incredible. Keep going, baby. More."

Shawn kissed Robin's inner thigh, drizzled a bit more lube, and then fucked Robin with a single digit. Mesmerized by the way his finger slid in and out of Robin's body, giving his boyfriend pleasure. Getting him ready for Shawn's cock.

Oh God, I'm really doing this. We're doing this.

And it was everything Shawn had ever wanted. On Robin's word, Shawn nudged two fingers inside, the pressure even more incredible. He studied Robin's blissful face for any hint of pain or displeasure and saw none. Only open joy and desire and trust.

Curious, Shawn stilled those fingers deep inside, then bent to suck on the head of Robin's cock. Robin cried out, hips jerking. "Oh fuck, yes! Please!" Shawn tried to match the swirls of his tongue around the glans with the thrusts of his fingers, but this was his first time and he wasn't very good at it. Didn't matter, though, with Robin falling apart in front of him. The usually put-together cowboy was a writhing, panting, begging mess, and Shawn adored the sight of him. It also stirred something new deep inside Shawn—a driving need to claim this man in the most intimate way possible.

To truly bring them together as one.

He flailed for the condom box with his left hand, but the damned thing was sealed so he reluctantly tugged free of Robin's body. Robin whined—actually fucking whined!—at the loss, but when he saw what Shawn was up to, he practically began to hump the bed. "Yes, need you in me."

"Soon." Shawn had only worn a condom once before, but the basic mechanics were easy enough. Pinch the tip to keep room for his come, then roll down his shaft. He was so hard he was scared he'd come just from smearing on more lube but the tight latex helped dull the sensations a bit. Good. He'd hate to shoot the minute he was inside Robin.

"You want to be on top?" Shawn asked.

"Just like this." Robin pulled his legs back, nearly to his own chest, red-cheeked and lust-drunk. "Please?"

"Anything you want." Shawn was eager for this part, to complete this journey they'd started together, and to give Robin all the pleasure he deserved. "Tell me if I'm doing something wrong, or it hurts."

"Baby, everything you do is exactly right."

Shawn grinned at the perfect words and knelt between Robin's lewdly spread legs. Took a moment to lick up the length of Robin's shaft to hear Robin gasp. Notched the head of his sheathed cock to Robin's shiny entrance. Held Robin's wide-eyed gaze. Robin gave him an encouraging wink.

He pushed, surprised by the resistance at first, just like with his finger, until Robin's body relaxed and accepted him inside. Into a sensation Shawn couldn't possibly describe beyond holy wow! The heat and pressure on his cock. How it changed as Shawn worked himself in and out with shallow thrusts, going a bit deeper each time. Taking care not to hurt Robin.

Robin took matters into his own hands by rocking his hips sharply upward, burying Shawn nearly to the root, and this time Shawn cried out. The intensity was almost too much, too fast, and when Robin clenched? Hot damn, Shawn saw stars. Nothing could have prepared him for how perfectly right this felt—not just the pleasure rolling through his body, but the emotions burning in his heart.

"Oh yeah!" Robin threw back his head, the fingers gripping his own thighs nearly bloodless. "Fucking hell, that's everything. Fuck."

Shawn clutched at Robin's left leg for balance, his entire world tilting a bit to the side, riding on the intense need to rut until he came.

"Fuck me, Shawn," Robin panted. "Please."

"Yeah." Shawn pulled back, Robin so tight around him he worried the condom would come off, but it stayed put. He thrust back in, going slow at first, getting used to it. Finding his rhythm and the confidence that he wasn't hurting Robin, before Shawn leaned down to kiss him. Robin's hot erection pressed between their bellies. Shawn rocked gently into Robin's body, trying to time it with his kisses. Robin wrapped his legs around Shawn's waist and held him tight while his hands raked up and down Shawn's back. Their bodies were sealed together and moving as one, and the depth of trust on display from Robin made Shawn love the man all the more. To give his body over to Shawn, knowing Shawn had all the power in this position.

Shawn would treasure that trust always.

They kissed until Shawn's body betrayed him with its own needs, so he raised up a bit more, giving him room to fuck Robin the way his body demanded. Hard slams of his cock, hips smacking into Robin's taut ass. The scent of sex filled the small cabin, the only sounds their strangled breathing and slaps of skin. Robin grabbed Shawn's ass and squeezed, encouraging him.

It was everything Shawn imagined it would be and more.

He wanted to stay here always, inside his boyfriend, making love to him, driving them both toward the precipice. But Shawn's orgasm barreled in out of nowhere and shattered him from the inside out. He stilled deep inside of Robin as his entire body shook from the force of it. Robin pulled him down, and Shawn collapsed onto his chest, unable to breathe properly from the force of both orgasm and his emotions. He pressed his nose into Robin's neck until the world made sense again.

"You with me, baby?" Robin whispered.

"Yeah. That was…wow." Shawn didn't have a lot of words right now, but those were good ones. Robin was still hard between them but Shawn didn't want to pull out. He loved being inside Robin, more than he ever expected to, and Robin definitely loved being fucked. They'd so be doing this again soon.

Robin lovingly helped Shawn hold the condom and pull out, and then rolled Shawn's boneless body onto his back. He shocked the hell out of Shawn by peeling off the rubber and using some of the come still clinging to Shawn's flagging cock to jerk himself off. The naughtiness gave Shawn the energy to reach out and pinch

Robin's nipple. Robin came on a shout, painting Shawn's chest with his spend before collapsing next to him.

Wrapped up in his boyfriend's arms, perfectly sated from sex, Shawn Matthews had never felt more safe, protected, or loved in his entire life.

I'm keeping you, Robin Butler. You're mine, and I'm yours.

Robin stroked Shawn's back as the smaller man dozed, overjoyed by the ache in his backside and the reason for it. So happy to have finally shared this beautiful thing with Shawn. And Shawn, for all his quiet strength, had shown hints of a dominant personality near the end, when he was pounding Robin's ass with all his might. The exact kind of fuck Robin loved most.

He hadn't expected this today. A small part of him had started to believe they'd never take this step, and he would have been totally okay with that. He owned a dildo for a reason. But Shawn had surprised him with the condoms, and Robin couldn't be happier.

They were also sweaty, sticky, and kind of a mess, so Robin hauled his slightly delirious boyfriend off the bed and into the bathroom. The small tub was awkward, but he made it work, scrubbing all the come off Shawn. Despite how hard he'd just come, Shawn started getting hard again from all the contact, so Robin rewarded his earlier performance with a soapy hand job. Robin's own dick perked up but he wasn't as young as he used to be.

The bedding wasn't too messy, so Robin pulled Shawn back under the covers with him, both still naked, and they dozed for a while. He loved that Shawn was a cuddler. Xander had been very tactile while awake—and definitely during sex—but he hadn't been a nighttime cuddler, despite the fact that they shared an RV's small, full-size mattress. He loved all the ways his relationship with Shawn was wholly unique to them.

Around eleven thirty, Shawn grumbled about lunch and they both reluctantly got dressed. Robin helped him make sure the hands who trickled in for sandwiches had enough sliced meats and cheese—Shawn, Patrice, and Judson were the only people allowed to operate the machines. The big tin of chips was nearly empty, but they had plenty of fresh fruit to nibble on if the sandwiches weren't enough.

Robin had definitely worked up an appetite. He piled two slices of marbled rye with ham, turkey, salami, and plenty of American cheese and mayo. He even sliced up one of the big dill pickles from the barrel for extra crunch. Shawn helped himself to the rest of the pickle.

If anyone else in the kitchen noticed a change in Shawn, no one said anything, not even Miles. But Robin saw it. Not really a glow, but a shift in his confidence. A smile that never seemed to leave his eyes.

Hugo still looked a tad hungover, so he nibbled on dry toast and lemongrass tea. Robin felt sorry for the kid, who probably needed some practice in drinking without the next-day regrets.

"Anyone got plans for the rest of the day?" Reyes asked as plates emptied. Other than exercising the horses, no one had any specific plans. "So who's up for a group trail ride this afternoon?"

Shawn shot Robin a curious look; Robin tried not to squirm. If Shawn wanted to go, Robin would suck it up and go. "Not us today," Shawn said, giving Robin a teasing wink. "We might take a trail walk, though."

Why was Shawn—oh. Oh! He probably thought

Robin's ass was too tender to sit in a saddle. And yeah, it was probably was. Robin kissed Shawn's cheek, then nuzzled the spot with his nose. "A trail walk sounds great."

Miles had arched an eyebrow in their direction, and he tossed Shawn a knowing smirk. The other guys made plans to meet up for a ride in thirty minutes. Once the kitchen cleared out, Robin said, "You could have gone with the group if you wanted to ride."

"I know, but I want to spend the day with you." Shawn kissed him on the mouth. "A walk on the trails feels like a good thing on the first day of a new year. Considering how our first walk went."

Robin chuckled. "Touché."

"Oh crap." Shawn clamped his back pocket where he usually kept his phone. "I left my phone in the cabin, and I really should call Granddad and wish him a happy new year."

"Go on back and make your call then. I'll finish cleaning up here."

"Are you sure?"

Robin waved him off. "I can handle storing cold cuts and wiping down a table. Go. I'll be down in a few."

"Okay, thanks."

After Shawn left, Robin took his time tidying up the kitchen, giving Shawn more privacy for his call. He was often subdued after these calls, so hopefully a walk would cheer him up. It was chilly but sunny, a good day to be outside for a while. Maybe make out under a tree. That could be fun. A picnic would have been fun, too, but Robin was stuffed, and Shawn had eaten a big sandwich himself.

Now that Robin knew Shawn had been homeless for

two years, his odd eating habits made more sense. When he first took over cooking from Patrice, Shawn would eat a decent portion of breakfast, maybe a half-sandwich at lunch if he ate anything, and then a larger meal at night. He seemed to ration what he ate and when, but as he eased into life on the ranch, three square meals a day was putting a bit of a curve on his skinny frame.

Eager to spend the afternoon doing nothing more taxing that holding his boyfriend's hand on the trail, Robin headed back to the cabin to collect said boyfriend. He opened the door and nearly tripped over Shawn, who was sitting on the floor a few feet inside, clutching his phone to his chest. Shawn's face was red, his breathing labored, and alarm shot through Robin like a bullet.

"What's wrong?" Robin dropped to his knees and clutched Shawn's trembling shoulders. "What happened?"

Shawn looked at him with agony in his eyes. "Nana died yesterday. Stroke. Oh God." He started sobbing then and threw himself at Robin. Robin struggled to hold him as Shawn broke down completely in his arms.

Shawn had dialed Granddad's line halfway back to the cabin, and he was a little surprised it rang for so long. Last week, he and Robin had transferred his old number to the new phone, and it had worked perfectly when Shawn test-called Granddad. He didn't worry over the long response time, though, because it was lunchtime, and Granddad could be in the middle of feeding Nana.

When the line finally picked up, a vaguely familiar female voice said, "Matthews residence."

"Um, hi? It's Shawn. Who's this?"

"Oh Shawn, hello. This is your mom's cousin Janet. From Reno."

"Hi." He kind of remembered Mom mentioning a cousin named Janet. "Are you in town visiting Granddad and Nana?"

"I am, but—" She made a soft, choking sound. "He didn't want to ruin your New Year's."

Shawn opened the cabin door and let it fall shut behind him, his stomach squirrely with nerves now. "What happened? Is Granddad sick?" He'd beaten throat cancer once, but it could reoccur and that would be awful to deal with on top of nursing Nana.

Janet's voice hitched. "Aunt Irma, your nana, she had a stroke late last night. I'm so sorry, Shawn, but she passed away."

"No, she didn't." Shawn swayed, and he barely felt the painful jolt that shot up his spine when his ass hit the wood floor. "No."

"I am so, so sorry. I kept asking your grandfather for permission to call you, but he didn't want you to know yet. I don't think he's fully processed it himself."

A bizarre anger combined with his refusal to believe this was true, and he snapped, "Why did he call you? Why are you there?"

"My mom was his sister, and I was closer, so I drove straight down to Breton. He's finally sleeping, or I'd let you talk to him."

"I'm coming up, first flight I can get."

I don't believe you. Nana isn't dead. She can't be. She can't...

But why would Janet lie? No one, not even a distant cousin, was that cruel.

"Are you sure that's a good idea, Shawn? We all know what happened with—"

Shawn hung up. His entire body was numb but somehow also shaking. He wanted to throw up everything he'd eaten for lunch. Nothing made sense. The world blurred behind a haze of confusion and denial.

No. No, no, no, no. NO!

The cabin door opened, spilling in sunlight and Robin's backlit shape. Robin's questions and concern finally penetrated the part of his brain that refused to accept the truth. "Nana died yesterday. Stroke." Saying it shattered something deep inside of Shawn's heart. "Oh God."

After those final two words, all he knew was the overwhelming agony of loss, the deep-wrenching sobs that burst from his chest, and the safety of Robin's arms around him…for a long, long time.

Chapter Nineteen

Shawn didn't remember a lot of the details of the next six or so hours of his life, because Robin took charge and made things happen. People spoke at and/or near him, and he knew the voices but the words made no sense. At some point, he was in a sitting room chair, a blanket around his shoulders and water in his hand. Miles was there. Judson, too, and probably Patrice. Offering condolences and assistance.

Through it all, he clung to the fact that Robin was always nearby, and then he was in a car. He and Robin were driving somewhere.

"What are we doing?" Shawn asked when he understood they were on the interstate.

"We're heading for the airport," Robin replied. "I've got us tickets north. We're going home, Shawn."

"Oh." He couldn't leave the ranch, though. "What about work?"

"Miles is going to pitch in with Patrice to keep everyone fed. Arthur, too. They've got four whole days before new guests arrive, and it's a small group."

That made sense, he supposed. "Your job?"

"The other horsemen are trickling back in, it's fine. Judson is completely okay with me taking extra time off

to help you through this. I couldn't imagine being anywhere else right now."

"But how? I never told you where I was from."

"I called Janet back. Got the address from her. I am
so fucking sorry, Shawn. You obviously loved her a lot."

For a split second, Shawn thought Robin meant he
loved Janet a lot, and he barely knew the woman. No,
Robin was talking about Nana. And yes, Shawn had
loved the woman. Her loss, on top of both his parents,
was almost too much to bear, and he was insanely grateful to Robin. "Thank you. I don't even know which end
is up right now."

"You're welcome, and you don't have to know. Just
try to relax and trust me to get us there safely."

"I do trust you." *I love you.*

Shawn dozed a bit until they arrived at the airport.
After parking in one of the paid lots, Robin grabbed a
single carry-on from the trunk and led Shawn into the
terminal. Shawn moved by rote, removing shoes and
doing all the random stuff he was told to do. Then they
were in seats, and eventually on a plane. The only other
time Shawn had flown had been the day he left Breton
at eighteen and went to live with Sheila.

God, my life has changed so much since then.

Hell, his life had changed completely since just this
morning. All the joy from everything he'd shared with
Robin was gone, sucked away by overwhelming grief.

It was a short flight, and Shawn simply followed
Robin through the terminal to the rental car counter.
Then out of the airport to their car. Robin used the
rental's GPS to navigate his way to Breton, driving
down streets Shawn knew by heart. It had snowed, and
Robin seemed a little nervous about the roads but he

did fine. Past signs for the ski lodge toward the wooded area where "the help" lived.

Granddad had worked hard his entire life, and he'd sacrificed a lot to make sure he and Nana stayed in the house they built when they first got married. Raised all their kids in. Went through fights and birthday parties and anniversaries. The familiar blue structure appeared on the street like an old friend. Its porch desperately needed a new coat of paint, and the flower beds hadn't been weeded in what looked like years. Things Shawn could have easily done. Long shadows stretched across the yard, and Shawn looked at the time.

Nearly six in the evening.

He didn't know how Robin had put this trip together so quickly, or what it had cost him, but Shawn would find a way to pay him back.

Two unfamiliar cars were parked next to Granddad's pickup, filling the driveway, so Robin parked on the street. Got out, grabbed the carry-on, and came around to Shawn's door. Opened it. Shawn hesitated, desperate to go inside and terrified a neighbor would see him. He couldn't take the looks.

They walked up the cracked pathway to the porch, and the front door opened before Robin could press the bell. A familiar, middle-aged woman opened it, and Shawn kind of saw his mom in the shape of her face and her curly brown hair.

"Shawn," Janet said. "And you must be Robin."

"Robin Butler, ma'am," he replied. Instead of shaking, he kissed the top of her hand, which charmed Janet instantly.

"Come inside, it's freezing out there."

Was it? Shawn hadn't noticed the significant temperature drop from getting on the plane to departing it.

"Pastor Schumer is here, too," Janet said as she closed the door. "He's speaking with Uncle Francis now. Apparently, they'd already made memorial and interment plans in case. You know. This."

"Makes sense that they'd have made arrangements," Robin replied softly. In Shawn's ear, he whispered. "Not how I imagined meeting your family, but I'm here. For anything you need."

Shawn could only nod that he understood. He squeezed Robin's hand once, then walked out of the small foyer and into the living room. Nana's hospital bed was still there, in the corner where they'd once had a love seat. Otherwise, the room looked exactly how Shawn remembered it—except for the two figures sitting close together on the couch.

Granddad looked up, his wrinkled face red, eyes swollen, right at Shawn. Shawn didn't think he had any tears left, but he was wrong. Granddad met him in the middle of the room in a fierce hug, and Shawn cried. He cried for all the years he'd missed, for the one loving grandparent he had left, for Granddad's own grief, which was wrenching out of him in ragged sobs.

They cried for a while, clutching each other, until Granddad let go. He looked like he'd aged twenty years in the last five, and a lot of that was Shawn's fault. "Look at you," Granddad said. "So grown-up. And a chef, to boot."

Shawn wasn't sure how to respond to that, so he waved Robin over. "Granddad, this is my boyfriend, Robin Butler."

"Ah, yes, the man you've spoken so highly of during our phone calls."

Robin's cheeks pinked up as he shook Granddad's hand. "It's a pleasure to meet you, Mr. Matthews."

"Pshaw, son, call me Granddad or Francis. None of this Mr. Matthews business."

"Francis, then."

"Good, good. Shawn, you remember Pastor Schumer."

The pastor had risen and stood slightly off to the side, his expression coolly neutral. "Of course," Shawn replied. Schumer made no move to approach or shake their hands, and Shawn didn't care. Let the asshole be quietly homophobic.

"I didn't want this to ruin your New Year's," Granddad said to Shawn. "But I'm awfully glad you're here."

"Me, too." He squeezed the elderly man's wrist. "Tell me what I can do."

"You being here is enough. We've got it all planned out. Small church service on Thursday, followed by a reception at the senior center. She wanted to be cremated and buried under her favorite tree out back."

"Sounds like Nana." Their backyard had a big old aspen tree in it that Shawn remembering climbing a few times as a kid.

"Have you boys eaten supper?" Janet asked. "I was just about to pop a casserole into the oven."

"Supper would be lovely, ma'am, thank you," Robin said. "Lunch feels like a lifetime ago." Shawn leaned into him, grateful to Robin for taking charge. He should eat, but Shawn wasn't hungry.

Shawn wandered down the short hallway that led to the three bedrooms and single bathroom. His room had been the first on the left, and he pushed open the door, unsurprised to find it exactly how he'd left it. Same furniture, same handful of comic books and scholar awards and participation trophies. Things he hadn't been able to take with him but couldn't manage to throw away.

"You played baseball?" Robin asked. He pointed at the trophies.

"Yeah, and I was pretty good at it, too. Quit when I started getting booed during games. It wasn't good for team morale, anyway." Ugh, the funeral and reception were going to be a nightmare, but Shawn had Robin. They'd get through it together.

"Huh. So what other hidden talents do you have?"

"I can roll my tongue and stick it out." Shawn demonstrated, and Robin chuckled.

"Outstanding trick."

"Can you do it?"

Robin tried and failed, and the silly exchange helped Shawn feel normal for a few seconds. Then he remembered why he was here. He sank down on the slightly musty full-size bed and dropped his face into his hands. Robin sat beside him and wrapped an arm around his waist. Leaned in close.

"You tell me what you need, okay?" Robin whispered. "Anything. That's a promise."

"You being here is all I need right now. Thank you."

"Of course."

They sat quietly until Janet called them for supper. Tuna noodle casserole was a familiar family dish, and Shawn accepted a small scoop. He hadn't eaten it in years, and he enjoyed the odd way canned tuna, cream of celery soup, egg noodles, and cheddar cheese came together to taste good. Robin sniffed at his first bite, and his surprised look after he tasted told Shawn this was his first time.

Probably didn't make a lot of casseroles on the road with Lucky's. And it struck Shawn that he didn't know what Robin had done during that mysterious year between Xander's death and Robin landing at Clean Slate. All Robin ever said about it was he'd been in a bad place, so Shawn didn't push.

No one really spoke during the meal, which was fine by Shawn. He had no idea what to say about anything. After dinner, Pastor Schumer excused himself, and Shawn was glad to see the man go. His quiet disapproval of Robin irritated him. Janet went into the guest room to call her husband and check in about Thursday's plans. Apparently, she was hanging around until then, which was nice.

Shawn, Robin, and Granddad watched a few game show reruns on GSN before Granddad excused himself to bed. Once they were alone, Shawn cuddled up closer to Robin, and they stretched out on the couch together to watch a movie. Shawn didn't pay much attention. Mostly, he existed here, among these familiar furnishings and photos and rugs. In some ways, no time had passed at all.

And then he noticed the hospital bed—apparently, it was being picked up tomorrow by the company they'd rented it from—and Shawn remembered how very much everything had changed. Some things for the worse, but so many, many things for the better.

Later, Shawn let Robin wrap his bigger body around Shawn in bed, and it didn't even feel strange spooning in his old room. He needed Robin, and Robin was there for him. Robin hadn't walked away or turned his back when things got hard, and that meant the world to

Shawn. Not having to handle this alone when he'd relied solely on himself for so many years.

Shawn shed a few more tears as he fell asleep that night. A mix of happy tears and sad ones. And in between, tears of hope for his future with Robin.

All the next day, Robin watched. He made it his mission to pay attention to Shawn and be there for whatever his boyfriend needed. Janet was polite and kind, and she took point on answering the doorbell whenever it rang. Often, it was a neighbor dropping off a casserole or freezer meal for Francis, sometimes baked goods. She put several wrapped loaves of banana bread right into the freezer. Most of the time, the guests stayed in the foyer. Francis occasionally spoke to them personally.

Shawn didn't…hide from the guests, but he also made no effort to engage them. Francis and Shawn spent several hours Wednesday morning poring over old photo albums for a poster collage to put in the church vestibule tomorrow. They'd already chosen the photo that they'd have blown up for the front of the church: Irma Worthington on her wedding day, dressed in white, and so beautiful with her styled hair and bright smile.

"No matter how she aged, that's how she always looked to me," Francis had said, and it had brought tears to Robin's eyes. The man spoke of his late wife of fifty-plus years with so much adoration in his voice. It was both humbling and inspiring.

After lunch, Shawn spent a lot of time prowling the house, both inside and out. Testing baseboards, poking at signs of water damage in one of the spare rooms, checking for termites on the front porch and other things like that. The house definitely needed work, and its condition bordered on disrepair. It wasn't falling down around Francis's ears but even Robin saw things that needed to be fixed, patched, or fully replaced, including that grease trap of an oven he cooked with.

That evening, Janet's husband and two tween sons arrived and the family shared one of the casseroles and a loaf of homemade apple bread for dinner. Robin made sure Shawn ate a decent portion of food. His appetite had been down since yesterday, and the younger man needed fuel. Janet's husband helped Robin wrangle the love seat out of the spare bedroom where it had been shoved a few years ago, and they put it where Irma's hospital bed had been. Francis got emotional over that and went to bed early.

The boys weren't excited about sleeping on the pull-out couch, but they were really into the fact that Shawn and Robin worked on a dude ranch, so Robin entertained the kids with stories until around nine, when the household seemed to mutually agree it was time to retire. Shawn was quiet as they climbed into bed, and he quickly turned into their familiar spooning position. Robin kissed the side of Shawn's neck, not worried exactly, but Shawn had been so quiet today...

"Penny for your thoughts?" Robin asked in the dark.

"I have so many, it'll probably cost you a couple of bucks."

"Totally worth it."

Shawn sighed. "I think my biggest regret right now is that Nana never got to meet you. She didn't get to see how freaking happy I am with you. And that's my fault."

"How's it your fault?"

"You offered to bring me up here to see them, and I said no."

"Hey, you had good reasons for saying no, and you also had no reason to suspect she'd pass so suddenly. Strokes just happen, baby. Same as heart attacks." Robin's thoughts shifted to this past summer when Arthur had suffered two heart attacks, one minor and one major. The entire staff had been terrified for the man, but he was bouncing back with lots of rest, a healthier diet, and a lot of determination.

"Yeah. I think a tiny part of me was also a little embarrassed. Huntington's takes so much away from you. The ability to function, to speak, to do so many things. Half the time, I could barely understand her when we spoke on the phone, and Granddad had to translate."

Robin considered a question he'd had in the back of his mind ever since Shawn mentioned his grandmother's affliction. "Did your mom have the gene?"

Shawn twisted around to face Robin, his expression difficult to decipher in the gloom. "Would you see me differently if I said yes?"

"Of course not. I'd heard of the disease, and I did a little digging." If one parent had it, then any children had a fifty percent chance of inheriting the gene, too, and eventually developing symptoms.

"I don't know if she had it," Shawn said. "Mom died before we knew Nana had it, so there was no chance to do the genetic test. And they're expensive, especially without insurance, so I've never taken it. I don't want to know. I want to live my life, Robin, and to be happy. Symptoms can manifest in the late twenties, but most don't until much later in life. So for now, I don't want to know."

"Okay. I hear you, and I respect that."

Shawn studied his face a beat. "Would me having the gene change how you feel about me?"

"Absolutely not," Robin said without a second's hesitation, and he meant it. He was in this with Shawn, period. "Even if you said you had it, I'm not going anywhere, I promise. Hell, I could be paralyzed in a car wreck tomorrow, or discover I have cancer next week. Part of life is taking the bad times along with the good." He pressed their foreheads together. "I'll weather any storm with you, Shawn Matthews."

Shawn sobbed once but didn't cry, and he pressed soft lips to Robin's. "Same. Have you always been this amazing?"

"Dunno. But you definitely bring out the best in me, so thank you for that."

"You bring out the best in me, too. I'm glad you're here. Tomorrow is really going to suck, and not just because it's Nana's funeral."

"Because of the thing that happened when you were a teenager?"

"Yeah."

Shawn didn't say anything else, and this probably wasn't the best moment to ask, so Robin left it alone. For now.

Robin didn't sleep well that night, likely because Shawn didn't, either. Shawn didn't usually toss and turn much but he couldn't seem to get comfortable. He rose before dawn, and Robin let him go, trusting his boyfriend to ask if he needed something from Robin. As the house came awake, seven people had to take turns showering and using the toilet of the single bathroom, and that became an interesting juggling act.

The service was scheduled at ten, with the reception directly afterward. After a light breakfast, Janet's clan headed for their car. Francis rode with Robin and Shawn in the rental, and Robin followed Shawn's directions to the church. Shawn was shotgun, and he got out to open Francis's door. The pair stuck close together, hands clasped, so Robin walked behind them, eyes open for anyone who might appear to be a threat to Shawn.

A small table in the vestibule had a guest book they all signed, next to the poster board of photos they'd put together yesterday. Their trio gazed at it with respect for a bit before moving into the sanctuary. Janet and her family weren't far behind. Robin had attended a few funerals as a kid, but all those had been in funeral homes with open-casket viewings. Not small services like this.

Shawn and Francis stopped just inside the sanctuary, which seemed to be their position for whatever came next. At the front of the church, next to the altar, was an enlarged copy of Irma's photo on an easel. The altar held a lovely arrangement of white roses and pink hydrangeas. Everything was simple and tasteful, as Robin imagined Irma had been as a young woman. Eager to marry and start a family. Family who had, according to Shawn, spread out across the States and rarely kept in touch.

The small sanctuary slowly filled with people, and Robin remained a steady presence on Shawn's right. He wanted to hold Shawn's hand, but Shawn hadn't reached for him, and Robin didn't want to push their relationship in these people's faces. Everyone who came in offered condolences to Francis. Women hugged him, men shook his hand. Many folks acknowledged Shawn with polite nods, but few engaged him in any meaningful way, and it irritated Robin on a cellular level. Shawn was grieving too, and the mood here stoked Robin's curiosity about Shawn's past.

At ten, their trio moved to sit in the front pew. Pastor Schumer made a show of shaking their hands, even Robin's, before moving behind the altar. Robin wasn't religious. He considered himself spiritual, but he respectfully went through the motions of an opening prayer and singing hymns. Schumer recited Bible verses. Another hymn, another prayer, and it was over.

The sanctuary slowly cleared out. Francis whispered something to Shawn. Shawn clasped Robin's hand and stood. Led him out into the vestibule to wait. "He wanted a few minutes alone," Shawn said. His eyes were red, his cheeks dry, and he leaned into Robin's chest.

Robin held him until Francis joined them.

The reception hall was modestly decorated with a buffet line of hot and cold dishes, and a drink station. Older women, who were probably church members, stood behind the line and were serving the guests. Some of the tables were already half-full of folks eating. Francis skipped the hot line and went directly to the dessert table for a big slice of chocolate cake. Robin loved that Shawn did the same, and they sat together at an empty table with their cake.

While they ate, people Robin didn't remember from the church came over to talk to Francis. A few folks spoke directly to Shawn, and Shawn even introduced Robin to a young couple about Shawn's age. An old high school classmate, he discovered. That couple was the most polite of the bunch, but Shawn didn't seem very bothered by the constant snubs.

He'd expected it, that much was clear.

"Well now," a deep voice said behind them. "If it isn't little Shawnie Matthews all grown up."

Shawn's entire body tensed. His breathing became labored as his face paled. Literally paled in front of Robin's eyes, and Robin knew without asking the voice belonged to the infamous Beck.

Oh shit.

Chapter Twenty

The only reason Shawn didn't flee the room the instant he heard Beck's voice was because of Robin. Robin was both his touchstone and his protector. And Shawn had returned to Breton today expecting some sort of confrontation with Beck. He was just glad Beck had waited to show up here, rather than at the church.

It still didn't stop his body's immediate panicked reaction or the cold ball of ice that landed in his gut.

Little Shawnie Matthews.

"Mr. Beckham," Francis said coldly. "Please offer your condolences and move along."

"But it's been so long," Beck replied in a familiar, too-charming-for-my-own-good tone. "Can't I say hello to the kid who tried to ruin my life?"

Next to Shawn, Robin stiffened, hands balling into fists in his lap. Shawn squeezed Robin's thigh briefly and then rose. Turned to face Beck for the first time in over five years. The man had aged well, only a bit more gray in his dark hair, a handful of new laugh lines around his eyes. Beck wasn't handsome, exactly, but he used natural charm to win people over and make friends, and he'd used that charm to turn half this damned town against Shawn.

For doing nothing more damning than telling the truth.

"Hello," Shawn said. He drew on all the confidence he'd been building by working at the saloon and the guesthouse. "Now *you* say hello, and we'll both go our separate ways."

Beck's left eyebrow twitched. "That's all I get? Not even a handshake?"

"Why would you want a handshake from someone you had branded a liar and opportunist? Especially when you're the fucking liar and we both know it."

God, but it felt good to say all this to Beck's face. To finally get this off his chest. During the court proceedings, they'd been kept apart, and after the dust settled, Shawn had kept his head down until he left town. There hadn't been a chance to defend himself, and even if there had been, Shawn hadn't been strong enough back then. But he sure as hell was strong enough to say it all now.

"I'm not the one who preyed on a fifteen-year-old and then lied about it to save his own ass. You did that. And you'll probably deny it until the day you die, but we know the truth. My conscience is clear. Is yours?"

Beck's face twisted in anger. The man's hands came up, but before Shawn could react to defend himself, Robin was there. Inserting his broader body between Shawn and Beck, and then Beck took a full step backward.

"Touch him," Robin snarled, "and you'll be eating your food through a straw while your two broken hands heal."

Holy hell. Overprotective Robin is hot.

In the tense silence that followed, Shawn realized that the confrontation had gained the attention of the entire room. Everyone had stopped talking and eating to watch. Shawn's face blazed with embarrassment, but he stepped out from behind the protective wall of Robin's body. "This is my grandmother's wake," Shawn said with steel in his voice. "Please leave. You are not welcome here."

Beck opened his mouth, then seemed to realize how many eyeballs were on him. Many pairs of them disapproving, too, which kind of pleased Shawn. Maybe they weren't all on Shawn's side, but they were not happy Beck had caused a scene. Beck's face clearly showed he understood the mistake he'd made, that even someone as popular in their small town as Roger Beckham needed to know when to show respect.

Head held high, Beck pivoted neatly on one heel and strode out of the room. Conversation levels returned to normal. Shawn took a few cleansing breaths, a little surprised his anxiety hadn't gone into self-destruct mode over this, but he was surprisingly calm. Because he'd faced his monster. And he'd won.

Robin turned to face him, his eyes silently begging for answers about what he'd just witnessed. "Granddad," Shawn said, "we're going to take a walk, okay?"

"Okay, son," Granddad replied. "You be safe."

"We will."

Shawn had no expectations that Beck was lying in wait to attack them. It wasn't the guy's style. He attacked using words. Threats. Not physical violence—which was exactly why Robin's words had made Beck back down. In his heart of hearts, Beck was a coward. And Shawn was done being afraid of him.

"Come on." Shawn took Robin's hand and led him through the maze of tables to the door. The cold air smacked him in the face and he inhaled deeply. Released the long breath through his nose.

The senior center was on the far end of town near a semibusy street. About five blocks from here was the hardware/general store where Shawn's nightmare had occurred, but he didn't want to take Robin there. So he took Robin in the opposite direction, down a residential street until he found a stone bench dedicated to the passing of some important person or another. Didn't matter.

Shawn sat and pulled Robin down beside him. Curled his arm around Robin's and stared out at the quiet street. With no idea how to begin, Shawn reached for the first starting point that came to mind. Some way to help Robin understand how things had unfolded.

"When I first came to live here with my grandparents, I already came with the baggage of a heroin addict for a father. Everyone knew he'd overdosed. I had trouble making friends at school, because everyone assumed I was a druggie, too. Granddad was already retired on a fixed income and struggling a bit with money, and I didn't want to be a burden. Plus, Nana's symptoms weren't under control and being in the house was... unpleasant. It was even worse in high school, and I wanted a distraction from how lonely I was, so when I was fifteen, I got an afterschool job."

"Working for Beck?" Robin asked.

"Yup. He owns the town's biggest store. It's a mix of hardware, groceries, general dry goods, and even has a small lending library inside. He needed a stock boy paid under the table, so he didn't have to worry about work permits from the school. I took the job. At first, he was this charming older guy who didn't treat me like gum on his shoe. He gave me candy bars and soda on my shifts.

After a few weeks working about five shifts a week, I started considering him a friend.

"And the shift was so gradual, I didn't see it as it happened. Looking back the signs were there, but I was a teenager desperate for attention, and I was just starting to realize I was gay. When Beck and I talked, he'd put his hand on my shoulder. Leave it there longer than most people might. Then it turned into his hand on my thigh. He'd give me long hugs when I left for the night. I craved the attention he gave me, because I still had no real friends. I spent some of my money on supplies to keep baking, practicing the recipes I used to make with Mom. A lot of it I gave to Granddad for groceries or the electric bill, especially when it was way higher in winter."

Shawn paused in case Robin had any questions, but Robin just listened. His eyes were sad, his smile encouraging. So Shawn kept telling his story. "I'd worked for him for about six months when he asked me to come in on a Saturday night to inventory the stockroom. It was something like eight to midnight, and the store closed at eight, so it was just us. He had pizza and beer, and having a beer at fifteen was like being one of the cool kids. So I drank two beers while we worked and it didn't seem weird when he'd brush his whole body against mine. Or when he'd lean over me, pressed in close. Looking back, I can see how he was testing me. Seeing how far he could go before I reacted badly."

"He's a fucking pervert," Robin said. "Coming on to a kid like that."

"Yeah, he was. And he knew he could get away with it, because of his popularity in town. He was everyone's buddy, knew all the locals. He even offered credit in the store when money got tight. To most people, Roger Beckham could do no wrong."

"But his behavior escalated?"

Shawn's skin crawled with old shame he tried to push away. "I was still about six weeks from turning sixteen, which is the age of consent in Nevada, the first time...he groped my dick. I freaked out a little, but Beck insisted it was an accident, joked about it, and I let it go. But on my next shift, he took me into his office upstairs and asked how badly I wanted to keep my job."

Robin growled softly.

"I said I'd do anything to keep my job. Besides baking, it was the only thing I had to look forward to and he knew it." Shawn let out a deep breath that did nothing to calm his nerves over this next part. "So I let him fondle me while he jerked off. That happened about once a week, usually when we were alone after closing, for several months. I got hard a few times because, you know, fifteen turning sixteen, and he used that biological function to tell me I enjoyed it. That I wanted it. That I was leading him on, giving him signals I wanted more."

"Shawn." Robin's voice was pitched low with horror. "Did he ever...?"

He didn't need to finish the question. "No, Beck never penetrated me. But he did manipulate me. Every time he got hard he said it was because I wanted it. If I tried to say no, he'd threaten my job. Or he'd threaten to out me as gay, even though I'd never come out to him. So I kept quiet about the abuse for about three months after I'd turned sixteen. It was late summer, and I'd started dreading going to work. Granddad noticed I was acting differently, but he was so overwhelmed with Nana."

"How did it all come out?"

Shawn rested his head on Robin's shoulder and told this final bit to his own feet. "The store was closed for Labor Day, but he insisted we both go in that morning to change displays and restock, and I tried to get out of it. I'd tried to avoid being alone with him but it didn't always work. When he said he'd fire me if I didn't come in, I went. And we worked. Actually worked, and it was totally normal, and it also fucked with my head a little. But when we finished, he insisted I go to his house for dinner. I said no, I was expected home. I was so confused by what was happening that when he said he'd fire me, I said I didn't care. I was…just so terrified to be alone with him in his house."

"It was probably a good instinct. Your self-preservation was kicking in."

"Probably so." Shawn didn't object when Robin rearranged them so his arm was across Shawn's shoulders, Shawn snuggled up close to his side. They were still on a public street, but he didn't care anymore. "The result of that argument with Beck was a forced blow job. I hated everything about it, and I started hating him for the first time. When I went home that night, I broke down. Told Granddad everything. He called the police. I confessed it all, and they were shocked when I said Beck had done it. But because I was fifteen when it started, they had to at least bring him in for questioning."

Robin let out a harsh sigh. "He denied it."

"Yup. That's when the shit hit the fan. I swore on and signed all kinds of things, and when we didn't relent, Beck painted me as the aggressor and a gay slut, swore it didn't start until I was sixteen. But I passed a polygraph and he didn't. Still, it divided the town. Here was this wholesome guy everyone liked being accused of molesting a teenager, and then there was me. Dead parents, one of them a drug addict. A loner with no friends. The whole thing embarrassed the hell out of my granddad but he stuck by me. He believed me, no matter what."

"Because he loves you, Shawn. You did the right thing by speaking up."

"In the end, it didn't matter, because I had no proof. No video evidence, no taped conversations." Not even Beck going on a drunken bender, throwing rocks at Granddad's house, and landing in jail for three nights straight made a difference in court. "Beck got a slap on the wrist for hiring a minor without the proper documentation, and I think a fine. A few people boycotted his store for a while, but mostly nothing changed. Once it was over I hated living here, and as soon as I graduated high school and was eighteen, I left. This is the first time I've been back since."

"I don't blame you for staying away from so many bad memories." Robin pulled him in for a proper hug, and Shawn melted against his broad chest. "I wish I knew how to make this better for you."

"You are." Shawn sat up so he could look Robin in the eyes, and he tried to project this truth with his own. "Because you believe me. You believe *in* me. What happened with Beck is the past, and for the first time since then, I know I can move on and be happy. Because of you. I don't want the things he did to control me anymore."

"I'm glad. I think we've both helped each other move on from the most painful parts of our pasts. So thank *you*, Shawn, for being you. And for sharing all this with me."

"It was time. You're the only person outside this town and my family who knows the whole story. Even last year when Miles was dealing with his ex, I sympathized with him so much because I knew what it felt like to have someone relentlessly coming at you, and all you want is to be left alone. I didn't report Beck to become famous or get a fast payday. I reported him because he finally pushed me too far."

"And you stayed away for over five years."

"I couldn't put anything else on Granddad's shoulders. But now he's alone and he needs me." Shawn managed a wry smile. "Plus I got to face down my bogeyman. Thank you, by the way, for standing up for me. It's refreshing to have someone on my side."

"I'll always be on your side."

"I know." It still felt too soon to say *I love you*, despite Shawn feeling the truth of those words in his soul. Right after such an emotional confession wasn't the right time.

"And for what it's worth?" Robin rubbed their noses together. "You coming back for the funeral and standing up to Beck? I have a feeling people who doubted you before may start changing their minds."

"Honestly? I'm not sure that I care anymore. If heaven exists, they'll have to answer for their own thoughts and prejudices. Like I told Beck, my conscience is clear. All I ever did was tell the truth."

"The truth is the easiest thing to remember."

Shawn snorted. "Unfortunately, some people are dedicated enough liars that they can make the worst lie sound like the truth. That's Beck. And I'm glad he's out of my life. I don't want to waste another minute thinking about him. I want to look forward now. It's going to be difficult for a while, helping Granddad adjust to his new life without Nana, but the ranch will be there when I come home. So will you."

"Yes, I will. Home is with you, Shawn. You've got my heart now. Be gentle with it?"

"As long as you're gentle with mine."

Robin brushed his lips lightly over Shawn's. "That's a promise."

Part of Robin wanted to set fire to this godforsaken town. Burn down everything that reminded Shawn of his painful past. Bring pain to the people who'd caused Shawn so much heartache. Maybe punch a few people in the face for good measure. But he didn't.

He stayed present for Shawn while he absorbed all the truths Shawn had lobbed at him today. Robin regretted not breaking both of Beck's hands back at the reception—or at least not punching the asshole right in the mouth. Shawn didn't seem to want revenge or retaliation, though, so Robin did his best to stay in the moment and not let his temper win.

They returned to the reception by the time it was winding down, and were able to collect Francis, as well as a few plates of leftovers. Francis wouldn't have to worry about cooking for at least two weeks, judging by all the food they'd collected at the house. Probably longer. Janet and her crew were home long enough to collect their things before heading back to Reno. Whatever. She was nice enough, but a small amount of tension left the house with her. Francis and Shawn seemed like they could breathe easier, and sometime late that afternoon, the pair brought out a chessboard.

Robin didn't pretend to understand the game, but he absorbed the lovely sight of grandfather and grandson studying the board and considering their moves for hours, while sharing hot tea and different slices of pie.

He also checked in with Colt at the ranch, who reported all was well, and they were ready for Sunday's group of six guests. Small but it was early January and still pretty cool during the day, which limited the guests' activities.

Judson hadn't given Robin a deadline for his return to the ranch, but the following morning, Robin rode shotgun while Shawn drove them to the nearest major home improvement store for a bunch of paint, plaster, caulking, and various other repair items. Shawn seemed to be hanging around for a while, and Robin didn't comment as they spent most of Friday doing small repairs around the house.

Francis heated up another casserole for dinner, and after their trio sat down to eat, Shawn said, "Granddad, I want you to think about moving to Garrett with me."

The elderly man's fork scraped across his plate. "What? Why?"

"So you aren't alone here. We can fix up the house and sell it. Maybe pay off the rest of our debt, start over."

"I'm seventy-four years old, Shawn. Not sure I can start over after all this time. No, this house is where I started my life, and it's where I'll end it. Just like my wife."

"Granddad—"

"No." Francis shook his head. "I love you, Shawn, but this is my home." With a soft sigh, Francis picked up his plate and took it into the living room.

For a split second, Shawn looked ready to burst into tears. A few hard blinks chased that away, and he kept eating. Robin wasn't sure what to say, so he stayed quiet for now. He completely understood Shawn's motives for moving Francis closer to Garrett, but he also understood why Francis would choose to stay. This town, this house, was the life he knew.

Both men were quiet the rest of the night, and while Robin knew how to play the clown to defuse tense situations, he didn't want to make things worse between the pair. This was something the Matthews men had to figure out on their own.

Francis went to bed first, leaving Shawn and Robin on the couch watching the end of a movie Robin hadn't been paying much attention to. They sat close to each other without really touching. Definitely not cuddling. Not that they cuddled much in front of Francis or anyone else, and Robin resisted dragging Shawn into his lap for a proper hug. Something about Shawn's posture screamed "don't touch!"

"A few dollars for your thoughts?" Robin said.

Shawn snorted. "You got change for a twenty?"

"Sure. Please, talk to me."

"It was a stupid thing to ask." Shawn flopped back against the couch cushions. "Him moving to Garrett. This is his home, and I know that. Being back just... reminded me how much I've missed him."

"That's natural." Visiting with Levi over Christmas had reminded Robin how much he missed Doug and the other rodeo performers. People he'd lived, worked, and traveled with for eight years of his life. "We all miss people we love when we're apart, but that's part of life, right? Before we go home, we can set your grandfather up with a good tablet so you guys can video chat when you get lonely."

Shawn flinched.

Robin didn't like that. "What?"

"I think I need to stay here for a while longer."

"How much longer?" It also didn't pass his notice that Shawn said "I need to stay," not we.

"A week, maybe two. The house still needs a lot of work, and even if I can't convince him to sell it and move, I can fix it up for him. Get it clean and tidy, and help him go through Nana's things."

"I can't stay that long."

"I know, and I didn't expect you to. Honestly, with guests coming on Sunday, you should probably fly back tomorrow. I'll call Judson and explain everything. I hate leaving the guesthouse in the lurch, but I'm needed here."

"Judson will understand that." Robin couldn't shake the sense that Shawn was dismissing him. Sending him away. Shawn was right, of course, that Robin should be back at the ranch, and he didn't want to take advantage of Judson's generous nature by asking for more time off. "Are you sure this is what you want?"

"Yes." Shawn reached out, and Robin squeezed his hand. "I love that you've been here for me these last few days, but you have a life back at Clean Slate."

My life is with you, Shawn.

"And I'll be back in Garrett before you have a chance to miss me," Shawn added.

Doubtful. I'll miss you the minute I get on that plane.

Robin didn't say any of those things out loud, because he didn't want to pressure Shawn into coming home with him, or into allowing Robin to stay and help. If this was what Shawn needed to process his grief, Robin would support him. He'd also carve a hell of a lot of chess pieces as a welcome home gift when his boyfriend came back to him.

"Okay," Robin said. "I'll look into flights for tomorrow evening."

"Thank you."

Later that night, after crawling into bed naked, they spent long hours kissing, touching, licking, and making each other come as quietly as possible. Everything about it was so familiar and tender and loving that Robin refused to feel like it had been goodbye sex. It was simply "until next time" sex.

Until next time.

Robin flew home late Saturday evening. Judson picked him up at the airport, and then he surprised Robin by saying they were waiting on another flight due to land in about forty-five minutes. So they chilled at a nearby convenience stop while they waited. Judson was cagey about who they were picking up, but Robin didn't think too hard about it.

His thoughts were too full of Shawn. They'd spent the morning and afternoon deep-cleaning the kitchen, and Shawn had a brand-new oven due to be delivered on Monday. Francis had helped some, but he mostly sat on the living room love seat and looked at photo albums. Robin had been impressed by the sheer number of them, curated over two lifetimes.

Shawn had also called Judson, who'd assured Shawn they would take care of the guesthouse cooking. To take all the time he needed. Shawn had helped them out of a jam after Patrice's accident, so they'd help him out now.

Robin sipped at a bottled water while they waited, until Judson's phone pinged with a text. "They landed," Judson said. "Let's go."

They?

Judson drove them back to the pickup area and found the terminal. Robin exited the front passenger seat out of habit, so he could politely greet whoever they were picking up. People with carry-ons streamed out of the doors and Robin absently glanced at faces—and then one face stood out. Slightly older but so familiar it socked Robin right in the feels.

Doug Peletier strode toward them with a green duffel bag in his hand and a watery smile on his face. He came straight for Robin, and Robin didn't even think. He flung his arms around the man he'd considered a father for years and hugged the life out of him. Emotion clogged his throat and threatened tears, and Robin didn't know what to say or do. He clung to Doug, who hugged him just as tight.

"It's been too damned long, son," Doug said. "Too long."

"Yeah." Robin pulled back so he could see Doug's face again, just to make sure, but he wasn't imagining this. "What are you doing here?"

"We'll explain in the car," Judson said. "Let's not hold up traffic."

"Okay."

Robin and Doug both got in the backseat, and Robin couldn't stop staring at the man. Couldn't stop marveling that he was here at all. "I spoke to your friend Mack a few days ago," Doug said. "I gotta say first, I'm really sorry for your boyfriend's loss."

"Thank you. I'll pass it along."

"So Mack and I got to talking, and even though he's sent me pictures and streamed live video, we agreed it would be a good idea for me to fly in for a few days. Go up myself and take a good look at where we'll be performing. I'd hoped to meet your Shawn but I understand he's still getting his affairs in order."

My Shawn.

"Yeah, he's staying in Nevada for another week or so."

"Well, I'm all yours until Wednesday."

Three whole days plus change. Robin couldn't believe his good luck. The only thing that could have made this surprise even better was springing Levi on him, too. But Levi did have a life and three cats back in Colorado to attend to. It was enough that he would be here for opening day and the big rodeo.

"This is the best surprise," Robin said. "I can't wait to see you guys perform again in a few weeks."

"You know, if you want to perform with us," Doug replied, "I'm sure we can work you into the show."

Robin stared at the man. Once Mack had made the change from Robin training horses and riders to having Lucky's do it, Robin had resigned himself to no longer actively participating in the show. "I haven't done more than basic roping tricks for tourists in three years."

"I can work with you, warm up those muscle memories. This is the kind of stuff you never completely forget."

"True."

"If you're worried about your job," Judson said from the front, "I'll work your schedule around it, no problem. You're doing Mack a huge favor by bringing Lucky's to town, Mr. Peletier, and Mack's like a son to me. We all want the ghost town to be a success."

Robin's eyes stung with grateful tears. He really did work for the most generous people on the planet. "I'd like to help, then. Thank you."

"You're welcome, son," Doug replied with a warm smile. "You are very welcome."

Chapter Twenty-One

Shawn didn't realize he could be jealous over someone thirty years older than himself, but he was insanely jealous of Doug Peletier, and he'd spent the last week solid working himself to death to try and kill that jealousy. When Robin called him late last Saturday to tell him all about Doug's arrival and Robin being in the eventual rodeo show, Shawn had been initially happy for Robin. He heard the joy in Robin's voice, and all Shawn wanted was for his boyfriend to be happy.

But during their infrequent phone calls between then and Doug's departure, all Robin seemed to talk about was Doug, the rodeo, the ghost town site, and everything related to opening day. Sure, Robin asked how Shawn and Granddad were doing, the progress on the house, et cetera, but it felt...forced?

Maybe Shawn was just being paranoid. Couples didn't grow apart in one week, did they? Nah, he was lonely, that was all. Shawn missed his friends at the ranch and the chaos of cooking for so many people. He missed the saloon kitchen and was glad they'd be reopening in three more weeks. Life could go back to seminormal.

At least Granddad's house was shaping up. Shawn had repainted the front porch, deep-cleaned all the carpets, dusted every single object within reach, and then used the stepladder to get everything else. Granddad said Shawn could do whatever he wanted with his old room, so Shawn hauled most of his old stuff to a thrift store. Personal objects he couldn't part with, he packed up in a plastic tote to take home with him.

That night, he and Robin had a Skype date, and Shawn recognized the walls of his own cabin as Robin's location. Which was totally fine with Shawn. They watched the same movie and commented like they were in the same room, and while it was a fun date, it also highlighted the physical distance between them. Maybe this was how they learned if they could manage long distance—especially with Robin's growing excitement over the rodeo.

What if he lost Robin to that life?

Shawn's promised "one week, maybe two," ended up being three. Granddad was slow to go through Nana's things, and every time Shawn turned around, he found a window that needed caulking, or a pipe that was leaking. Shawn had no handyman training whatsoever, but it was way cheaper to bust out Granddad's toolbox and watch a YouTube video than hire someone else.

On Thursday afternoon, the three-week anniversary of Nana's funeral, Granddad sat him down in the living room and said, "It's time for you to go home."

Shawn frowned. "What?"

"The house is as good as it's going to get, considering its age, and you need to go home to your ranch. And your boyfriend."

"He understands why I'm here."

"I know he does. But you're unhappy here, Shawn, I can tell. You have such a big, loving heart, and you're trying to do right by me. I cannot thank you enough for all the work you've done, but it's time to stop giving. You need to go invest in your own life and future, and I don't just mean by not giving me your money anymore. I'll be fine, I promise. Go be happy."

"I am happy."

"No, you are not. Not completely. Not like before when we talked on the phone and I heard the joy in your voice. Joy I never really heard until you met Robin. You miss him."

Shawn couldn't argue the positive effect Robin had had on his life these last two months, but still... "I do miss Robin. A lot. But sometimes I'm not sure how much he misses me."

"How's that?"

"I don't know. When we talk, all he ever really talks about is the rodeo. His phone calls with old friends, building the corral they'll need up at the site, stuff that feels so disconnected from our relationship. He's even stopped asking when I'm coming home."

"Maybe he expects you'll tell him when you're ready. Or maybe he's hoping you'll just show up at his door with a smile on your face."

That sounded more like a romantic gesture that Robin would pull. Shawn didn't want to have to rent a car to drive from San Jose to Garrett. Maybe he could enlist Miles's help in surprising Robin with his return.

"You're no quitter, Shawn," Granddad said, his voice serious now. "Never have been, no matter how many losses or curveballs life throws at you. No matter how bad the case against Beck got, you never backed down. You get knocked down, you dust off and get back up

You got that stubbornness from your mom. If you want
Robin, you go and get him, you hear me?"

"I hear you." Shawn flung his arms around his grandfather's waist and hugged him tight. "I hear you loud and
clear. Thank you."

Granddad patted his back. "You're welcome. Now
get on that complicated phone of yours and make plans
to go home."

Home. Shawn gazed around the house where he'd
lived for roughly five years of his life. Memories lingered here, both good and bad, but this wasn't his home.
His home was a small cabin on a dude ranch outside
Garrett, California. Home was Robin.

Yes, it was beyond time for Shawn to go home to
Clean Slate Ranch where he belonged.

Shawn had his flight booked and arrival time on hand
later that day when he called Miles about a ride tomorrow. It was about four, and with Miles helping out in the
guesthouse kitchen, he may or may not be able to talk.
But now that Shawn had a plan to surprise Robin, he
wanted to put it into gear.

"Hey, man, how are you?" Miles asked after a handful of rings.

"Good, actually, thanks. How are things at the ranch?"

"Can't complain. We've got a good batch of guests,
and we've been talking up the ghost town reopening next
Saturday. You're coming home by then, right?"

"Yes, that's why I called. Are you able to pick me up
from the airport tomorrow at three in the afternoon? I
want to fly in and surprise Robin by just showing up
unannounced."

Miles was silent for several long beats. "Um, I can

definitely pick you up, but...have you talked to Robin today?"

His stomach shriveled in on itself. "No. Why? Did something happen?"

"Kind of. I mean, Robin's not hurt or anything, I promise."

"Then what's wrong?"

"I think you should call Robin, okay?"

"Fine, thanks." Shawn hung up without saying good-bye, which was rude, but his nerves were jangling all over the place now.

Robin picked up quickly. "Hey, gorgeous, I was just thinking about you."

"Good, because I was just talking to Miles about you." Shawn regretted how harshly that had come out, but too late now.

"What did he tell you?"

"Not much. I called because I wanted to fly home tomorrow and surprise you, and I was asking Miles for a ride, but I got the impression that's not going to happen. What's going on?"

"Look, it's nothing bad, and I was going to call you before dinner. I just now finalized my plans."

Shawn glared at his bedroom wall. "Plans for what?"

"I'm, uh, flying to New Mexico tomorrow morning so I can drive up with Doug and the rest of the rodeo. It's a two-day trip with one overnight stop. We leave early Saturday and we'll get in late Sunday, which gives the crew time to get set up and practice. Spend some time at the ranch, too."

"I see." Shawn's stomach got impossibly tight, and his hands started to tremble. Robin had planned to be away for the weekend, and he hadn't even consulted Shawn about it? Shouldn't partners talk about things like that before plans were made? Or were they too casual in Robin's mind for that?

No, that's not fair. He had no idea when I was coming home.

"Are you mad?" Robin asked.

"No. Disappointed, I guess. It's been so long since we've seen each other."

"I know, and I miss you like crazy. It's just a few more days, right? And I love that you wanted to surprise me. That's supersweet, Shawn, honest."

"It was Granddad's idea. We both agreed it was time for me to go home."

"I'm glad you're finally coming home. Everyone's missed you around here. I think Miles was getting a little stressed that you weren't ever coming back, and he'd have to run the saloon without you."

"Never. I love that job too much. Besides, my life is in Garrett." *With you.*

"Good. How's the house look?"

They chatted for a bit about casual things, and Shawn tried to shove his disappointment away and enjoy talking to Robin. But his attempt at being romantic had backfired, and it would be three more days before he saw Robin again. Days Robin would be spending on the road with his old employer and employees. Reliving the good old days...

Shawn didn't sleep well that night, and in the morning, he packed up his storage tote and had it shipped to the ranch. Then he and Granddad spent the rest of their time together playing an ongoing game of chess. They'd started up in the evenings two weeks ago, and they didn't finish today's game before it was time for Granddad to drive him to the airport. But they left the board as-is on the kitchen table.

It would be there the next time Shawn came for a visit this spring. He'd work in time before the ghost town got too busy with summer tourism.

They'd said their goodbyes at the house, so at the drop-off, Shawn simply kissed his grandfather on the cheek and climbed out of the car with his stuffed gym bag. Robin had taken the small suitcase they'd shared back with him, and Shawn had picked up a few extra sets of clothes so he wasn't doing laundry every other day to have clean underwear. New stuff he was now taking home with him.

Miles had texted him that Avery would pick Shawn up at the airport, since he was driving out to spend the weekend with Colt up at Mack's cabin. Saved everyone extra driving, and while Shawn saw his point, he'd wanted to talk to his friend. Get some advice on all his conflicting feelings over Robin and the rodeo. He could probably ask Avery for advice, but Shawn didn't know the guy as well as he knew Miles.

So the drive to Garrett was mostly silent between them with the radio blasting a classic rock station. As soon as the familiar town came into view, something loosened inside of Shawn's chest. A band of tension he'd worn for weeks and was now free of because he was home. Well, almost home. Avery carefully navigated the pitted dirt road up to the ranch. Guests hung out on the front porch of the guesthouse, where Avery dropped him off. Shawn went directly around to the rear kitchen door, needing the familiarity of that space right now.

Patrice and Miles chatted while they worked on tonight's spread for hands and guests, and Patrice let out

a happy little squeak when she saw him. "Shawn, welcome home, honey." Her right arm was no longer in a
sling, but she had…an oven mitt duct-taped to her hand?
"It's so I don't forget I can't put a lot of weight on my
right arm yet. Miles insisted."

"Oh." Shawn hugged her gently, then hugged Miles,
too. "Miss me?"

"You know it." Miles winked at him. "I keep getting
picked on because I can't seem to get Patrice's corn bread
recipe to taste as good as you do."

"It's all in how much you love your baked goods,
Mr. Savory Cook. Seriously, though, how is everyone?"

"Can't complain," Patrice replied. "Arthur took in a
new rescue yesterday, and he's happy as fish in water
down there working with her. Former racehorse, no
abuse, so he thinks she'll be a good fit as a riding horse
for our guests."

"That's great for Arthur. And the horse, too."

"Patrice, can I have fifteen minutes?" Miles asked.

"Sure, sure," she said. "The stew's in the pot, so all
I have to do is stir once in a while."

Miles followed Shawn back to his cabin, where
Shawn dumped his bag on the bed and then sank into
one of the chairs. Miles took the other one. "You need
to talk?"

Shawn snorted sharply through his nose. "Yeah, I do,
and I need to be talking to Robin, but he's obviously got
other things to do."

"He didn't leave to be cruel. Robin's not that guy."

"I know. And I love that he's doing everything he can
to help opening day be successful and safe for everyone
involved, but… I guess I'm frustrated he didn't ask me

before agreeing to drive west with the rodeo. He just decided to leave the state."

"If it helps, Robin was…kind of a grumpy bear while you were away. Colt asked Ernie, who said Robin slept here every night. He keeps switching duties so he's stuck in the barn, mucking stalls, exercising the horses, doing everything except being around the tourists. He missed you a lot."

"And I missed him. So much. I didn't stay in Nevada to be cruel or to hurt him. My grandfather needed my help, and I had to be sure he'd be okay when I left."

"Robin understands that. I'm sure if he'd known you were coming back today before he committed to the New Mexico trip, he'd have stayed."

Shawn wished he was as certain of that. "Am I being a brat about this?"

"No. You guys had a miscommunication, and you've been apart for weeks. It's natural to resent him a little for going away, just remember he didn't do it to hurt you back for staying in Nevada for so long."

"I know he didn't. That's not what worries me." Shawn huffed, which fluttered his bangs. He needed a serious haircut soon. "I'm worried he'll remember everything he used to love about touring with the rodeo, and that he'll leave with them." *That he'll leave* me.

Miles studied him silently for several long moments. "Do you think he's likely to?"

"I don't know. He left the rodeo because he had this huge fight with Doug after Xander died, and now Robin and Doug have mended things. Robin and Levi, too. There's nothing keeping him from going back to that life. These three weeks without him have been stressful, and I can't imagine staying here while he's on the road for months at a time doing dangerous tricks. Especially when I still don't know how Xander died."

"He hasn't told you that yet?"

Shawn shrugged. "I know it was an accident that had some connection to the show, but I can't make myself ask directly. Always felt like he'd tell me when he was ready. Maybe it just hurts too much to talk about."

"I'm sure it does hurt. We all have painful things in our past, but it's important to share that stuff with the people you love. Speaking hugely from experience here."

"I know. I did tell Robin the truth about my past, and I want to tell you, too, because I kind of fudged the truth when I said I had an ex who spent three nights in jail. The jail thing was true, but he wasn't an ex. Not really."

"Okay." Miles's expression went soft, patient. "We're friends, Shawn, so anything you tell me stays between us. Promise."

Shawn took a slow, cleansing breath, and then told Miles what really happened with Beck. Miles's face remained stoic, but his eyes blazed with anger and a kind of commiseration that came from experience. They shared similar pain. Shawn ended with his confrontation with Beck at the reception, and the peace he'd found in finally standing up for himself.

"I'm so sorry that happened to you," Miles said. "But I am also so freaking proud of you for standing up to Beck. Seriously. It's not easy to stare your abuser in the face."

"Yeah. And even though I don't care what people in that town think of me anymore, I hope I've got a few more folk there who are on my side."

"Well, you'll always have me on your side. And Robin

and Mack and Wes, et cetera. We're both part of the Clean Slate family now and always will be."

"I'm glad. It's nice having a family again. I also did finally tell Robin about being homeless for two years, so if it happens to come up in casual conversation, it's not a secret anymore."

"Good." Miles reached over to squeeze his knee. "I better get back to the kitchen. Do you feel any better about Robin?"

"A little. I still hate that's he's gone but he is coming back."

Hopefully, he'll be back to stay.

But they hadn't been dating long enough for Shawn to demand any promises from Robin. If Robin decided to leave with the rodeo, Shawn couldn't make him stay. And he wouldn't try. Shawn didn't want to be the guy who stopped someone else from reaching for their dream. And if Robin's dream was to go back on the road, Shawn wouldn't stop him from leaving.

He'd enjoy all the time he had with Robin while he could and stand tall no matter what life threw at him next.

Chapter Twenty-Two

Robin's favorite part of his two-day road trip was the familiar camaraderie with the Lucky's Rodeo riders—not only the guys he'd worked with, like Petey and Harold and Frank, but also the new folks Robin met when he arrived at the winter site outside of Santa Fe. Friday night was filled with storytelling of all kinds. Robin went on and on about Clean Slate Ranch, and the guys filled him in on their own stories these last three years.

Saturday morning, Robin was reintroduced to the horses as they were loaded into trailers for the trip. The gorgeous black mare he'd done most of his tricks on had been retired last year and was living her life on a ranch in Arizona, so there were a handful of new horses, too. He rode in one of the RVs with four other folks, including a spirited young woman named Chelsea who'd been hired on as the new "clown." She had a wicked sense of humor and knew how to whip up a crowd before the show, and despite knowing she had taken Xander's job… he liked her.

He talked to Shawn as frequently as he could, depending on cell signal and who was where in the RV. While Doug would never hire anyone openly homophobic, some of the new riders looked at Robin funny whenever he talked about Shawn. So Robin tried not to throw too much light on the relationship.

Fuck them anyway if they had a problem with Robin being happy and in love.

And he did love Shawn. A lot. He'd realized how much these last three weeks without him. Sure, they'd talked every day, sometimes multiple times a day, but the physical distance hurt. Like a part of Robin was missing from his body, and he wouldn't be whole again until he got that piece back. Until he could hug and kiss Shawn again.

He also had a nice little stash of chess pieces completed that he couldn't wait to gift to his boyfriend. He worked on a second bishop during the trip, careful to keep his wood shavings in a neat little pile so no one stepped on them, Petey especially. Them joking about shavings and toenail clippings was so familiar Robin felt like no time had passed. Like he was back working for Lucky's and these last three years had been a weird dream.

On Sunday, Robin was insanely excited to finally cross into California, knowing home was only a few more hours away. Since it was after dark and late when they finally arrived in Garrett, Doug had previously agreed with Mack that they could set up camp along the road leading up to the ranch. Mack would take them up to the ghost town site in the morning.

And since that week the guesthouse only had ten guests, Doug, Chelsea, and a few of the other riders had been invited to stay at the guesthouse for the week. Mack drove down to get them in one of the ranch pickups. Robin was a little annoyed Shawn wasn't in the truck cab with Mack, but maybe Shawn was planning a surprise back in his cabin?

Please, let it be naked sexy times.

He'd missed their naked sexy times, and jerking off to the memories of making love on New Year's Day just wasn't the same. Robin was kind of sick of his own right hand.

He rode in the bed of the pickup with his friends, new and old, and he nearly vibrated with joy at the sight of the guesthouse. Barely three days away, but he'd missed this place. This land that still whispered to him sometimes. Reassured him he was home.

Once Mack pulled up and parked by the guesthouse, Robin said a hasty goodnight to everyone, grabbed his small duffel bag, and bolted for cabin row. The lights were on in their cabin, and Robin rushed inside. Shawn was stretched out on their bed on his stomach, playing something on his phone—a phone he immediately dropped when he saw Robin. A relieved smile shifted into a simmering, lusty gaze, and Shawn launched himself off the bed. Robin caught him in a fierce hug, and that missing thing inside Robin clicked back into place. They stood there for a while, soaking in each other's body heat. Shawn smelled deliciously of wood smoke, probably from that night's welcome barbecue. Some of that flavor lingered in the far corners of Shawn's mouth as Robin plundered him, reacquainting with lips and a tongue he'd missed so much.

With the man he'd missed so much.

"Welcome back," Robin said once he'd kissed them both breathless, and his dick throbbed for relief.

"I could say the same to you." Shawn rubbed his own erection against Robin's thigh. "God, I missed you."

"Me, too. I'm so glad we're both finally home."

"Yeah?" Shawn boldly groped Robin's ass, and Robin leered at him. "So am I. It felt really weird being here without you."

"Same." Robin decided to let his inner caveman out to play, and he scooped Shawn up into a fireman's carry. Shawn laughed at the treatment, and then laughed again when Robin deposited him on the bed. Climbed right on top and rubbed their hard cocks together. "Hello."

"This is a new side of you," Shawn said with a chuckle. "I like it."

"Tell the truth. You didn't ride down to get us with Mack because you knew the minute we saw each other again, we'd be all over each other."

"Guilty." He leaned up to kiss Robin. "Can we make love tonight? We only ever have that one time."

"Absolutely we can." Robin wanted nothing more in that moment than Shawn inside him, pushing them both to climax.

And that's exactly what happened…about an hour later. They took their time undressing each other, kissing swaths of bared skin. Licking nipples and pinching butt cheeks and simply exploring. Sharing. Shawn fingered his hole for ages, getting him wet and ready for when he eventually slid home in Robin's body. Robin on his back, Shawn looming over him so they could kiss. Look into each other's eyes.

Shawn took him apart bit by bit, moving so slowly Robin's entire body shook with the need to come. But he didn't beg or demand, he just took what Shawn gave him, and it was everything Robin had ever wanted or needed out of sex. This was joy and pleasure and possession.

This was love.

They both did come eventually, but Robin was so drunk on endorphins he wasn't sure in which order. Only that once he had some sense again, Robin rolled them so he could smother Shawn into the mattress and hold him tight. In his arms, exactly where Shawn belonged.

Despite having plenty of food, Shawn kind of resented the fact that he had six extra people staying in the guesthouse—and that the news had been sprung on him Sunday afternoon while that week's paying guests explored the ranch and settled into their assigned rooms. But he got over it quickly when, on Monday morning, Doug assured him that they had plenty of food of their own to cook up for their lunches and dinners up at the site.

Extra people for breakfast was way less annoying than three full meals. And Shawn was only cooking for a few more days. On Thursday, he and Miles were returning to Bentley to reopen the saloon, draw up a supply order, and get their kitchen set back up for Saturday's big opening day. Patrice would once again reign as den mother supreme for the guests, with some additional help with heavy stuff from Hugo.

Shawn liked Doug Peletier instantly. He was an older version of Levi, but with more wrinkles and a deeper tan. Doug seemed pleased that Robin was dating again, which relaxed Shawn even more. He couldn't imagine how strange it was to know your former son-in-law was with another person.

After breakfast, Robin and Mack drove everyone back down to the campsite where they'd left the RVs and trailers, and the entire production moved up to the ghost town. This morning while they were showering,

Robin had dropped the bomb that he was thinking of taking part in the show, but he needed to practice first. Shawn had tried to be happy for Robin, because Robin dripped excitement over the idea.

All Shawn could see was the beginning of the end of their relationship, because everyone he loved eventually left him. Mom. Dad. Nana.

He tried to push that depressing thought away and enjoyed every free moment he had with Robin, which was usually mornings through breakfast, and maybe an hour or so at night before Robin fell asleep from exhaustion. Robin was working his ass off—and landing on his ass quite a lot, or so he complained—relearning some riding tricks so he could be part of the show. Shawn didn't like the bruises that kept showing up on Robin's body, but Robin was happy. So happy to be near his old family again.

By Thursday, Shawn's mood was pretty crappy as Miles and he drove up to open the saloon. Neither of them had seen the new corral yet. It had been built to the west of the main town, in a large open field they'd used for kids games and line dancing last year during their July fourth celebration. Oval-shaped and about a hundred feet long at its widest, the simple wood structure was surrounded by the Lucky's staff. Different horses were either tethered to the corral or being ridden around the hard-packed earth.

Their campsite was near the rear of the parking area, and Shawn spotted a row of blue tents with gates on the front—temporary housing for the horses, most likely. He couldn't imagine that kind of existence, where you took your entire life state to state, never putting down roots. Okay, he could kind of imagine it after living in his car, but it wasn't the same.

Walking into the saloon's kitchen boosted Shawn's mood a little bit, and he enjoyed the quiet way he and Miles reassembled their kitchen. After two months away, Shawn was glad to be back. And twice as glad that when he left at the end of the day, he had a real home to return to, and not his car parked on the side of the road.

Since they were starting from scratch, Miles had a pretty long list of things to order tonight, so they could start food prep on the beans and chili tomorrow. Mary-Ellen Hurley stopped by with a load of jarred pickles and jams, both for the saloon and the general store. Since Megan wasn't on the grounds until tomorrow, they stored her stuff in the kitchen for now, instead of tracking Mack down so he could unlock the general store.

Tasks completed by three, Miles suggested they check out what was happening down at the corral. "I'm crazy curious about what they'll be doing while we're stuck in our kitchen," he said. "You game?"

"Sure." Shawn's response had lacked real enthusiasm, because Miles studied his face a beat.

"Are you and Robin okay?"

"We're fine. I mean, we aren't fighting or anything, and I'm glad he's having fun working with the old crew and all."

"But?"

"Same fear, different day, I guess. They're my issues, though, and Robin has to do what makes him happy. I refuse to smother him or make demands because I have abandonment issues." Shawn froze, surprised he'd said that out loud. He had never been so blunt about the true root of his fears.

"Have you talked to Robin about this?"

"When? He works so hard here all day that he pretty much passes out at night after a few kisses, and he's barely half-awake in the mornings. The rodeo's only here for a few more days, and then our lives can go back to normal."

"Unless Robin goes with them?"

Shawn grunted. "I keep trying not to think about that."

"Has Robin ever said anything that specifically makes you think he'd leave?"

"No. Like I said, it's my issue. I'm just jealous of all the time he's not spending with me while he's here practicing, but now that I'm working in the saloon again, we won't see each other at every meal like we used to, so we both have to adjust to being apart more than we're together."

"Yes, you will, and trust me, it is a big adjustment. After being technically off work for the last two months, seeing Reyes whenever I wanted, it's going to be hard only seeing him in the morning and at night. But that's part of most adult relationships when both parties don't work in the same place."

"You're right, as usual."

"I know." Miles's teasing smile took any smugness out of his tone. "But this is your first real relationship, Shawn. You're still feeling your way through it, so trust me on something. You need to talk to your partner about your doubts before they fester."

Shawn nodded, and with the conversation over, they locked up the saloon's kitchen and strode down Main Street toward the active corral. A couple of guys were finishing up construction of a set of wooden bleachers for the audience, but most everyone else was standing outside the corral, while a man whose name Shawn didn't know rode around the corral on two horses.

Standing on two horses, one foot on each horse wearing a special kind of harness instead of a regular saddle, and holy crap. Hearing Robin talk about it and even watching videos online was not the same as seeing it in person. No special effects or wires hanging from the ceiling. This was real life.

And it was a little bit terrifying. Mack, Wes, and the ghost town's head actor, Colin James, stood with Doug, Chelsea, and some other folks. Wes noticed their pair approaching and waved them over. Shawn and Miles reached the group just as the rider expertly switched to only standing on one horse, and then eased himself down so he rode to scattered applause.

"Where's Robin?" Shawn asked.

"He's getting ready," Wes replied, his blue eyes sparkling with excitement. "I think he's up next."

"He's doing this as a surprise for Levi," Doug added. "Robin and Levi used to do coordinated trick riding the crowd just ate up, so Robin's doing part of their routine solo."

"That's really cool," Shawn said. "When does Levi arrive?"

"He's driving in tomorrow."

"Driving?"

"Yup, he decided to leave Colorado for Northern California for a while."

Levi was coming to town to stay? When had that happened, and why hadn't Robin told Shawn about it? What else was going on that he didn't know about? "Where's he, um, parking his house?"

"He'll be up here with us through the weekend, and then I think Robin said something about helping him check out nearby campsites."

Okay, well, at least Levi wasn't parking his tiny home right on the ranch. And maybe Shawn was being a little bratty about this, but his time with Robin was already going to be limited without having to share Robin with the man's former best friend. Miles must have seen something of his thoughts in his expression, because he squeezed Shawn's wrist.

Jealousy is not attractive. Get it together, Matthews.

Shawn spotted Robin at the far end of the corral near a gate, and he was leading a chestnut-brown horse forward. From their distance apart, Shawn wasn't sure if Robin could see him or not, but he pretended Robin could and that he was performing for Shawn only. Robin gave the audience a deep bow before moving to the horse's left side. He held on to the saddle like he was about to mount the beast, but instead, the pair both started to run.

In a shocking display of strength and physical dexterity, Robin used their momentum and both feet to jump high enough to plunk down into the saddle. He then continued to shock the hell out of Robin by using both hands on the saddle—and a crap ton of core strength—to lift himself up, legs spread, while the horse continued to run!

His entire routine lasted maybe two minutes, but he was fast, graceful, and looked so free as he performed that a rock landed squarely in Shawn's stomach. Robin was still this good after three years away and only four days of practice? Insane. He executed a fancy dismount and stumbled a bit on the landing, but his huge smile told Shawn everything.

Shawn clapped for the performance, so proud of Robin and a little worried what this might mean. But he pushed that aside, because Robin spotted him, handed the horse off to someone else, and raced over. Climbed right over the corral fence to hug Shawn, red-faced and still panting from his exertion.

"You were incredible," Shawn said. "Holy crap."

"It's not as fancy as the routine used to be." Robin gulped in air and then kissed him. "But damn, it felt great to get through it without falling. First time. Must be because you were here. My good luck charm."

"I've never seen anything like that before," Miles said. "You really used to do that all the time?"

"Yup. Like I said, it's watered down a bit because I'm not as flexible as I used to be, and I'll never have the body of a twenty-four-year-old again, but it felt great being out there. Performing."

Miles flashed Shawn a "you need to talk to him about this" look.

"Well, now I know why you've been so sore every night this week," Shawn quipped instead.

Robin laughed and kissed his cheek. "Yeah. The good news is I only have to get through tomorrow's final rehearsal and then the performance on Saturday. Maybe you and I can spend some daytime together tomorrow after lunch?"

"I can't. I have to help Miles prep for Saturday. We're starting from scratch with everything from sauces and biscuits, to making the buffalo burger patties." Shawn winked at Miles, even though he was not feeling it. "I have a very demanding boss who needs those patties just so."

Miles stuck his tongue out at him. "It helps get the temperature right."

"What about dinner?" Shawn asked Robin. "We haven't had dinner together in a month."

Robin's expression went instantly guilty, and that did not make Shawn feel better. "Um, can we do after dinner? Levi should be rolling in around four, and I promised him and Doug the three of us would go out to dinner someplace. Not all the way to San Jose, but the three of us haven't had a meal in years."

Years definitely trumped Shawn's month, and he held back a grumble of irritation. "Then you three should have dinner. You and I will have time to eat dinner once the craziness of opening day is behind us."

"Are you sure? You could come with us."

Shawn wasn't going to be a pathetic fourth wheel to this three-man family reunion in order to assuage Robin's guilt. "No, you guys go. Be a family again."

Robin hesitated, his eyes uncertain. "Okay. Thanks. Listen, I have to take care of my horse, but I'll be back in ten minutes or so. Wait for me?"

"Of course." Shawn kissed him again, hoping to go for easygoing when he was tied up in knots inside. "See you soon."

"Yeah." Robin headed to the opposite end of the corral, where someone waited with the chestnut-colored horse. They had a trailer and temporary fencing set up near the far gate, which appeared to be the tack area.

The next event had several men standing on wooden barrels, with a rider coming at them, and the point was for the standing man to climb onto the moving horse behind the first rider. For the live show, Doug would ask the audience to vote for the best duo based on applause. Shawn couldn't imagine how many times the jumper had fallen trying to mount a moving horse...

Then again, Shawn wasn't the most coordinated person on the planet and he was still mastering riding a horse.

A young, blond man brought a white-and-brown-speckled horse to Doug, who stood facing the "audience."

"This is when I'll ask for a volunteer," Doug said, mostly for Shawn, Miles, Wes, and Colin's benefit. "Someone without a lot of riding experience."

Wes immediately put his index finger over his nose. "Not it."

"I did dressage as a kid," Miles said, clearly uncomfortable with being stared at by a bunch of strangers.

Shawn shrugged and raised his hand. "I'm still learning." And he had plenty of past experience being stared at. It didn't bother him much, as long as he wasn't about to be embarrassed.

"Then come on up and join me, Shawn," Doug said with a big grin.

The width between the fence slats was enough that Shawn could climb through, instead of trying to climb over or circle to the gate. He approached Doug and the horse, who Doug introduced as Fiona. "So what we're gonna do," Doug said, "is put you up on Fiona here, and then you'll hold this here stick out at an angle, about forty-five degrees from your head." He demonstrated. "Our men are going to ride past and try to throw rubber rings on that stick. All you need to do is hold real still. Fiona won't bolt."

"Okay." Sounded easy enough. Shawn had ridden enough that he could finally haul his butt up without using steps or a boost, and he was proud of himself for that. After he got comfortable in the saddle, Doug handed him the painted stick. Helped him adjust how he sat so even if a ring missed, it wouldn't hit him in the face. He was a little nervous about men charging at him on galloping horses, but Doug was calm and encouraging, so Shawn settled in to see how good these ring throwers were.

Doug approached the fence and raised his hand to signal the riders.

"What the fuck!?" Robin's furious voice boomed across the corral and turned heads, and Shawn nearly fell out of the saddle. Robin easily leapt over the fence and charged toward Shawn, his face a scary mixture of fear and rage. "Get down right now."

"What? Why?" Shawn was not prepared for Robin physically dragging him down off Fiona, and he stumbled a bit getting his feet back under him. Robin cut off Doug's approach with a scowl and snarl, and he pulled Shawn away by the elbow. "What the hell is wrong with you, Robin?"

"You shouldn't have been up there," Robin snapped. "Doug should have known better. You're terrified of horses."

"No, I'm not." Shawn yanked his arm out of Robin's bruising grip, confused and angry at the bigger man's handling. "Robin, calm down and think. The horse barely blinked at me, I was fine."

Robin stared at Shawn with naked terror in his eyes. Terror that melted into bright confusion and then shock. "Oh shit. Shawn."

Everyone was gaping at them, and Doug seemed poised to insert himself into the situation at any moment. The entire site was silent except for Robin's heavy breathing. Shawn could barely hear over his own racing heartbeat. And then it clicked. "You thought I was Xander again, didn't you?"

Grief filled Robin's eyes then, and Shawn's temper ignited. Shawn didn't know for sure what this entire conniption fit had been about, but he had an idea, and it pissed him off. He was not a Xander substitute, goddamn it, and if Robin still saw him as such, he could fuck right off. Shawn turned and stormed toward the corral fence. Slipped between the slats easily and kept going.

Miles caught up with him a few yards away. "Are you okay?"

"I have no idea." Shawn didn't stop striding toward his car. "I don't know what the fuck just happened, but if I don't get out of here, I will punch Robin in the face."

"Okay."

Miles took Shawn's keys from his trembling fingers and drove them both back to the ranch. He didn't push, didn't ask any more questions, he was just there for Shawn. And Shawn appreciated it more than he could say. His phone rang once but he ignored it when he saw it was Robin. He did not want to speak to the man right this second.

After Miles parked his car in the barn-shaped garage, he led Shawn back to his and Reyes's cabin, instead of letting Shawn go back to his own. Shawn paced the living area, his mind a tangled mess of anger and confusion. Miles handed him a beer, which Shawn didn't normally drink, but he appreciated the gesture and gulped down several long pulls without really tasting it.

"I've never seen Robin act like that before," Miles said.

"Me, either. It was like he thought I was in danger by being up on that horse. For a few seconds, I think he really did believe I was his husband, Xander, because he said I was scared of horses, and I'm not. But Xander was." A horrifying thought occurred to Shawn. "Oh God. What if a horse was involved in how Xander died? The first time Robin met me, I was up on a horse and he reacted really weirdly."

"It's possible. He probably didn't expect Doug to have you out into the corral like that. Put up on that horse. Maybe it triggered an old memory."

"I just… That was so embarrassing." Shawn rubbed his elbow, which was still sore from where Robin had dragged him—yes, dragged him—off Fiona and ten feet away from the sedate horse. For a few seconds, and for the only time since Shawn had met him, Robin had genuinely scared him. And Shawn didn't want to fear his boyfriend, not for any reason. Not ever.

Someone knocked a split second before the cabin door opened. Shawn braced for the intruder to be Robin, but it was Reyes, whose expression was schooled. "Are you two all right?" he asked. "Mack called and said Robin and Shawn had some kind of confrontation at the ghost town." Reyes's dark brown eyes zeroed in on Shawn. "Did he hurt you?"

"No." Shawn's arm still ached a little but he didn't think Robin had been trying to hurt him. "He scared me a little, and I don't completely understand what happened. I just needed space."

Miles filled Reyes in on the last ten minutes, while Shawn resisted the urge to keep pacing. "It definitely sounds like some sort of flashback," Reyes said when

Miles finished. "But Robin and I aren't close, so I couldn't begin to guess."

"I think it has to do with how his husband died," Shawn replied. "And probably being around the Lucky's employees again...it made everything even worse. Maybe I shouldn't have walked away like that. Maybe I should have stayed and talked to him."

"Hey, you needed to protect yourself." Miles looped his arm around Shawn's. "Believe me, we both get that. It's okay to put yourself first. Talk to Robin when you're ready."

"Honestly, I think I'm ready now. I don't like knowing he's upset, and I don't know exactly how his husband died." Shawn palmed his phone, intent on calling Robin, when another knock sounded at the door.

Reyes opened it, and no one was surprised to find Robin on the porch, his face as pale as Shawn had ever seen. Robin's gaze went directly to Shawn's, asking a silent question. Shawn nodded and said, "Can we have a few minutes?" Fully aware this wasn't his cabin.

Miles took Reyes by the hand and led him outside. Robin came in and shut the door. "I am so sorry for what I did," Robin said. "So fucking sorry."

"Tell me why you did it." Shawn needed to hear the words from Robin.

"I panicked." Robin approached, his expression tentative and sad, and his hands twitched as if wanting to reach for Shawn. "Xander died during a rehearsal for that trick. We needed someone to play the inexperienced audience member, and Xander hated horses. Was terrified of them." Real grief fractured his face. "I goaded him, said Xander getting up a horse just this once would be the best Christmas present ever. He agreed. For me."

Shawn closed his eyes as grief for both Xander and for Robin pressed in on him from all sides. "How did he die?"

"Truck backfired. Spooked the horse, who threw him. Xander broke his neck when he landed." Robin choked. "He died in my arms before an ambulance could get there."

"Oh, Robin." Shawn surged forward and caught Robin around the waist as the bigger man collapsed. Eased them both to the floor as Robin sobbed twice without actually crying. As if his body needed to expel the negative energy somehow. "I am so sorry. God."

"It's why..." Robin pressed his forehead into Shawn's neck. "When I first saw you that day up on Valentine, I honestly thought you were Xander. Come back to me, about to fall and break your neck all over again. It's why I was so rude that first hour or two."

"Now it makes more sense. Why you acted so oddly. Oh, Robin, you could have told me that."

He drew in a ragged breath and let it out slowly. "I know. I just... I blamed myself so hard for Xander's death. I was the reason he was on that damned horse. If I hadn't goaded him, he wouldn't have died. He didn't know how to do stunt falls or twist on a landing so he didn't hurt himself."

"It's not your fault."

"I spiraled hard, Shawn. So fucking hard. I fought with Levi and with Doug. I couldn't look at myself in the mirror anymore without seeing the face of a killer. We were in Wichita when Xander died, and after a huge blowout with Doug, I packed a bag and left. On foot. Headed west with no idea what I wanted to do other than die."

Shawn shivered at the bald emotion in those words—
and for how deeply Robin's pain had dragged him down.
"But you didn't die."

"Not for lack of trying." Robin let out an angry snort.
"I drank. Heavily. Hitchhiked. Fucked around. Did all
the things that could have landed me in a morgue, but I
woke up every morning and kept walking. Or hitching.
All I wanted to do was die, but I was too fucking scared
to swallow pills, or jump in front of a bus. I wanted
something or someone else to take me out. There are
chunks of time I don't even remember, and it lasted for
close to a year."

A year. A year of chasing death, only for death to
dodge out of reach over and over. Shawn couldn't imagine the pain of such an enormous loss. For something
so devastating to happen that he'd want to end his own
life. For all of Shawn's own personal losses, he'd never
wanted to die. Every single time he was knocked over,
he got back up and kept trying. Kept fighting.

Robin quit. Holy shit.

It completely reset his image of the man shivering in
his arms, clutching at his waist, dropping these intense
truth bombs all over the place. "All I knew for sure was
that I was in California," Robin continued. "In the mountains, surrounded by trees. No cars, no people. Back
roads. I walked until I collapsed in a ditch, and I really
thought that was it. I was broke, hadn't eaten in days,
no fresh water. I wanted it to be over."

Twin tear tracks ran down Shawn's cheeks, and he
tried to hold Robin tighter. Hearing how far someone
he considered his own rock had fallen? Devastating.
Knowing Robin trusted him enough to finally unload
these burdens?

Priceless.

"And then a truck pulls up on the side of the road," Robin said. "I was pretty delirious, but these two men picked me up and got me into their truck. Took me back to this ranch, and they helped me get sober. Gave me a job and place a live. A purpose again. A second chance I wasn't sure I deserved, but I took it. Arthur and Judson literally saved my life that day." He sat up and met Shawn's eyes, so much love and devotion shining in Robin's that Shawn wanted to cry. "Somehow I got here so I could meet you, Shawn. I might have given up on life, but life didn't give up on me. And I truly hope you don't, either."

"Never." Shawn cupped Robin's cheeks in his palms. "I'm heartbroken that you gave up so completely. But I am also grateful you're in my life." Robin had been incredibly honest with Shawn today. It was time for Shawn to be honest in return. To say the things he felt in his heart and soul. "I love you, Robin Butler. Please don't leave me."

"I'm not going anywhere, Shawn. And I love you, too. Have for a while but I haven't been able to say it. Not sure why."

"Maybe you needed to share this final secret with me first."

"Could be. I'm sorry I acted like a possessive nutcase earlier."

"Forgiven. It hurt but now I understand where that fear came from. And now that I know this secret, do you think you and I could go riding together sometime?"

"Yes, we can do that. I didn't lie about preferring to ride alone, but I did use it as an excuse not to see you on a horse. But you aren't Xander, and I can't live my life being terrified of losing you every single second. I want to live and love you freely. Without fear."

"So do I." Time to put Shawn's final fear to rest. "Are you considering leaving with Lucky's when they go back on tour?"

Robin gaped at him. "What? Of course not."

That final knot of tension unfurled and drifted away, leaving Shawn relaxed and proud. "Good. I want you here."

"I want me here, too. Baby, I have had a blast this week being around the guys again. Being around Doug and the horses. But I will never be the rider I was in my heyday, and my aching bones will be very glad when Saturday's show is over."

"I can't imagine." Shawn brushed his lips over Robin's. "I love you, and I know in my heart we can make this work."

"Me, too."

They sealed the promise with a long, sensual kiss, and then they held each other for a long time. Existing as a couple with no more secrets between them. They were both in this for the long haul, and Shawn very much looked forward to whatever came next.

Epilogue

"You may now kiss your spouse."

Loud cheers rose up in the crowd as the two now-married couples kissed in front of their guests. Robin had a slight sense of déjà vu over the entire production, because this was the second wedding he'd attended up here at Bentley Ghost Town in the last two years. The first wedding had a been a straight couple, and Robin had been here with Colt and the other hands. Today, Robin was here with his boyfriend watching Colt kiss his husband senseless on the saloon porch.

The other happy couple, Reyes and Miles, shared a shorter, but no less intense kiss of their own. Beside him, Shawn wiped at his eyes with a tissue, clearly overjoyed by the beautiful celebration of love they'd both witnessed. Robin could see himself and Shawn sharing those kinds of vows one day. Not anytime soon, but one day.

And the man who'd married the pairs? Arthur Garrett himself. He'd taken it upon himself to get certified online, and when Miles had absently mused during a movie night at Mack's place that he didn't want a big wedding, he just wanted to be married, Mack had gone to Arthur. Two weeks later, Mack closed the ghost town early on a Saturday so they could have the private celebration.

Colt's entire family was here for the wedding, and they'd overtaken the guesthouse for the night, along with the Bentleys and Masseys. Avery's parents. Miles's parents had been invited, and apparently they'd sent a check as a congratulations. Whatever, because Miles had plenty of family here, surrounding him with love and affection.

Not standing much on ceremony, Arthur shooed the wedded pairs off the porch and into the crowd of guests to be hugged and congratulated. Robin was so happy for his fellow hands that he could barely see straight, and he hugged whoever came at him for one. Even Sophie Massey, their first ghost town bride, who was heavily pregnant and due to give birth in about two weeks. Her husband, Conrad, watched her like a hawk.

Robin gave Derrick a firm hug and handshake. "You gonna put a ring on it now, too?" Derrick asked, inclining his head in Shawn's direction. Shawn was talking to Hugo and Wes a few feet away.

"Not yet," Robin replied. "It hasn't even been five months. We'll know when it's right. How about you? Seeing anyone special?"

"Nah. Being single suits me."

"Sure it does. Suited me just fine, too, until I met Shawn. There's someone out there for you, too, Derrick."

"We'll see." Derrick moved on to speak to other people.

Megan Landsdowne took his place, and she handed him an envelope. "For you. We sold the other horse carving right before close."

"Really?" Robin tucked the envelope, which felt like it contained a check and not cash, into his jeans pocket. At Shawn's insistence, Robin had started carving horse or Old West-themed items to display in the ghost town's general store. After the first two times Megan called Robin about someone interested in buying the items, he let her sell them. It wasn't making him a gold mine, but the extra cash helped pad his bank account.

Money he hoped to use on a down payment one day soon—when he got up the nerve to finally ask Shawn about them getting their own place together. A real house in town, not just a cabin on Arthur's property.

"Thanks so much, Megan," Robin said. "I've got a wall piece I'm almost finished with. Should be able to get it to the store by Tuesday."

"Works for me. You should think about doing commissions."

Robin chuckled. "Maybe I'll do that this coming winter when I'll be out of work for two months. It'll keep me busy."

Megan laughed and moved on, and Robin's gaze landed on Levi, who was chatting amiably with Wes and Sophie's parents. Having Levi around these last two months had been fantastic, and it had led to a minor career switch for Robin. After a long chat with Mack and Judson, Robin had quit as an official horseman for the ranch and gone to work for Mack up here at Bentley.

Robin and Levi had found their trick-riding groove quickly, as if no time had passed, and they now performed twice a day for ghost town guests. They also offered horse rides around the corral, did a few of the simpler acts such as ring tossing while riding, and gave lectures on how they'd learned what they knew to interested guests.

Levi was an incredibly patient teacher, and he seemed to find an inner peace working in a less chaotic format than the traveling show had been. Mack had generously offered to let Levi park his tiny home on a piece of the land Arthur had given to him, out of view of both the ghost town road and Mack's own cabin. Levi's three cats were left free to wander via a cat door and they always returned home each night. And while Levi kept to himself and rarely accepted invitations to dinner or a movie night, he seemed happy.

Robin was beyond happy. He was content, settled, and loved his new role at the ghost town. Not only because he saw new faces every single day, but because he was closer to Shawn. They rode up to the site every day on the horses Robin and Levi used in their demos, taking the now-familiar path through the wilderness.

At first, Robin had been nervous to ride with Shawn, but Shawn was a natural with horses. He was a fast learner, at ease in the saddle, and he'd even expressed interest in maybe learning some of the easier tricks Robin knew. Robin wasn't so sure if his blood pressure could handle that, but he'd deal with it if Shawn insisted.

Or he'd let Levi teach him. He absolutely trusted Levi to teach Shawn.

Speaking of whom…

He cast about until he found Shawn, who was now in a tight huddle with Wes, Mack, Conrad, and Sophie. Wes's eyes were bugging out and Conrad looked equal parts excited and terrified, and what—? Sophie.

Robin made his way over to the group, and sure enough, Sophie—whose much shorter body had been blocked from view until now—was breathing hard, both hands clasped over her round belly. Shawn met Robin's eyes and he mouthed "contraction" at Robin.

Holy shit.

"Derrick's getting a car," Shawn whispered. "We're trying not to make a scene."

Robin looked at Wes, who seemed ready to burst from excitement. "I can tell."

"Don't want to make this about me," Sophie wheezed. "Ooh, where's my mom?"

"I'll get her."

Robin found the Bentleys conversing with Colts parents, and he whispered what was happening into Leta Bentley's ear. She gasped, and it probably took every ounce of her self-control not to race over to her baby girl, who was now having a baby of her own. Derrick was back with a car, and a car on Main Street finally got the crowd's attention. Conrad climbed into the backseat with Sophie and Leta. Mack drove with Wes shotgun. Derrick promised he and the other in-laws were right behind them.

Not that there was a huge rush, because didn't babies take a long time to actually come out? Robin's own mom had been in labor for hours giving birth to his younger siblings. A mom and siblings Robin still hadn't reached out to. He wasn't sure if he ever would. No big reunion like with Colt and the extended Woods clan. Robin's family was here and he could live with that.

"Oh my gosh," Shawn said. "I can't believe Sophie went into labor in the same place she got married."

Robin slipped an arm around Shawn's waist and pulled him closer. "And if she gives birth before midnight, today's going to be a busy day for years to come. Two wedding anniversaries and a birthday."

"It's crazy."

Miles and Reyes came over, both of them grinning like fools. "Did Sophie really go into labor?" Miles asked. Off Shawn's nod, he added, "Wow, I bet Wes is a hot mess right now. He's been worrying about this for weeks."

"Why?" Robin asked. "It's not like Wes has to do any of the hard stuff, like pushing."

"She's his baby sister. He's always fussed over her. Hell, he's the one who came up with us vacationing on a dude ranch as her bridal party, just because he knew it would make her happy. Back then, Wes was not about horses or dirt."

Reyes snickered. "He still isn't, but he did make Mack the happiest man alive." He squeezed Miles's hip. "Well, second happiest."

Miles beamed at his husband.

With the gathered guests now buzzing about Sophie, Robin pulled Shawn into the shade of the sheriff's office porch. "So, I've been thinking," Robin said.

"Uh-oh." Shawn grinned at him and rested both hands on Robin's hips. "About weddings or babies?"

Robin laughed. "Neither. I know we've been living together in the cabin, and it's great, but I also sometimes feel guilty about taking up a cabin when neither of us technically work at the ranch anymore."

"Same. It's why I've been paying Judson a bit of rent. I don't like charity, and I can afford it now." A flash of sadness was there and gone quickly. Shawn still regularly tried to urge his granddad to move to Garrett, but the stubborn old man refused. And with Francis no longer paying extra for Irma's care, Shawn kept more of each paycheck for himself.

"I know." Robin took a breath. "Shawn, I want to look for a place to live, either in Garrett, or maybe over in Daggett, since it's not too far. I want us to buy a house together."

Shawn blinked hard several times. His lips parted. "You do?"

"I do. We can still commute every day together, except in a car instead of horses. We'll have our own kitchen to cook meals in. You can keep teaching me how to bake. It doesn't have to be big or fancy, as long as it's ours and—"

Shawn cut him off with a kiss. The hands on his hips circled to cinch around his waist and haul Robin closer. Shawn plundered his mouth with his tongue, and Robin didn't have to ask to know this was a resounding "yes" to his unasked question.

Yes, Shawn would move in with him. Yes, Shawn would buy a house with him. Yes to the beautiful future Robin had painted for them with his words. Robin had never owned a home before, and neither had Shawn, and this was an adventure he very much wanted them to take together.

The first of many, many more to come.

* * * * *

Reviews are an invaluable tool when it comes to spreading the word about great reads. Please consider leaving an honest review for this or any of Carina Press's other titles that you've read on your favorite retailer or review site.

For more information about A.M. Arthur's books, please visit her website here:
https://amarthur.blogspot.com/

Or like her on Facebook:
https://www.facebook.com/A.M.Arthur.M.A/

Watch for **Hard Ride**, *the next book in the Clean Slate Ranch series, coming from A.M. Arthur and Carina Press in February 2020.*

When my editor and I first brainstormed this series, I initially envisioned it as a trilogy. A trio of best friends who work on a ranch, find their perfect someone, and fall in love. And yet, as I wrote the series, Clean Slate Ranch took on a life of its own. So did various secondary characters who kept popping up book after book. And when my publisher asked if I was going to write more books, I was thrilled at the chance to feature quiet sous chef Shawn Matthews. To learn his secrets and give him an HEA. Many, many thanks to readers who've already fallen in love with this series, and who continue to support a ranch and ghost town I truly wish were real.

Hugs and puppy snuggles to my longtime editor, Alissa Davis. This one was lucky number thirteen! You are always a pleasure to work with, and your thoughts and notes make each manuscript shine. Thanks to the team at Carina Press for continuing to support me and my beautifully broken characters. Thank you to everyone who has ever read, reviewed, or raved about one of my books. You're why I do this crazy thing called publishing.

About the Author

A.M. Arthur was born and raised in the same kind of small town that she likes to write about, a stone's throw from both beach resorts and generational farmland. She's been creating stories in her head since she was a child and scribbling them down nearly as long, in a losing battle to make the fictional voices stop. She credits an early fascination with male friendships (bromance hadn't been coined yet back then) with her later discovery of and subsequent love affair with m/m romance stories. A.M. Arthur's work is available from Carina Press, Dreamspinner Press, SMP Swerve, and Briggs-King Books.

When not exorcising the voices in her head, she toils away in a retail job that tests her patience and gives her lots of story fodder. She can also be found in her kitchen, pretending she's an amateur chef and trying to not poison herself or others with her cuisine experiments.

Contact her at am_arthur@yahoo.com with your cooking tips (or book comments). For updates, info and the occasional freebie, sign up for her free newsletter: https://vr2.verticalresponse.com/s/signupformynewsletter16492674416904.

Turn the page for an excerpt from
Come What May *by A.M. Arthur,*
now available at all participating e-retailers.

**Now Available from Carina Press and
A.M. Arthur**

*Jonas needs Tate. He just doesn't know it yet.
Or at least, he doesn't want to admit it.
Read on for an excerpt from* Come What May

Chapter One

The last time Jonas Ashcroft had taken money from someone and made change had been during a drunken game of Monopoly at the Delta Theta house sophomore year. Everyone was wasted enough that they didn't care Jonas was probably giving the wrong bills back half the time, and eventually they'd abandoned the game in favor of beer pong and more tequila shots.

Staring down the ancient cash register behind the main counter at All Saints Thrift Store was like facing off against an old enemy. Jonas and math did not get along. Never had.

The teenage girl with spiky hair who'd handed him a ten-dollar bill to pay for three T-shirts glared at him over the top of her cell phone, waiting for him to make change. The register told him that three shirts at two-fifty each was seven dollars and fifty cents. It didn't tell him what to give her back.

He knew this. He wasn't a total idiot, no matter what his father seemed to think. Two quarters made it eight. Two dollars made ten. Right?

The girl took the change he offered without remark, then fled the store with her bag, the overhead bell announcing her departure.

Jonas slammed the register drawer shut with clammy hands. First transaction down. He could survive a few more, until Aunt Doris got back and took over running the till. She'd shown him how to use it yesterday, and while it seemed pretty simple, he flat out sucked at math. Thank God his father hadn't insisted Jonas go for a business degree, because he'd have flunked out the first semester.

Not that it mattered. Junior year was less than a month old and instead of living it up with his frat buddies and getting the Communication Arts degree he desperately needed so he could get a real job and be independent, he was stuck working at his aunt and uncle's thrift store on a run-down side of Wilmington, Delaware. A shitty fate, and exactly what he deserved.

"I can't have your recklessness interfere with my chances at Congress," his father had said last week. "You need to learn some responsibility for once in your life." Angry words lobbed at him from behind his father's walnut desk, moments before Jonas was stuffed in a car and stranded here for the next nine months.

Jonas poked at the cash register. He had another hour until Aunt Doris returned. She and Uncle Raymond had driven out to some person's house to pick up a load of shit for the shop.

Or something. She might have mentioned books.

He had no idea how people made an actual living running a thrift store, much less one that donated some of its money to charity, but they'd been at it all Jonas's life. Probably why Jonas's own parents had little to do with them.

Appearances and all that crap.

The store itself was clean and organized and smelled

like some kind of floral incense. The merchandise was sectioned into departments. A pretty typical thrift store.

Like you know what a typical thrift store looks like. Yesterday was your first time in one, asshole.

His mother hadn't come from money, but his father had, and Jonas had never worked a day in his life until today.

They'd opened twenty minutes ago and so far he'd had one customer. Good thing he had his iPhone.

He pulled his earbuds out of his pocket and was about to turn up some music when a shadow fell over the front door. It opened with the ding of a metal bell, and his second ever customer stepped inside.

"Good morning—" The guy faltered, eyes going wide behind a pair of round, black-framed glasses. "Um, hi, person I don't know."

Jonas grunted a greeting, then decided Aunt Doris would give him that sad puppy look if she found out he was being rude to her customers. "Hi."

About Jonas's age and a few inches shorter, the maybe-customer let the door fall shut and slid his hands into the pockets of very loose, very worn jeans that hung low on narrow hips. "Doris isn't in this morning?"

Does it look like she's here? "No, she's out picking something up."

"Oh, okay. Did she happen to mention a basket of sheets for Tate?"

Jonas had no idea what any of that meant. "No."

"Okay, let's try this again. Hi, I'm Tate Dawson." He held out a hand.

"Jonas Ashcroft." Jonas took the guy's hand briefly. "I'm Doris's nephew."

"Oh hey, cool. I've never seen you around before."

"That's because I've never been here before."

Tate opened and closed his mouth a few times, probably unsure how to proceed. Yeah, Jonas was kind of being a dick. He wanted the guy to do whatever he needed to do and leave so Jonas could turn on his music and hope this day ended as quickly as possible.

"Yeah, okay," Tate said. "Listen, I help run the homeless shelter across the street, and Doris was supposed to bring in a basket of sheets for me today."

Jonas stared.

Tate's hands went from his pockets to his hips. A line creased his forehead, and his cheeks pinked up. "Could you check the back room, maybe? Or should I look myself?"

"I'll check. Jesus."

"Tate, not Jesus, and thank you."

Jonas resisted rolling his eyes. He took his time strolling to the back of the shop, and then ducked through a beaded curtain doorway. The back room was neatly organized with dated shelves for new stock, empty hangers for clothes, cleaning supplies and a recycle bin for things they simply couldn't sell. He found a plastic laundry basket of folded sheets on one of the shelves with a piece of paper taped to it that said "Tate" in Aunt Doris's careful handwriting.

"Found it," he announced upon his return to the main room.

"Hope you didn't hurt yourself." Tate's words were soft, but they carried in the quiet store.

Jonas liked the snark. Made needling the guy more fun, and it gave him something more entertaining to do than stare at racks of used women's clothing. He carried the sheets to the counter and set the basket down. "Do you need some kind of receipt for these?"

"Nah, Doris was just doing me a favor."

"Why do you work at a homeless shelter?"

I need to get my brain-to-mouth filter checked.

Tate tilted his head, apparently not offended in the least. "Why *not* work at a homeless shelter? There are a lot of people these days with nowhere to go, especially teenagers."

Jonas glanced out the front window at the brick building across the street. "You get a lot of teens there?"

"I would hope so." Tate arched one eyebrow impressively high. "We're a homeless shelter for LGBT teenagers." Jonas's confusion must have been all over his face, because Tate sighed. "Gay teens. Gay, lesbian, trans, whatever end of the spectrum they identify on."

"I know what LGBT stands for. I didn't know there were enough of them that they needed their own homeless shelter."

"Where the hell did you crawl out of, a rock in Siberia? Gay teens make up almost forty percent of the homeless youth population in this country. Their asshole parents kick them out and a lot of them have nowhere to go except the streets. We may not be a big operation but we help as much as we can."

Jonas made a time out gesture. "Okay, sorry, Christ. I just…" *I don't think about those issues because they don't directly affect my life.*

So, did working in an LGBT shelter mean Tate was gay?

Tate crossed his arms and settled his weight on one foot, his gaze roving over Jonas like he was studying him for a quiz later. "Let me guess. Rich boy. Privileged life.

Great future ahead of you until you... What? Crashed your BMW into a tree while driving drunk? Knocked up a sorority girl and you're being punished?"

Jonas stared, both impressed by and annoyed with Tate for reading him so easily. "You have no right to my life story."

"Ha, I got close. You don't want to be here, do you? Not even a little bit."

Nope. Well, maybe a little bit. Even though expulsion hadn't been at the top on his list of ways to remove himself from the role he'd played at college—the horny frat boy who would eventually find a girl, get a great job, settle down, make babies and maybe make his father proud of him.

He'd pledged the fraternity because his father had demanded it. Here, no one expected anything from him except that he do his job and respect his curfew. "It's not so bad here."

Tate's brow furrowed. "Where are you from?"

"Lake Bluff, Illinois. It's near Chicago."

"Ah. City boy."

"So? You some grass-fed country boy?"

"Hardly. I grew up in Wilmington. Been in or around it my entire life."

"All eighteen years of it?"

"Twenty-three."

Tate was older than him. Why the hell did that matter?

"And you're what?" Tate smirked. "Thirty?"

Ouch. "Ha ha. Twenty-one."

"Out of college?"

Time to change the subject, like, now.

Except he answered, instead. "I have two years left. I'm, uh, taking a break."

"You're twenty-one and still a junior?"

"Yes." No way was Jonas admitting he'd been kept back in fourth grade because he sucked so badly at math.

"Uh-huh. You're going to be around the rest of the year?"

"Probably until next summer, yes. Why?"

"Then, as it seems we'll be seeing more of each other, we should grab lunch or something one day. I can show you around the neighborhood. Maybe you'll realize it's not the slum you seem to think it is, that there are some great people here." Tate flashed him a cocky smile that irritated him to no end. "Believe it or not, there's a fantastic coffee shop two blocks from here."

"I'm, uh, pretty busy here most days." He also had no intention of letting Tate find out how close to the mark some of his comments were.

"Come on, man, even thrift store employees get days off."

He had to give Tate something so he would go away. "Maybe. We'll see."

"*Maybe* is not *no*." He pulled out a clunky flip phone that was probably on a monthly minutes plan. "Give me your number."

Jonas had no good reason to do that, but he did. And he put Tate's number in his own phone, a little embarrassed by his top-of-the-line model and unsure why.

"I've gotta get these back to the shelter," Tate said as he picked up the basket of sheets. "It was nice meeting you, Jonas. I'll see you around."

"Yes, um, you, too." That didn't make a whole lot of sense as a response, but something about Tate made him fumble around even though he usually had no problem talking his way through a social situation. That kind of pissed him off.

He tracked Tate's easy stroll across the street. He had just enough sway to his hips to make Jonas wonder...

Didn't matter. He and Tate were not now, nor were they ever going to be friends. If Tate actually called about coffee, he'd find a way to get out of it. Eventually Tate would get the message and back off.

He hoped.

Tate punched the lock code into the shelter's back door harder than necessary, taking his confusion over the last ten minutes out on the keypad with trembling fingers. Holy fucking hell, Jonas Ashcroft was gorgeous. Like, model gorgeous with a perfectly contoured face, high cheekbones, thick brown hair, the prettiest hazel eyes he'd ever seen on a human being. And the faint "I forgot to shave today" scruff?

Yeah, scruff always did it for Tate. Just enough to feel it when they kissed or to tickle between his—nope. Pointless fantasy. Tate was interested, but everything about Jonas—from his perfect posture to his pointed stares—screamed "straight."

Except for the handful of times he'd caught Jonas holding eye contact longer than most straight guys would with a gay one. Not that Jonas had any reason to guess Tate was gay. Tate wasn't obvious about it, and it wasn't like he'd gone in with any serious flirting. And a lot of straight people were staunch allies. Hell, they'd actually exchanged phone numbers, even though Tate had figured the coffee shop thing to be a long shot. Especially after he'd kind of insulted Jonas while delivering the invitation.

Tate was too busy with the shelter and his sisters to bother dating, but if Jonas could smooth out some of his prickly edges, Tate wouldn't mind being friends.

A friend you want to lick from top to bottom.

"Tate? You back?" Marc's shout echoed down the corridor from the direction of the kitchen, and he followed the sound.

When he and Marc had decided to go all in on the shelter two years ago, it was through determination—and maybe a tiny bit of luck—they'd landed this location. Not only because it helped tie them to the thrift store, but because the building had once been a restaurant and it came with a full kitchen. He found Marc in there with a clipboard in hand, going over the racks of metal shelves that stored their food donations. Their budget for purchasing food wasn't what Tate wanted it to be, so they relied heavily on the generosity of a few frequent donors.

"Oh good, you got the sheets," Marc said after a quick glance in his direction.

"Yep."

"How's Doris? Gout any better?"

"Not sure. She wasn't there."

"Yeah? She left Raymond in the store alone?" Marc chuckled.

Raymond Burke was good people, but Tate had witnessed him fussing with the registers—and customers—enough to know why he stuck to the back room and donation pickups. He'd been a construction foreman in his early life, until a back injury forced him to find new work. Doris had already been working for the owners of All Saints Thrift Store, and they'd wanted to sell and move to Florida. Doris possessed, according to herself, all of the business sense, so they'd taken a chance.

Money wasn't always free-flowing in the Burke house but they both seemed to enjoy the challenge. The store was open Wednesday through Sunday so she could supervise almost all business hours, unless their daughter, Claire, volunteered to help. But Claire was pretty busy lately surviving her senior year of high school, so Tate hadn't seen her around much.

"Her nephew is staying here for the year." The memory of Jonas's beautiful face made Tate smile. "I can't decide if he's an asshole or not."

"Uh-oh." Marc turned around to face him, lips twisted in a familiar smirk. "Don't tell me you're crushing on him already."

"You would too if you saw him. He could give Matt Bomer a run for his money in the drop-dead-stunning department."

"Oh yeah?" Marc straightened. "When you're done, can I have him?"

"You wish."

"He'd be so lucky. Unless…"

Tate stared at Marc's amused face until he finally gave in and asked, "Unless what?"

"Unless you think this one's gonna be more than your usual habit of pump and dump. You thinking about getting serious for a change?"

"Asshole. No. He's probably straight anyway."

"Doesn't mean you can't admire the goods."

"So true. Did Lilah strip the beds yet?"

"Yeah."

"Cool."

Tate used his elbow to push open the door from the

kitchen to the main area of the shelter. With planning help from Raymond and the design expertise of their third partner, Dave, they'd redesigned the open floor plan to make five smaller rooms with three sets of bunk beds each. Thirty beds that allowed them to create safe spaces for girls, boys and everyone in between, depending on who showed up for the night. They also had two separate bathrooms with showers, and a large living area with donated couches and picnic tables for eating breakfast.

They didn't have the resources yet to offer more than one meal, but they always had snacks available at night. The doors opened at eight and closed at nine, and everyone had to be out by eight the next morning, until the weather turned. Once the cold set in, they'd open the doors at six. In the two and a half months since they'd officially opened their doors, all thirty beds had been full every night.

All it had taken was word of mouth.

As much as Tate loved helping these kids, his heart also broke for each and every one of them. He knew what it was like to work the streets for meal money. He knew what it felt like to offer up your mouth for a twenty-dollar bill, and how dirty that money was in your pocket. So did Marc.

They both had their own reasons for doing this every day.

Lilah had stripped the beds, as promised, and they smelled faintly of lemon disinfectant. The mattresses were thin, college dorm style, and each one was encased in a rubber cover to protect against lice, scabies and anything else the kids might bring in with them. Cleanliness standards were huge, especially when it came to a nonprofit like All Saints House. Even the smallest violation could get them shut down.

Tate remade the beds with the freshly laundered sheets. They couldn't afford their own washer and dryer yet, so Doris had very generously offered to let them use her set at home. Sometimes Tate did them himself, sometimes another person in the Burke household helped out, but every single morning the shelter had clean sheets for the beds.

He bumped into Lilah in the main area, where she was wiping down the picnic tables with disinfectant. A retired school counselor with a husband who made good money working for the city, Lilah had plenty of free time to help with the shelter.

She'd also been friends with Doris forever.

"Did you know Doris and Raymond have a nephew?" he asked.

She paused in her work and looked up, her wire glasses halfway down her nose. "Yes, Raymond's sister's son. He's about your age, I think."

Jonas had seemed genuinely affronted when Tate teased him about being thirty, and Tate kind of liked that he was older than Jonas. "I met him today at the shop."

"I'd heard something about him staying with the Burkes for a while. Some kind of trouble at college."

"Oh yeah?" Tate's instincts had been spot-on, then. "He knock up some mayor's daughter?"

Lilah laughed. "No, nothing like that. Doris isn't one to gossip, especially about family. You'd have to ask her for the details. Or her nephew, I suppose."

"I tried. Jonas didn't seem keen on talking about it."

"Oh, Jonas, that's right. You two get along well?"

"He's a little rude, but he agreed to let me show him around. Get to know the neighborhood."

"That was generous of you."

"Well, he's easy on the eyes, so it's not a hardship, trust me."

"So you do have an ulterior motive."

"Don't I always?"

Tate went off to finish making the beds, the sound of Lilah's laughter trailing behind him. Tate had always had a plan, ever since he was fourteen years old and had become the man of the household. It had helped him and his two sisters survive their father's death, and two years later, their mother's.

First step in Tate's new plan: figure out just how straight Jonas Ashcroft really was.

***

Don't miss Come What May *by A.M. Arthur,*
Available now wherever
Carina Press ebooks are sold.

www.CarinaPress.com